W.H.G. Kingston

Will Weatherhelm

W.H.G. Kingston

Will Weatherhelm

ISBN/EAN: 9783337337575

Printed in Europe, USA, Canada, Australia, Japan

Cover: Foto ©Raphael Reischuk / pixelio.de

More available books at **www.hansebooks.com**

WILL WEATHERHELM.

WILL WEATHERHELM

THE YARN OF AN OLD SAILOR

BY

W. H. G. KINGSTON

AUTHOR OF
"THE THREE MIDSHIPMEN," "THE MISSING SHIP,"
ETC., ETC.

NEW EDITION

*WITH ILLUSTRATIONS IN COLOUR BY
ARCHIBALD WEBB*

LONDON
HENRY FROWDE
HODDER AND STOUGHTON
1915

PREFACE.

The favourable reception the early part of my old friend Will Weatherhelm's adventures met with, has induced me to add a further and very considerable portion, derived from the same source as the first.

It contains accounts of some of the most remarkable naval events which occurred during the early part of that great war when all the world was in arms against Old England, among which I may mention the masterly retreat of Vice-Admiral Cornwallis from an overwhelming French fleet, and the gallant action fought by Captain (afterwards Sir Henry) Trollope in the *Glatton*, a fifty-gun ship, once an East Indiaman, with four French frigates,—one of greater size than his own, and the same number of smaller vessels,—when he compelled them, shattered and defeated, to seek for safety by flight. Many other equally interesting events are recorded in the narrative.

From the large amount of fresh matter which I have introduced, it must be looked upon as a new work rather than as a second edition.

I desire to dedicate the present work, as I had the pleasure of doing the former, to my old friend Charles Gilbert Duncan, Esq., of Lerwick, a countryman of Will Weatherhelm, as true and kind-hearted an Islander as ever stepped; but as he is a man whose modesty is equal to his worth,—for both of which qualities his countrymen and his fair countrywomen are especially known wherever they go,—I before merely gave his initials, but I hope that he will now allow me to mention his name in full.

He will, I am sure, recognise the scenes described in the history of my hero during his visit to Shetland. And I must here advise those who have a few weeks to spare from their daily toils, before they wander away south, to go to that beautiful group of islands and judge of their correctness; and besides enjoying some most lovely and picturesque scenery, if they are as kindly welcomed as I was, they may well be content. All I have now to do is to bespeak the same reception for *Will Weatherhelm* from those for whom it is my pride to write, as has been obtained by *Peter the Whaler, Neil D'Arcy, The Three Midshipmen*, and several other voyagers and travellers who have placed their memoirs in my hands for publication.

WM. H. G. KINGSTON.

LONDON, 1879.

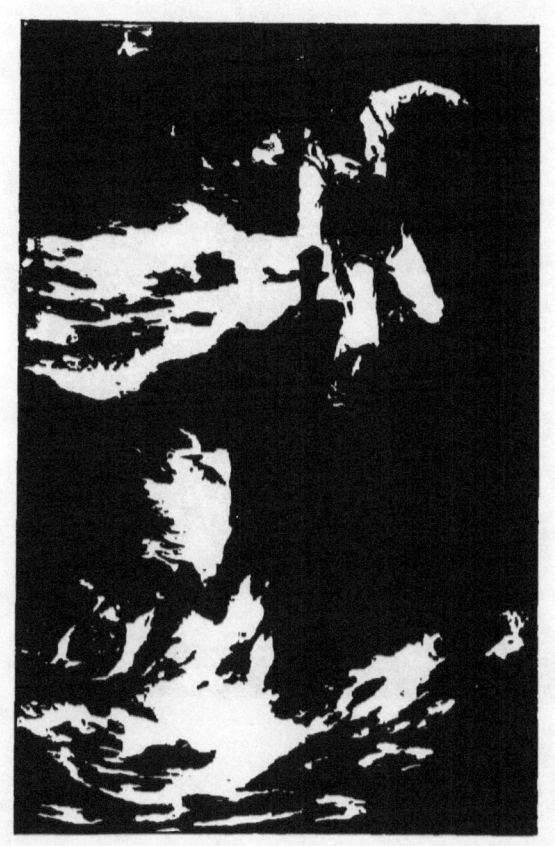

WILL WEATHERHELM.

CHAPTER 1.

My father's land—Born at sea—My school life—Aunt Bretta—Spoilt by over-
indulgence—Enticed to sea—The *Kite* schooner—Contrast of a vessel in port
and a vessel at sea—My shipmates—My name fixed in more ways than one—A
gale—Repentance comes too late—Suspicious customers—A narrow escape—Naples
and its Bay.

My father, Eric Wetherholm, was a Shetlander. He was born in the
Isle of Unst, the most northern of those far-off islands, the Shetlands.
He loved his native land, though it might be said to be somewhat
backward in point of civilization, though no trees are to be found in it
much larger than gooseberry bushes, or cattle bigger than sheep;
though its climate is moist and windy, and its winter days but of a few
hours' duration. But, in spite of these drawbacks, it possesses many
points to love, many to remember. Wild and romantic, and, in some
places, grand scenery, lofty and rocky precipices, sunny downs and
steep hills, deep coves with clear water, in which the sea-trout can be
seen swimming in shoals, and, better still, kind, honest, warm hearts,
modest women with sweet smiles, and true, honest men.

Once only in my youth was I there. I remember well, on a bright
summer's day, standing on one of the highest of its lofty hills, sprinkled
with thousands of beautiful wild-flowers, and. as I looked over the

hundreds of isles and islets of every variety of form, grouping round
the mainland, as the largest island is called, I thought that in all my
wanderings I had never seen a greener or more lovely spot floating on
a surface of brighter blue; truly I felt proud of the region which my
poor father claimed as the place of his birth. I knew very little of his
early history. Like the larger proportion of Shetland men, he followed
the sea from his boyhood, and made several voyages, on board a
whaler, to Baffin's Bay. Once his ship had been nipped by the ice,
whirled helplessly against an iceberg, when he alone with two companions escaped the destruction which overwhelmed her. Finally he
returned home, and, sickened of voyages in icy regions, became mate
of a merchantman trading out of the port of Hull round the English
coast. On one occasion, his brig having received severe damage in
a heavy gale, put into Plymouth harbour to obtain repairs. He there
met an old shipmate, John Trevelyn, who had given up the sea and
settled with his family on shore.

John had a daughter, Jannet Trevelyn, and a sweet, good girl I
am very certain she must have been. Before the brig sailed my father
obtained her promise to marry him. He shortly returned, when she
became his wife, and accompanied him to Shetland. But the damp,
cold climate of that northern land was a sore trial to her constitution,
accustomed, as she had been, to the soft air of her native Devonshire,
and she entreated that he would rather take her with him to sea than
leave her there. Fortunately, as he considered it, the owners of the
brig he had served in offered him the command of another of their
vessels, and he was able to fulfil the wishes of his wife, as well as to
please his own inclination, though for her sake he would rather have
left her in safety on shore, for he too well knew all the dangers and
hardships of the sea to desire to expose her to them.

My father had very few surviving relatives. His mother and sister were the only two of whom I know. His father and two brothers had been lost in the Greenland fishery, and several of his uncles and cousins had been scattered about in different parts of the world, never to return to their native islands. When, therefore, he found that Shetland would not suit my mother's health, he tried to persuade my grandmother and Aunt Bretta to accompany him to Devonshire. After many doubts and misgivings as to how they could possibly live in that warm country far away to the south among a strange people, who could not understand a word of Erse, they at length, for love of him and his young wife, agreed to do as he wished. As soon as he was able he fetched them from Shetland to Hull, whence he conveyed them to Plymouth in his own vessel, and left them very comfortably settled in a little house of their own in the outskirts of the town. Though small, it was neat and pleasant, and they soon got accustomed to the change, though they complained at first that the days in summer were very short compared to those in their own country. This was the year before I was born. My mother, though she had now a home where she could have remained, was so reconciled to a sea life, and so fond, I may say, of my father, that she preferred living on board his vessel to the enjoyment of all the comforts of the shore. On one memorable occasion, a new brig he commanded, called the *Jannet Trevelyn*, in compliment to my mother, was bound round from Hull to Cork harbour in Ireland, and was to have put into Plymouth to land her, seeing that she was not in a fit state to continue the voyage, when a heavy south-westerly gale came on, and the brig was driven up channel again off the Isle of Wight. During its continuance, while the brig was pitching, bows under, with close-reefed topsails only on her, with a heavy sea running, the sky as black as pitch, the ocean a mass of foam, and with the wind howling and whistling as if eager to carry the masts out of her, I was born. My poor mother had a heavy time of it, and it was a mercy she did not die. But oftentimes delicate, fragile-looking women go through far more than apparently strong and robust persons. She had a fine spirit and patient temper, and what is more, she put a firm trust in One who is all-powerful to save those who have faith in him, both for this life and for eternity.

The brig was hove to, and though more than once she narrowly escaped being run down by ships coming up Channel, she finally reached Plymouth, and my mother and I were landed in safety. Thus I may say that I have been at sea from my earliest days. Old Mrs. Wetherholm was delighted to receive my poor mother and me, and took the very fondest care of us, as did Aunt Bretta, while my father proceeded on his voyage.

Soon after this I was christened under a name which may sound somewhat fine to southern ears, Willand Wetherholm; but, as will be seen, I did not very long retain it.

My mother had another trial soon after this. My grandfather, John Trevelyn, who had for some time been ailing, died and left her without any relations that I ever heard of on his or her mother's side of the house. Thus she became more than ever dependent on my father and his mother and sister. She had no cause to regret this, however, for kinder, gentler-hearted people never existed.

Two years more passed away, and I throve and grew strong and fat, and what between grandmother, and mother, and aunt, ran a great chance of being spoilt. My father had been so frightened about my mother before, that he would never take her to sea again; but he often said that he would endeavour, when he had laid by a little more money, to give it up himself and to come and live with her on shore. It is a dream of happiness in which many a poor sailor indulges, but how few are able to realize! He was expected round at Plymouth, on his way to the Mediterranean, but day after day passed and he did not arrive.

My mother began to grow very anxious, so did my grandmother and aunt. A terrific gale had been blowing for some days, when the Eddystone was nearly washed away, and fearful damage was done to shipping in various parts.

At length the news reached them that the brig had put into Salcombe range. It is a wild-looking yet land-locked harbour on the Devonshire coast. Black rocks rise sheer up out of the water on either side of the entrance, and give it a particularly melancholy and unattractive appearance. One of the owners had come round in the brig, but he had landed and taken a post-chaise back towards London. In the morning the brig sailed, and by noon the gale was blowing with its fiercest violence. In vain my poor mother watched and waited for his return; from that time to the present neither my father nor any of his crew were again heard of. The brig with all hands must have foundered, or, as likely as not, been run down at no great distance from Plymouth itself. My mother, who had borne so bravely and uncomplainingly her own personal sufferings, sunk slowly but surely under this dispensation of Providence. She never found fault with the decrees of the Almighty, but the colour fled from her cheeks, her figure grew thinner and thinner. Scarce a smile lighted up her countenance, even when she fondly played with me. Her complaint was incurable, it was that of a broken heart, and I was left an orphan.

Most of my father's property had gone to purchase a share in the brig, which had been most fatally uninsured, and thus an income remained barely sufficient for the support of my grandmother and aunt. They, poor things, took in work, and laboured hard, night and day, that they might supply me with the food and clothing they considered I required, and, when I grew older, to afford me such an education as they deemed suitable to the son of one holding the position my father had in life. Aunt Bretta taught me to read pretty well, and to write a

little, and I was then sent to a day-school to pick up some knowledge
of arithmetic and geography. Small enough was the amount I gained
of either, and whether it was owing to my teacher's bad system or to my
own stupidity, I don't know, but I do know that I very quickly lost all
I gained, and by the time I was twelve years old I was a strong, stout
lad, with a large appetite and a very ill-stored head.

Though I had not picked up much information at school, I had some
companions, and they were generally the wildest and least manageable
of all the boys of my age and standing. The truth was, I am forced to
confess, my grandmother and aunt had spoilt me. They could not
find it in their hearts to deny me anything, and the consequence was
that I generally got my own way whether it was a good or bad one. I
should have been altogether ruined had they not set me a good example,
and instilled into my mind the principles of religion. Often the lessons
they taught me were forgotten, and years passed away, when some
circumstance recalled them to my mind, and they brought forth a
portion, if not all, of the fruits they desired. Still I grew up a way-
ward, headstrong boy. I heard some friends say that my heart was in
its right place, and that I should never come to much harm, and that
satisfied me; so I did pretty well what I liked without any qualms of
conscience or fears for the consequences.

I am not going to describe any of my youthful pranks, because I
suspect that no good will come from my so doing. If I did not reap
all the evil consequences I deserved, others might fancy that they may
do the same with like impunity and find themselves terribly mistaken
One of my chief associates was a boy of my own age, called Charles
Iffley. His mother, like mine, was a Devonshire woman, and his father
was mate of a merchantman belonging to the port of Hull, but trading
sometimes to Plymouth, and frequently to ports up the Straits of
Gibraltar. Charley and I had many tastes in common. He was a

bold dashing fellow, with plenty of pluck, and what those who disliked him called impudence. One thing no one could deny, that he was just the fellow to stand by a friend at a pinch, and that, blow high or blow low, he was always the same, merry-hearted, open-handed, and kind. These qualities, however, valuable as they are, if not backed by right principle and true religion, too often in time of temptation have been known miserably to fail. On a half-holiday, or whenever we could get away from school, Charley and I used to steal down to the harbour, and we generally managed to borrow a boat for a sail, or we induced one of our many acquaintances among the watermen to take us along with him to help him pull, so that we soon learned to handle an oar as well as any lads of our age, as also pretty fairly to sail a boat. When we returned home late in an evening, and I went back to supper, my poor old grandmother would complain bitterly of the anxiety I had caused her; and when I saw her grief, I used to promise to amend, but I am sorry to say that when temptation came in my way I forgot my promise and repeated my fault.

At length the schooner to which Charley's father belonged came into Plymouth harbour. I went on board with my friend, and he showed me all over her; I thought her a very fine vessel, and how much I should like to go to sea in her. The next day he appeared at our house in great glee, and told my grandmother and Aunt Bretta that he had come to wish them good-bye, that his father had bound him apprentice to the owners of the schooner, and that he was to go to sea in her that very voyage. I was sorry to part with him, and I could not help envying him for being able to start at once to see the world. When he was gone, I could talk of nothing else but of what Charley was going to see, and of what he was going to do; and I never ceased trying to persuade my grandmother and aunt to let me go and be a sailor also. Poor things, I little thought of the grief I was causing them.

'Willand, my dear laddie, ye ken that your father, and your grandfather, and two uncles were all sailors, and were lost at sea,—indeed, I
may well say that such has been the hard lot of all the males of our
line,—then why should ye wish without reason or necessity to go and do
the same, and break your old grandmother's heart, who loves ye far
better than her own life's blood,' said the kind old lady, taking me in
her arms and pressing me to her bosom. 'Be content to stay at home,
laddie, and make her happy.'

'Oh, that ye will, Willand dear,' chimed in Aunt Bretta; 'we'll
get a wee shoppie for ye, and may be ye'll become a great merchant, or
we'll just rent a croft up the country here, and ye shall keep cows,
and sheep, and fowls, and ye shall plough, and sow, and reap, and
be happy as the day is long. Won't that be the best life for Willand,
grannie? It's what he is just fitted for, and there isn't another like it.'

I shook my head. All these pictures of rural felicity or of mercantile
grandeur had no charms for me. I had set my heart on being a rover,
and seeing all parts of the world, and I believe that had I been offered
a lucrative post under Government with nothing to do, without a
moment's hesitation I should have rejected it, lest it might have prevented me from carrying my project into execution. Still for some
time I did not like to say anything more on the subject, and the kind
creatures began to hope that I had given up my wishes to their
remonstrances. Had they from the first taught me the important
lessons of self-denial and obedience, they might have found that I was
willing to do so; but I had no idea of sacrificing my own wishes to
those of others, and I still held firmly to my resolution of leaving home
on the first opportunity.

I was one day walking down High Street, Plymouth, when I saw
advancing towards me a fine sailor-like looking lad, with a well-bronzed
jovial countenance.

'Why, Will, old boy, you don't seem to know me?' he exclaimed, stretching out his hand, which seemed as hard as iron.

'Why, I scarcely did, Charley, till I heard your voice,' I answered, shaking him warmly by the hand. 'You've grown from a boy almost into a man. There's nothing like the life of a sailor for hardening a fellow, and making him fit for anything. I see that plainly.'

'Then come to sea with me at once,' he replied; 'I can get you a berth aboard our schooner, and we'll have a merry life of it altogether, that we will.'

I liked his confident and self-satisfied way of talking; but I said I was afraid I could not take advantage of his offer, though I would try and get leave from my grandmother.

'Leave from your grandmother!' he exclaimed with a taunting laugh; 'take French leave from the old lady. You are far better able to judge what you like than she is, and she can't expect to tie you to her apron-strings all your life, can she?'

'No, but she is very kind and good to me, and I'm young yet to leave her and Aunt Bretta. Perhaps, when I am older, she will not object to my going away,' I replied.

'Pooh, pooh! feeds you with bread and milk, and lollipops; and as to being too young—why, you are not much more than a year younger than I am, and fully as stout, and I should like to know who would venture to say that I am not fit to go to sea. I would soon show him which was the best man of the two.'

These remarks, for I will not call them reasons, had a great effect on me. I thought Charley the finest fellow I had ever known, and I promised to be guided by him entirely. I did not consider how ungrateful and foolish I was. How could he really care about me, or know what was for my best interests? He only thought of pleasing himself by getting a companion whom he knew from experience he could generally induce to do what he liked. I forgot all the love and affection, all the tender care I had received from my grandmother and aunt since my birth, and that I ought on every account to have consulted their feelings and opinions on the most important step I had hitherto taken in life. Instead of this, I made up my mind if they should say no, as Charley expressed it, to cut my stick and run. Many have done as I did, and bitterly repented their folly and ingratitude every day afterwards to the end of their lives. It stands to reason that those who have brought us up and watched over us in helpless infancy or in sickness, instructed us and fitted us to enter on the active duties of life, must feel far greater interest in our future welfare than can any other person. We, as boys, are deeply interested in a shrub or a tree we have planted, in a dog we have brought up from a puppy; and we may be certain that our parents or guardians are far more interested in our welfare, and therefore I repeat, do not go and follow my example, and run counter to their advice and wishes.

I spent the afternoon with Charley Iffley on board the *Kite* schooner, of which his father was mate. She was a fine craft, with a handsomely fitted up cabin. She had been a privateer in the last war, and still carried six brass guns on deck, which were bright and polished, and took my fancy amazingly. She also had a long mahogany tiller bound with brass, and with a handsomely carved head of a kite which I much admired. These things, trifles as they were, made me still more desire to belong to so dandy-looking a craft. The captain was on shore, but Mr. Iffley, the mate, did the honours of the vessel, and talked largely of all her good qualities, and finally told me that for the sake of his son, who was my best friend, if I had a mind to go to sea, he would make interest to get me apprenticed to her owners. I did not exactly understand what that signified; but I thanked him very much, and said that I left the matter in his and his son's hands.

'All right, Will, we'll make a sailor of you before long!' exclaimed Charley, clapping me on the back.

Mr. Iffley was not a person, from his appearance, very well calculated to win the confidence of a young lad. He was a stout, short man, with huge, red, carroty whiskers, and a pock-marked face, small ferretty eyes, a round knob for a nose, and thick lips, which he smacked loudly both when speaking and after eating and drinking. However, Charley seemed to hold him in a good deal of respect and awe, an honour my friend did not pay to many people. This I found was owing much to the liberal allowance of rope-end which the mate dealt out to his son whenever he neglected his duty, or did anything else to displease him; but of course Master Charley did not confide this fact to me, but allowed me to discover it for myself. In the evening I went back to my grandmother's. I wanted Charley to accompany me, but he said that he thought he had better keep out of the way, or out of sight. This I have since found the Tempter—that great enemy of man—always does when he can. He does his best to hide the hook with which he angles for souls, as well as to conceal himself; and we may justly be suspicious of people who dare not come forward to explain their objects and intentions regarding us. Even in a worldly point of view, the caution I give is very necessary. It was not, however, till long, long after that I found all this out. I had not been seated at the tea-table many minutes before I opened the subject which lay nearest my heart. My kind grandmother and Aunt Bretta used all the arguments they could think of to induce me to stay at home, and so powerful and reasonable did they seem, that had I not been ashamed of facing Charley and confessing that I was defeated, I should, at all events for the time, have yielded to their wishes. They pictured to me all the horrors of being shipwrecked and being cast on a barren island, or tossed about at sea on a raft, or having to live among savages, or being half starved or parched with

2

thirst,—indeed, they had little difficulty in finding subjects on which to enlarge. They also reminded me that, as I had no friends and no interest, if I went to sea they could do nothing for me, and that though Mr. Iffley might be a very kind man, he could not be expected to care so much for me as he would for his own son, and perhaps I might have to remain before the mast all my life. All this I knew was very true, but I could not bear the idea of being laughed at by Charley and his father, and in my eagerness I swore vehemently that go to sea I would, in spite of everything they could say; and I declared that I didn't mind though I might be cast away a dozen times, or go wandering about the ocean and never come back,—indeed, I scarcely know what wicked and foolish things I said on the occasion.

My poor grandmother and aunt were dreadfully shocked at the way I had expressed myself. They had too much respect for an oath themselves, even though it was as rash as mine, to endeavour to make me break it, and with tears streaming down her face my grandmother told me, that if such was my resolution, she had no longer the wish to oppose it. There was something very sad in her countenance, and the words trembled on her lips as she spoke, I remember. It was not so much, however, because of my wish to go to sea, as of my rank ingratitude and want of tenderness.

'Oh, Willand! ye dinna ken what harm ye have done, laddie,' said Aunt Bretta, as I parted from her to go to roost in my little attic room, which she had fitted up so neatly for my use.

At first I was inclined to exult at having made the first step towards the accomplishment of my wishes, and I was thinking how proud I should be when I met Charley the next morning, to be able to tell him that I had triumphed over all difficulties and was ready to accept his offer; but then the recollection of what Aunt Bretta had said, and a consciousness of the nature of my own conduct came over me, and I began to be sorry for what I had done. In the morning, however, before breakfast, Charley called for me, and when I told him that I had got leave to go, he said he would come in and comfort the poor women. This he did in a rough kind of way. He told them that we were going to make only a short summer voyage—out to the Mediterranean and back; that if I liked it I might then be apprenticed, and if not, that I might come on shore; that I should have seen a little of the world, and that no great harm would be done.

The matter once settled, no people could have exerted themselves more than did my two kind relatives to get me ready for sea. They knew exactly what was wanted, and in three or four days my entire kit was ready and stowed away in a small sea-chest, which had belonged to some member of my family who had escaped drowning. It received no little commendation when it was hoisted up the side of the *Kite*.

'That's what I like,' said Mr. Iffley; 'traps enough, and no more. It speaks well for your womankind, and shows that you come of a sea-going race.'

I told him that I was born at sea, and that my father was drowned at sea.

'That's better than being hung on shore,' he answered with a loud laugh; and I afterwards found that such had been the fate of his father, who was a noted pirate, and that he himself had enjoyed the doubtful benefit of his instruction for some time.

While we lay at Plymouth we received orders to call in at Falmouth, to carry a cargo of pilchards, which was ready for us, to Naples, in the south of Italy. The people in that country, being Roman Catholics and having to fast, eat a great quantity of salt-fish. They have plenty of fish in their own waters, but they are so lazy that they will not be at the trouble of catching them in sufficient quantities to supply their wants. Falmouth was a great fishing place in those days, and full of

vessels going to all parts of the world. There had been some heavy
rain in the night, and as they lay with their sails loosed and the flags
of all the civilized nations in the world flying from their peaks, I
thought that I had never seen a more beautiful sight.

Mr. Tooke, our captain, was a very good sailor. He was a tall, fine
man, with black hair and huge whiskers, like his mate's, and a voice,
when he liked, as loud as thunder—a quality on which he not a little
prided himself. I thought when I went on board that I was to live in
the cabin and be treated like a young gentleman. Charley had not said
anything about the matter, but he had showed me the state rooms, as
they were called, and I had sat down in the cabin and taken a glass of
wine with him there, so I took it for granted that I was to be a sort
of midshipman on board.

The first night, when the middle watch was set, and I began to grow
very sleepy, I asked Charley in which of the cabins I should find my
bed. He laughed, and told me to follow him. I did so, and he
slipped down a little hatchway forward, just stopping a minute, with
his head and shoulders above the deck, to tell me that I must not be too
squeamish or particular, and that I should soon get accustomed to the
place to which he was going to take me. He then disappeared, and I
went after him. I found myself in a dark hole, lighted by a very dim
lantern, with shelves which are called standing bed-places, one above
the other, all round it, and sea-chests lashed below. In the fore part
were two berths, rather darker and closer than the rest.

'That's where you and I have to sleep, old boy,' said Charley. 'I
didn't like it at first; but now I would just as soon sleep there as
anywhere else. But, I say, don't make any complaints; no one will
pity you if you do, and you will only be laughed at for your pains.'

I found that he was right with regard to my getting accustomed to
the place, though sheets were unknown, and cleanliness or decency was

but little attended **to**. Not only were the habits of many of the crew dirty, but their manners and ideas were bad, and their language most foul and obscene; cursing and swearing went on all day long, just as a thing of course. It might seem strange to some who don't know much about human nature, that I, a lad decently brought up by good, religious people, and fairly educated, should have willingly submitted to live along with such people. At first I was startled,—I won't say shocked, —but then I thought it fine and manly, and soon got not only accustomed to hear such language, but to use it with perfect indifference myself.

We are all of us more apt to learn what is bad than what is good I have mentioned Captain Tooke and our first mate. We had a second mate, old Tom Cole by name. He was close upon sixty years of age He had been at sea all his life, and had been master of more than one vessel, but lost them through drunkenness, till he got such a name that no owners would entrust him with the command of another. He was a good seaman and a fair navigator, and when he was sober there wasn't a better man in the ship. He had been to sea as first mate, but lost the berth through his besetting sin. I believe Captain Tooke engaged him from having known him when he himself was a young man, and from believing that he could keep him sober. He succeeded pretty well, but not always; and more than once, in consequence of old Cole's neglect of his duty, we very nearly lost our lives, as many lives have been lost before and since. The two mates messed with the captain, but the apprentices lived entirely with the men forward. Besides Charles Iffley, there was another, Jacob La Motte, a Guernsey lad. He was a far more quiet and steady fellow than either of us. In my wiser moments I learned to like him better than Iffley; and perhaps because I was better educated than most of the men, and, except when led away by bad example, more inclined to be rational, he associated more with me than with them. The best educated and the most steady among the

bands forward was a young man, Edward Seton. He was very well-
mannered and neat in his person, and I never heard him giving way to
profane swearing or any other gross conduct, and he tried, but in vain
to check those who indulged in it.

I had not been long at sea, though time enough to have any pride I
might have possessed knocked out of me, when I was accosted by old
Ned Toggles, one of the roughest of the rough hands on board, and
generally considered the wit of the crew, with, ' And what's your name,
youngster ?   Did any one ever think it worth while to give one to such
a shrimp as you ?'

' Yes,' said I, firing up a little ; ' I should have thought you knew it
by this time.'

' Know it !   How should I know whether your name is Jack, or Tom,
or Bill ?   Any one on 'em is too good for you, I should think, to look at
you,' remarked old Toggles, with a grin and a wink at his companions.

' Thank you for nothing,' said I, feeling very indignant at the
gratuitous insult, as I considered it, thus offered to me. ' If you want
to know my name, I'll tell it you. It is Willand Wetherholm.' The
last words I uttered with no little emphasis, while I looked at my shipmates as much as to say, ' There ! I should like to know who has got
as good a name as that !' I saw a grin on the countenance of old
Toggles as I spoke.

' Will Weatherhelm !' he ejaculated. ' A capital name, lad.   Hurrah
for Will Weatherhelm.   Remember, Will Weatherhelm is to be your
name to the end of your days.   Come, no nonsense, we'll mark it into
you, my boy.   Come, give us your arm.'   What he meant by this I
could not tell ; but after a little resistance, I found that I must give in.
' Come, it's our watch below, and we have plenty of time to spare ; we'll
set about it at once,' said he, taking my arm and baring it up to the
elbow.   One of the other men then held me while Toggles procured a

sharp needle, stuck in a handle, and began puncturing the thick part of my arm between the elbow and wrist. The operation cost me some little pain; but there was no use crying out, so I bore it patiently. When he had done he brought some powdered charcoal or gunpowder, and rubbed it thoroughly over the arm. 'There, my lad,' said he, 'don't go and wash it off, unless you want a good rope's-ending, and you'll see what will come of it.'

I waited patiently as I was bid, though my arm smarted not a little, and in three days Toggles told me I might wash as much as I liked. I did wash, and there I found on my arm, indelibly marked, my new name, WILL WEATHERHELM!* and at sea, wherever I have been, it has ever since stuck to me.

If one of my old shipmates were to be asked if he knew Willand Wetherbolm, he would certainly say, 'No; never heard of such a man.' 'But don't you remember Will Weatherhelm?' 'I should think so, my boy,' would be his reply, and I hope he would say something in my favour.

We had a quick run to the southward till we were somewhere off the latitude of Lisbon, when a gale sprung up from the eastward which drove us off the land, and not only carried every stitch of canvas clear of the bolt-ropes, but very nearly took the masts out of the vessel. It was my watch below when the gale came on, and I was awoke by the terrific blows which the schooner received on her bows; and what with the

* Weatherhelm is a sea term. A vessel, when not in perfect trim and too light aft, has a tendency, when on a wind, to luff of her own accord, or to fly up into the wind. To counteract this tendency it is necessary to keep the helm a-weather, and she is then said to carry a *weather helm*. It is not surprising, therefore, that Toggles should at once catch at my name, and turn it into one which is so familiar to a seaman's ear. Indeed, to this day, I have often to stop and consider which is my proper name, and certainly could not avoid answering to that of Will Weatherhelm.

darkness and the confusion caused by the noise of the sea and the
rattling of the blocks aloft, the stamp of feet overhead, and the
creaking of the bulkheads, I fully believed the ship was going down, and
that my last moment had come. I thought of my poor old grandmother's warnings, and I would have given anything if I could have
recalled my oath and found myself once more safe by her side. 'All hands
shorten sail!' soon sounded in my ears. I slipped into my clothes in
a moment, and hastened on deck. The sky overhead was as black as
pitch, and looked as if it was coming down to crush the vessel between
it and the ocean, and every now and then vivid flashes of lightning
darted forth from it, playing round the rigging and showing the
huge black seas as they came rolling up like walls capped with white
foaming tops, with a loud rushing roar, as if they were about to overwhelm us. A rope's-end applied to my back made me start, and I
heard the voice of old Cole, saying, 'Hillo, youngster, what are you
dreaming about? Up aloft there, and help furl the topsails.' Aloft
I went, though I thought every moment that I should be blown away
or shaken from the shrouds; and when I got on the yards, I had to
hold with teeth and eyelids, as the saying is, and very little use I
suspect I was of. Still the sails, or rather what remained of them,
were furled, and I had been aloft in a gale. I very soon learned to
think nothing of it.

We were many days regaining our lost ground, and it was three
weeks after leaving Falmouth before we sighted the Rock of Gibraltar.
We did not stop there, but the wind being then fair, ran on through
the Gut towards our destination. Inside the straits, we had light and
baffling winds, and found ourselves drifted over to the African shore,
not far from the Riff Coast. We kept a sharp look-out and had our
guns ready shotted, for the gentry thereabouts have a trick of coming
off in their fast-pulling boats if they see an unarmed merchantman

becalmed; and, as a spider does a fly caught in his web, carrying her off and destroying her. They are very expeditious in their proceedings. They either cut the throats of the crew or sell them into slavery, carry all the cargo, and rigging, and stores on shore, and burn the hull, that no trace of their prize may remain. Charley told me this; but we agreed, as we were well armed, if they came off to us, they might find that they had caught a Tartar.

The captain and mates had their glasses constantly turned towards the shore. The sun was already sinking towards the west, when I heard the captain exclaim, 'Here they come! Now, my lads, let's see what you are made of.' We all, on this, gave a loud cheer, and I could see six or eight dark specks just stealing out clear of the land. Charley and I were in high glee at the near prospect of a skirmish, for we both of us had a great fancy for smelling gunpowder.

Old Cole heard us boasting of what we would do. 'Just wait, my boys, till you see some hundreds of those ugly blackamoors, with their long pikes, poking away at you, and climbing up the side of the schooner, and you will have reason to change your tone, I suspect,' said he, as he turned on his heel away from us.

'Here comes a breeze off the land!' exclaimed Mr. Iffley; 'we may wish the blackguards good-bye before they come up with us.' The breeze came and sent us a few fathoms through the water, and then died away and left the sails flapping as before idly against the masts, while at the same time the row-boats came nearer and nearer. The captain walked the deck with his glass under his arm, every now and then giving a glance at the approaching boats, and then holding up his hand to ascertain if the breeze was coming back again. Once more the sails filled, and his countenance brightened. Stronger and stronger came the breeze. The schooner felt its force, and now began to rush gaily through the water. 'Hurrah! she walks along briskly!' he exclaimed, looking over the side. 'We may wish the gentlemen in the boats good evening.'

I was surprised to find the captain so glad to get away from the pirates. I thought it was somewhat cowardly of him, and that he would rather have stopped and fought them. Charley laughed when I told him this. 'He is as brave a man as ever stepped,' he answered. 'He has his own business to attend to, and that is to carry his cargo to the port we are bound for. What good would he have got had he fought the pirates, even though he had knocked them to pieces?'

The breeze continuing, and darkness coming on, we very soon lost sight of the boats. It was nearly a fortnight after this that we made the coast of Sicily, and saw Mount Etna towering up with a flaming top into the clouds. We stood on towards the Bay of Naples. A bright mist hung over the land as we approached it soon after sunrise, like a veil of gauze, but still thick enough entirely to conceal all objects from our view. Suddenly, as if obeying the command of an enchanter's wand, it lifted slowly before us and revealed a scene more beautiful that any I ever expected to behold. On the right was the bright green island of Capri, with Sorrento and its ruined columns beyond it. Before us was the gay white city of Naples, with its castles and moles below rising upwards out of the blue sparkling waters on the side of a hill, amid orange groves and vineyards, and crowned at its summit by a frowning fortress, while on the left was the wildly picturesque island of Procida and the promontory of Baiæ, every spot of which was full of classic associations, which, however, the little knowledge I had picked up was scarcely sufficient to enable me to appreciate, and in which even now, I must own, I could not take the interest they deserve. Still the beauty of the scene fixed itself on my memory never to be eradicated.

CHAPTER II.

Greek pirates—A suspicious stranger—My first fight—Desperate encounter—Our fate sealed—The sinking vessel—The mate's death—We secure a boat—Down she goes—Our perilous voyage—Loss of another shipmate—Death of Edward Seton—My promise—A strong breeze—A gale springs up—A heavy sea.

HAVING discharged our cargo at Naples, the captain, finding that we could get no freight home from thence at the time, determined to go to Smyrna, where he knew that he could obtain one of dried fruit, figs, currants, and raisins. We spent ten days there, and on our homeward voyage, keeping somewhat to the northward of our course, got among the islands of the Greek Archipelago. At that time a great many of the petty Greek chiefs, driven by the Turks from their hereditary domains, had established themselves on any rocky island they could find, with as many followers as they could collect, and nothing loth, used to carry on the respectable avocation of pirates. Some possessed only lateen-rigged craft, or open boats, but others owned fine large vessels, ships and brigs, strongly armed and manned. Though they attacked any Turkish vessels wherever they could find them, they were in no respect particular, if compelled by necessity to look out for other prey, and the merchantmen of any civilized nation which came in their way had but a small chance of escape.

I observed some little anxiety on the countenances of the officers, and a more careful watch than usual was kept on board at night, while in the day-time the captain or first mate was constantly aloft, and more than once the course was changed to avoid a strange sail. The winds were light and baffling, so that we were detained among the islands for some time. At last we got a fair breeze from the northward, though it was light, and we were congratulating ourselves that we should have a quick run to the westward. We had been standing on for a couple of hours or so, when I saw the master and mates looking out anxiously ahead. I asked Charley Iffley what it was they saw.

'An ugly-looking big brig, which has a cut they don't like about her,' was the answer. 'When we were out here the last time, we sighted just such another chap. A hundred or more cut-throat-looking fellows were dancing on her decks, and we had every expectation that they would lay us aboard, when a man-of-war hove in sight, and she prudently cut her stick. The man-of-war made chase, but a Thames barge might as well have tried to catch a wherry. The pirate was out of sight in no time.'

'But if this stranger should prove to be a gentleman of the same profession, what shall we do, Charley?' I asked.

'Run away if we can, and fight him if he comes up with us,' he replied.

I thought he did not seem quite so anxious about fighting as he had been when we were off the Riff coast. Indeed, from what I could learn, should the vessel in sight prove to be a Greek pirate, we might find a struggle with her no joking matter. That she was so, I found the captain and officers entertained not the slightest doubt. The schooner was brought on a wind and stood away to the southward, but the brig immediately afterwards changed her course for the same direction. The captain on this called the crew aft, and told us that he intended to try and make his escape, but that if he did not succeed, we must fight for our lives, for if overcome we should all have our throats cut. Charley and I, and La Motte, gave a shrill cheer, in which we were joined by two or three of the other men, but the old hands merely growled out, 'Never fear; no man wants to get his throat cut, so we'll fight.' I was surprised at their want of enthusiasm; but when men have been much knocked about in the world, and have all their finer feelings blunted, that, among other sentiments, is completely battered out of them.

When Captain Tooke saw the brig change her course, he hauled the schooner close on a wind, but the brig instantly hauled her wind also, and we very soon saw that she was rapidly overhauling us. The truth is, that English merchantmen of those days were mere tubs compared to those of foreign nations; and even the *Kite*, though a fast vessel of her class, was very inferior to the craft of the present day of the same rig. Thus we saw that there was little chance of escaping a fight should the stranger prove to be a pirate, unless a man-of-war or large merchantman, able to help us, might heave in sight.

While we were trying the speed of our heels, every possible preparation was made for fighting; boarding nettings were triced up; our two guns were carefully loaded; the small arms were got up and distributed among the people, who fastened on the cutlasses round their waists and stuck the pistols in their belts. Charley and I had got hold of a pistol apiece, and purposed committing great execution with them, but I was condemned to help La Motte to hand up powder and shot from below, greatly to Master Charley's amusement, who looked down and asked how I liked being a powder-monkey. As I every now and then shoved my head through the hatchway, I saw that the brig was coming up rapidly after us. I had been down some little time, when just as I came up and was looking about me, my ears were saluted with a loud hissing whirl, and I saw our main gaff shot away at the jaws and come tumbling down on deck. This made the schooner fall off the wind somewhat.

'Fire, my lads! fire!' shouted Captain Tooke, 'and see if we can't repay them in kind.'

Our lee-gun had been run over to the weather side, and both guns were fired at once, discharged by some of our best hands, old men-of-war's men. Still, as no cry of satisfaction followed, I suspected that they had not succeeded in damaging the enemy. A whole broadside from the Greek now came rattling down upon us. I could not resist giving a look up on deck. Several of our poor fellows had been knocked over, and lay writhing in agony. Some were binding up their wounds, and one lay half hanging over the hatchway shot through the body. Such another iron shower would speedily clear our decks of every living being. As to striking our flag, or crying out for mercy, that was out of the question; we were contending with people who had received none from their oppressors, and had not learned to show it to others. Those not required to work the two guns, began blazing away with the muskets, but in that arm also the pirate was infinitely our superior. Her shot from another broadside came rushing fiercely over us. This time no one on deck was hit, but the effects aloft were disastrous. Both our topsail-yards were wounded, and several braces and much of our standing rigging shot through. Our people fought as well as any men-of-war's men, and our captain showed that though he was a rough diamond he was a brave fellow. A third broadside reduced our rigging to a perfect wreck, and masts, and spars, and blocks came tumbling down from aloft in melancholy confusion. All this time the wind had been increasing, and it now blew a pretty smart breeze. We might have still a chance if we could knock away some of the enemy's spars, and keep him from boarding us. Our hull had received no material injury, and if a gale came on we might weather it out till perhaps some ship might come to our rescue. Having got up all the powder and shot required, I came on deck. I asked Charley what he thought of the state of things. He was looking very pale; his shirt-sleeve was tucked up at the elbow, and there was blood on his arm, which a musket-ball had just grazed.

'Don't ask me, Will,' said he.   'What can we do against that big fellow ?   We shall all be food for fishes before long, I suppose.'

I looked at the brig, which was twice our size and uninjured in rigging, and was closely approaching us, while I could make out that her decks were crowded with men in a variety of Eastern costumes, mostly such as I had seen on board the Greek vessels at Smyrna. By this time it was blowing fresh, and a good deal of sea had got up.   The schooner, having no canvas aloft to steady her, was pitching and tumbling about in an awful way.   Our fate was sealed.   I remembered all the dreadful stories I had heard, and the atrocities committed by these Greek pirates; but I had little time for thought. On came the pirate; showers of musket-balls swept our decks, and round shot came crashing through our side.   In another instant her grappling-irons were thrown aboard; and as a huge spider catches a miserable fly, so did our big antagonist hold us struggling and writhing in his grasp.

We had fought as long as we could; but what could we do against such overwhelming numbers?   We did not strike to the villains at all events, for we had not a man by this time left on his legs to haul down the flag, even had we wished to do so.   The pirates, with fierce shouts, waiting till the sides of the vessels rolled together, leaped, sword in hand, on our decks.   The captain and mates continued fighting to the last, as if resolved to sell their lives dearly. Some were driven overboard, several were knocked down below, and so saved their lives for the moment, while the greater number were unable to lift hand or foot in their defence.   I was among them.   A shot grazed me, I could scarcely tell where, my whole body was in such agony; but overcome with it I lay without power of moving

This was fortunate, for had any of us shown signs of life, the pirates would have despatched us at once. As it was, they merely shoved us out of the way, while they set to work to get out the cargo. Though I could not move, my eye was able to follow them, and from the expeditious way in which they proceeded about their work, they were evidently well practised in it. Every moment I expected to find my existence finished by having the point of a sword or a pike run into me. I suppose after this that I went off into a swoon, for when I again looked up, the pirates had left the vessel, and I could see the topsails of their brig, just as they were sheering off. My first impulse was that of joy to think that I was saved. I tried to rise, and fancied that I might have strength sufficient to do so; but then I thought it better to be perfectly still, lest the pirates should see me moving about, and take it into their heads to fire and perhaps finish me. My feelings were very dreadful. I knew not how many of my companions might have escaped. Perhaps I might be soon the only survivor left alone on the shattered wreck, for the groans of my companions still alive showed that they were desperately wounded; or perhaps my doom was already fixed, and my hours were drawing to a close. I could scarcely bear to hear those sounds of pain, yet I dared not move to render assistance. I waited for some time, and then I slowly turned round my head, and ventured to look if the vessel could be seen from where I lay. She was not visible, so I crawled to a port through which I could see her about a mile off, standing away to the eastward. I now felt that, provided no one showed their heads above the bulwarks, we should be safe. A cask of water stood on the deck for daily use. I crawled to it, and swallowed some of the precious fluid, which much revived me. I never tasted a more delicious draught in my life. I took the tin cup, and crawled to the nearest person who appeared to be alive. It was the captain. He was groaning heavily, 'Here's a cup of water, sir,' I said; 'it will do you good. The pirates are off, and I do not think they are coming back again.'

At first he did not seem to understand me; then he took the mug of water, and drained it to the bottom.

'What, gone, are they?' he at length exclaimed. 'Ah, lad, is that you? Well, what has happened? Oh! I know. Help me up, and we'll see about it.'

I did my best, hurt as I was, to raise him up. In a short time he very much recovered. Both he and I, it appeared, had been knocked over by the wind of a round shot, and had been rather stunned than seriously hurt.

The captain, as he lay on the deck, bound up my wound for me with a kindness I did not expect from him. As soon as he was somewhat recovered, he told me to come with him and examine into the state of affairs. Many of the crew lay stiff and stark on deck—their last fight over. We carried the water to the few who remained alive, and very grateful they were for it. Among the killed was the first mate; but poor Charley I did not see. I observed another man moving forward. I crawled up to him. He was Edward Seton. I gave him the mug of water. He thanked me gratefully.

'I'm afraid that I am in a bad way, Weatherhelm,' said he; 'but see what you can do for me, and I'll try and get about and help the captain: tell him.'

Under his directions I bound up his wounds as well as I could, and in a little time he began to crawl about, though it seemed to give him great pain to do so. On looking into the hold we found that several men were there. The captain hailed them, and gave the welcome news that the pirate was off, and that they might venture on deck. As soon as they heard his voice they sprang up, but looks of horror were on their countenances

3

'It's all over with us, sir,' said they. 'The villains have bored holes in the ship's bottom, and the water is rushing in by bucketsful.'

I accompanied the captain below. Unhappily he found that what they said was too true, and at the first appearance of things it looked as if the schooner could not swim another half hour. On further examination, however, it appeared that, whatever might have been the intention of the villains, they had not bored the holes very cleverly. Some of them were through the timbers, and others were even above the water line, and they had providentially been prevented from finishing their work by breaking their auger, the iron of which was sticking in one of the timbers. When this had occurred they made the attempt to knock a hole through the ship's side; but they had found the ribs and planking too strong for their axes, and had been compelled to desist before accomplishing their purpose. They had, however, effectually destroyed the pumps,—a few strokes of their axes had done that,—so that we had little hope of freeing the vessel of water, as it would take long to repair them. Why they did not set her on fire I do not know. Perhaps because they were afraid that the blaze might attract the attention of any ship of war which might be in the neighbourhood, and bring her down upon them. At all events, they refrained from no tender feeling of love or mercy for us.

'Don't give in, my lads,' cried the captain, after he had examined the state of affairs. 'All who can manage to move, come with me; we may still have a chance of saving our lives. See if any of you can find an axe and wood to make plugs to drive into these holes.'

The pirates had of course intended to heave overboard everything of the sort; but fortunately, without loss of time, a hatchet was found under the windlass forward, where one of the men recollected he had left it, after chopping wood for firing, and another discovered an axe in the carpenter's store-room, under a number of things which had been routed out of the chests by the pirates in their search for money. With these two tools we set to work, and as soon as a plug was cut, we drove it into such of the holes as let in the greatest quantity of water. There was no difficulty in finding them, for the water spouted up in jets in all directions in the hold.

It must be understood that what was already inside had not yet got to a level with the sea. Indeed, if it had, we should very soon have gone down. We succeeded in stopping the greater number, but unfortunately two or three had been bored low down, and some of the cargo having washed over them, we could not contrive to reach the places to plug them. I guessed, when the fact was discovered, that all hopes of ultimately saving the vessel must be greatly diminished, though what we had done would enable her to float for some time longer.

I have before been prevented mentioning anything respecting those of my shipmates who had escaped with their lives. The first person I saw below was old Cole. He was unhurt, and seemed to take matters as coolly and quietly as if they were of ordinary occurrence. He had, as I afterwards discovered, directly he saw the pirate brig running us aboard, gone below and stowed himself away. I ventured to ask him, on a subsequent occasion, how it was that he had not remained on deck and fought on like the rest. 'Why, I will tell you, Will,' said he; 'I have found out, by a pretty long experience, that if I don't take care of number one, no one else will; so, when I saw that nothing more could be done to beat off the pirates, I thought to myself, there's no use getting killed for nothing, so I'll just keep in hiding till I see how things go.' La Motte, the Guernsey lad, was unhurt, but we picked up poor Charley Iffley with an ugly knock on his head, which had stunned him. He didn't know that his father was killed. We let him perfectly recover before we told him. I wished to have kept back the knowledge of this fact from him, but of course as soon as he came on deck he could not fail to discover it, so La Motte and I broke it to him gently. I was somewhat shocked to find how little effect it had on him.

'What, father dead, is he? Well, what am I to do then, I wonder?' was his unfeeling observation.

'And this is the person whom I thought so fine a fellow, and by whom I was guided rather than by those who loved me best in the world,' I thought to myself. Still, I could not help feeling compassion for my friend, and I believe he really did feel his father's loss more than his words would have led me to suppose.

Having done what we could below, the captain called us all on deck to examine into the state of the boats, and to see if any of them were fit to carry us to the nearest shore. A glance showed us their condition. The spars which had fallen from aloft, and the shot of the enemy, had done them no little damage, and the villanous pirates, before leaving us, had stove in their sides and hove the oars overboard, to prevent any of us who might survive from making use of them. I felt my heart sink within me when I saw this, but none of us gave way to despair. It is not the habit of British seamen, while a spark of life remains in them, to do so. The long boat was in the best condition, but with our yards gone we could not hoist her out, even had we had all the crew fit for the work, so that we were obliged to content ourselves with trying to patch up the jolly-boat, which we might launch over the side.

The carpenter was among the killed, so that had the pirates left us all his tools, we could not have repaired the boat properly, and the captain therefore ordered us to set to work to cover her over with tarred canvas, and to strengthen her with a framework inside. Thus prepared, there were some hopes that she might be able to float us, provided the weather did not grow worse.

While the captain and old Cole, with the more experienced hands, were patching up the boat, he sent La Motte and me to try and find a spy-glass in the cabin. After some search we discovered one and took it to him. He watched the pirate brig through it attentively. 'Hurra, my lads, she'll not come back !' he exclaimed. 'She's stand ing under all sail to the eastward, and soon will be hull down.' This announcement gave us all additional spirits to proceed with our work. La Motte and I were next sent to get up some mattresses from below on which to put the wounded men; we also bound up their hurts as well as we could, and kept handing them round water, for they seemed to suffer more from thirst than anything else.

My own wound hurt me a good deal, but while I was actively employed for the good of others, I scarcely thought about it. I found that much progress was being made with the boat. There was plenty of canvas, and a cask of Hockholm tar was found. After paying both the boat and a piece of canvas sufficiently large to cover her over with the tar, the canvas was passed under her keel and fastened inside the gunwale on either side. It went, of course, from stem to stern, and the thickly tarred folds nailed over the bows served somewhat to strengthen them. In our researches La Motte and I had found a hammer and a pair of pincers, which were very useful, as they enabled us to draw out the nails from the other boat with which to fasten on the canvas. As the boat would require much strengthening inside, a framework of some small spars we had on board was made to go right round her gunwale, from which other pieces were nailed down to the seats, and two athwart, inside the gunwale, to prevent her upper works from being pressed in. Besides this, some planks were torn from the long-boat, and with them a weather streak was made to go round the jolly-boat, and this made her better able to contend with a heavy sea.

When we had performed our first task, the captain sent us with the second mate to get up such provisions and stores as we might require.

with some small beakers to fill with water. He then came himself to judge how fast the water was gaining on us, and seeing that the schooner would swim some time longer, he had another thick coat of tar put on, and an additional coat of canvas nailed over the boat. It was lucky this was done, for as the tar had not time to sink into the canvas, I do not think the first would for any length of time have kept the water out. We had still much to do, for we had neither oars, spars, nor sails fitted for the boat. In half an hour more, however, we had fashioned two pairs of oars, in a very rough way certainly, but such as would serve in smooth water well enough. We had stepped two masts and fitted two lugs and a jib. Fortunately the rudder had not been injured, so that we were saved the trouble of making one. I felt my heart somewhat lighter when the work was finished, and we were able to launch the boat over the side where the bulwarks had been knocked away when the enemy ran us aboard. She swam well, and we at once began putting what we required into her. The pirates had carried off all the compasses they could find, but the captain had a small spare one in a locker which had not been broken open, and this he now got out, with a chart and quadrant they had also overlooked. Thus we might contrast our condition very favourably with that of many poor fellows, who have been compelled to leave their sinking ships in the mid Atlantic or Pacific hundreds of miles from any known coast, without chart or compass, and with a scant supply of water and provisions.

We had no difficulty in stowing water and provisions for the remnant of the crew to last us till we could reach Zante or Cephalonia, or some part of the Grecian coast; for that, I heard the captain say, would be the best direction to steer. We first put the wounded who could not help themselves into the boat, and the rest were following, when the captain stopped us.

'Stay, my lads,' said he. 'The schooner will float for some time longer, and we must not leave the bodies of our poor shipmates aboard her to be eaten by the fish with as little concern as if they were animals.'

'All right, sir,' answered the men, evidently pleased. 'We wouldn't wish to do so either, sir, but we thought you were in a hurry to be off.'

We set to work at once, for all hands knew what he meant, and we sewed each of the bodies up in canvas, with shot at their feet.

'Can anybody say any prayers?' asked the captain.

No one answered. Of all the crew, no one had a prayer-book, nor was a Bible to be found. I had one, I knew, which had been put into my chest by my grandmother, but I was ashamed to say it was there, and I had not once looked at it since I came to sea. Edward Seton, however, who had been put into the boat, heard the question. 'I have a prayer-book, sir,' he said. 'If I may be hoisted on deck, I will read the funeral service.' The captain accepted his offer. He was taken out of the boat and propped up on a mattress. He read the Church of England burial service with a faltering voice (he himself looking like death itself) over the bodies of those whom it appeared too probable that he would shortly follow.

It might, perhaps, have been more a superstitious than a religious feeling which induced my rough, uneducated shipmates to attend to the service, but it seemed to afford them satisfaction, and it may, perhaps, at all events, have done some of us good. Then the poor fellows were launched overboard, with a sigh for their loss, for they were brave fellows, and died fighting like British seamen. Charley stood by while his father's body was committed to the deep, and he cried very heartily, as if he really felt his loss. Then, slowly, one after the other of us went into the boat. The captain was the last to quit the schooner. For some time we held on. The captain evidently could not bring himself to give the order to cast off—

indeed, it was possible that the vessel might still float for some time longer; still it is difficult to say when a water-logged vessel may go down. Had we hung on during the dark, we might have been taken by surprise, and not have been able to get clear in time. I heard the captain propose to Mr. Cole to set her on fire, in the hopes that the blaze might bring some vessel down to our relief; but I suspect that he had not the heart to do it. At last, as night was coming on, he gave the order, 'Cast off.' I suspect he never gave a more unwilling one. Not another word did he say, but he gave a last lingering look at the craft he had so long commanded, and then turned away his head.

Our lugs were hoisted, for the wind had come round to the southward, and away we stood for Cephalonia. It was a beautiful night, the sea was smooth and the wind was light,—indeed, we would rather have had more of it,—the stars came brightly out of the clear sky, and there was every appearance of fine weather. There seemed no reason to doubt that all would go well, if the wind did not again get up; and, as we had just had a strong blow, there was a prospect of its continuing calm till we got to our destination. The night passed away pretty well—all hands slept by turns, and, for my own part, I could have slept right through it, had it not been that the groans of one of my companions, who lay close to me, sounded in my ears and awoke me. I sat up and recognised the voice of poor Edward Seton. La Motte and I, who were closest to him, did all we could to assuage his pain. We bathed his wounds and supplied him with drink, but his tortures increased till towards the morning, when on a sudden he said that he felt more easy. At first, I fancied that all was going right with him; but soon the little strength he had began to fail, and as the sun rose, and fell on his pale cheeks, I saw that the mark of death was already there. I spoke to him and asked him what I could do for him. He was perfectly conscious of his approaching death.

'You have done all you could for me, Will,' he answered, in a low faint voice, not audible to the rest. 'It is all over with me in this world. I am glad that you are near me, for you think more as I do, and you know better what is right than the rest of our shipmates; but, Weatherhelm, let a dying man warn you, as you know better than others what is right, so are your responsibilities greater, and thus more will be demanded of you by the Great Judge before whom I am about to stand, and you will have to stand ere long. Oh! do not forget what I have said. And now I would ask a favour for myself. I have a mother living near Hull, and one I love still better, a sweet young girl I was to have married. Find out my mother—she will send for her—see them both—tell them how I died—how I was doing my duty faithfully as a seaman, and how I thought of them to the last.'

'Yes, yes,' I answered, 'I'll do my best to fulfil your wishes.' I took his hand and pressed it. A fearful change came over his countenance, and he was a corpse. I hoped to be able to keep my promise, for often the only satisfaction a dying seaman has, is to know that his shipmates will faithfully carry his last messages to those he loves best on earth. The body was dragged forward into the bow of the boat, for rough as were the survivors, all esteemed Edward Seton, and no one liked to propose without necessity to throw his remains overboard before they were cold.

At noon the captain took an observation, and found that since leaving the schooner the previous evening we had run about forty miles, which showed that we had been going little more than two and a half knots an hour—for the wind had been very light all the time. Still we were far better off than if it had been blowing a gale. As, however, the day drew on, clouds began to collect in the horizon, forming heavy banks which grew darker and darker every instant. I saw the captain and mate looking at them anxiously.

'We are going to have another blow before long,' observed Mr. Cole. 'If we could have got under the lee of some land before it came on, it would have been better for us.'

'No doubt about that, Mr. Cole; but as we have no land near us, if the gale catches us we must weather it out as men best can,' answered the captain.

The mate was unfortunately right, and somewhere about the end of the afternoon watch a strong breeze sprung up from the southward, which soon caused a good deal of sea. The boat was hauled close to the wind on the larboard tack, but she scarcely looked up to her course, besides making much lee-way. She proved, however, more seaworthy than might have been expected, but we shipped a good deal of water at times, to the great inconvenience of the wounded men, and we had to keep constantly baling with our hats, or whatever we could lay hold of. As it became necessary to lighten the boat as much as possible, the captain ordered us to sew the body of poor Seton up in his blanket, and to heave it overboard. No one present was able to read the burial service over him, and he who had so lately performed that office for his shipmates was committed to the deep without a prayer being said over him. I thought it at the time very shocking; but I have since learned to believe that prayers at a funeral are uttered more for the sake of the living than the dead, and that to those who have departed it matters nothing how or where their body is laid to rest. Of course we had no shot to fasten to poor Seton's body. For a short time it floated, and as I watched it with straining eyes, surrounded by masses of white foam blown from the summits of the rising waves, I thought of the awful warning he had lately uttered to me, and felt that I, too, might be summoned whither he was gone.

The wind and sea were now rapidly rising. In a short time it had increased very much, and as the waves came rolling up after us, they threatened every instant to engulf the boat. She had begun to leak also very considerably, and do all we could, we were unable to keep her free of water.

'We must lighten the boat, my lads,' said the captain. 'Don't be down-hearted, though; we shall soon make the land, and then we shall find plenty of provisions to supply the place of what we must now cast away.'

Some of the men grumbled at this, and said that they had no fancy to be put on short allowance, and that they would keep the provisions at all risks. I never saw a more sudden change take place in any man than came over the countenance of the captain at this answer. Putting the tiller into the mate's hand, he sprung up from his seat. 'What, you thought I was changed into a lamb, did you?' he exclaimed in a voice of thunder. 'Wretched idiots! just for the sake of indulging for a few hours in gluttony, you would risk your own lives and the lives of all in the boat. The first man who dares to disobey me, shall follow poor Seton out there—only he will have no shroud to cover him. You, Storr, overboard with that keg; Johnston, do you help him.' The men addressed obeyed without uttering another word, and the captain went back to the stern-sheets, and issued his orders as calmly as if nothing had occurred.

'The captain was like himself, as I have been accustomed to see him,' I thought to myself. 'Sorrow for the loss of his vessel and his people changed him for a time, and now he is himself again.'

I was not quite right, though. Rough as he looked, he was born with a tender heart; but habit, example, and independent command, and long unconstrained temper, made him appear the fierce savage man I often thought him. A large quantity of our water and provisions, and stores of all sorts, were thrown overboard, as was everything that was not absolutely necessary, to lighten the boat as much as possible. Yet, do all we could, there appeared to be a great probability that we should never manage to reach the shore. The water had also somehow or other worked its way between the canvas at the joints in the fore and after parts of the boat, in addition to the seas which came in over the gunwale. To assist in keeping it out we stuffed everything soft we could find, bits of blanket, our shirt-sleeves and handkerchiefs, into the holes in the planks, though of course but little good was thus effected. In vain we looked round on every side, in the hope that our eyes might rest on some object to give us cause for hope. Darker and more threatening grew the sky, louder roared the wind, and higher and higher rose the seas. Scarcely half an hour more remained before darkness would come down on us. With no slight difficulty the boat had been kept steadily before the seas with the advantage of daylight; at night, with the sea still higher. we could scarcely expect that she could be kept clear. It was indeed with little hope of ever again seeing it rise that we watched the sun sinking towards the western horizon.

CHAPTER III.

A LOOK of blank, sullen despair was stealing over the countenances of most of the crew. Charley Iffley sat with his hands before him and his head bent down, without saying a word, and seemingly totally unconscious of what was taking place. When I spoke to him he did not answer or look up. I suppose that he was thinking of his father, and grieving for his loss, so, after two or three trials, I did not again attempt to rouse him up. La Motte and I occasionally exchanged remarks; but when the wind again got up and we expected every moment that the boat would founder, we felt too much afraid and too wretched to talk. The captain was the only person who kept up his spirits. Once more he rose from his seat, and stepped on to the after-thwart, holding on by the mainmast. I watched his eye as he cast it round the horizon. I saw it suddenly light up. 'A sail! my lads, a sail!' he exclaimed, pointing to the westward. Not another word was spoken for some time. We kept on our course, and we were soon able to ascertain that the stranger was standing almost directly for us. The captain at once resolved to try and get on board her, whatever she might prove, rather than run the risk of passing the night in the boat. He on this put the boat about, for had we continued on the course we were then steering she might have gone ahead of us. Our great anxiety was now to make ourselves seen before the night closed down upon us. We had a lantern, but its pale light would not have been observed at any distance. Just before the sun sank into the ocean we were near enough the stranger to make out that she was a large brig, apparently a ship of war, and by the cut of her canvas, and her general appearance, she was pronounced to be French. Though all my younger days we were at loggerheads with them, there happened just then, for a wonder, to be a peace between our two nations, so there was no fear but what we should be treated as friends.

The sun sank ahead of us with a fiery and angry glow, while the clouds swept by rapidly overhead, and every now and then a flash of lightning and a loud roar of thunder made us anxious to find ourselves on board a more seaworthy craft than the frail boat in which we floated. We had no firearms with us, for the pirates had carried away or thrown overboard all they found on board the schooner, so we had no means of making a night signal. However, as there was still a little light remaining, we lashed two oars together, and made fast at one end an ensign, which had fortunately been thrown into the boat. The captain then stood up and waved it about to try and attract the attention of those on board the brig. I felt inclined to shout out, under the feeling that far off as she was my feeble voice would be heard. On we flew through the water at a rate which threatened every instant to tear the canvas off the boat's bottom, while the seas at the same time constantly came on board and nearly swamped us. Time passed away; the gloom of evening thickened around us. Our hearts sank within our bosoms. It seemed too probable that the stranger would pass without observing us. We were again almost in despair, when the boom of a gun came rolling over the water towards us. To our ears it was the sweetest music, a sign that we were seen, and a promise, we believed, that we should not be deserted. On stood the man-of-war directly for us; but it had now grown so dark, that though we could see her from her greater bulk, we could scarcely hope that those on board her could see us. We had two serious dangers to avoid. If we stood directly in her course, so rapidly was she going through the water, she might run over us before we could possibly make ourselves heard; while, if we kept too much out of her way, she might pass us, and we might miss her altogether. Fortunately we succeeded in getting our lantern lighted, and the captain sent me to hold it up forward as soon as we drew near her. On she came; another minute would decide our fate; when we saw her courses hauled up, her top-gallant sails furled, and coming up on the wind, she hove to on the larboard tack, scarcely a cable's length from us. We stood on a little, and then putting the boat about, we fetched up under her lee-quarter and ran alongside. A rope was hove to us, and lights were shown to enable us to get on board.

Our captain spoke a little French, though it was of a very free-and-easy sort, I suspect. The brig proved to be, as he had thought, of that nation; and such a jabbering and noise as saluted our ears I never have in all my life heard on board of a man-of-war. However, they wished to deal kindly by us. They at once sent us down ropes with which the wounded men were hauled up, though there was great risk of getting them hurt in the operation. When this was done, the rest of us set to work to hand up all the more valuable things we had in the boat,—not that the pirates had left us much, by the by. While we were thus engaged, a squall struck the brig, and almost laid her on her beam-ends. We had just time to clamber up on board, when a sea swamped the boat, which was directly afterwards cut adrift; the helm being then put up, the brig righted, and off she flew before the wind. The squall was quickly over (we had reason to be grateful that we had not been compelled to encounter it in the boat), and the brig was once more brought up on her course. We found that she was the *Euryale*, of eighteen guns, and then bound for Smyrna. Though we would rather have been put on shore at Cephalonia, we were certain of their finding a vessel to carry us to Malta, if not home direct to England.

The French captain and officers treated us very kindly, and the surgeon paid the greatest attention to the wounded; but though I have been on board many a man-of-war since, I must say that I never have seen one in a worse state of discipline. One-half of the officers did not know their duty, and the other half did not do it; and the men did just what they liked. They smoked and sang and danced the best part of the day, while the officers played the fiddle or the guitar, or gambled with cards and dice, and very often danced and smoked with the men, which at all events was not the way to gain their respect. The captain was a very gentlemanly man, but had not been to sea since the war, and could not then have known much about a ship, so he did nothing to keep things right, and the great wonder to us was how he had managed not to cast her away long before we got on board her.

We had no reason to complain. Both the officers and men treated us very kindly, and were thoroughly good-natured. Since those days, too, a very great change has taken place in the French navy. Their officers are, as a rule, very gentlemanly men, and the crews are as well disciplined as in our own service—indeed, should we unhappily again come to blows, we shall find them the most formidable enemies we have ever encountered.

We arrived at Smyrna without any adventure worthy of note. Just as we entered the port, the *Ellen* brig, belonging to Messrs. Dickson, Waddilove, and Burk, the owners of the *Kite*, came in also, and we at once went on board her. Captain Mathews was her master; he was one of the oldest and most trusted captains of the firm, and acted as a sort of agent for them at foreign ports. Whatever he ordered was to be done. He could send their vessels wherever he thought best, and had full control, especially over the apprentices. Thus Charley, La Motte, and I at once found ourselves under his command. He was a good-natured, kind sort of a man, therefore I had no reason to complain. We found lying there another brig belonging to the same owners. She was called the *Fate*. It was the intention of Captain Tooke to return home in the *Ellen*, and to take us three apprentices with him, while of course the rest of the men would be left to shift for themselves; but there is a true saying that man proposes, but God disposes.

We soon recovered from our fatigues and hardships, and got into fine health and spirits. The crews of the two brigs were allowed a considerable amount of liberty, and did not fail to take advantage of it. Altogether we had a good deal of fun on shore. Charley and I were generally together. We had not much money between us, but we contrived to muster enough to hire a horse now and then; and as we could not afford to have one apiece, we used to choose a long backed old nag, which carried us both, and off we set in high glee into the country. The grave old Turks looked on with astonishment, and called us mad Giaours, or some such name; and the little boys used to throw stones at us, or spit as we passed, but we did not care for that; we only laughed at them, and rode on. Once we rode into a village, and seeing an odd-looking building, we agreed that we should like to have a look inside. We accordingly tied up our long-backed horse to a tree, and as there was no one near of whom to ask leave, in we walked. It was a building with a high dome, and lamps burning, which hung down from the ceiling, and curtains, but there was not much to see, after all. Presently some old gentlemen in odd dresses appeared at the further end, and as soon as they saw us standing and looking as if we did not think much of the place, they made

4

towards us with furious gestures, so we agreed that the sooner we took our departure the better. When we turned to run, they came on still faster, and as we bolted out of the mosque—for so we found the building was called—they almost caught us. We ran to our horse; while Charley leaped on his back, I cast off the tow-rope, and then he caught my hand and helped me up behind him, and away we galloped as hard as we could go through the village. The old gentlemen could not run fast enough to overtake us, but they sang out at the top of their voices to some men in the street, and they called out to others, and very soon we had the whole population after us with sticks in their hands, heaving stones at our heads, and shouting and shrieking at us. Luckily the hubbub frightened the old horse, and he went faster than he had done for many a day, and amid the barking of dogs, the shouts of boys, the crying of children, and the shrieking of women, we made our escape from the inhospitable community. I had a good thick stick with which I belaboured the poor beast to urge him onward. After some time the Turks, seeing that they could not overtake us, gave up the chase, and we agreed that we had better not enter into their village till they had forgotten all about the circumstance. When we got on board, we were told that we were very fortunate to have escaped with our lives, as many Englishmen had been killed by the Turks for a similar act of folly.

Two days after this, one of the *Ellen's* men came on board, complaining of being very ill. In a short time another said he felt very queer, and both of them lay down on their chests and could eat no food or keep their heads up. Before long, Captain Mathews came below, and finding that they both had something seriously the matter with them, sent on shore for an English doctor who resided at the place. After some time the doctor came, and told the men to turn up their shirt-sleeves and to show him their arms.

'I thought so.' said he, turning to the captain; 'it is my unpleasant duty to tell you that you have got the plague on board. We have it bad enough on shore.'

I thought the captain would have fallen when he heard the news. 'The plague!' he gasped out. 'What is to be done, doctor?'

'Send the men on shore; purify your ship, and get to sea as soon as you can,' was the answer.

But the plague is a conqueror not easily put down. Before night two more men were seized, and the two first were corpses. The captain of the *Fate* heard of what had happened, and sent his boats alongside to inquire how we were doing, but with strict orders that no one should come on board. No boat came the next day; the plague had paid her a visit, and three of the crew were corpses. The moans and shrieks of the poor fellows were very dreadful when the fever got to its height. One moment they might have been seen walking the deck in high health and spirits, and the next they were down with the malady and utterly unable to move. Sometimes three or four hours finished their sufferings, and the instant the breath was out of their bodies we were obliged to heave them overboard. One after the other, the greater part of the crews of the two brigs sickened and died. We three apprentices had escaped, and so had our captain and Mr. Cole. The mate said he was not afraid of the plague or any other complaint, as he had got something which would always keep it away. Charley Iffey and I frequently asked him what it was. It was a stuff in a bottle which he used to take with his grog, and we suspected that he took it as an excuse for an extra glass of spirits. One cause why he escaped catching the plague was, that he never was afraid of it,— either he trusted to his specific, or felt sure that he should not catch it; also, he never went on shore among the dirty parts of the town the men had frequented, and also lived separate from them on board.

At length my companion Charley got ill. We lads had been removed to some temporary berths, put up in the hold, where we could have more air than forward. One day after I had gone on shore with the captain to bring off the doctor, not finding Charley on deck, I went down to look for him. I found him in the berth tumbling about in bed and his eyes staring wildly.

'Oh, Will! I am going to die, and there's one thing weighs so heavy on my mind that I cannot die easy till I tell it to you!' he exclaimed, in a tone of anguish. 'Just for my own pleasure I persuaded you to come to sea, and ever since you have had nothing but danger and trouble. You'll forgive me, won't you? That's what I want to know.'

I told him, of course, that I forgave him heartily; indeed, that I had never accused him of being the cause of the sufferings which I had endured, in common with him and others. Then I told him that he must not fancy that he was going to die just because he felt a little ill, and that as the doctor was on board I would go and fetch him at once.

The doctor came immediately, and, after examining him, applied some very strong remedies. I followed him on deck to inquire whether Charley really had the plague. 'No doubt about it,' was his reply; 'but if he drops into a sound sleep, I think he may throw it off without further evil consequences.'

Anxiously I watched at the side of poor Charley's bed. He talked a little—then was silent—and I found that he slept. I did not dare to leave his side lest any one should come into the berth and awake him. Hour after hour I waited, till at last I sank back on the chest on which I was sitting and fell fast asleep. When I awoke the sun was shining down through the main hatchway into the berth. I heard Charley's voice. It was low but quiet

'I am quite well now, Will,' he said. 'If the doctor, when he comes, will let me get up, I think I could go about my duty without difficulty.'

I was very glad to hear him speak in that way, but I told him that his strength had not returned, and that he must remain quiet for a day or two. From that moment, however, he got rapidly better, and in a week was almost as well as ever. He was the last person seized with the complaint on board the two brigs. On board the *Fate*, the master, and mates, and half the crew died; and had not we and the other survivors of the *Kite's* crew arrived at Smyrna, it would have been difficult to find hands to take her to sea. Captain Mathews, however, directed Captain Tooke to take command of her, and sent Mr. Cole as mate, with Charley Iffley and me, while most of our men shipped on board her. I thought that we were to go home, but I found that my summer cruise was to be a very much longer affair than I had expected. Had I gone home then, I think that I should have followed my kind grandmother's wishes and given up the sea. Instead, however, of returning to England, the brig was employed running from place to place, wherever she could secure a freight. In that way I visited nearly every part of the coast of the Mediterranean. Sometimes we went up the Adriatic; then across to Alexandria; then to some port in Greece, or to one in Italy; then up to Constantinople, and away over to the ports on the northern coast of Africa. I saw a number of strange people and strange sights, but have not now time to describe them.

I wrote home several times to my grandmother and aunt, but, as I was always moving about, I got no answers. I thought very likely that my letters or their replies had been wrongly directed; still I began to grow very anxious to hear what had become of the only two relatives I had on earth, and whom alone I had really learned to love. After I had been out about a year I asked leave, if I could find the chance to go home. The captain on this laughed at me, and reminded me that apprentices were not their own masters, and that I must make up my mind to stay where I was till the owners wanted the brig home.

Three years passed away so rapidly that I was astonished to find how long I had been out in those seas. During all that time no accident had happened, and I began to hope that I was not going to suffer any further misfortunes in consequence of my rash oath. I expressed my feelings to Charley Iffley. He laughed at me, and said that had nothing to do with the matter, that there was no great harm in what I had said, and that, consequently, I could not expect to be punished for it. I thought differently. I knew that there was harm, and felt that I might justly be punished. At first, after Charley had recovered from the plague, he appeared to have become a thoughtful and serious character, but unhappily he very soon fell off again, and was now as reckless as ever. At length the order came for us to return home. Merrily we tramped round at the capstan bars to a jolly song, as we got in our anchor for the last time, and made sail from the port of Leghorn. We passed the Straits of Gibraltar, and with a smooth sea and southerly wind we had a quick run to the Land's End, while our crew sang—

> To England we with favouring gale
> Our gallant ship up Channel steer;
> While running under easy sail,
> The snow-white western cliffs appear.'

CHAPTER IV.

WE made the Land's End one morning in the middle of March, when a strong north-easterly gale sprung up in our teeth, and threatened to drive us back again into the middle of the Atlantic. After the bright sunny skies and blue waters of the South, how cold and bleak and uninviting looked our native land! But yet most of us had friends and relations whom we hoped to see, and whom we believed would welcome us with warm hearts and kindly greetings; and we pictured to ourselves the green fields, and the shady woods, and the neat cottages, and picturesque lanes to be found inside those rocky barriers, and we longed to be on shore. The captain was as eager as any of us to reach home; so, the brig being close-hauled, with two reefs in her topsails, we endeavoured to beat up so as to get close under the land in Mount's Bay. It was a long business, though—tack and tack—no rest and wet jackets for all of us; but what cared we for that? We had an important object to gain. Old England, our native land, was to windward. There we hoped to find rest from our toils for a season; there each man hoped to find what in his imagination he had pictured would bring him pleasure, or happiness, or satisfaction of some sort. I've often thought how strange it is, that though men will toil, and labour, and undergo all sorts of hardships, to obtain some worldly advantage, some fancied fleeting good, and to avoid some slight ill or inconvenience, how little trouble do they take to obtain perfect happiness —eternal rest—and to avoid the most terrific, the most lamentable of evils, the being cast out for ever from the presence of the great, the glorious Creator of the universe, to dwell with the spirits of the lost.

I gave a short account of Captain Tooke and Mr. Cole, as they appeared to me when I first joined the unfortunate *Kite*. They had in no way altered. The captain was the same bold, daring seaman as ever, without any religious principle to guide him; and though his heart was not altogether hard or unkind, his manners were rough and overbearing, and he was often harsh and unjust to those below him. I have met numbers of merchant masters just like him from the same cause. They are sent early to sea, without any proper training, and without any right principles to guide them. If they are sharp, clever lads, they soon are made mates, and before they have learned to command themselves they are placed in command over others. In most instances, their fathers, or relatives, or friends are masters or owners of vessels, and are in a hurry to get them employed. The vessels are insured, so that if, through their carelessness or ignorance, the vessels are cast away, that matters little, they consider. If the crew are lost, that is the fate of sailors. If the master escapes, they can easily get him a new vessel; and as he has learned a lesson of caution, he will be all the better master for some time to come till the vessel is worn out, and then there will be no great harm if she is lost also. I speak of things as they were in my day. I am glad to say that a very great improvement has taken place of late years.

Our old mate held the master in great awe and respect. This

was fortunate, as it generally kept him sober; still the old man never lost an opportunity of getting hold of his favourite liquor, and he would seldom leave the bottle while a drop remained. However, he generally contrived to get tipsy in harbour just before he was going to bed, so that he could turn in and sleep off the effects; and when now and then he was overtaken at sea, the men knew how to manage him; and, as he was good-natured and indulgent, they generally contrived to conceal his state and save him from the anger of the captain. Something of this sort had occurred the very day we made the land. While the captain was on deck, he had gone into the cabin, where, in an open locker, he had discovered two bottles of rum. It was too tempting a prize not to be seized, and he carried off both the bottles to his own cabin, carefully closing the locker. The captain did not discover his loss. The old man went on deck, but soon making an excuse to go below, broached one of the bottles. He had made some progress through it before he was recalled on deck, and the condition on which he was verging did not then appear. The brig was kept beating away across the seas, the wind shifting about and every now and then giving us a slant which enabled us to creep up closer to the land. We continued gaining inch by inch, showing the advantage of perseverance, till just about nightfall we got fairly into Mount's Bay. We thought ourselves very fortunate in so doing, for just then a strong breeze which had before been blowing grew into a downright heavy gale, against which we could not possibly have contended. It seemed, however, to be veering round more to the northward, and the captain, hoping that it would come round sufficiently to the westward of north to enable us to stand up Channel, instead of running in and bringing the ship to an anchor, determined to keep her standing off and on the land during the night, that he might be enabled to take immediate advantage of any change which might occur.

As he had been on deck for many hours, he went at last below, leaving the brig in charge of the mate. Now the old man found the weather cold, and bethought him of his bottles of rum. He knew the importance of keeping sober on such an occasion especially, but he thought that a little more rum would do him no harm, and would make him comfortable, at all events. He did not like to send for a bottle, so he went below himself to fetch it. It was his business to keep a constant watch on the compass, so as to observe any change of wind. He was not long gone below, that I remember. When he came on deck, he brought a glass and a bottle, but he had brought the full bottle instead of the half-emptied one. He asked Charley to bring him a can of hot water. Of course the fire had long been out, and there was none at that hour of the night. He stowed his glass and bottle away in a pigeon-hole under the companion-hatch, but every time he took a turn on deck he went back to it and had a taste of the liquor. He very soon forgot that he had put no water to it. This went on for some time till he sat himself down and forgot another thing—that was, that he was in charge of a vessel on a dark night, with a heavy gale blowing, and close in on a dangerous coast. We had gone about several miles without any difficulty, when, as we were once more standing in for the shore, a squall heavier than any we had yet experienced struck the vessel and laid her over almost on her beam-ends. At that moment the captain rushed on deck with the look of a half-frantic man. He cast one hurried glance forward. 'About ship! about ship! down with the helm!' he shrieked out in a voice of terrific loudness.

'All right—no fear, cap'en,' cried the old mate, staggering up to him. 'I've taken very good care of the barkie.'

At that instant a loud, grating, crushing sound was heard, and the brig seemed to be about to spring over some obstacle in her way. Then she stopped. Loud cries of horror arose from all hands, and the watch below rushed on deck. All knew full well what had occurred. The brig was on the rocks, and the sea, in dark masses with snowy crests, came roaring up around us, threatening us with instant destruction. What reply the captain made to the old man I dare not repeat. Before I thought of anything else, I remembered my own rash oath. 'Am I doomed to cause the destruction of every vessel I sail aboard?' I said to myself, with a groan of anguish, and a voice within me seemed to reply, 'Yes—that is to be your fate; but leap overboard and end it, and you will disappoint the malignity of the monarch of the tempest.' Happily the prayers my good grandmother had taught me had not all been forgotten. At that moment I uttered a prayer for mercy and forgiveness, and I knew then for certainty that the instigation had come from the evil one for the purpose of destroying me body and soul. 'O God, have mercy on me; do what is best,' I cried. Just then I was aroused by hearing the loud voice of the captain ordering the crew to get out the long-boat. I hurried to lend a hand at the work. It seemed, however, almost a hopeless undertaking, so high ran the sea around us. Fortunately the masts still stood. We got the tackles hooked on to the yards, and, casting in oars and boat-hook and sails, hoisted away with a will. The boat swung clear of the side, and the moment she touched the water, the old mate, with Charley and I, and the greater number of the men, leaped into her. We were expecting the captain and the rest of the crew to follow, when a heavy sea, with a terrific roar, came rolling up towards us. We heard shrieks and cries for help from our shipmates. Both the masts went by the board, the boat narrowly escaping being crushed by the mainmast, and the brig instantly began to break up. We got out our oars, and pulled back the distance

we had drifted, shouting out to the captain, and to any who might
have remained on board, but no reply reached us. Again and again
we shouted louder than ever, still there was no response. The old
mate sat like one stupefied; but the catastrophe his neglect had
caused had had the effect of sobering him. One of the men who
was more intelligent than the rest, and often had charge of the deck
at sea in the place of a second mate, said that he thought we had
struck on the Rundle Stone, which is near the shore, between
Mount's Bay and the Land's End, though we ought to have been a
long way to the eastward of it.

We had hard work to keep our own near the wreck; but still we
did not like to pull away while there was a chance of picking up
any of those who might have remained on board. We did our best
to keep our eyes on it through the darkness, with the wind and
rain and spray dashing in our faces. Another huge sea came
rolling on. The crashing and tearing of the timbers reached our
ears, and the water which washed round us was covered with fragments of the wreck, among which we ran a great risk of having the
boat stove in; but no voice was heard, nor could we see any one
clinging to them. We had now to abandon all hope of saving any
more of our unfortunate shipmates, and had to think of our own
safety. Just as we had come to this resolve, another sea rolled
towards the wreck, and when it passed over not a fragment of her
remained hanging together. We were in a sad plight. None of us
had saved more than the clothes we had on our backs, and some of
the watch below had not had time even to put on all theirs. In
getting into the boat I had lost my shoes, which I thought a great
misfortune, as my feet felt very cold, and I fancied when I got on
shore that I should not be able to walk. We bent manfully to our
oars, and tried to pull in for the shore; but the gale came down

stronger than ever on us, and we could not help being conscious
that at all events we were making very little way. Still we persevered. We hoped there might be a lull—indeed, we had nothing
else to do but to pull on. Bitter, however, was the disappointment
which awaited us when the morning broke, and we looked out
eagerly for the land. Instead of being nearer we were much further
off (six or seven miles at least), and were still rapidly drifting away
to sea. The further we got off the land, the greater danger there
would be of the boat being swamped; besides, we had saved no
provisions, and we had the prospect of a fearful death staring us
in the face from hunger and thirst. The old mate had by this
time been sufficiently aroused to comprehend clearly the state of
affairs. As I have said, he was, when sober, a good seaman, and
thoroughly acquainted with the coast. As day drew on, it cleared a
little, and looking round, he made out the Scilly Islands directly to
leeward of us. He watched them earnestly for some time, and throwing off his hat and putting back his grey hairs with his hand, he
sat upright, and exclaimed, 'Never fear, my lads, we've got a good
port under our lee! I know the passage through the channel leading
to it. Trust to me, and I'll carry you safely there.'

Though after what had occurred we had no great confidence in him,
yet as none of us knew anything about the islands, we had his
judgment and experience alone to trust to. So we watched our opportunity, and bringing the boat's head carefully round, pulled in the
direction he pointed out. A break in the clouds, through which the
sun gleamed forth glancing over the white foam-topped seas, showed
us the land in bold relief against the black sky.

'Ah! there's St. Martin's and St. Mary's Islands,' observed the old
man. 'Ah! I know them well. Many's the time I've run between
them up Crow Sound. Let's see—what's the time of day? There

will be plenty of water over the bar. We shall soon have a glimpse of the Crow rock, when we get in with the land; and if only the Big Crow shows his head above water, we may cross the bar without fear of breakers. Once through it, we shall soon be on shore at Grimsby, and there are several people I know there who will give us all we can want to make us comfortable.'

The Crow, to which old Cole alluded, is a somewhat curious rock at the entrance of the Sound. It has three heads, called the Great Crow, the Little Crow, and the Crow Foot. When the Great Crow is even with the water's edge there will be twenty-one feet of water on the bar, when the second point appears there will be sixteen, and when the Crow's Foot is visible there will be ten feet only. These are the sort of particulars which a good coast pilot has to keep in his memory, with the appearance of the numberless landmarks on the shore, and their distances one from the other.

As we drew near the entrance of the Sound, through which if we passed we hoped all our misfortunes would end, the weather came on to be very thick again, so that we could scarcely see a dozen yards ahead. Still the mate seemed so sure of the passage that we steered on without fear.

'Are you certain, sir, that we are heading in for the right channel?' asked Wilson, the man I before spoke of, looking round over his shoulder at the mass of foam which he saw leaping up just ahead of us. 'Round with her! round with her, lads!' he shouted, 'this isn't the channel.'

'All right, all right,' persisted the old mate. But it was all wrong. A sea came rolling up, and hove us in among a mass of rocks over which the breakers dashed with terrific fury. In vain we endeavoured to pull round. Over went the boat, and we were all thrown here and there, shrieking in vain for aid, among the foaming mass of broken waters. I struck out to keep my head above water if I could, and in another instant found myself hove against a steep rock to which I clung with all the strength of despair. I had thought the loss of my shoes a great misfortune. I now found it the cause of my preservation. Had not my feet been naked, I never could have clung to the slippery rock, or freed my legs from the tangled seaweed which clung round them. I struggled on—now a sea almost tore me off, and then I made a spring, and scrambled and worked my way up, not daring to look back to watch the following wave, or to observe what had become of my companions. At length I reached the top of the rock. It seemed an age to me, but I believe it was not a minute from the time I first grasped hold of the rock till I was in comparative safety. Then I looked round for my companions in misfortune Dreadful was the sight which met my eyes. There they were, still struggling in the waves — now touching some slippery rock, and hoping to work their way on to where I was, and then borne back again by the hungry sea. In vain they struggled. I could afford them no help. One by one, their heavy boots impeding all their efforts, they sank down, and were hid to view beneath the waters Two or three still remained alive, though at some little distance. One I recognised as our old mate, the cause of our disaster. He had contrived to kick off his shoes, and was swimming towards the rock. Poor old man, he struggled hard for life. In a moment I forgot all the mischief he had caused, and considered how I might help to save him. Undoing my neck-handkerchief, I fastened it to another I had in my pocket, and secured the two to the sleeve of my jacket. I watched him anxiously as he drew near, crying out to encourage him. Then I lowered the handkerchiefs, and as a sea washed him up towards the rock he caught hold of them, and with great care, lest we should both fall in, I helped him up the side of the rock. I had not time to say anything, for I saw another person struggling in the water. I was afraid that he would never reach the rock, for his strength seemed almost exhausted. I shouted to him. He looked up. It was Charley Iffley. I own that I was now doubly anxious for his safety. Just then an oar washed by him. He was just able to grasp it. It enabled him to recover his strength, and in a short time another sea drove him close up to the rock. I hove the end of my handkerchief to him, he caught it; and the old mate and I leaning over, hauled him, almost exhausted, out of the reach of the sea. We looked round. We were the only survivors out of all the crew. The strong men had lost their lives. The oldest and weakest, and the two youngest, had alone been saved. Whether we should ultimately escape with our lives seemed, however, very doubtful. There was barely space enough for us to sit clear out of the wash of the sea; and should the tide be rising we might be washed off. We found, however, that the tide was falling, and this restored our hopes of being saved. As the tide ebbed, the water got a good deal smoother, and the weather once more clearing, we were able to consider our position and what was best to be done. We judged that we were three-quarters of a mile from the island of St. Mary's, but we could make out no habitations, and we thought it very probable night might come on before anybody would see us, while we felt if we remained on the rock that we could scarcely hope to survive.

We were already benumbed with the cold, and almost perishing with hunger. 'We must try and reach the island,' said Mr. Cole; 'are you inclined to try it, lads?' We of course said we were. He looked at his watch, which being an old silver hunting one, was, in spite of the wet, still going, and found that it was two o'clock. 'In another half hour we must make the attempt,' said he; 'so, lads prepare as best you can. It won't be an easy job.' The time to wait seemed very long. We watched the tide ebbing, and rock after rock appearing. At last he said, ' We cannot hope for a better opportunity than now. I'll lead the way. Lend me a hand, lads, if I want it.'

We promised him that we would, and slipping down the rock on the land side a much greater distance than we had come up, we found our feet touching the bottom. There was no sea to speak of, so on we went pretty confidently. The old man advanced very cautiously, but Charley Iffley, thinking that we might move faster, said he would go ahead. He did, and went head under also immediately afterwards. He came up again directly, and struck out towards the next rock. We took to swimming at once, to save the loss of breath, and all reached the next rock without difficulty. After resting a little, we started again. We had no wish to remain longer than we could help with a north-easterly gale blowing on us in the month of March. The cold, too, was very bitter. Yet at the time I fancy I scarcely thought about it. Thus on we went, sometimes wading, sometimes swimming, and sometimes scrambling along the ledge which the receding water had left bare. Often we had to assist each other, and I believe none of us alone could have performed the task. Once Mr. Cole was very nearly giving in, and twice Charley declared he could not go on, and must stay on the rock where we were resting till we could send him aid. We soon showed him that the rock would be covered long before assistance could reach him, and in another instant he was as ready as either of us to proceed. Once I almost gave in, but my companions roused me up, and again I set forward with renewed strength.

It was not, however, till six o'clock in the evening that we reached the shore, and as we found ourselves on dry land we staggered up

5

the beach, and the old mate fell down on his knees, and in a way I did not expect of him, thanked the Almighty for the mercy He had shown us. It was a wild, desolate place, with only high rocks about on every side, without trees, and no roads that we could discover to guide us to any habitation. We went on a little way, and then the mate and Charley said they could go no further. I also felt my strength almost exhausted, but I knew that it would not do for all of us to give in, so I roused myself to exertion. That I might try and learn our position before night completely overtook us, I climbed up to the top of the highest rock I could find and looked around me. Not a habitation or a sign of one could I discover, or a road or path of any sort,—while wild heath, or sand, or rock stretched away on every side, looking cold and bleak as well could be, in that dark, dreary March evening. With this uncheering information I found my way back to my companions. We could not attempt to move on in the dark, so we looked about for some place where we might find shelter during the night.

'Oh, Will, I wish we had some food, though,' said Charley; 'I am dying of hunger.'

So was I, and before moving further I returned to the beach, and with my knife cut off a number of shell-fish from the rocks, and filled my pockets with them. With this provision I returned to my companions, and sat down by their side. We ate a few, which much refreshed us, and Charley said he could go on, but the old mate declared his inability to move further.

Accordingly, Charley and I hunted about in every direction, and at last came on a shallow cave on the lee-side of a rock. The sand inside was dry, and after being exposed so long to the cold wind we thought the air warm, so we helped the old man into it, and placed him in the warmest and driest spot we could find out. He did not seem to care about eating, but complained bitterly of thirst. Charley could no longer move, so I went out to try and find some water. As I was groping about, almost giving up the search in despair, I felt my foot splash into a puddle. I knelt down. It was clear, pure water, and I drank as much as I required. How grateful I felt! I thought that I had never tasted a more delicious draught. I had saved my hat, and filling it from the pool, I carried the water to my two companions. We longed to be able to light a fire, but we had in the first place no flint and steel to produce a flame, so of course it was not worth while to search about for fuel. At last, finding I could do nothing else for the comfort of my companions, I sat down beside them and opened some more of the shell-fish, which we ate raw. They served to stay our hunger, but I cannot say that eaten raw, without vinegar, or pepper, or bread, they were particularly palatable.

We had promise of a dreary night, and this was only the commencement. The poor old mate was very ill. Deprived of his usual stimulants, he could badly support the cold and wet to which he had been so long exposed. He began to shiver all over, and complained of pains in every part of his body. Then he was silent, and would do little more than groan terribly. At last his mind began to wander; he did not know where he was nor what had happened, and he talked of strange scenes which had occurred long ago, and of people he had known in his youth. I could not help listening with much interest to what he said. By it I made out that he was by birth a gentleman; that he had gone to sea in the navy with every prospect of rising in it, and that he had been in one or two actions in which he had distinguished himself. But a change came over him. He had begun by small degrees, just taking a nip now and then, till he had become—and that very rapidly—a hard drinker. From that time all his prospects in life were blighted. From some misconduct he was dismissed the ship to which he belonged, and soon afterwards, for similar behaviour, the navy itself. Then he squandered away in vice and sensual indulgence the whole of his patrimony, and at last went to sea in the merchant service as the only means of obtaining support.

His career has been that of many young men who have begun life with as fair prospects, and ruined them all from their own folly and imprudence. Poor old man, when I heard all this, and feared that he was dying, I could not help pitying him, and feeling still more sad when I thought that the last act of his life was a strong evidence that he had in no way reformed as he advanced in years.

At length he slept more quietly, and, overcome by weariness, I too fell fast asleep. I did not awake till the sun was up and glancing on the tops of the rocks before our cave. Charley awoke at the same time, and began to rub his eyes and to wonder where he was. The old mate was awake. There was a dull, cold look in his eye, and his brow was wrinkled with pain. He groaned when I spoke to him, but after a little time he aroused himself and spoke. He said that he could not move a limb, much less walk; but he begged that Charley and I would try and find our way to the nearest village and bring him assistance.

'Make haste, that's good lads,' said he, in a trembling voice; 'my days are numbered, I fear; but I am not fit to die. I don't want to die, and I would give all I own to save my life.'

I did not want any pressing. I got up, and though my limbs were stiff, after moving them about a little I found that I could walk. Charley at first thought that he could not move, but on making one or two trials he discovered that he was able to accompany me. So we set off together to try and find our way to Grimsby, which the mate told us was the nearest village he knew of.

After wandering about and missing our way, and having to sit down frequently from weakness, we reached Grimsby. Our appearance excited a good deal of compassion among the people, who came out of their houses to inquire about the wreck. The chief man of the place was a Mr. Adams; he took us into his house and sent for shoes and clothing for us, and had us washed, and dressed in fresh dry clothes, and put food before us. When I told him about the old mate, he said that he knew the place, and that he could not let us go back, but that he would send some men with a litter who would bring him in much sooner than if we were to go for him. He was as good as his word, for not long after we had done breakfast Mr. Cole appeared; he seemed very ill, but he was able to take a little food, and drink some spirits and water. He was put at once to bed, and Mr. Adams sent over to St. Mary's, the chief town in the island, for a doctor to see him. The doctor came, and shook his head and said that he saw very little prospect of his recovery. All the time we remained at Grimsby, we were treated with the greatest kindness. We had the best of everything, comfortable beds, and nothing to do. Charley and I sat up by turns by the side of the old man's bed. He grew worse and worse; we soon saw that his days were drawing to a close.

A week passed away, and still he lingered on. I asked the doctor if he did not think that he might recover.

'No; it is impossible,' he answered.

'Does he know, sir, that he is going to die?' I asked.

'Every man knows that such will be his lot, one day or other,' he replied, 'though many try very hard to forget it.'

'Shall I tell him, sir, what you think?' said I; for I could not bear the idea of allowing the old man to go out of the world without any preparation.

'It will do him no harm,' said the doctor. 'If it would, I could not allow it. My duty is to keep body and soul together as long as I can.'

I thought even at the time that something more was to be done. It was not, however, till many years afterwards that I discovered it was far more important to prepare the soul for quitting the body, than to detain it a few hours or days longer in its mortal frame, with the risk of its losing all the future happiness it is so capable of enjoying. When I went back to the old mate I told him that the doctor thought he was in a very bad way, and that he would never be on his feet again.

'Well, Will,' said he, 'it's a hard case; but I've known men as ill as I am get well again, and I don't know why I shouldn't recover.'

'But if you don't recover,—and the doctor, who ought to know, thinks you won't,—wouldn't it be well to prepare for death, sir?' said I boldly; for, having made up my mind to speak, I was not going to be put off it by any fear of consequences. He was silent for a long time.

'I'll think about it,' he said at last.

He little thought how short a time he had to think about it. So it is with a great number of people. They'll tell you that they will not think about dying, but think whether they will make preparation for death; and they go on thinking, till death itself cuts the matter short, and the right preparations are never made. So it was with the poor old mate. He said that he had no friends,—no relations who would care to hear of him,—and that he had no message to send to any one. He intended, however, to get well and to look after his own affairs. In the evening he got worse. I suspected that he thought he was dying, because he gave his watch to Mr. Adams, who had been so kind to us, and divided a few shillings he had in his pockets between Charley and me. The next day he died. Though I had no respect for him, I felt a blank as if I had lost an old friend. Charley and I saw the poor old man buried, and then we agreed that it was time for us to be looking out for a vessel to get back to our masters.

The next day a brig called the *Mary Jane* put into the harbour, bound round from Bridgewater to London. Though I wanted to get to Plymouth to see my grandmother and aunt, and Charley wished to go to Hull, to stay with his widowed mother, as another chance might not occur for some time, we shipped aboard her. Before going we told Mr. Adams the name of the firm to which we were apprenticed, that he might recover from them the sums he had expended on us; but he replied, that he had taken care of us because it was right to succour the distressed, and that he required no reward or repayment. He was a good man, and I hope he enjoys his reward.

The desire to see my only relations grew stronger every day, and I thought how happy I should feel if I could but get landed at Plymouth, to run up and take them by surprise. This, however, could not be. When we reached London I found that the *Mary Jane*, as soon as she had discharged her cargo, was to sail again for the westward; and as she this time was to touch at Plymouth, so the captain said, I asked him to give me a passage. He replied, that as I had behaved very well while with him he would, so I remained on board. Here I parted from Charley, who got a berth on board a vessel bound for Hull, where he wanted to go. We sailed, and I hoped in a few days to have my long-wished-for desire gratified. When, however, we got abreast of the Isle of Wight, we met with a strong southwesterly gale, which compelled us to run for shelter to the Motherbank. While lying there the captain received orders from his owners not to touch at Plymouth, but to go on to Falmouth. This was a great disappointment to me. Still I thought that I could easily get

back from Falmouth to Plymouth, so that it would be wiser to stick
by the ship.

The old brig was not much of a sailer, but still, after running
through the Needles, we had a quick passage till we got a little to
the westward of the Eddystone. The captain, for some reason or other,
expecting a south-westerly breeze, had been giving the land a wide
berth, when the wind, instead of coming out of the south-west, blew
suddenly with terrific violence from the north-east. The old tub of a
brig did her best to beat up towards the land, but without avail. A
squall took all her sails out of her, and away we went driving helplessly before it, as if we were in a hurry to get across the Atlantic.
Our master, Captain Stunt, though a good seaman, was nothing of a
navigator, and we could scarcely tell even where we were driving to.
The vessel also was old, and had seen a good deal of hard service.
Our condition, therefore, was very unsatisfactory. We had no quadrant
on board, and if we had possessed one there was no one to use it—
indeed, it was many days before the sun appeared, and all we knew
was that, by the course we had drifted and the rate we had gone, we
were a considerable distance from any land. Still the captain hoped,
when the weather moderated, to be able to beat back and get hold of
the Irish coast, as the phrase is. At length the wind lulled a little,
and we once more made sail on the brig. We got on pretty well for
a few hours, when down came the gale once more on us, and before we
could shorten sail, a heavy sea struck the vessel, and she was turned
over on her beam-ends, a sea at the same time knocking our boats to
pieces and washing everything loose off the deck. There she lay like
a log, the water rushed into her hold, and every moment we expected
she would go down. Terror was depicted on every countenance. The
only person who remained cool and collected was the old master.

'My lads, we must cut away the masts—there's no help for it!' he sang out in a clear voice. He himself appeared directly afterwards with an axe in his hand, but it was some time before others could be found. The first thing was to cut away the lee rigging and then the weather, that the masts might fall clear of the hull. A few well-directed strokes cut nearly through them, and with a crash the remaining part broke off, and the vessel lay a dismasted hull amid the high-leaping and foaming waves. She righted, however, and we had now to hope that, if she weathered out the gale, some vessel might fall in with us and tow the brig into harbour, or at all events take us off the wreck. The next thing to be done was to rig the pumps to get the vessel clear of the water which had washed into her. We all pumped away with a will, for we knew that our lives depended on our exertions. Pump as hard as we could, however, we found that we made no progress in clearing the wreck of water. At last the mate went down to ascertain the cause of this. In a few minutes he rushed on deck with a look of dismay.

' What's the matter, Ellis ?' asked the captain.

' It's all up with us, sir,' answered the mate. ' A butt has started, and it is my belief that the brig will not swim another half hour.'

' Then let us get some grog aboard, and die like men,' cried some of the crew.

' Die like brutes, you mean, my lads !' exclaimed the old master. ' No, no, we will have none of that. Let us see what we can do to save our lives. What, do you call yourselves British seamen, and talk of giving in like cowards ! Don't you know that there's " a sweet little cherub that sits up aloft" to take care of the life of poor Jack. That means that God Almighty watches over us, and will take care of those who trust in Him.'

These remarks from the old man had a good deal of effect with the sailors. ' What is it you want us to do, sir ?' they asked.

'Why, build a raft, my lads, and see if it won't float us.'

Encouraged by the spirited old man, we all set to work with a will. With our axes some of us cut up the deck and bulwarks, and collected all the remaining spars, while the rest lashed them together. The mate and a boy were employed meantime in collecting all the provisions and stores he could get at and in stowing them away in a couple of chests, which formed the centre of our raft. In a very short time nearly everything was ready. The raft was, however, so large that we could not attempt to launch it, but we hoped that it would float when the brig sank under us. We had all been so busy that we had not observed how rapidly the vessel was sinking. Suddenly the old master gave a loud shout, 'Now, my lads, now, my lads! to the raft, to the raft!' Some of the men had gone forward to get hold of their clothes or some money, or anything they could find, against his advice. Some of them were seen at this moment leisurely coming up the fore hatchway. Even when he shouted to them they did not hurry themselves, any more than sinners are apt to do when warned by their faithful pastors to flee from the wrath to come. Mr. Ellis and I, with two other men, were near him at the time. We leaped on to the raft as he spoke, and seizing some oars which had been placed on it, we stood ready to shove it clear of the wreck as she sank. The vessel gave a plunge forward. The other men on deck rushed aft with frantic haste, but the waters were around them before they could catch hold of the raft. The look of horror on their countenances I cannot even now forget. One was a little before the others: he clutched at one of the oars. With our united strength we hauled him in. Then down went the brig. The cry of our companions was quickly stifled. The raft rocked to and fro as the wild seas tossed up fiercely round us. Now one came sweeping on. 'Hold on! hold on!' shouted the old master. One of our number did not attend to him. The sea passed over the raft, almost blinding us.

When we looked up, the man was gone. Five of us only remained alive. How soon more of our number might be summoned from the world, who could tell? I dare not dwell on the dreadful thoughts which passed through my mind. Was I truly under the ban of Heaven? Was I to prove the destruction of every vessel I sailed aboard? This was the fourth time I had been shipwrecked. 'Oh, my oath! my oath!' I ejaculated. 'Could I but retract it! But how is that to be done?' Uttered once, there it must remain engraven in the book of heaven. As I lay on that sea-tossed raft, in the middle of the Atlantic, I pondered deeply of those things in my own wild untutored way. Did but men remember always that every word they utter, every thought to which they give expression, is entered on a page never to be erased till the day of judgment, how would it make them put a bridle on their tongues, how should it make them watch over every wandering emotion of their minds, and pray always for guidance and direction before they venture to speak!

For several days the gale continued. We scarcely ventured to move for fear of being washed away. Now the raft rose on the side of a sea —now rocked on its summit—now sunk down into the trough, but still was preserved from upsetting—had which event occurred, we must have been inevitably lost. We had food in the chests, but we had little inclination to taste it. Water was our great want. Our supply was very scanty. By the master's urgent advice, we took only sufficient at a time to moisten our tongues. For a few days we bore this with patience. Then the wind went down, and the sea grew calm, and the hot sun came out and struck down on our unprotected heads. The weather grew hotter and hotter. The men declared they could stand it no longer. One seized the cask of water, and before the master could prevent him, took a huge draught: then the others followed his example

The mate for some time withstood the temptation, but at length he yielded to it.

'Are we to die without a prospect of prolonging existence, because these men consume all the water?' I said to myself, and taking the cask, drew enough to quench my thirst. I offered it to the master. 'Come, sir,' said I, 'take the water, it may revive you, and perhaps to-morrow help may come.'

He could not withstand the appeal. Perhaps some men might have done so, from a high sense of the necessity of adhering to a resolution once formed. In two days we had not a drop of water left. There came horrors unspeakable. Madness seized the poor mate. Before he could be restrained, he leaped from the raft and sunk below the waves. The other two men sickened. First one, then the other died. The captain, though the oldest of all, kept his senses and his strength. He was a calm, even-tempered, abstemious man. Still, as he sat on the chest in the middle of the raft, of which he and I were the only occupants, he spoke encouragingly and hopefully to me. I listened, but could scarcely reply. I felt a sickness overcoming me. I thought death was approaching. I sank down at his feet with a total unconsciousness of my miserable condition.

CHAPTER V.

My last thoughts had been, before I lost all consciousness, that death was about to put an end to my sufferings. I remember then hearing a rush of waters—a confused sound—rattling of blocks—human voices— cries and shrieks. I looked up—it was night. A dark object was towering above my head. I fancied it was a huge black rock, and that it was going to fall down and crush me. 'To what strange shore have we drifted?' I thought. I cried out with terror. 'Never fear, my lad,' said a voice. 'It's all right.' I found myself gently lifted up in the arms of a person, and when I next opened my eyes, I discovered that I was on the deck of a large ship and several people standing round me. The light of a lantern fell on the face of one of them. I looked hard at the person. Was it only fancy? I was certain that it was the countenance of Charley Iffley. I pronounced his name. He had not before recognised me.

'Why, Will Weatherhelm, how did you come out here?' he exclaimed, in a tone of surprise. But a gentleman, whom I found to be a doctor, told him that he must not now talk to me, and that he would find out all about it by and by.

I was then carried below, and placed in a berth, and very kindly treated. In a few days I was sufficiently recovered to go on deck. I was glad to see old Captain Stunt there also, looking well and fresh. I found that we were on board a large West India trader, the *Montezuma*, belonging to the firm to which I was apprenticed, Messrs. Dickson, Waddilove, and Buck. I little knew what additional cause for gratitude we had for our escape, for the ship coming on the raft at night while Mr. Stunt was asleep, we were not observed till she actually grazed by it. The noise awoke him, when he shouted out, and the ship being close-hauled, and having little way, was immediately luffed up, and without difficulty we were taken on board.

'Well, Charley, how did you come to be on board the *Montezuma?*' I asked.

'That question is very simply answered,' said he. 'When I got home I found that my uncles and aunts and all my first cousins looked upon me as a very troublesome visitor, and hinted that the sooner I took myself off to sea again the better. It is not comfortable to feel that everybody is giving one the cold shoulder, so I begged to have a new kit, and offered to look out for a ship. It was wonderful how willingly everybody worked, and how soon my outfit was ready. My eldest uncle hurried off to Mr. Dickson, and as they were just sending the *Montezuma* to sea, and had room for an apprentice, I was immediately sent on board, and here I am. Now you know all about me. I thought I was going to change and become a better character. I was sorry for many things I had done, and if my relations had treated me kindly at first, I think they would have found me very different to what I was. How ever, give a dog a bad name and it sticks to him like pitch.'

'But I am afraid, Charley, from what you have told me, that you gave yourself the bad name,' said I. 'You should not blame others.'

'I do not,' he answered. 'All I blame them for is, that they did not soften their hearts toward me, and try to reform me. They might have done it, and I could have loved some of them tenderly; but others are harsh, stiff, cold, very good people, who have no sympathy for any who do not think like themselves, and make no allowances for the follies and weaknesses of those who have not had the advantages they have enjoyed.' And Charley put his head between his hands and burst into tears.

I was very glad to see this. It made me like him more than I had ever before done. I have since often thought how very different many young people would turn out if they were spoken to by their elders with gentleness and kindness—if sympathy was shown them, and if their faults were clearly pointed out.

Our owners were very respectable people, and understood their business, so they were generally well served. Captain Horner, of the *Montezuma*, was a good sailor. The crew consequently looked up to him, though he kept himself aloof from them. He was what the world calls a very good sort of man, but as to his religion and morals I was not able to form an opinion. It may seem strange that I, a young apprentice, should have thought at all on the subject. Perhaps, if those in command knew how completely their conduct and behaviour are canvassed by those under them, they would behave very differently to what they do. Our second mate, Josias Merton by name, was a man worthy of remark. He was a very steady, serious-minded person, and yet full of life and fun. He prided himself on his knowledge of his profession in all its details. His heart was kind and gentle, and he was at the same time brave and determined, active and prompt in action. He never undertook what he did not believe, after due consideration, he could accomplish, and therefore seldom failed in what he undertook. Both Charley and I owed him much, for he spared no pains to improve us and to instruct us in our profession.

As soon as I was well, I was placed in a watch and had begun to know and to do my duty. The Atlantic afforded me the sight of many objects to which I had been unaccustomed in the Mediterranean. I remember one night coming on deck, and after I had looked to see what sail was set, and how the ship was steering, I cast my eyes over the calm ocean. It was very dark. There was no moon, and clouds obscured the stars. I gazed with amazement. The whole surface of the deep, far as the eye could reach, was lighted with brilliant flashes. I bent over the side. The sea was alive with fish of every size and shape. Some were leaping up, ever and anon, out of the water; others were chasing their smaller brethren through it; others, again, rolled over in it, or lay floating idly near, as if looking up with their bright eyes to watch the ship, the invader of their liquid home. People talk of the lack-lustre of a fish's eye. They are acquainted only with a dead fish. Did they ever remark the keen, bright, diabolical eye of a shark watching for his expected victim? I know nothing in nature more piercing, more dread-inspiring. Here were collected sharks, and pilot-fish, and albicores, bonettas, dolphins, flying-fish, and numberless others, for which old Mr. Stunt, to whom I applied, could give me no name. The very depths of the ocean seemed to have sent forth all their inhabitants to watch our proceedings.

'I suppose that it is the shining copper on the ship's bottom attracts them,' said the old man. 'They take it to be some big light, I conclude.' Whether he was right or not I have never since heard any one give an opinion.

The first place at which we touched was Bridgetown, in the island of Barbadoes. I thought the Bay of Carlisle, with the capital Bridgetown built round its shores, and the fertile valleys, and rich fields of sugar-cane, altogether a very lovely spot. The West India Islands are divided into what are called the Windward and Leeward Islands. The wind, it must be understood, blows for nine months of the year from the east. The most eastern islands are therefore called the Windward Islands, and those in the western group the Leeward Islands. Of all the Caribbean Islands, Barbadoes is the most windward, and the Havannah the most leeward. We had to land cargo and passengers, and to take in cargo at several islands. We commenced, therefore, at the windward ones. In that way I became acquainted with a considerable portion of the West India Islands, and very beautiful places I saw on them. The *Montezuma* was not long in getting a full cargo, and then she prepared to return home. The last place at which we touched was Kingston in Jamaica. At length, I thought to myself, I shall once more see Old England, and satisfy my kind grandmother and Aunt Bretta that I am still alive. I hope that I may leave this vessel without her being shipwrecked, as has been the fate of every one I have yet been on board. Just as this idea had crossed my mind the captain sent for me, and said that he was going to leave Mr. Merton in charge of a small schooner, which was to be employed in running between the different islands to collect cargo to be ready for the return of the ship, and that he wished me to remain.

'You will be soon out of your indentures, and if you behave well, as I have no doubt you will, I will promise you a mate's berth,' he added.

This was indeed more than I could have expected; and though I was disappointed in not going home, I thanked the captain very much for his good opinion of me and kind intentions, and accepted his offer. The *Montezuma* sailed for England, and I found myself forming one of the crew of the *Grogo* schooner. We had a very pleasant life of it, because the black slaves did all the hard work, taking in and discharging cargo, and bringing water and wood off to us.

I might fill pages with descriptions of the curious trees and plants

6

and animals I saw in the West Indies. There is one, however, which
I must describe. I was asking Mr. Merton one day the meaning of
the name of our schooner. He laughed, and said that grogo is the
name of a big maggot which is found in the Cockarito palm or
cabbage tree. This maggot is the grub of a large black beetle. It
grows to the length of four inches, and is as thick as a man's
thumb. Though its appearance is not very attractive, it is considered
a delicious treat by people in the West Indies, when well dressed,
and they declare that it has the flavour of all the spices of the East.
These maggots are only found in such cabbages as are in a state of
decay. The Cockarito palm often reaches fifty feet in height. In the
very top is found the most delicate cabbage enclosed in a green husk,
composed of several skins. These are pee'ed off, until the white
cabbage appears in long thin flakes, which taste very like the kernel
of a nut. The heart is the most delicate, and, being sweet and crisp,
is often used as a salad. The outside when boiled is considered far
superior to any European cabbage. One of the most important trees
in the West Indies is the plantain tree. It grows to the height of
about twenty feet, and throws out its leaves from the top of the
stem so as to look something like an umbrella. The leaves when
fresh are of a shining sea-green colour, and have the appearance of
rich satin. When the young shoots come out, they split and hang
down in tatters. From the top grows a strong stalk about three
feet long, which bends down with the weight of its purple fruit, each
of which is in shape like a calf's heart—a considerable number form
one bunch. Each tree produces but one bunch at a time. The
plantain, when ripe, forms a delicious fruit, and when boiled or
roasted, it is used instead of potatoes. It forms a principal portion
of the food of the negroes. The cassava forms another important
article of the food of the blacks. The plant grows about four feet

high; the stem is of a grey colour, and divides near its top into several green branches, from which spring red stalks with large leaves. There are two species, the sweet and bitter cassava. The bitter is excessively poisonous till exposed to the heat of fire. The root is like a coarse potato. It is dried and then grated on a grater formed by sharp pebbles stuck on a board, and the juice which remains is then pressed out by means of an elastic basket, into which the grated root is stuffed. The farina thus produced is made into thin cakes and baked. Tapioca is the finer portion of the farina.

I might, as I was saying, fill my pages with an account of the wonderful productions of those fertile islands, of the value of which I do not think even now my countrymen are fully aware. One curious circumstance I must mention in connection with them and my paternal country, Shetland, though I did not hear it till very many years afterwards. It shows how intimately the interests of distant parts of the world are united. The slaves in the West Indies were supplied by their masters with salt fish, which fish were caught by the Shetlanders off their coasts. When the slaves were emancipated, they refused any longer to eat the description of food which they had been compelled to consume during their servitude, and the Shetland fish-dealers had not thought in the meantime of looking out for fresh markets. The consequence was, they were ruined; the herring boats were laid up, and the fishermen had to go south in search of employment.

However, that has nothing to do with my story. The *Grogo* was very successful, and we were looking forward every day for the return of the *Montezuma*. I could not help telling Mr. Merton one day of my rash oath which I had made in the presence of my grandmother, and how I had been wrecked in every vessel I had sailed in from the time I came to sea. He tried to reason me out of the belief that I

was the cause of the loss of the vessels. He said the oath was
wicked, there was no doubt of that, but that others had lost their
lives and some their property, while I each time had suffered less
than anybody else. I saw the strength of his reasoning, but still I
was not convinced. I felt that I had deserved all the hardships I
had endured, and I fully expected to be wrecked again. What
followed may seem very strange. All I can do is to give events as
they occurred. Two days after this we lay becalmed about ten miles
from the land off Port Morant, to the eastward of Kingston in
Jamaica. We had an old man of colour, who acted as pilot and
mate on board. He had been below asleep. At last he turned out
of his hot, stifling berth, and came on deck. He looked round the
horizon on every side.

'Captain,' said he, 'I wish we were safe in port. There's something bad coming.'

'What is it, Billy?' asked Mr. Merton.

'A hurricane!' was the answer.

The hurricane came. The spirit of the whirlwind rode triumphantly
through the air. Earth and ocean felt his power; trees were torn up
by the roots; houses were overthrown; the water rose in huge waves
—hissing, and foaming, and leaping madly around us. Our topmasts
had been struck; every stitch of canvas closely furled, and everything
on deck securely lashed. The fierce blast of the tempest struck the
little vessel; round and round she was helplessly whirled. Away we
drove out to sea, and we thought we were safe; but our hopes were
to prove vain. Once more we approached the shore with redoubled
speed; the frowning rocks threatened our instant destruction; we could
do nothing for our preservation. To anchor was utterly useless. We
shook hands all round; on, on we drove. A yellow sandy bay
appeared between two dark rocks; a huge sea carried us on; safely

between the two rocks it bore us; up the beach it rolled. The schooner drew but little water. High up the sea carried us stem on. We rushed forward, and springing along the bowsprit, leaped on to the sand, and before another sea could overtake us we were safe out of its reach. We fell down on our knees and uttered a prayer of thanksgiving for our preservation. In ten minutes not a fragment of the schooner held together. We had truly reason to be grateful.

'Another time wrecked,' said I to Mr. Merton.

'Yes, Will; but another time saved,' was his answer.

We got safe to the village of Morant Bay, where we were very kindly received, and the next day were forwarded over land to Kingston, there to await the arrival of the *Montezuma*. She came into Port Royal Harbour in about a week, not having felt the hurricane. As the agent had a full cargo for her, she only remained a short time, and at length I found myself on the way to the shores of old England.

'There is no fear now but what I shall get to Plymouth at last,' I thought to myself as I walked the deck in my watch the first night after we had got well clear of the land, and were standing out into the broad Atlantic. Then I remembered my rash oath, and in spite of all Mr. Merton's reasonings, I could not help believing that its consequences would still follow me. 'Home! home! with all its endearments, is not for you. The time of your probation is yet unfulfilled!—your punishment is not accomplished!'—a voice whispered in my ear. I could not silence it. Still I thought that it was only fancy. Just then Charley Iffley joined me in my walk; we were in the same watch. Hitherto I had never told him of my belief that a curse was pursuing me. I should have been wiser not to have mentioned the subject to him; still I thought that he was so much changed that he would sympathize with me. I told him all that had occurred from the moment when I first expressed my wish to go to sea to my grandmother and aunt, and reminded him of all the sufferings I had endured, and the number of times I had been shipwrecked. Instead, however, of treating the subject in the gentle, serious way Mr. Merton had done, he burst into a loud fit of laughter.

'Nonsense, Will,' he exclaimed, 'you'll next accuse me of being your evil spirit, and of tempting you to sin. Many a man has been shipwrecked as often as you have who has been sent to sea against his own will; and if he swore at all, it was that he might speedily get on shore. Get that idea out of your head as soon as possible.'

I was anxious enough to follow Charley's advice, but do all I could, the idea came back and back again whenever I found myself during my watch at night taking a turn by myself on deck.

Charley was already out of his indentures, and as he had become a steady fellow and a good seaman, he hoped to be made mate on his next voyage. At last the day arrived when the term of my apprenticeship expired, and I was to be a free man, able to take any berth offered to me. My only wish, however, after I had paid my family a visit, was to be employed in the service of my present owners. To commemorate the event, Charley proposed having a feast in our mess, and he managed to purchase from the third mate, who acted as a sort of purser, various articles of luxury and an additional bottle of rum. We were very jolly, and very happy we thought ourselves, and blew all care to the winds. The passengers and the captain were making merry in the same way in the cabin, drinking toasts, and singing songs, and making speeches, and telling funny stories, so the cabin-boy told us as he came forward convulsed with laughter. The wind was fair and light, the sea was smooth, and no ship floating on the ocean could have appeared more free from danger. Suddenly there was a cry—a cry which, next to 'Breakers ahead,' is the most terror-inspiring which can strike on a seaman's ear. It was, 'Fire! fire! fire!' Who uttered it? A man with frantic haste— horror in his countenance—rushed up from the after hold. 'Fire! fire! fire!' he repeated. In an instant fore and aft the revellers in dismay sprung from their seats and hurried on deck. The captain was calm and collected, had he lost his presence of mind, who could have hoped to escape? With rapid strides he reached the after hatchway, out of which streams of smoke were gushing forth. He summoned the passengers and some of the crew to provide themselves with buckets, and to heave water down upon the spot whence the smoke seemed to come, while the rest of the crew were employed in pumping water into the hold. Wet sails and blankets were brought, and, led by Mr. Merton, some of the more daring of the men leaped down with them, in the hopes of stifling the flames before they burst forth. I followed the second mate; I knew the risk, but I resolved to share it with him. 'More blankets! more sails!' we shouted. They were hove down to us; but in vain we threw them over the lower hatchway. Thicker and thicker masses of smoke came gushing forth, and we were obliged to cry out to be drawn up, and were almost overpowered before we reached the deck. Two of our number had been left behind. Mr. Merton and I were about to return, when a loud explosion was heard. Part of the deck was torn up, and flames burst fiercely forth through the hatchway. It was very evident that some of the rum casks had ignited, as was afterwards ascertained, by a candle having been carelessly left burning in the hold.

All hopes of saving the ship were now abandoned. The boats could not carry the entire crew and passengers. They were, however, instantly lowered into the water with a boat-keeper in each, while the rest of the people were told off, some to get up provisions and water, and others to construct a raft. I was engaged on the raft, but remembering what I had suffered on former occasions, I urged the people to take an ample supply of water in each of the boats. Scarcely was the long-boat in the water than the flames burst forth through the main hatchway, and had not the captain been prompt in his orders, the boat itself would have been lost. Provisions for the raft were put into the long-boat, while we were working away at its construction. Every moment we expected to see the flames burst forth from under our feet. We worked with might and main; with our axes we cut away the after-bulwarks, so as to launch it overboard. We had crowbars in our hands. It was barely finished.

'Heave away, my lads, heave away!' shouted the captain. 'Now, gentlemen; now, my men; those told off for the boats, be smart! Get into them! No crowding, though.'

The orders were obeyed, for everybody had learned to confide in the captain's judgment. We meantime were urging the raft over the side. 'Quick! quick!' was the cry. With reason, too. The flames burst forth close to our heels. With mighty efforts, by means of our crowbars, we prized on the raft, it being balanced over the sea, yet the flames almost caught it. One effort more. It plunged into the water. A rope brought it up. Almost before it again rose to the surface we were compelled by the devouring element behind us to leap on to it. The deck gave way with a crash as we left it, and two more poor fellows sank back into the flames. The painter was cut, and as the ship drove slowly away from us, another loud explosion was heard, and fore and aft she was wrapped in flames, which rose writhing and twisting up to her topgallant masts.

'And there's an end of the fine old *Montezuma*. Well, she was a happy ship!' exclaimed a seaman near me, passing his hand across his brow. 'You know, Weatherhelm, I've sailed in her since I was a boy, and I have learned to look upon her pretty much as if she was my mother.' I never heard warmer praise bestowed on a merchantman.

Thus was I once more floating on a raft in the middle of the Atlantic. 'I thought it would be so,' I muttered to myself. 'My oath, my oath!'

While watching the conflagration of the ship, we had had no time to think of our own condition. The boats had pulled off to some distance from the burning ship, and we were left without oars, or sails, or provisions. Night, too, was coming on. The dreadful idea occurred to some of us, that those in the boats with their eyes dazzled by the glare of the burning ship might not see the raft. The captain, by the urgent request of the people, had gone in the long-boat. Mr. Merton had remained with us. We shouted—but in vain—the boats were too far off to allow our voices to be heard. The night came on, but still we could see the burning wreck, and we felt sure that while that beacon was in sight, the boats would not give up their search for us. We forgot how fast the wreck had been drifting away. Ours seemed a hard fate. Without food or water, unless picked up we must evidently soon perish. Mr. Merton addressed us in a spirited, manly way. He told us not to despair—that many poor fellows had been much worse off than we were, and that certainly by daylight we should be seen by our shipmates in the boats, and be supplied with what we wanted. If not, we were exactly in the track of homeward-bound vessels coming from America, and that we should be certainly fallen in with.

It was a very dreary night, though. All we could do was to sit quiet and watch the burning wreck. Gradually the flames burnt lower and lower. Then a huge glowing ember appeared, and that suddenly sank from sight. In spite of our position, I had fallen asleep, when I was aroused by a loud shout from my companions. It was in answer to a cry which came floating over the water from a distance. We waited eagerly listening. Again the far-off cry was repeated. Loudly we

cheered in return, for we were very hungry, and had not yet had time to
grow weak from hunger. In less than twenty minutes the boats came
dashing up round us, and we found ourselves amply supplied with
provisions, which we discussed with no small appetites. The captain
then addressed us all; he told us that we must husband our provisions
and water, as we could not tell when any vessel might fall in with us.
He then urged the people in the other boats to remain by the raft, and
suggested that in the day-time they should extend themselves about ten
miles on either side so as to have a wider field of observation, but in
the night that they should come back and hang on to the raft.

I ought to have said there were four boats, and thus we were able to
command a range of vision of at least fifty miles. That is to say—the
raft being in the centre—the boats were twenty miles apart, and from
each boat a sail of fifteen miles off could at all events be seen. The
plan was agreed on. We had secured a long spar, which we set up as
a mast in the centre of the raft, with a flag at its head, so that the boats
could always have us in view; besides which, several compasses had
been saved which would enable them to find us even in thick weather.
All we had now, therefore, much to fear from was bad weather and a
long detention, when we might run short of provisions. The day passed
away, and no sign of a vessel was perceived. The mate kept up our
spirits by every means in his power. He encouraged us to sing songs
and tell stories to each other, and to give an account of our adventures,
and then he told us some stories, and some of them were very funny, and
made us laugh, and I must say that I have passed many duller days
than were those which I spent on that raft. 'And now, my lads,' said
he, 'as we cannot steer our course across the ocean without a compass,
no more can we our course through life without principles to guide us.
Now the only book which can give us right principles—can show us
how to live—the port we are bound for, and how to gain it, is one J

have in my pocket.' We all wondered what he was aiming at, and he was silent for some little time to allow our thoughts to settle down after the joking we had had. Then he pulled out of his pocket a Bible, and took his seat on a cask in the middle of the raft. 'I am going to read to you from this Holy Book, my lads, and I hope that you will listen to what I read—try to understand it—think over it—and do what it tells you.' I've often since heard the word of God read to sailors, but never more impressively; never to better effect, I believe, than I did on that raft in the Atlantic.

Just at nightfall all the boats came back, and hung on to us during the night, and nearly all the people went soundly to sleep. The captain in the morning proposed that those in the boat should change places with those on the raft, but we said that we were contented to be where we were, and that we preferred remaining with Mr. Merton. The next day passed away much as the first, so did a third and fourth. In the evening, however, of that last day, three boats only came back; the whale-boat, commanded by the fourth mate, did not make her appearance. Various were the surmises about her. Some thought that an accident had happened to her; many expressed their fears that the mate had deserted us, and abuse of no gentle nature was heaped on his and his companions' heads. The only people who made no complaints, and only seemed anxious to find excuses for him, were those on the raft. Why was this? Because, as I fully believe, they were influenced by the principles of Christian charity which the mate had been explaining to us, that principle which thinketh no wrong, until evidence indubitable is brought that wrong has been committed. Although we on the raft did not abuse the first mate and those with him, we could not help feeling anxious for his return. An hour of darkness passed away, and then another and another, and still the whale-boat did not appear. She had gone, I ought to have said, on the lee side of the raft; but the wind was light, so that she could have had no difficulty in pulling up to it. No one this night felt inclined to go to sleep. We were all too anxious about our companions. I saw Mr Merton turning his eyes with a steady gaze away to the south-east. I looked in the same direction. Gradually I saw emerging out of the darkness an opaque, towering mass. At first I thought it was a mere mark in the clouds, and then it resolved itself into the form of a tall ship close-hauled under all canvas. A shout from the boats showed that they had discovered the stranger. Again we shouted, and a cheer came up from her to show us that we were seen and heard. In a few minutes she hove to, and our own whale-boat appeared from alongside her, accompanied by another boat. The mate explained, as he made a tow-rope fast to the raft to tow us alongside the ship, that he had seen her just before nightfall, and by pulling away to the southward had happily succeeded in cutting her off.

We soon found ourselves on board a large ship, the *Happy Relief*—and a happy relief she was to us—bound homeward from Honduras with logwood. They were a rough set on board, from the master to the apprentices, but they treated us kindly, as most sailors treat others in distress, and we had every reason to be grateful to them. We had still greater reason to be thankful that we got on board their ship that night, for before the morning a gale began to blow, and a heavy sea soon got up, which would have swept us all off the raft, and in all probability swamped the boats. It continued blowing for several days. The ship laboured very much, and soon all hands were called to the pumps. She had proved a fortunate ship to us, and it was a fortunate circumstance for her that she had fallen in with us; for all hands had to keep spell and spell at the pumps, and even so we were only just able to keep the leaks under. Had she not had us on board, she would very soon, I suspect, have been water-logged. At length the gale abated, but we, notwithstanding, had to keep the pumps going night and day.

By the time we reached the Chops of the Channel, having a fair breeze, we were looking out every instant to make the land, when a big ship hove in sight, standing directly across our course. The people on board the Honduras ship had told us that a few days before they fell in with us, they had spoken an outward-bound brig, from which they gained the news that war had broken out between England and France and Spain. We made out the stranger to be a heavy frigate, but as she showed no colours, to what nation she belonged we could not tell. Some on board thought we ought to haul our wind on the opposite tack to that she was on, so as to avoid her altogether. She was standing with her head to the north. Our captain soon after gave the order to brace up the yards on the larboard tack, hoping to run into Mount's Bay or Falmouth harbour. We soon had proof that those on board the frigate had their eyes on us. The smoke of a gun was seen to issue from one of her bow ports, as a sign for us to heave to, but the captain thought he should first like to try the fleetness of his heels before he gave in. So we continued our course to the northward. The frigate on this braced her yards sharp up, and showed that she was not going to allow us to escape her, and, by the way she walked along, we soon saw that we should without fail become her prize.

All the men who had got two suits of clothes went and put them on, and stowed away all their money and valuables in their pockets, and we all of us began to think how we should like to see the inside of a Spanish or French prison. For my part, I had heard such stories about the cruelty of the Spaniards and French that I began to wish I was back again on the raft in the middle of the Atlantic. One thing is certain,— there is nothing harder than to become a prisoner at the beginning of a war, to an enemy who hates you, with very little prospect of being exchanged. All the glasses in the ship were turned towards the frigate as she drew near, to try and make out what she was. Presently she

fired another gun across our bows, and this time she was within shot
of us, and at the same moment up went the British ensign. Seeing that
there was no chance of escape, our captain hove to. I thought that as
she was an English ship, all was right, and could not make out the
reason of the agitation some of the older hands were in. In a quarter
of an hour or so, a boat with a lieutenant and a pretty strongly armed
crew came alongside. As he stepped on board, he went up to the
captain and told him about the war, and asked where he had come from,
and whether he had fallen in with any strange ships. 'And now,
captain,' said he, quite calmly, 'I should just like to see your crew.
Muster them on deck, if you please. You've a large number,' he
remarked, as soon as we all appeared. The captain told him how he
had picked so many of us up at sea. 'Ho, ho!' said the lieutenant;
'come here, my lads; you'd be glad to serve his Majesty, I know.'
And he told all the crew of the *Montezuma*, except the captain and first
mate, to get into his boat.

There was no little grumbling at this, but he did not appear like a man
who would stand any nonsense of this sort, so it went no further. 'But
those two are apprentices,' said Captain Horner, pointing to Charley and
me, and forgetting that we were both out of our indentures.

'Stout lads for apprentices,' remarked the lieutenant. 'Let me see
your papers.'

Now it might have been said, as we had been wrecked, that we had
lost them, but I would not tell a lie to gain any object.

'Please, sir,' said I, 'the captain makes a mistake. I was out of my
indentures a few days ago. I've no protection, and I don't want
any. I, for one, am ready to serve his Majesty and to fight for my
country.'

Charley hearing me say this, declared himself of the same mind, and
wishing Captain Horner and the captain of the Honduras ship good-bye,

and thanking them, we went over to the side ready to step into the boat. The lieutenant said he liked our spirit, and that he should keep his eye on us, and if we behaved well he should recommend us for promotion. This was satisfactory, but still I felt that all my prospects of becoming a mate were blown to the wind. The person who felt it most was Mr. Merton. From being an officer (and a gentleman he always was) he was reduced to the rank of a common seaman. What was far worse, too, he was engaged to be married, as soon as he returned home, to the daughter of a clergyman, who, Charley told me, was quite a lady. Now, poor fellow, for what he could tell, years might pass before he would be able to return on shore.

'Well, my man, are you ready to go?' said the lieutenant to him.

'I was second mate of the ship, and have private affairs which require my presence in England, sir,' he answered, quite calmly; and his voice showed that he was a man of education.

'That is no protection, I am afraid,' said the lieutenant. 'Duty is not always pleasant, but it must be done.'

'Very true, sir,' said Mr. Merton; 'but let me write a line to send home, and speak a few words to my late captain. I will not detain you.'

'I can give you five minutes,' said the lieutenant. pulling out his watch.

Mr. Merton thanked him and hurried below.

'Poor fellow! What words of anguish and sorrow did he pour out in that letter; yet, I doubt not, he expressed his own resignation, and endeavoured to encourage her to whom it was addressed to hope that yet happy days were in store for them. He entrusted the letter to the captain, and begged him to go and see and comfort the lady to whom it was addressed. Then with a calm countenance he appeared on deck, and signified to the lieutenant that he was ready to

accompany him. I doubt not he felt like a brave man going to
execution.

The frigate we were on board was the *Brilliant*, of forty guns, and,
as I looked round and saw what perfect order she was in, I thought her
a very fine ship, and except that I regretted not being able to return
home, I was perfectly content to belong to her. Men-of-war in those
days were very different to what they are at present. Men of all classes
were shipped on board, often out of the prisons and hulks, and the
sweepings of the streets. Quantity was looked for because quality
could not be got. An able seaman was a great prize. The pressgangs
were always at work on shore, and they thought themselves fortunate
when such could be found. Now, with such a mixture of men, the
bad often outnumbering the good, very strict and stern discipline was
necessary.

The very first day I got on board I saw five men flogged for not
being smart enough at reefing topsails. I thought it very cruel, and it
set me against the service. I did not inquire who the men were. I
found afterwards that they were idle rascals who deserved punishment, and always went about their duty in a lazy, sluggish way. However, there was no doubt that our captain was a very taut hand. The
ship had just come out of harbour. He had found out that the greater
part of his crew were a bad lot, and he was getting them into order.
He treated us who had belonged to the *Montezuma* in a very different
way. He saw that we were seamen, and he valued us accordingly.
Still I think there was more punishment on board than was absolutely
necessary. We had nine powerful fellows doing duty as boatswain's
mates on board, and there was starting and flogging going on every day
and all day long. The first time I ever saw a man punished I felt sick
at heart, and thought I should have fallen on deck, but I recovered
myself and looked on afterwards with very little concern.

The frigate I found was bound on a six months' cruise in the Bay of Biscay, not the quietest place in the world in the winter season. Mr. Merton was very soon made captain of the fore-top, and Charley and I were stationed on the top with him. Owing to him, I believe, we avoided being flogged, for he was always alive and brisk and kept us up to our duty. After all, there's nothing like doing things briskly. There's no pleasure in being slow and sluggish about doing a thing, and a great waste of time. Mr. Merton soon attracted the notice of the officers, and they used to address him very differently to the way they spoke to the other men. There was in the top with us a young midshipman: he was a fine little lad—full of life, and fun, and daring. He was the son or heir of some great lord or other, and a relation of the captain's, who had promised especially to look after him. Well, one day the ship was running before the wind with studden sails set alow and aloft and every sail drawing, so that she was going not less than eight or ten knots, when this youngster, with two or three others, was sky-larking aloft. He had gone out on the fore-topsail yardarm, when somehow or other he lost his hold and down he fell. Fortunately, he struck the belly of the lower studden sail, which broke his fall and sent him clear of the ship into the sea. Just at that moment Mr. Merton was coming up into the top. He saw the accident. Almost before the sentry at the gangway could cry out, ' A man overboard!' he was in the water striking out to catch hold of the youngster, who couldn't swim a stroke. At that moment the captain came on deck. He was in a great state of agitation when he heard who it was who had fallen overboard. Studden sail-sheets were let fly. No one minded the spars, though they were all cracking away; the helm was put down, the yards were braced sharp up, and the ship was brought close on a wind.

Meantime Mr. Merton was striking out towards where young Mr. Bouverie had gone down. All eyes were directed to the spot. 'Now

7

he sees him. He strikes out with all his might to catch him before the youngster sinks again. He has him—he has him, hurra!' Such were the cries uttered on every side, for the youngster was a favourite with all hands. A boat was instantly lowered, and Mr. Merton was brought on board with the youngster he had rescued, both of them nearly exhausted. The midshipman was carried into the captain's cabin. Mr. Merton, when he had shifted his wet things, returned on deck to his duty. The captain, however, immediately sent for him, and told him that he could not find words to express his gratitude. Mr. Merton thanked him, and said that he had merely done his duty, and did not consider which of the midshipmen it was he was going to try to save.

'Well, you have prevented a mother's heart from being wrung with agony, and a noble house from going into mourning,' said the captain. 'You deserve to be rewarded.' Mr. Merton thanked him, and went about his duty, thinking little more of the matter.

Now, although seamen know how to value a man who has leaped overboard, at the risk of his own life, to save a fellow-creature from drowning, they do not make much fuss about it, because most of them would be ready to do the same thing themselves. Still, it was easy to see that Joe Merton, as he was called by the ship's company, was raised yet higher in their estimation.

After we had been at sea some time we stood away to the westward. One forenoon, a shout from the masthead announced a sail in sight.

'Where away?' asked the officer of the watch.

'On the weather bow,' was the answer. 'There are two—three—four—the whole horizon is studded with them,' cried the look-out.

The officers were pretty quickly aloft to see what the strangers could be, for some thought perhaps it was an enemy's fleet. As they drew near, however, they were pronounced to be merchantmen, and before long we ascertained by their signals that they were part of a homeward-bound West India convoy, which had been separated in a gale of wind, off the banks of Newfoundland, from the ships of war in charge of them. Finding that they were totally unprotected, our captain made up his mind that it was his duty to see them safe into port, and signalling to them to keep together and put themselves under his orders, he invited some of the masters of the vessels near him to come on board to give him the news. Among other things, he learned that a fast-sailing French privateer had been hovering about them for some time, and had already picked off two, if not more, of their number, both heavily laden and valuable ships belonging to London; and the masters were of opinion that she had carried them into Santa Cruz, a harbour in the island of Teneriffe, one of the Canaries, because they had spoken an American vessel, the master of which told them that he had passed two such ships, accompanied by a craft answering to the description of the privateer, steering for that place. This information made the captain in a greater hurry than ever to get back to England, as he had made up his mind, as it afterwards appeared, to go and try to cut the ships out.

A strong westerly wind sprang up soon after this, and carried us in five days, with all our convoy, safe into Plymouth Sound. Now, for the first time after so many years, I found myself back at the place where I had passed my childhood, and where the only relations I had ever known, the only beings whose love I had any right to claim, resided. How eagerly I gazed on the shore, and I thought even that I could make out the little neat white row of cottages outside the town, in one of which my grandmother and aunt lived! But now came the question, how could I hope to get on shore? It was not likely that any leave would be granted, as we guessed that the frigate would not remain more than a day or two in harbour. The captain had gone on shore to see the admiral, and the first lieutenant was also called away, so that the

ship was left in charge of the second lieutenant, who had pressed me.
I knew that I was not likely to get what I wanted by holding back, so
I made bold and went up to him and told him how I had left my grandmother when I was a boy, and had been kept knocking about ever since,
and had only once, for a few hours, set my foot on English ground in
the London docks, and how I would give anything if I might just run
up and see how the old lady and my aunt were, and show them that I
was alive.

'I think I may trust you, my lad,' said the lieutenant, looking hard at
me. 'But who will be answerable for you?'

'Mr. Merton, sir. I know he will. He has known me for some time,
I answered earnestly. The lieutenant smiled; he was not accustomed to
hear a topman have a mister put to his name. 'I mean Joe Merton—
beg pardon, sir,' said I, 'he was my officer for some years.'

'No offence, my man; I like to hear a person speak respectfully of
those above him,' answered the lieutenant. 'He is your officer still, I
fancy. Well, if you can get him to be answerable for you, you may go
on shore for ten hours. I cannot give you longer leave than that.'

'Thank you, sir; thank you,' said I, and I hurried below to look for
Mr. Merton. I found him hard at work writing a letter to send on
shore; but he instantly jumped up, and accompanied me on deck to
assure the lieutenant that I would return. So on shore I went with
great joy; but my knees almost trembled as I walked up the steep
streets towards the part of the town where my grandmother and aunt
lived. I had seen a good many strange places since last I walked down
those streets on my way to join the *Kite*, and though, after thinking a
moment, I easily found the road without asking, the houses seemed
changed somehow or other. They were lower and narrower and less
fine-looking than I expected. At last I reached the quiet little house I
knew so well. By climbing up an iron railing before it I could, when a

boy, look into the parlour over the blind. There was no necessity to climb now. By holding on by the rail, and stretching myself upon my toes, I could easily look in; I could not help doing so before knocking. There I saw an old lady with a neat white cap and dressed in black, bending over her knitting. Her back was towards me; but somehow or other I did not think that it could be Granny. Her figure was too small and slight for that of Aunt Bretta. Who could it be then? My heart sank within me. It was some minutes before I could muster courage to knock. At last I went up to the door. A little girl opened it. She was deaf and dumb, so she did not understand what I said, and I could not understand her signs.

'Come in,' said a voice from the parlour. 'Who is that? what does he want?'

On this I pushed open the parlour door, and then I saw the old lady whom I had observed through the window, seated in an arm-chair, with her knitting in her hand. I looked at her very hard. 'I am Willand, your grandchild, Granny!' I exclaimed, springing across the room.

'Young man, you have made a strange mistake,' said the old lady, in a voice which sent a chill through my heart. 'I never had a grand-child. You take me for some one else.'

'Beg pardon, marm,' said I, trying to recover myself. 'I took you for my grandmother, Mrs. Wetherholm, who once lived here. I have been at sea for many years, and have never heard from her or my aunt. Can you tell me where they are gone?'

'Sit down, young man, and let me think. I cannot answer all in a hurry,' said she, and I thought her tone was much pleasanter than at first. 'Your name is Wetherholm, is it? and what ship did you go to sea in?' I told her. 'The *Kite!* That is strange,' said she. 'I should know something about that vessel. If Margaret were here, she would tell me, but my memory is not as good as it was. You want to know where your relatives are. Now I come to think of it, the old lady who lived in this house before me had a daughter. They came, I have heard, like my poor niece's family, from Shetland. Wetherholm was her name. Then I am sorry to say, young man, that she is dead.'

'Dead!' I exclaimed. 'Dear Granny dead!' And my heart came all of a sudden into my throat, and I fairly burst out crying as I should have done when a boy. For some time I could not stop myself; but I put my face between my hands, and bent down as I sat, trying to prevent the tears finding their way through my fingers. I hadn't had such a cry since I was a little boy, and then I felt very differently, I know. The old lady did not say a word, but let me have it out.

'That will do you good, young man,' said she at length. 'I don't think the worse of you for those tears, remember that.'

I thanked her very much for her sympathy, and then asked her if she could tell me anything about Aunt Bretta.

'I can't tell you myself,' she answered; 'but Miss Rundle, who lives next door, knew her well; and I'll just send and ask her to step in, and she will give you all the information you want.'

The old lady summoned her little deaf and dumb girl, and signing to her, in two minutes Miss Rundle made her appearance. I remembered Miss Rundle, and used to think her a very old woman then, but she did not look a day older, but rather younger than when I went away. I had no little difficulty in persuading her who I was, and at first I thought she seemed rather shocked at seeing a common sailor sitting down in her friend's parlour. However, at last I convinced her that I was no other than the long-lost Willand Wetherholm. She told me how my grandmother had long mourned at my absence, still believing that I was alive and would return, and always praying for my safety. At length she sickened—to the last expecting to see me. She had died about two years before; 'and then,' added my old acquaintance, 'the good old lady sleeps quietly in the churchyard hard by. I often take a look at her tombstone. Her name is on it; you may see it there.'

'That I will,' said I. 'It will do my heart good to go and see dear Granny's tombstone, as I cannot ever set eyes on her kind face again.' When I asked about Aunt Bretta, Miss Rundle bridled up a little, I thought.

'Well, she was my friend,' said she; 'and she was a very good woman, and I used to have a great respect for her. Nobody made orange marmalade better than she did, or raspberry jam; and as for knitting, there was no one equalled her in all the country round. I have several of the bits of work she gave me, and I value them; but still I don't see what right one's friends have to go and demean themselves.'

Rather astonished at these remarks, I asked what had happened.

'Why, young man, she went and got married,' said Miss Rundle, drawing herself up.

'I don't see any great harm in her doing that,' remarked the old lady.

'No, marm, not in marrying,' answered Miss Rundle, somewhat sharply. 'It's a very lawful state to get into, I dare say; but I find fault with her in respect to the person to whom she got married. I don't want to offend the feelings of this young man, her nephew; but what was he but a common sailor, and more than that, he had a wooden leg.'

'Aunt Bretta married to a common sailor with a wooden leg!' said I, scarcely knowing what I was saying, yet not thinking that there was anything very shocking in the matter. 'What sort of a man was he, marm? and can you tell me where they are gone, and where I shall find them? I long to see Aunt Bretta again.'

'I won't deny that he was a pretty good-looking man enough, and as we do now and then exchange letters, I can tell you where she is to be found,' answered Miss Rundle, softening down a little. 'They live at Southsea, near Portsmouth. Her husband was an old shipmate of one of her brothers—your father, perhaps—and that is the way they became acquainted. His name is Kelson; you'll find them without difficulty.'

'Aunt Bretta hasn't any family?' said I. 'I should like to have a dozen little cousins to play with when I go to see her.'

Miss Rundle looked very much shocked at the question, and said that as she had not been married much more than a year, that wasn't very likely.

Well, though all Miss Rundle's talk had for the moment driven away my sad thought, as soon as we were silent I felt very low-spirited and melancholy. I said that I would go up and have a walk through the churchyard, and the old lady begged that I would come back and take tea with her, when her niece would be there, who would be glad to hear me talk about the sea. Miss Rundle said that she had an engagement, and was very sorry she could not stop; but the old lady signed to the little girl to accompany me to point out my grandmother's tomb, remarking that I might otherwise have some difficulty in finding it.

The child tripped away before me, and we soon reached the churchyard. She pointed out an unpretending white little slab of stone in a quiet corner, with a number of wild-flowers growing round it, and then, looking up into my face with an earnest, commiserating look, she nodded and ran off. I walked up to the stone and read a short inscription—

'ELLA WETHERHOLM LIES BENEATH.
HOPE, IF ON ME YOUR HOPE IS PLACED.'

I felt very sad and grave, but I had no longer an inclination to cry.

'She wrote that for herself,' I thought. 'I'll try and hope as she hoped, and perhaps her prayers may lighten, if they do not remove, the heavy curse I brought down on my head.'

With regard to the curse I fancied was following me, I now know that I was entirely mistaken. Our loving Father in Heaven does not curse His creatures, though He permits for their benefit the consequences of sin to fall on their heads.

I will not repeat all the ideas which passed across my mind. I was not nearly so sad as I might have expected. I had met with sympathy and kindness, though from a stranger, and that lightened the burden; and then, though Miss Rundle was an odd creature, I could not help feeling pleased at seeing her again, and hearing from her about my aunt. I had little fear about her marriage, and I had every expectation of finding the sailor she had married, some fine old fellow well worthy of her, even though he had been all his life before the mast. While I was sitting down beside my grandmother's grave, and thinking of the years that were past, the days of my childhood, and the many strange things which had since occurred to me, every now and then reading over the words on the tombstone: 'Hope!—if on me your hope is placed,' and trying to understand their full meaning, and very full I found it, I happened to look up, and then I saw at a little distance a young woman who seemed to have been passing along a path across the churchyard, regarding me attentively. She was dressed in black, which made her look very fair and pale, and certainly I had never seen anybody else in all my life who came up in appearance to what I should fancy an angel in heaven would look like. This is what I thought at the moment. When she saw that she was observed, she drew her shawl instinctively closer around her, and moved on.

CHAPTER VI.

First introduction to Miss Troall—Happy evening—Return on board—An expedition planned—Attack on privateers—The boat sinks under me—Meet an old friend—Follow his advice—Join an American vessel—Chased again—The action between the British and French ships—Land our passengers—Loss of our vessel—Get on shore at Guernsey—La Motte and his family—Sail for Portsmouth.

AND so at length the dream in which I had so long indulged was realized. Once more I trod my native shores. Once more I had visited the home of my childhood. What a blank I had found! My lot has been that of thousands of seamen—of thousands of poor wanderers over the face of the globe, of every rank and in every clime. It is the tale which many and many a shipmate has told me in our midnight watch :—' I got back to the place where I was born. I thought to find it a home, but most of those I left were dead ! the rest removed. All were gone. The spot which once I knew so well, knew me no more ; so I fell in with an old messmate. We had a jovial spree on shore, and then, when all our cash was gone, we went to sea again.' Such was not my lot, though. Had I been inclined for a spree, which I was not, I had not time to indulge in it. I took a walk through some of the beautiful green lanes about Plymouth, and filled my hat full of wild-flowers, and then came back to the old lady's house to take my tea, as I had promised. I opened the door without ceremony, for I forgot entirely that it was not my own home, and walked into the parlour, expecting to find the old lady. Instead of her, what was my surprise to see seated at the tea-table

113

the very young woman who had been watching me in the churchyard I was regularly taken aback, and stammered out—

'Beg pardon, Miss, I didn't know that there was anybody here but the old lady who asked me to tea.'

'You need not offer any excuse; my aunt told me you were coming,' she answered, in just such a voice as I should have expected to hear when looking at her.

In a very few minutes she made me quite at home, and her aunt came in, and we soon were talking away just as if we were old friends. I will not say that I forgot my grandmother and aunt, but I should be wrong if I did not confess that my sorrow was very much soothed, and what is more, that in some respects I felt happier than I had done for a very long time. Tea was made, and I began to talk to them about my adventures and my shipwrecks.

'The most dreadful,' said I, 'was the first, when I and all my companions nearly lost our lives aboard the *Kite*.'

'The *Kite!*' exclaimed the young lady, 'the *Kite!* What do you know about her? Oh, in mercy tell me, young man!'

I saw she was very much agitated, but as I could not tell what part of the narrative to pass over or to touch on slightly, I told her all about the vessel from the time we left Plymouth till we got aboard the French brig; especially I could not help speaking of Seton and his bravery, and how he was wounded, and how he entreated me to bear his dying messages to his family, and to the girl to whom he was to be married. She seemed almost breathless as I proceeded with my story, but every now and then she would say, 'Go on—in mercy go on.' So I continued with my story to the end; 'and,' said I, 'the first time I have freedom on shore, I will, please heaven, go and fulfil my promise to poor Seton. I remember the young lady's name—Margaret Troall.'

'You have fulfilled it already,' said the young lady, with a faltering voice, and bursting into tears; 'I am Margaret Troall.   And oh, believe me, I am most grateful to you.'

I was astonished.   I found that the rest of her family in England were dead, and that she and her aunt had come to live at Plymouth just as my aunt and her husband had left the place, and they had taken my grandmother's house, which was then vacant.   At first, after all this, the young lady was very sad, but by degrees she recovered her spirits, and we talked on very pleasantly till Miss Rundle came in.

She wasn't half as stiff as at first, when she saw how well I was received by Mrs. Sandon (that was the name of the old lady) and her niece, and she promised to write to my aunt to tell her that I was alive and well, and that she might expect to see me some day.

'When you see her, as I hope you will soon,' said she, 'remember to tell her that I am looking well, and that you knew me at once.'

'That I will, Miss Rundle,' said I; 'I'll tell her that you look as young and handsome as you ever did, and for that matter younger to my eyes,—and that's the truth.'

So it was, for a boy always thinks an oldish woman older than she really is.   Miss Rundle drew herself up, and looked quite pleased, and smiled and smirked, and I saw that my joking had gained me a place in her good graces which I never enjoyed in my boyish days.   Well, I was very sorry when the time came for me to get up and return on board the frigate.   I put my chair back against the wall, and shook hands with all the ladies round, and they charged me to come and see them without fail when I returned to Plymouth.   Somehow or other I found myself shaking hands twice with Miss Troall, and she again thanked me for bringing her the message from him who was gone; and I heard Miss Rundle remark as I went out, that I was a very well-mannered young man, though I was a common sailor.

It was rather later than I intended.   I hurried down to the harbour, jumped into a wherry, and promised the waterman half-a-guinea if I got on board before dark.

'Why, lad, there's no great hurry, I should think,' said he; 'the frigate won't sail without you.'

'No; but a shipmate pledged his word for me that I would be back, and I must not let him break it, you know.'

'Well, we wasn't so particular in my time,' said the old man. 'But as your gold is as good as that of any other man, I'll do my best to put you on board.'

The wind was against us, so his mate and I took the oars while he steered, and by dint of hard pulling we got on board just about ten minutes before my time was up. I told Mr. Merton how it was I had run the time so short, and gave him an account of all that had happened to me. He was very much pleased with me at finding that I had been so anxious to come off in good time, and urged me on all occasions to make every sacrifice, rather than break a pledge of any description. Charley and I were in the same watch, and he was very anxious to hear how I had fared on shore. Of course, he could not care about my grandmother's death, but he was very much amused with my account of Miss Rundle, whom he remembered well.

'I must go and pay her a visit the next time I can get on shore, and if I can take her some wonderful present from the other side of the world, I expect to cut you out in her good graces,' he said, laughing. I asked him what he proposed taking. 'An alligator, or a shark, or a mermaid, or an orang-outang, or something of that sort—stuffed, I mean,' he answered.

I remembered Charley's love of a practical joke in our younger days, and I did not wish to interpose between him and the venerable spinster. I thought that he would not do anything really to annoy her.

Our captain came on board the next morning in high spirits. He had got leave to go to Teneriffe, in company with his Majesty's sloop-of-war *Talbot*, to cut out the two West Indiamen taken by the French privateer. No sooner, however, did we get out of the Channel than we met with strong westerly winds, which nearly blew us back into its chops again. However, not to be daunted, we kept hammering away at it, and though we in the frigate made tolerably fine weather, those on board the sloop had wet jackets for many a day. We had been out about ten days when two sails hove in sight, running with canvas set before the wind. One we made out to be a large brigantine, the other was a ship, evidently an English merchantman. The ship stood on, and when we fired a gun to make her heave to, let all fly, while the brigantine hauled her wind and tried to make off. We sent a boat aboard the ship, and found that she was an English merchantman belonging to Bristol, which had been captured by the brigantine. The privateer herself belonged to St. Malo, and was the very vessel which had taken the two West Indiamen we were going to cut out. The Frenchmen taken in the prize gave us some useful information as to where the two West Indiamen were lying.

The *Talbot* meantime was proceeding in chase of the privateer, and very soon coming within shot, knocked away the head of her mainmast and brought her to. She was an important capture, for she had committed a great deal of mischief, and, to our no small satisfaction, she had a considerable sum of money on board her, which she had taken from various captured vessels. Prize crews being put on board the two vessels, we proceeded on our course, thrashing away in the teeth of the south-westerly gale. However, at last, in about three weeks, we sighted the island of Teneriffe, and hove to that we might make arrangements for the attack. This was on the 8th of December. At about four o'clock in the afternoon, all the boats assembled round the frigate under the command of our first lieutenant. We had four boats, and there were three belonging to the corvette. I was in the boat with the first lieutenant She was a very fine, fast boat, pulling six oars. Merton, who had volunteered, was in one of the other boats, under the command of one of the master's mates of the frigate, and Charley Iffley was with him. When all was ready, the signal was given, and with three hearty cheers we shoved off from the frigate's side. We acted as a sort of whipper-in to the other boats, and we kept pulling about among them to keep them together, our lieutenant dropping a word to one and then to another, just to make the people laugh and to keep them in good spirits. It was some hours after dark, and nearly ten o'clock, as we approached the harbour of Santa Cruz. We then had all our oars muffled, and in perfect silence we entered the harbour, all keeping close together. As we got well in we lay on our oars for a minute, to make sure which were the two ships to be attacked. We made them out through the darkness. Four boats were to attack one ship, under the command of our lieutenant, while the three others pulled away to the second ship. The signal was given, and dashing off at full speed, we were alongside in a moment.

The Frenchmen little expected us, but they flew to their arms and made a stout resistance. Some were cut down—others were hove overboard—the cables were cut—our men flew aloft to loosen sails, and as quickly almost as I take to tell the story the ship was under weigh and standing out of the harbour. The other three boats were not so fortunate. The noise we made in attacking the first ship, our shouts, and the cries and curses of the enemy, aroused the people of the second ship, so that they had time to man their guns, of which she carried ten, before the boats got alongside. Our commanding officer, seeing this, ordered one of the midshipmen to take charge of his boat, in which I was, and of another in which was Mr. Merton, to go to the assistance of our shipmates. With hearty cheers, to show that aid was coming, we pulled away towards them, but as we advanced we were received with a hot fire of musketry and round shot. The officer in the other boat, which was close to us, was killed, but Merton sprang to the helm, and cheering on the men, they pulled up towards the ship. Just then a round shot struck our boat, cutting her right in two, killing one man, and wounding two. Instantly she began to fill, and very soon we could not move her through the water. She was sinking under us. The shot came round us thick as hail. I could not see where the other boats were, or what had become of my shipmates, but I caught a glimpse of the ship standing out of the harbour. I thought I heard Mr Merton's voice shouting out to the people, and I was pretty certain he was doing something ; but what with the darkness, and the firing, and the confusion and noise, it was some little time before I could decide in which way to strike out. What became of my companions in the boat I could not tell. Looking up, I saw a vessel not far off from me, and so I swam away with all my strength towards her. I got hold of her cable and rested myself, hoping to see some of the boats, or perhaps the second ship; but when I looked round I saw that there was little chance of our people taking her, for she mounted, as we knew beforehand, ten guns, and that a strong crew had been put on board her was evident from the hot fire she kept up.

The Spaniards had aroused at last, and the forts were blazing away at the boats which were pulling with all their might down the harbour. All hope of regaining the frigate must therefore, I saw, be abandoned. The vessel I was hanging on to was a large schooner. Her people were all on deck, and, to my great satisfaction, I heard them talking English. By this I knew that she was an American, and I determined to trust to their kindness. I therefore hailed, ' Schooner, ahoy ! Just heave me a rope, will you, to save me from drowning.'

' Well, I don't mind if I do,' said a man, looking over the bows ; and he heaving me a rope's-end, I quickly hauled myself up on board.

I found myself among three or four of the schooner's crew. ' You must come along aft to the mate,' said one of them.

I accordingly accompanied them aft, where we found the mate, who asked all about me, and I told him how we had come into the harbour to cut out the two West Indiamen.

'Well, small blame to you, my man,' said the mate. 'We don't wish you ill, but we must see what the captain has to say to you.'

The captain was on shore, but as soon as the firing was over he came on board. Meantime I watched as far as I could what was taking place, and I had the satisfaction of seeing one of the ships get out of the harbour, and I hoped the boats had reached her also. The American crew seemed inclined to treat me very civilly; and when the captain came off, and I told him all that I had told the mate, 'Well, my man,' said he, 'I am sorry for it, but I am afraid that I must take you before the Spanish governor to-morrow morning; because if I do not, I may get myself into trouble. However, go below, and get your wet clothes shifted. You shall have some food and a glass of grog, and we'll see about it in the morning.'

I went below. I was soon rigged out in warm, dry things, had a jolly hot supper, and I must say was never more kindly treated in my life. When I turned in, I felt that I ought to be thankful that I had not been killed like some of my shipmates. But still I could not help thinking, 'The curse is still following me—the boat I was aboard was the only one destroyed.'

The next morning, when I went on deck, I saw one of the officers doing duty. I looked at him hard. I was certain I knew his face. I put out my hand. 'La Motte,' said I, 'do you know me?'

'I should think I did indeed, Weatherhelm,' he answered, laughing, and shaking my fist warmly; 'it is a good many years since we saw each other.' I told him that the captain said he would have to take me to a Spanish prison. 'Oh, that is all nonsense,' he answered; 'I'll soon manage that. All you have to do is to join this craft, and we can protect you.

8

I'll just say that you are an old shipmate of mine, and I'll soon make it all right.'

Accordingly he took me to the captain, who was too glad to get an able seaman on board his vessel, and he promised me if I would sign the articles that I should have thirty dollars a month. I had not much difficulty in balancing this offer against the prospect of a Spanish prison. Now I honestly believe, that had she been a privateer, and I should have had to fight against my own countrymen, nothing would have tempted me to accept the offer. However, I decided at once. ' I'll join you,' said I, ' and am ready to sign the articles whenever you like.'

That evening I found myself, like many other British seamen, converted suddenly into an American. La Motte told me that he had been wrecked on the American coast, and having been kindly treated, he had joined one of their merchantmen, when shortly afterwards he was made a mate. The schooner was called the *Skylark*, and was a remarkably fine and fast vessel. At that time, while all the rest of the world were at war, the Americans remained neutral, and their merchantmen made a great deal of money by becoming the carriers for all the belligerent parties. This was a wise policy in all respects, but still wiser would they have proved themselves had they adhered to it. While it brought wealth and prosperity to their newly established republic, it laid the foundation of that naval power which enabled them to contend for a time even with England herself, and has since enabled them to take an important part in the transactions of the world. The schooner had been employed to bring out a new governor for the islands from Cadiz, and she was waiting to convey the former one back to Spain. He, however, was not ready, and the schooner was detained a long time. Still I had no reason to complain. Teneriffe was a very pleasant place; the captain and first mate of the schooner were very kind sort of men, and La Motte, for old friendship's sake, did his best to make my life agreeable. Perhaps, had we been less idle, it would have

been better for us all. The great difficulty the officers had, was to find
work for the men. We painted and polished, and scrubbed and used up
every particle of rope-yarn, and turned in all the rigging afresh before
Senor Don Longwhiskerandos announced that he was ready to take his
departure.

The voyage was not to be without danger, for there were English
cruisers watching all the Spanish and French ports; and though they
could not have touched us on the high seas, they would have made prize
of us, had they caught us trying to enter an enemy's port. I never heard
the real name of the governor. We called him Don Longwhiskerandos
just for shortness' sake, for it was fully three times as long as that. He
looked a very important personage, and awfully fierce, and did little else
than smoke cigars, and let a black man attend on him as if he was a mere
baby. We had fine weather, and the Don sat on the deck in great state,
when a sail was made out on our weather quarter. As she drew near
there could be little doubt from her appearance that she was an English
frigate. I borrowed a glass from La Motte. I took a long, steady look
at her, and I felt certain that she was my old ship the *Brilliant*. Meantime our helm was put up, and off we went before the wind to endeavour
to increase our distance. She made sail of course in chase, and I began
to consider whether it would not have been better to have gone to a Spanish
prison than be taken as a deserter, and cruelly flogged, if not hung. I
pictured all sorts of dreadful things to myself, and earnestly prayed that
the schooner might escape the frigate. If I was in a fright, Don Longwhiskerandos was in a still greater. He tore his hair and wrung his
hands, and walked about the deck uttering all sorts of extraordinary expressions, calling on I don't know how many saints to come and help
him—while blackie followed him with his snuff-box and a handkerchief,
and seemed trying to console him. La Motte, however, laughed at my
apprehensions. He said that of course it was known that I had not

willingly left the ship, and that I had a right to save my life in the best way I could. Still I was not satisfied. On came the frigate. We pressed the schooner with all the canvas she could carry. She walked along at a great rate, and so did the frigate. A stern chase is a long chase, but I had very little expectation that we should escape. If we could keep ahead till night, then we might have a better chance.

It was well on in the afternoon when we saw two sail ahead. From the whiteness of their canvas and the squareness of their yards, they were evidently men-of-war. If they should prove English cruisers, we were fairly caught in a net, and Don Whiskerandos would have very little chance of seeing his wife and family for a long time to come. Still our captain was a resolute man, and one who would never give in while a prospect of escape remained. The helm was put down, and we kept up five or six points towards the French coast, thinking that we might keep clear of them all till night set in, and might then escape in the darkness. The officers kept their glasses on the strangers. One was a frigate, the other a corvette. They made sail when they saw us. Evening was closing in. 'Hurra, my lads,' shouted our captain, ' up go the French colours. I thought by the cut of their canvas they were Frenchmen, and our friends!' How strangely those words sounded in my ears! To be glad to fall in with Frenchmen, and to call them our friends!

Once more we altered our course. In a short time the ships of war made out the English frigate, and allowing us to go ahead, then clewed up their topsails and waited for her. She saw them, and nothing daunted, under all sail stood on to close them before nightfall. Now, for the first time, I felt a little regret that I was not on board my own ship, she looked so proud and bold going into action against so superior a force. Oh, how I wished that I could find myself on her deck alongside my former shipmates, whom I pictured to myself standing at their guns, bared to the waist, with handkerchiefs round their heads, looking stern and grim as became men about to fight with heavy odds, yet every now and then cutting a joke with each other in the exuberance of their spirits. I thought if I could now but jump overboard with something to float me till she came up, and then I would climb up her side, and say that I had come to join them. Still, when I thought again, I knew that she was not likely, even if I was seen, to heave-to to pick me up, and I abandoned the idea as too hazardous. As the frigate got up to them, the two French ships let fall their canvas, and began to manœuvre to gain the weather-gage; but she was too quick for them, and getting up to the corvette first, gave her such a dose from her broadside as must have made the Frenchmen dance to a double-quick tune. Our captain's object was to land his passengers, so of course he could not stop to see the result of the action. As we ran out of sight, all three ships were hotly engaged. 'Well, if there's one man on board who will do his duty, and show what real English-men are made of, its Joe Merton,' I said to myself.

For some time after nightfall I could hear the sound of their guns borne over the calm waters, and then all was silent, and we continued our course to the French coast. Two days after this we were again chased by an English sloop of war; but the *Skylark* showed a faster pair of heels than she did, and we ran her out of sight. At length, after being chased away from various ports, we entered the mouth of the Gironde river in France, which runs down from Bordeaux. We were some days getting up to Bordeaux, where we landed Don Longwhiskerandos and his black slave and all his property, and hoped to get a return cargo. But there were no freights to be had; so, as the Don described the schooner as being a very fast craft, the French Government offered a large sum for her, which our captain was too glad to accept. The mates and crew accordingly received their wages, and we were all turned adrift. Now I found that there was a great chance of my being in a much worse condition than ever. Of course I hailed as an American, and if the police had found me on shore without a ship, I should have been seized and sent to serve on board a French man-of-war. On every account I must avoid that, I felt. In the first place, I did not wish to serve with Frenchmen; and in the second, had any ship I might have been in been captured, I should have been looked upon as a deserter and a traitor, and very likely shot.

La Motte, as an English subject, was in the same condition, except that he had never served on board a man-of-war. Accordingly he and I talked the matter over before we left the schooner, and agreed that it would never do to trust ourselves on shore. We saw ahead of us a ship under Hamburguese colours, taking in a cargo of wine for Hamburg, which was a free port. When, therefore, we left the schooner, we pulled alongside, and asked if she wanted hands. The captain said yes; he would ship us at once. He spoke very good English, and the mate we had reason to suspect was an Englishman, as were several of the crew. So much the better, we thought. I at all events was very glad to get to sea. Four or five days afterwards, just as we got into the English Channel, the captain called us aft, and told us that, instead of going to Hamburg, he expected to proceed to London; but that he had received directions to put into the Island of Guernsey first to wait for orders. I was very glad to hear this news, for I thought there was a chance of my seeing old England again sooner than I had expected.

'Yes, that may be very true,' observed La Motte. 'But how will you see it? The first night you put your foot on shore you will be pressed to a certainty, and quickly find yourself on board a man-of-war, and a slave as before.'

'No, not a slave,' said I indignantly. 'I'd rather go and serve willingly than be pressed, that's the truth; but no one has a right to call British men-of-war's men slaves. They may be pretty hardly tasked sometimes; but they get pay and prize-money and liberty, and if they did but know how to take care of their money, and would but conduct themselves like rational beings, the good men would have no reason to complain.' The truth was, that La Motte had got the notion entertained by most merchant seamen, and encouraged by shipowners as well as masters and mates, that men-of-war were all alike, little better than hells afloat; that all naval officers were tyrants, and all men-of-war's men miserable, spiritless slaves. Why, even in those times they were generally better treated than merchant seamen, and now the lot of the two cannot be compared. There's no class of men better cared for, better fed, better clothed, and more justly treated, than the British man-of-war's man. I don't want to cry down the merchant service, or owners or officers of merchant ships, but this I will say, that the most comfortable, happy merchantmen I have seen have been those commanded by naval officers.

We were within half-a-day's sail of Guernsey, and were expecting to get in there next morning, when a heavy gale sprang up from the north-west, and before we could take the canvas off the ship—for we were very short-handed—every yard of it was blown out of the bolt ropes. We were in a bad way, for we were already too much to the southward. Still our captain hoped, if we could bend fresh sails, to weather the islands; but all that nook of the coast is full of rocks and dangers, and tides setting here and there, so that it is difficult to tell where a ship will be drifted to. Twice we tried to bend fresh sails; but each time they were blown away, before we could hoist them to the yards. Darkness came on. Two of our shipmates were hove off from the lee yard-arm, and their despairing shrieks reached our ears as they drifted away, a warning to us of what might be our fate.

'We have some Jonah on board,' I heard the first mate observe to the second. He was a rough sailor, such as are not often met with now-a-days, though then they were common. 'If we could find him, we would heave him overboard.'

I remembered too well what I had often thought about myself, and felt

thankful that I had kept my own counsel since I was on board, and had
not told my story. The night came on very dark. I do not believe
anybody in the ship knew exactly where we were. Several hours of
deep anxiety passed away. The ship began to labour dreadfully. All we
could hope was that, when daylight returned, we might find ourselves
clear to the northward of all dangers, and then with tolerable sea-room
we might expect to make sail so as to carry the ship into an English
port. Vain were our hopes. Suddenly there was a cry, 'Breakers
ahead! breakers on the lee beam!' The ship struck, again and again,
with terrific violence. The masts went by the board; then she seemed
to be lifted over the ledge, and we found her floating in smoother water.
We hoped that we were in some bay where we could bring up and ride
out the gale; but it was too dark for us to distinguish our position.
The captain had just given the order to let go an anchor, when the fearful
cry was uttered, 'The ship is sinking! the ship is sinking!'

'Get the boats out, my men; no hurry, now!' cried the captain; but
it was not quite so easy to obey the order or to follow the advice. The
long-boat was stove in; but we had a gig and a whale-boat hanging to
the ship's quarters. We ran to the falls. La Motte and I, with some
others, leaped into the whale-boat just as the ship sank beneath our feet.
We shouted out to the rest of our shipmates that we would try to pick
them up, but we could see no one. Though I said the sea was calmer
than on the other side of the reef, still we had no little difficulty in keeping the boat from swamping. We could not tell either in which direction
to pull. All we could do, therefore, was to keep the boat's head to the
sea, and wait till daylight, which we knew was not far off. At length it
came, as it always comes at last to the weary and the watchful, if they
will but patiently wait for it. As the dawn gradually broke we found
that we had been drifted into a bay, and that the shore was not four
hundred fathoms from us. There was a good deal of surf breaking on

It, so that it was necessary to use caution in landing. Waiting our opportunity, we gave way and drove the boat high up on the beach. A sad sight met our view; the sand on each side was covered with portions of the wreck and casks of wine, many of them stove in; but sadder far it was to see the bodies of our late shipmates hove up dead on the beach, while one or two were still washing to and fro in the surf, as if the sea were yet loth to give up its dead. Perhaps there is no more melancholy sight than that for a seaman to behold. We examined the bodies; they were all dead; but as we looked about we came upon some marks of feet in the sand, leading up the beach, and this gave us hopes that some of our companions had escaped. I saw La Motte looking inquiringly about him. I asked him if he knew where we were.

'Yes, that I do,' he answered. 'At no great distance from my home. Come along with me, Weatherhelm. My family will be glad to welcome an old shipmate.'

Just as the sun got up we saw several people approaching, and were truly glad to find among them our captain and three of the crew. They took charge of the men who had been saved with us, while I set off with La Motte to his home. It was a large farm-house standing by itself. He looked round the building, and in at one or two of the windows, but could not make up his mind how to announce himself. 'I am afraid of giving some of them a fright if I were to appear too suddenly,' he said. At last he told me that I must go in and tell them that I was a shipmate of his, and that he would be there soon. So I opened the door, and an old lady came out and spoke to me, but I could not understand a word she said, and then an old gentleman made his appearance, with white hair, with a long red waistcoat and greatcoat, but he could not help on the conversation. At last they went to the back of the house, and called Janette! Janette!' and a young girl, with her petticoats tucked up, came tripping in, as if she had just been milking the cows, and she asked me, in broken English, what I wanted; and when I replied that I knew Jacob La Motte, and was a shipmate of his, they seemed very much interested, and not a little agitated. When I saw this, I thought the sooner I told them that he was all right and well the better, and then, to their astonishment, I ran out of the house and called him, and he soon had both them and several other young boys and girls all hanging round his neck, and kissing him and asking him all sorts of questions. I envied him—I could not help it. I had no father or mother, or brothers or sisters, to care for me, so even at that moment I felt very desolate and forlorn. However, they soon recollected me, and then they all did their best to make me happy and comfortable.

The days passed very quickly away. I never had been so happy and merry in my life. Though the old people could not speak English, they understood it a little, and I soon picked up French enough to make out what I wanted to say; and then all the younger people could talk English, though among themselves they always spoke French. As we lived on so quietly and peaceably in that pretty farm-house, no one would have supposed that all the horrors of war were being enacted in the surrounding seas. It might have been supposed that neither of us would ever have wished to leave those quiet scenes, but after a time La Motte began to grow fidgety, and said he must think of getting employment. At last away he went to Peter-le-port, the only town in the island. He was away three or four days, and when he came back he told me that he had taken service on board a privateer, one of the fastest craft out of the island. 'She is called the *Hirondelle*,' he said. 'You never set eyes on a more beautiful craft. She is lugger-rigged, mounts sixteen guns, and will carry a hundred and twenty hands, all told, fore and aft. There is nothing will look up to her. I could not resist the temptation of joining her. Her crew will have six months' protection from the pressgang. That alone is worth something. Now is your opportunity, Will, for making your fortune. Don't throw it away. By the time you are paid off you'll have your pockets full of money, and then come and settle down here. That is what I intend to do.'

His reasonings and arguments seemed irresistible. Still I held off. I was balancing between my wish to go and see Aunt Bretta at Southsea and the old lady and her niece at Plymouth, and trying to find my way back to my ship. I had an idea that the latter was the right thing to do. Still, unhappily, I had not always been accustomed to do what was right, and now found it easy to do what was wrong. I told him, in reply, what I wished to do, and what I thought I ought to do; but he laughed at all my reasonings, and before the day was over I had consented to go and enter on board the lugger. In those days not many people thought there was any harm in privateering. Many do not think so now. Still there were some who looked upon it as little better than a sort of lawful piracy, and made but little scruple in running down an enemy's privateer.

I found the *Hirondelle* everything La Motte had described her. We had not been out a week before we had taken a couple of prizes, and we recaptured a number of English vessels which had been taken by the enemy and were on their way into French ports. As we were low in the water and had short stumps for masts, by lowering our sails we could lie concealed till we could make out what sort of craft were heaving in sight. We therefore ran but little risk of catching a Tartar, as privateers very often do.

I remained in the privateer upwards of a year and a half, and at last peace came, and the crew were paid off, and she was laid up. Though I had spent my money pretty freely when I was on shore, still I found that, what with wages and prize-money, I had fully four hundred pounds in my pocket. This I might well look on as a handsome fortune to begin life with on shore, and carefully managed it was enough to set a

young man up in business. I have known numbers of seamen go on
shore with far larger sums, and spend the whole in the course of a few
days, but then they have never—poor ignorant fellows!—read the book
of Solomon, or, if they have, profited by the wise advice contained in it.
I spent a few days with the La Motte family, but the thoughts of Aunt
Bretta, and still more, perhaps, that quiet evening spent at Plymouth,
were constantly coming into my mind; and wishing him and them
good-bye, I shipped myself and my fortune aboard a cutter bound for
Portsmouth.

CHAPTER VII.

ON reaching Portsmouth, I buttoned my money tight up in my pockets,
for, thought I, ' I'll have no land-sharks taking it from me in the way
many poor fellows have lost all the profits of their toils.' I had no
difficulty in finding my way through the gate under the ramparts to
Southsea Common, and then I turned to the left till I reached a number
of small, neat little houses. The fine big mansions and great hotels
which stand there now were not built in those days. I walked up and
down for some time trying to discover the house my aunt lived in from
what Miss Rundle had told me, but I could not make up my mind to
knock at any door by chance to inquire. At last I saw a stout, fine
sailor-like looking man come stumbling along the road on a wooden
leg. I looked at his face. He had a round, good-natured countenance,
somewhat weather-beaten, with kind-looking eyes, and a firm mouth,
full of fine white teeth.

' You're the man who will give me a civil answer at all events, and
maybe help me to find my aunt, so I'll just speak to you,' I thought to
myself. ' Please, sir,' said I, stepping up to him, ' can you tell me if a
young woman called Bretta Wetherholm lives any way handy here?'
He looked at me very hard as I spoke, with some surprise in his countenance. Then I recollected myself; ' that was her name, I mean, sir,' said

I; 'it's now Mrs. Kelson, I am told. Her husband is Tom Kelson. Yes, that's his name.'

'I think I can show you the house, young man,' said the stranger, casting his eye all over me. 'You are a stranger here.'

'Yes, sir,' said I, 'this is the first time I have been at Portsmouth. I've been knocking about at sea all my life. There are very few days in which I have set foot in England since I was a little boy.'

'Just paid off from a ship?' I suppose.

'Yes, sir,' said I, 'a few days ago.'

'Ah, I see, come round from Plymouth,' he remarked, stumping on at a pace which kept me at a quick walk.

I always addressed him as sir, for I thought very likely he was a post-captain, or perhaps an admiral. I did not like, therefore, to say that I had just come from Guernsey, as he would at once have guessed that I had been serving on board a privateer, and I knew that many officers did not at all like the calling. I therefore said, 'I beg pardon, sir, but I fear that I am taking you out of your way.'

'Not in the least, young man,' he answered in a good-natured tone. 'Your way is my way.'

'Well, you are indeed a very civil, kind gentleman,' I thought. Then all of a sudden I remembered the land-sharks I had been warned against, but when I looked in his face I felt certain that he was not one of them.

'And so you have heard speak of Tom Kelson,' said he, looking at me.

'Not much, sir,' I answered. 'There's a lady down at Plymouth whom I know, Miss Rundle, who just spoke about him, and told me about my aunt's marriage, and how she didn't quite think '——

'Oh, never mind what Miss Molly Rundle thought,' said he, laughing, as he pushed open the door of a house and walked in. 'You'll find Mrs.

Kelson in there,' and he pointed to a parlour on one side of the passage.
'Here, Bretta, come down; here's a young man come to see you. Who
he is I don't know. He's a friend of Molly Rundle's, that is all I can
make out,' I heard my new friend hail at the foot of the stairs.

I found myself in a very pretty, neat little sitting-room, with the
picture of a ship over the mantelpiece, and lumps of coral and large
shells, and shell flowers, on it, and bows and arrows, and spears and
models of eastern craft, and canoes from the Pacific, and some stuffed
birds and snakes, and, indeed, all sorts of curious things arranged in
brackets on the walls, or nailed up against them, or filling the shelves of
cabinets. Indeed, the room was a perfect museum, only much better
arranged than museums generally are. I had some little time to look
about me. 'Well, Aunt Bretta is comfortably housed at all events,' I
thought to myself.

At last the door opened, and a portly fair dame, with fair hair and a
pleasant smile on her countenance, entered the room. 'Who are you
inquiring for, young man?' said she, dropping a sort of curtsey.

I looked at her very hard without answering. 'Yes, it must be Aunt
Bretta,' I thought. 'But if it is her, she is a good deal changed. And
yet I don't know. Those kind eyes and that smile are just the same.
Oh, yes, it is her.' 'Aunt Bretta,' I exclaimed, running towards her;
'don't you know me? I'm Willand Wetherholm, your nephew!'

'You my nephew! I heard that without doubt he was dead. Yet
let me look at you, boy!' she exclaimed, taking both my hands and
fixing her eyes on my countenance. 'Yes, you are Willand—you are
my own dear boy—welcome, welcome back to life, and to one who loved
you as her own son!' And she flung her arms round my neck and burst
into tears. 'Oh, Willand, had but dear mother been alive, how it would
have done her heart good to see you! She never ceased talking of you,
and always felt sure that you would come back when you could.'

I will not describe the scene any farther. I pretty nearly cried too—indeed I am not certain that I did not, but they were tears of happiness, and not yet entirely of happiness. There was sorrow for one I had lost—regret for my own obstinacy and thoughtlessness, and many other emotions mingled with the satisfaction of finding myself under the roof of one in whom I had the most perfect confidence, who I knew loved me sincerely. I think I have said it before, but if not, I now urge those who are blessed with real friends, to prize the love their hearts bestow as a jewel above price, which wealth cannot purchase, and which, let them wander the world round, they may never find again.

After my aunt and I had sat a little time, in came the fine old gentleman I had met. I now guessed who he must be. He very quickly understood who I was. 'You are not the first seaman I have known who has been lost for years, and has at last turned up again when he was least expected,' said he; 'but welcome, Willand, I'm very glad to see you, and to own you for my nephew.' He very soon gave evidence of the sincerity of his words, for a kinder, better-hearted man I never met, and I felt thankful that Aunt Bretta had married a man so well worthy of her.

My uncle accompanied me back to the inn where I had left my chest and bag, and we got a porter to carry them to his house; and now, for the first time since I went to sea, I found myself settled with my relations quietly on shore. I had been very happy with the La Mottes, but still they were strangers. My kind aunt never seemed tired of trying to find out what would please me. She had done something to spoil me as a boy—it appeared as if there was a great probability of her spoiling me as a man. We had much to talk about. I told her of my falling in with the old lady at Plymouth, and of my visit to my grandmother's tomb. I found that Miss Rundle had never written to her, or if she had written, the letter had not reached her.

'I suspect that she was afraid I might answer her letter, and she did not like the idea of having to pay the return postage. It shows that she does not consider my friendship worth ninepence.'

Still I was surprised that Miss Rundle had not written, as she had so positively promised to do. I could not exactly make it out. I found that my aunt knew nothing of old Mrs. Sandon and her niece. She was very much interested with my description of the young lady. 'So, Willand,' said she, 'I hope you will go back to Plymouth and find her out again. There are very many good girls in the world, but, like sweet violets, they often bloom unseen, and it is not so easy to find them. From what you tell me of her, and I can bring her clearly before my mind's eye, she is just the sort of person to make a man a good wife, and I hope that you may be able to win her.' Now, when my aunt spoke thus, I laughed, and said that I had not thought of settling, and that it was not likely I should win a young lady like her, who was a great deal too good to be the wife of a foremast man like me, and anything else I never expected to be.

'You need not say that, Willand,' replied Aunt Bretta. 'I have something to say to you on that subject. You must know, Willand, that your father left some money to your grandmother for her life, and afterwards it was to go to you; but when you were supposed to be dead I took possession of it. Now, my dear boy, that you have come back, your uncle and I have been preparing to give it up to you. It is yours by every law of right, so do not say a word about it. We can manage very well without it.'

'Indeed, I will not deprive you of a farthing of it, dear aunt!' I exclaimed. 'I would rather go to sea for a dozen years longer and never come back again, than take the bread out of your mouths. I won't take it, so don't be pressing it on me. I have got plenty without it. There, take care of that.' And I gave her the cash I had been carrying

9

in my pocket. 'You can make me your heir, if you like, and I hope it will be a very long time before I come into my fortune.'

My uncle soon after came in, and we had a long talk over the matter. I succeeded at last in making them keep the money. The fact was, I knew myself better than they knew me, and I felt pretty certain that some day or other I might spend it all, and nobody would be the better for it. This affair settled, we lived together still more pleasantly than ever, for they had it off their minds, and I felt that I had done what was right. I found that my uncle had once been what Miss Rundle called a common sailor— that is to say, he had been mate of a merchantman, and had been pressed on board a man-of-war, where he had obtained a warrant as boatswain. While acting as such, he had lost his leg. After he had recovered he got command of a large merchantman, for he was a good navigator as well as a first-rate seaman. He was not very refined, according to some people's notions, I dare say, nor were some of his acquaintance. He valued them, as he did all things, for their sterling qualities, and cared very little for their outside. A good many of his old friends and shipmates used to look in on him, and I was much struck by the kind and hospitable way in which my aunt always received them. 'They are my husband's friends, and I inquire no further,' she used to say. 'I know that he will never ask anybody I shall not be glad to receive.'

Scarcely an evening passed without our having one or more guests, and this made it very pleasant. Just as we were sitting down to tea one evening, a ring was heard, and on my uncle's opening the door (I found that he always did that sort of work), I heard him exclaim, 'Come in, Jerry! come in, old boy! There is only my nephew here, and he won't be sorry to hear you talk, I'm sure.' There was a shuffling and cleaning of shoes, and then my uncle ushered in as odd a looking old man as I ever saw. He was of diminutive figure, very wizzened and wiry, with long grizzly hair and small bright eyes, with a wonderfully roguish expression in them.

'This is Jerry Vincent, an old shipmate of mine, nephew,' observed my uncle, as he placed a chair for the old man. 'He can tell you more curious things than most people when he has a mind. Can you not, Jerry?'

Our guest nodded, and his eyes twinkled curiously.

'Sarvant, missus; sarvant, all,' said he, pulling a lock of his hair and putting his tarpaulin hat under the seat which had been offered him. 'Why, old ship, I've seen some rum things in the course of my life, and I don't forget them, like some does,' he remarked, smoothing down his hair with his long, rough, bony hand.

I told him that I should much like to hear some of his adventures, but he did not become loquacious till my aunt had served him out three or four cups of tea, into which she poured, as if it was a usual thing, a few drops of cordial, a proceeding which always made the old man's eyes twinkle cheerily. During the course of conversation, I found that Jerry Vincent was not only peculiar in his appearance but in his habits also. He never by any chance, from choice, slept in a bed. When at sea, a caulk on a locker was the only rest he took, and most of his nights, in summer, were passed under the thwarts of his boat. My uncle told a story of him, to the effect that one cold winter's night he had gone to sleep under his boat, which had been hauled up and turned over on the beach, and that when he awoke in the morning his dog had been frozen to death, while he was only a little stiff in the neck. At all events, it was evident that he was a very hardy old man.

'There are many like to hear my yarns,' he observed. 'Now, for example, there was a gentleman down here from Lunnon, and he used to go out in my boat off to Spithead, and sometimes across to the Wight. One day I thought I would try one of my yarns on him, so I spun it off the reel. He said, when I had finished, that it was a very good one, though it was very short, and when he stepped out of the boat he tipped me half-a-crown. The next day I took him out again, and spun him another yarn rather tougher than the first, and he gave me three shillings. Ho, ho, thought I to myself. If you pay according to the toughness of a yarn, I'll give you something worth your money. Well, the third day down he came, and said he wanted to go across to Cowes, if the tide would suit, and I told him it would; and now, I thought, here's a fine time for spinning a long yarn. I'll give you a tough one, and no mistake. Well, I spun away, and my eye if it didn't beat the two others hollow! We had a pretty quick run to the Wight and back, and just before I landed him, "I hope you liked the story, sir," says I. "Very much," says he. "And by the by, I should pay you for it. Here's a couple of shillings." I looked at the coin with disdain. "Pardon, sir," says I; "that story is worth five shillings if it's worth a penny, and I can take nothing less." "Are you in earnest, my man?" says he. "Yes, sir," says I; "the story, if written down, would be worth ten times the money." "Then you are an extortionate old scoundrel, without a scrap of a conscience," says he. "Hard words, sir," says I; "but it can't be helped. We poor fellows must submit to great people." But all I could say wouldn't do. He vowed that he would never give me anything again, and what is more, he never did, and never again would take my boat.'

'Served you right too, old ship,' said my uncle. 'You learned by that, I hope, that moderation is the best policy. But heave ahead. You are not to charge us at the rate of a shilling a fathom for your yarns, remember that.'

Old Jerry cocked his eye with a knowing wink, and began. 'Well then, one morning after I had been sleeping up at my uncle's, for some reason or other—it might have been that I'd had a drop too much the night afore, but I can't say, as it's some time ago—I don't score those things down in my log, d' ye see—I was going down the street with my

boat-hook in my hand—I know that I had the boat-hook because I took
it up with me. It was rather dusky, so to speak, because the sun wasn't
up, nor would be for some hours to come, when, as I was passing a
house with a deep porch before the door, what should I see but a big
pair of fiery eyes glaring out at me like hot coals from a grate in a
dark room. Never in all my life did I see such fierce red sparklers,
but I never was a man to be daunted at anything, not I, so I griped
my boat-hook firmly in both hands and walked towards it. I wasn't
given to fancy things, and I had never seen any imps of Satan, or Satan
himself, and never wished to see them, so I thought this might be a dog
or a cat, maybe, troubled with sore eyes, which made them look red. On
I marched, therefore, as steady as a judge or a grenadier on parade,
when, just as I got near the door, a dark shaggy form rose up right
before me, the eyes glowing redder and hotter than ever. It grew, and
it grew, and grew, every moment getting taller and bigger, till it
reached right up to the top of the house. I kept looking at it, thinking
when it would have done growing ; but as for running away, even if I
had had any fancy for running, I knew that it would have come after
me and would overhaul and gobble me up, in a quarter less no time, so
I stood where I was, considering what would happen next. At last,
thinks I to myself, you are not going to look at me in that way whatever you are; so, shutting my eyes, for I couldn't for the life of me bear
its glare any longer, I made a desperate dash at it with my boat-hook.
You should have heard the hullabaloo there was, and I found the boat-
hook dragged right out of my hands. I opened my eyes just in time
to see the monster, big as he was, bolt right through the door, carrying
my boat-hook with him. I rushed after him to try and get it back, for
it was a new ash one I had bought but a few days before, and I did not
want to lose it, but I only knocked my head a hard rap against the
door, and though I looked about everywhere I never could find it from

that day to this; and that, mates, mind you, is the circumstantial and voracious way Jerry Vincent lost his boat-hook.' And the old man gave one of his comical and expressive winks, and a pull at the glass of swisell which my uncle had placed by his side.

'Don't you all acknowledge that that story was well worth half-a-crown to a Lonnoner, seeing as how it was quite new, and he could never have heard it afore? Of course you'll all agree with me, now, to my mind, those Lonnoners are generally such know-nothing sort of chaps, though they think themselves so wise that they never will believe what you tell 'em. They are just like the old lady whose nevy had just come from sea. When he told her that he'd seen flying fish scores of times, she said he was trying to hoax her, and wouldn't listen to him, but when he said he'd been up the Red Sea, and that the water there was the colour of a soldier's coat, she said that she had no doubt about that, and that she was glad to listen to him when he spoke the truth. But,' continued Jerry, who had now got into his talkative vein, 'what I have been telling you is as nothing to what happened to me soon after then. I had been ill for some time, and could not tell what was the matter with me, when I happened one day to go to Portsdown fair. I thought the walk would do me good, and I wanted to see some of the fun going on. Well, after I had been to see the beasts and the raree shows, and the tumblers, and theatres, and conjurers, and taken a turn in a round-about, on a wooden horse, which I found more easy to ride than a real one, because, do ye see, the wooden one never kicks, while, to speak the truth, whenever I've got on a regular-built animal, he to a certainty has shied up his stern and sent me over his bows, sometimes right into a hedge, or a ditch, or a pond, or through a window, into a shop, or parlour, I happened to catch sight of a man standing at the end of an outlandish sort of a cart or a van, painted all over with red and yellow, and blue and gold, with a sort of a Chinaman's temple at one end of it.

'"Now, ladies and gentlemen," says he, for he was a very polite sort of a chap, "here's the universal 'lixier of life; it cures all complaints, and takes a man, if he has a mind to it and has proper faith in what it will do for him, right clear away to the end of the world. It's as infallible as the Pope of Rome and all his cardinals, and is patronized by all the first haristocracy and clergy in the country. Only one shilling a bottle, ladies and gentlemen; taken how you will and when you will—it's all the same—in a glass of grog, a bowl of punch, or a basin of pap; for old or young, for boys or girls, it will cure them all and they will never feel ill again as long as they continue to take it. Take enough of it, and take it long enough, and you will see the wonders it will work."

'On hearing all this, I asked of those who were looking on, who the chap was, and they told me he was the celebrated Doctor Gulliman, who was going to send all the old regular practitioners to the right about, and it was wonderful what good he did, and how much more he would do if people would but trust him. I afterwards found out that the fellow who told me this was a friend of the doctor's, and stood there on purpose to say a good word in his favour, though he pretended to have nothing at all to do with him.

'Well, thinks I to myself, maybe he'll know how to cure me; so I made bold and went up to him.

'When he saw me he stooped down from his carriage, and says he, "Well, my good fellow, what's the matter with you? But never mind, whatever it is I'll cure you. Trust Doctor Gulliman for that."

'I didn't much fancy having to tell my complaint among so many hearers. You see my modesty stood in my way.

'"Come, come, tell me all about it, my good man," says he in an encouraging tone.

'So I put my hand on my bread-basket, and told him that I was troubled with pains in them parts, and that for the life of me I couldn't get well, though there was seldom a night I didn't take half-a-dozen tumblers of grog to set me to rights.

' " Put out your tongue, my man," says he.

' I stuck it out so that from where he stood he could look right down my throat.

' " Oh, oh! my dear man, I guessed what it was that ails you. But never fear, I'll cure you in a jiffy. You're troubled with smoke-worms. That's it. And they are very dangerous things if you don't get rid of them, mind that. You see this invaluable stuff which I hold in my hand. If you want to get cured you must take six bottles of it. I don't say but that it would be safer for you if you took twelve. But do as you like about that. Mix each of them in a stiff glass of grog. You may take three a day if you like, and then come back to me for more. At the end of three days—trust the word of an honest man and a true friend of the whole human race—you will be clear of them all, and every complaint you have at the same time."

' Well, thinks I to myself, " in for a penny, in for a pound,' though there is a difference between the shilling my friend in the crowd said I should have to pay and the twelve shillings the doctor demands. But then, to be sure, the stuff can't be unpleasant, and the grog, at all events, is no bad thing. " Well, doctor," says I, " I'll take the twelve bottles, but I should like to know what the stuff you give me is made of ?"

' " What !" he sings out, drawing himself up and looking as proud as a prince. " What! Do you just imagine for one quarter of a moment that I would tell you, or any man like you, alive on this terrestrial sphere, what my infallible Obfucastementiscoposis is composed of ? No; not to satisfy the gaping curiosity of twenty such wretched creatures as you are would I reveal that golden, all-important, mysterious secret. If you are not content, go! Give me back my invaluable 'lixier and cut."

'" Yes, doctor," says I, going to give him the twelve bottles, "and just do you in return hand me out my twelve shillings."

'" Your twelve shillings! you audacious rascal. Here's a man asks me for twelve shillings in exchange for my 'lixier, which is worth twelve pounds at least. Ladies and gentlemen, he ain't fit to be among such as you. Hoot him—hoot him—hiss him—kick him out from among you."

'On this my friend in the crowd, who advised me to buy the stuff, began to hoot and to hiss and to shove me about, and others followed his example, till I saw that there was no use of attempting to hold my own, and I wasn't sorry to be able to get clear of them, and to bolt with a whole skin on my body, though two of the bottles were broken in the row.

'I got home at last, not over well pleased with Doctor Gulliman and the way I had been treated. However, as I had paid for my whistle, I thought I might as well try if the stuff would do me any good. As soon as I got into Portsmouth I bought a bottle of old rum ; for, thinks I to myself, if I am to take the stuff, the sooner I begin the better.

' When I reached my boat, I recollected that I was engaged to go out to Spithead to bring on shore an officer from one of the ships lying there, so I stowed away a glass and a can of water, not forgetting the rum and 'lixier, and shoved off. I just paddled down the harbour, for I was in no hurry, and the ebb was making strong. At last says I to myself, just as I got off the kickers, " I'll just take a bottle of the 'lixier and see how I feel after it." So I got a bottle, and poured it out, and put in some old rum, just on the top of it, to take the taste away, and then I took the can of water, but I found that there was a hole at the bottom of it, and that most of the water had leaked out. So, do you see, I was obliged to be very careful of the water, and couldn't put much of it at a time in the glass. If I had, you see, I shouldn't have had any of the precious fluid, as they calls it, left for another glass. Well, I tossed off the liquid, and when I had smacked my lips, I began to think much better of the doctor. His stuff, you see, wasn't so bad after all. Thinks I to myself, "If one glass is good, two must be better; so, before I take to the oars again, I'll have another." Somehow the second was even better than the first. Then it struck me all of a heap like, that the doctor said I should take three bottles of his stuff in a day; so, as it was now getting towards sundown, thinks I, "The sooner I takes the third the better."

'Howsomedever, when I came to look at the can, I found that every drop of water had leaked out, so I had no help for it but to fill the tumbler up with the rum. I can't say it tasted bad, though it was, maybe, rather stiffish. Well, as the tide was sending me along nicely, I didn't get out the oars again, but sat in the boat meditating like, when all of a sudden I felt myself very queer in the inside, and pains came on just for all the world as if I had swallowed a score or two of big mackerel, and they were all kicking and wriggling about in my bread-basket. "They are the smoke-worms the doctor told me about," thinks I. "They don't like the taste of his stuff, that's the truth of it." Well, I felt queerer and queerer, and Southsea Castle began to spin round and round, and the kickers went dancing up and down, and the ships in the harbour were all turning summersets, and every sort of circumvolution and devilment you could think of took place. Thinks I to myself, "There's something in that doctor's stuff, there's no doubt about that, though whether its worth a shilling a bottle is another matter." Just then I felt more queer than ever. "Heugh! heugh!" There was a rattling and a kicking, and such a commotion in my inside, and up came what I soon knew was the smoke-worms right out of my mouth, and overboard they went as I put my head over the gunwale. There was a bushel of them if there was one.

'Never afore nor since have I seen such things, for every mother's son had hairy backs and forked tails. Yes, gentlemen and ladies, forked tails and hairy backs. Believe Jerry Vincent for the truth of what he says. The moment they got into the water they began to frisk and frolic about as if it was natural to them, and to grow bigger and bigger and bigger, till the first which came up was as big as a frigate's jolly-boat. I made short work of it, and threw them all up till I felt there wasn't another morsel of any one of them in my locker. Then thinks I to myself, "It's time to look out sharp, or some of these merry chaps with forked tails will be playing me a trick;" for you see that they'd already begun to open their mouths very wide, and to splash the water right over me as they whisked about round the boat, just like sharks in the West Indies. So I got out my oars pretty sharp, and began to pull away towards Spithead, thinking to get clear of them, and to carry my freight ashore as I'd engaged to do. But I soon found that the smoke-worms weren't quite so ready to part company with me, and as my boat began to gather way, they began to swim after her. The big fellow led, and all the others followed. There was hundreds of them, of all sizes, and one little chap, who brought up the rear, was no bigger than a sprat. After me they came with open mouths and big red eyes, all the hair on their backs standing up, and their tails whisking about like the flukes of a whale in a flurry. Didn't I just pull for dear life, for I knew what they'd be after if they once grappled me. They would have swallowed me, every one of them. I soon gave up all thoughts of fetching up the ship I was bound for. It would never have done to have gone alongside one of his Majesty's crack frigates with such a train after me. I should have lost my character, you know. On I pulled;

I didn't spare the oars, depend upon it; but, somehow or other, the way in which the tide set, and the manner in which the brutes dodged me, made me go right out to Spithead, and there I found myself pulling among a whole fleet of men-of-war and Indiamen. The officers and ships' companies crowded into the hammock nettings and rigging to see me pass, and never have I heard such shouts of laughter as they raised as I pulled by. Neither to the one side nor to the other could I turn; for if I did, as surely one of the beasts would instantly swim up, with open mouth, and make a grab at my oar to keep me going straight ahead. I sung out to the people aboard the ships in mercy's name to take a shot at some of the bigger brutes, for I thought that I could grapple with the little ones; but either they didn't or wouldn't hear me; so away I pulled right out towards the Nab. Thinks I to myself, " Perhaps the people in the lightship will lend a helping hand to an old seaman; " but not a bit of it. When they saw me coming with my train of forked-tailed brutes after me, they sung out that I must sheer off, or they would let fly at me. So there I was fairly at sea, followed by as disagreeable a set of customers as a man ever had astern of him.

'I didn't bless Doctor Gulliman exactly, for I could not help thinking that somehow or other he had had a hand in the mystification. I now pulled up my larboard oar a little, and found that I was going right round by the Culver cliffs. " Well, I'll get on shore at the back of the Wight anyhow, and do them," I thought to myself. But what do ye think; the moment I tried the dodge, the cunning brutes kept edging me off the land, till I saw that there was no hope for me but to go on. All the time they made such a tremendous hissing and splashing and whisking, that you'd have thought a whole ship's company was washing decks above your head, and heaving water about in bucketsful. It was now night, but there was light enough and to spare to enable me to see the beasts as they kept way with me. I passed Sandown and Ventnor and

Steephill, and could see the lights in the houses all along the shore; but as to being able to land, the wriggling brutes in my wake, as I said, took good care that I shouldn't do that. By the time I got off St. Catherine's my arms began to ache a bit, and I felt as if I couldn't pull another stroke; but when I just lay on my oars to take breath and to knock the drops off my brow, which were falling down heavy enough to swamp the boat, the look of their wicked eyes and big mouths, as they came hissing up open-jawed alongside, set me off again pretty fast. I passed Black-gang Chine, and caught a sight of Brooke, and then I thought I would try to pull into Freshwater Gate, when I would beach the boat, and have a run for my life on shore, for I didn't think they would come out of the water after me. The truth was that I couldn't bear the look of them any longer; but the wriggling beasts were up to me, and before I had so much as turned the boat's head towards the Gate, three or four of the biggest fellows ranged up on my starboard side, and cut me off. I sung out in my rage and disappointment, but this only made matters worse, and my eyes if they didn't begin to laugh at me, and such a laugh I never did hear before, and hope I never may again. It was like ten thousand donkeys troubled with sore throats trying which would sing out the loudest, and twice as many jackals mocking them, all joined in chorus. At last I got to Scratchell's Bay. " Now's my time," thinks I, " if they once get me on a course down Channel, they may drive me right round the world, or over to the coast of America at shortest." I knew well the passage through the Needle rocks. The flood was about making. There might be just water for the boat, but none to spare. " No odds," thinks I. So, while I pretended to be steering for Portland, I shoved the boat round, and then gave way with a will. " If I knock the boat to pieces against the rocks, I shall not be worse off than I am now," I said to myself, as I pulled for the passage. I just hit it. The keel of the boat grazed over a rock below water ; but the tide was running strong, and I shot through like an arrow, and there I was in Alum Bay. Now the passage was too narrow, you see, for the forked-tailed beasts to get through, and they had a good chance of hurting themselves on the rocks if they attempted it; so, if they had been as wise as I took them for, I knew that they would go all the way round the outer Needle rock, and that this would give me a great start. Instead of that, in their eagerness to follow me, what should they do but bolt right at the passage. The big fellow stuck fast, and the little ones couldn't get by him, and there they were, to my great delight, all knocking their noses against the rocks, and wriggling and hissing and struggling and kicking up such a row, that I thought the people at Milford and Yarmouth, and all along the coast, would be awoke up out of their quiet sleep to wonder what it was all about. However, it would never have done for me to lay on my oars to watch the fun, because I thought it just as likely as not, when the tide rose, that the noisy brutes might shove through and be after me again, so I pulled away as hard as ever right up the Solent, till I got safe back again into Portsmouth harbour. Luckily, I had the whole of the flood with me, or I never could have done it. My arms ached as it was not a little. I moored my boat securely, and as it wasn't yet daybreak, I lay down in the bottom of the boat, and fell asleep. I never slept so soundly in my life, and no wonder, after the pull I had had.

'When I awoke the sun was shining out brightly, and I heard some one on board a vessel coming up the harbour hail and call somebody or other a drunken old rascal. Who he meant of course I couldn't tell; that was nothing to me. At last I sat up in my boat, and rubbed my eyes, and there was the doctor's bottles and the empty rum bottle and the can, without any water in it, just as I left them when I was taken ill. I half expected to see the whole troop of wriggling, twisting, forked-tailed smoke-worms coming up the harbour with the last of the flood;

but though I looked out till the tide had done, they didn't come, and it's my belief that they knocked themselves about so much against the Needle rocks, that they put about and went down Channel; and all I can say is that I hope that every one of 'em was drowned or came to some other bad end out at sea, and that I may never as long as I live have such a night as the one I spent after taking Doctor Gulliman's physic. Sarvant, marm and gentlemen, you'll agree that story is worth five shillings. Howsomedever, I never charges my friends, but gives them all free gratis and for nothing.' And old Jerry gave one of his most knowing winks as he finished off his glass and took up his hat to prepare for his departure.

I ought perhaps to apologize for giving such a story; but it is a fair specimen of the style of narrative in which old seamen of Jerry Vincent's stamp are apt to indulge, and I have heard many such, though seldom told with so much spirit, during my career at sea.

CHAPTER VIII.

Visit to Plymouth—Bitter disappointment—Miss Rundle's account of Charley—Voyage to Shetland—Wrecked again—Fall among friends—Near death's door—Happy encounter—Description of Shetland—My residence there—Married—Summoned southward.

I DID not think that I should ever have got tired of living at Southsea with my kind aunt and fine hearty old uncle, but I had been so accustomed to a roving life and active employment, that in a little time I began to consider that I ought to be looking out for something to do. What to do was the question. I had a fancy for staying on shore after having been knocked about at sea for so many years, and setting up in some business.

'What, have you forgotten Margaret Troall?' said my aunt to me one day.

The chord was struck. 'No, indeed, I have not,' said I; 'I'll go and find her, and bring her back to you as my wife if she will have me.'

I had given all my money to my uncle to have put safe in a bank for me. The next day I drew thirty pounds of it, and shipped myself aboard a smack bound for Plymouth.

Strange as it may seem, all the time I had been on shore I had never once thought of my oath and its consequence, but scarcely had I got to sea than the recollection of it came back, and I fully expected that some accident would happen to me before I reached my destination. It did not, however. I landed in safety, and walked immediately up to the house where I hoped to find the old lady and her niece. How strange it seemed! I never felt in such a way before in my life. A child might have knocked me down. I got to the house. How well I knew it! I looked in, as I had done before, at the parlour window. I fully expected to see the old lady sitting in her arm-chair and knitting, as I had when I was last there. My heart jumped up right into my throat, and then down it went I don't know where. There was no old lady there; but there were three little children, fat, chubby, merry things, tumbling about head over heels on the floor, and shouting and shrieking with laughter, while a young woman sat on a low chair knitting and encouraging them in their gambols, while she rocked a c..dle with her foot. 'All sorts of strange thoughts came into my head. Who can she be, I wonder? Can it be?' I said. I looked at her very hard, but the glass was thick and dirty, and I could not make out her features. With a trembling hand I knocked at the door. A servant girl, after a little delay, opened it.

'Does Mrs. Sandon live here?' I asked.

'No, she doesn't,' was the short answer.

'Can you tell me where she lives?' I said.

'No; she does not live anywhere, she's dead,' said the girl, who seemed determined not to throw a word away.

'Dead!' said I. 'Dead! just like Granny,' I muttered, scarcely knowing what I was saying. The girl was going to slam the door in my face. 'Can you tell me, my good girl, who that lady is in the parlour?' said I, stopping her.

'Yes, that's Mrs. Jones,' was the answer.

I was no wiser than before. 'Can you tell me what her maiden name was?' said I, in a low, trembling voice.

'Missus never was a maid-servant; she was always a lady, as she is now,' answered the girl, with a toss of her head, again attempting to slam to the door.

10

'Stop, stop!' I exclaimed, in an agitated manner. 'Can you tell me whether she was Mrs. Sandon's niece?'

'She'd nothing to do with Mrs. Sandon that I knows on,' said the girl; 'you're asking a lot of questions. You wouldn't, if master was at home.'

I was fairly beaten. Just then I heard a footstep behind me, and on looking round, who should I see but Miss Rundle, tripping along the pavement up to her own door, looking as brisk and young as ever.

'Oh, Miss Rundle, I'm so glad to see you!' I exclaimed, forgetting all the proprieties, and running after her. 'Can you tell me anything about my kind friends who lived in our old house, and where I met you last at tea?' I thought she would have shrieked out when she saw me —she looked so astonished.

'Why, who are you? where did you come from? What do you want? Why, I thought you were dead. You are not alive, are you?'

'I hope so, Miss Rundle. I fancy I am. I've done nothing to kill me lately, and I know that I was alive a short time ago,' I answered, laughing in spite of my agitation.

'Well, if you are sure that you are alive, come in here and sit down and tell me all about it,' said the little old lady, opening the door of her house with a latch-key which she drew from her pocket, and pointing to the parlour, which she signed to me to enter.

I took off my hat and sat down, wondering what strange news I was to hear. She presently made her appearance, having laid aside her walking dress. I felt myself completely at home in a moment, she looked so exactly as she had done when I last saw her on that delightful evening I spent at Plymouth, and I so well remembered her in the days of my boyhood.

'Well, Willand, I am glad to see you,' said she in a kinder tone than usual. 'A young man whom you know, and whose name I would rather not repeat,—indeed I do not like thinking about him,—told us that you were dead—drowned or killed somehow or other at sea. Perhaps he had his own selfish ends to serve, or perhaps he believed it; we will hope for the best.'

'Who do you mean? What do you speak of, Miss Rundle?' I exclaimed, in a voice full of agitation.

'I speak of that false deceiver, that bad, heartless fellow, Charles Iffley,' she answered, in a tone which showed her strong dislike to my former friend. 'Do you know, some time after you were here he returned from sea, and came up here to visit me, and talked of old times and old friendships, and how I had known his poor mother and his friends, till I was quite taken with him; and then he presented me with a stuffed parrot and two little pets of Java sparrows he called them (which certainly were very merry and hopped about gaily in their cage), and a dried snake, which he told me was a great curiosity; and he used to drop in to tea nearly every evening, and certainly he used to talk very pleasantly. However, it is not always the talkers that are the best doers or the best people. Then he began to inquire about the ladies next door, and I invited them in to meet him, and he made himself still more agreeable than ever. This went on for some time, till I saw that he admired Miss Margaret, old Mrs. Sandon's niece; however, as he had plenty of money, that was no business of mine. I must say that by this time I did not think so well of him as at first. Many things he said were very incorrect, and the snake he gave me began to be so disagreeable that I was obliged to throw it away, and my maid told me that she was certain the sparrows were no great things, so we examined them carefully, and there could be no doubt about it, they were merely common English sparrows painted. When he came in and was waiting for me sometimes (for he used to watch when I was out on purpose), he used to give them a touch up, and tell me that he had been washing them

and restoring their plumage, and in that way he kept up the deception
so long.   An old gentleman, a friend of mine, who used to be fond of
poking about and looking into old curiosity shops, happened to call, and
I showed him the parrot which Charles Iffley told me had come from
some part of Africa or South America round Cape Horn, only that it
had died before he could give it to me.   When my friend saw the stuffed
parrot, he turned it about and examined it, and then showing me a ticket
fastened to its claw, told me that he knew the old Jew's shop where that
bad fellow had bought it, and to a certainty that he had not given more
than a shilling for it.   All this was very provoking, and made me begin
to think very differently of him to what I had done at first.   I did fancy
that he might have had some regard for an old friend.'   And the old
lady drew herself up and uttered a gentle sigh.   'Such a dream was
soon blown to the winds,' she continued.   'I found that he was constantly going and calling at Mrs. Sandon's, and very often he did not
look in on me at all.   It did not seem to me, however, that Margaret
liked him, though I think her aunt thought well of him, and encouraged
him to come to the house.   He had never spoken of you, I found, till
one day I mentioned your name, when he said, "Ah, poor fellow! he
was a great friend of mine.   I first got him a ship, and helped to make
a sailor of him.   I was very sorry to lose him."   "How lose him?"
asked Miss Margaret gently.   Then he told them how you had been
sent away in a boat expedition in Teneriffe, to cut out some prizes, and
that the boat you were in had been knocked to pieces, and that you had
been either killed by the shot of the enemy or drowned, and that nothing
since had been heard of you.'

'I cannot blame Charley, then,' said I to Miss Rundle.   'I have no
doubt that he fully believed the statement he made.   Had I not succeeded in getting on board another vessel, I should have been drowned,
and we have never met since.   But what occurred after this?—go on.'

'You shall hear. When he saw that Miss Margaret took some interest in you, he began to talk of you in a disparaging way, as a poor sort of a fellow, easily led, and that you had all sorts of strange fancies, which he said he supposed had come to you with the northern blood which flowed in your veins, and then he spoke in no complimentary way of Scotland and the Orkney and Shetland people. He said he forgot to which you belonged. I saw the colour come into Miss Margaret's cheeks. "I belong to Shetland myself," said she. "It is a country I love dearly." On this, the young man began to apologize, and said that he was speaking without consideration; that he had known one bad Orkney man, and that was all, whereas he had known hundreds of bad Englishmen, and he hoped Miss Margaret would pardon him. She bowed, but said nothing. He did his best to make amends for what he had said, and certainly if attention would have won a woman, he would have won her. I could not help seeing that was his aim. However, his behaviour to me had not made me wish to give him any help. And, do you know, I found that he had been speaking in a very disrespectful way of me. I cannot repeat the names he called me. It showed me clearly what he was, and, though I did not like to interfere, still I only hoped he would not succeed in winning that sweet girl.'

'Did he succeed, though?' I exclaimed, in a voice choking with agitation. 'Oh! tell me, Miss Rundle.'

'You shall hear,' answered the old lady, who was not to be hurried with her narrative. 'Of course, having won the good opinion of the aunt was a great point in his favour. So he used to continue to go to the house as often as ever. He took the aunt all sorts of pretty presents. though he did not venture to offer them to Margaret. At last, however, he seemed to think that the time was come when he must try his chance. So he walked in and found Margaret in the room alone, and he told her, in an off-hand sort of way, that he loved her, and that, if she would

marry him, he would give up the sea and live on shore, and make her
comfortable and happy for the rest of her days.'

'Did she accept him? did she marry him?' I exclaimed, interrupting
the old lady.

'You shall hear, Mr. Wetherholm,' she answered quietly. 'What
woman does not feel flattered by receiving a proposal of marriage from
a fine-looking, free-spoken young man. I'm sure I should.' And she
put her hand mechanically before her face to hide the gentle blush which
the thought conjured up on her cheek. 'She thanked him, but entreated
him not to persist in his offers. Then she frankly told him that one she
had loved had died at sea; that her heart was buried with him in his
ocean grave; and that she could not marry a man she did not love. She
was very firm, and Charles Iffley could not help seeing that he had very
little chance of success. She told me this shortly afterwards. He, it
seems, did not give up his attempt to win her. Somehow or other, he
had taken it into his head that she was speaking of you, though he was
puzzled to know how you had won her heart. He returned several
times to the house, but his chief occupation seems to have been in abusing
you. This made poor Miss Margaret fancy that you all the time were
alive, and that he knew it; and this, of course, made her still less inclined
towards him. The less way he made in her affections, the more bitter
he became against you, till at last she had to tell him that his conversation was disagreeable, and that he must never come to the house again.
He still did come to the door several times, but the maid told him that
he must not come in, and that she would scream out murder if he
attempted it. Soon after this, poor old Mrs. Sandon fell ill and died,
and poor Miss Margaret was left alone without any one to assist her or
protect her. I asked her to come and live with me till she could make
arrangements what to do. She had friends in Shetland, though that is
a long way off, and I could not think what help they could afford her.

They wrote back begging that she would come to them, and that she should be like their daughter, and they would be parents to her. Well, against my advice, she resolved to set off, and away she went. She kindly wrote to me once, to tell me of her safe arrival, and she thoughtfully paid the postage, which was just like her, and very right. You shall see her letter, for I do not think she would object to my showing it to you.'

I thanked Miss Rundle very much for the account she had given me, but I could with difficulty reply to her for thinking what I would do. All sorts of ideas crowded into my mind. I scarcely, however, recollected Charley Iffley and his behaviour. My thoughts flew off to Shetland, and to Margaret Troall. Miss Rundle gave me her letter. I read it over and over again. I made a note of the place from which she dated it. Miss Rundle saw me, and asked me if I was going to write to her.

'No; I intend to go to Shetland,' I answered promptly. 'I have made up my mind to that. After all you have told me, I shall not rest happy till I have seen her. Perhaps I shall take up my abode there altogether. My father's family come from Shetland, and if I could get Aunt Bretta to come up there also, we might all be very happy.'

I was much pleased by the kind way in which Miss Rundle seemed to sympathize with me, and entered into all my views and plans, though she herself had no personal interest in them. She told me, in course of conversation, that she had not since seen Charles Iffley, but that she believed he belonged to some man-of-war or other, at the time of which she had been speaking, and that she understood he was still in the service.

My plan once formed, I lost no time in putting it into execution. That very evening I found a smack sailing for Portsmouth, and took my

passage by her. On reaching Southsea, and telling my aunt all that
had occurred, she very much approved of my plans, and encouraged me
to set off at once for Shetland. She sent all sorts of messages to old
friends, and to the children of old friends; for, as she remarked with a
sigh, it was too probable that many of the parents would have been
called away from the world.

Drawing a further supply of money from the bank, I went up to
London by the coach next morning. I won't stop to describe how I
was bothered and confused in London, and how heartily I wished myself
out of it. I found my way to London Bridge, and, after making many
inquiries, I reached a place where there were several Leith smacks
moored together. One was going to sail the next tide. I joyfully
stepped aboard of her, and still more happy was I to find myself clear
of the Thames and out at sea We were just a week making the
passage, which was very well, considering that we had a foul wind for some
hours and had to bring up in Yarmouth Roads. From Leith I got on
by another vessel to Aberdeen. In that port I found a regular trader
which sailed once a month to Lerwick, in Shetland. She was a smack,
but not equal in size to the craft in which I had come down from
London to Leith.

We had been out about three days when very heavy thick weather
came on, and a south-westerly gale sprung up, which came sweeping
through the passage between Orkney and Shetland, kicking up a terrific
sea. The smack behaved very well, but at last all that could be done
was to set a try-sail and to heave her to, and away we drifted we knew
not where. I had never before been in the North Seas, so I was not
accustomed to such dark gloomy weather—not but what it is bad
enough in the English Channel now and then—still it does not often last
so long as it does up in the north.

Day after day the clouds hung down over our heads, and the wind howled, and the dark green seas kept leaping up around, as if eager to draw us down under their angry foaming bosoms. We had a hard matter to cook our provisions, and no very easy one to eat them raw or cooked. Suddenly the wind shifted and blew as strongly as ever from the eastward, and then from the northward, and then got back again into the old quarter, and the master confessed that, for the life of him he could not tell where he had drifted to.

'On which side of Shetland are we, do you think?' said I.

'I only hope that we are still to the eastward, but at all events I believe we are well away to the northward of the islands.'

'I hope so,' I answered. 'But look, captain, what huge and unbroken seas come rolling in from the west; if we are not to the northward, it is my opinion that we have got the islands under our lee, and if this gale is to continue, I would rather have them anywhere else than there.'

'So would I, young man; but I have made this trip pretty often, and I don't think that I can be so far out in my calculation, was the answer.

All I could say was that I hoped that I was wrong and he was right, as, whichever was the case, there was nothing we could do till the weather moderated. On we drove. I did not like the look of things. When night came on I did not turn in, but sat down below out of the cold, ready to spring on deck in a moment. I had fastened my money in a belt round my waist, and kept my shoes ready to kick off, and my jacket loose to throw easily aside. I was certain that the vessel would be wrecked. I felt no fear for my own life, though I remembered my rash oath and what had occurred so often before, and the gloomy weather had indeed increased the conviction that I was under a sort of curse, and that I should have no rest till it was fulfilled. I am just saying what I then thought. I cannot even now be surprised at the idea gaining such powerful possession of my mind, while everything that had happened to me had tended to strengthen it.

Night came on. Pitchy darkness surrounded the storm-driven little smack. The cry of 'Breakers! breakers!' and piercing shrieks made me spring on deck. At that moment the vessel struck. The foaming seas came hissing and roaring up after her. We were among a dark mass of rocks; no fabric formed by human hands could have withstood the violence of those terrific waves. I held on to the last moment, while the huge foaming seas washed over my head, almost drowning me, as I clung to the wreck. Then I felt the deck quiver and shake, and the stout beams and timbers were wrenched and torn asunder under my feet, and I was hurled onward among the broken fragments by a roaring sea, which must have well-nigh completed the destruction of the craft. I lost all consciousness.

My last thought had been that at length the angry sea was about to claim me as a victim. There was a hissing, roaring sound in my ears; I felt myself tossed to and fro, knocked and battered, but I made no attempt, that I am aware of, to save myself. At length I opened my eyes. It was daylight. Some men were bending over me.

I heard a voice say, 'Here is one who seems to have still some life in him.' And another person came and took my hand, and after waiting a minute, said, 'Yes, carry him up to the house.' And I was put on a litter and borne up a steep path among some cliffs; and then across a high, wild down till I reached a substantial, strongly-built stone house. The movement of the litter had a very good effect on me, so that by the time I reached the house, my chest was relieved from the salt water I had swallowed, and my senses had completely returned. I was therefore saved the ceremony, very common in those days, by which a good many people were killed, of hanging nearly drowned men up by the heels, under the idea that the water would more quickly run out of their months. I was carried into a large boarded room, out of which several others opened. In one of those there was a bed. After my wet clothes had been taken off me I was placed in bed, carefully wrapped up in blankets, and directly after some warm drink was brought me.

I remember struggling somewhat when I found my money-belt being removed, and trying to possess myself of it.

'Never fear, young man; it will be all safe,' said a voice. 'We are not wreckers, and we no longer fancy that you will work us harm because we help to save your life.'

This satisfied me. I knew that there were honest people as well as rogues in the world, but I had often met with honest ones, so I hoped that I had now fallen among such. One thing, at all events, was very evident, they seemed anxious to save my life. After this I fell into a sound sleep.

It was nine o'clock in the evening when I awoke; but the summer days are very long in those regions, and even then the evening sun was shining into the window. A stout, white-haired, kindly-looking old gentleman came in to see me with a younger man, whom I took to be his son, and a servant girl brought in a tray with some tea, and some barley scones, hot and buttered. I thought that I had never tasted anything nicer in my life.

'I hope you are better now after your sleep, young man,' said the old gentleman. 'If fever can be kept off, I think you will do well; but we have sent for the doctor to look at your hurts. There are two or three other people who want his aid.'

'What, only two or three escaped out of all those on board the smack?' said I.

'It is a mercy that any one came on shore alive; and you will say so when you see the place in day-time,' said the younger man.

'We won't speak about it at present,' said the old gentleman. 'The less he talks or hears others talk, the better just now. We bid you good-night. Sleep again, if you can; some one will look in on you to see how you are going on, now and then.'

With these words my hospitable friends left me once more to myself.

I suspected, indeed, that I should be better for a doctor's care, for I felt that I had been bruised and battered dreadfully; my head had been bandaged, and when I tried to stir I found all my limbs sore and stiff,— indeed, it was not without great pain that I could move either an arm or a leg. I slept through most of the night. When I did awake, I began to wonder where I had got to, for the old gentleman had remained in the room so short a time, that I had not been able to ask any questions.

I had little doubt that I had been cast away on the coast of Shetland, but whether on the northern or southern end I could not tell, any more than I could who was my kind host.

The next day the doctor arrived. He had ridden over from Lerwick, with only the rest of half-an-hour for his steed, he said; so I knew that I must be at some distance from that town, and yet on the big island called the mainland. He dressed my wounds and bruises, and told me that one or two of my ribs were broken, but that I might consider myself fortunate that matters were no worse; and remarked that he had no doubt I had lived a prudent, careful life, as I was perfectly free from all signs of fever, which would not otherwise have been the case; and then giving me some bottles of medicine to take, he left me to look after his other patients. He spent two or three days in the house, for the islands are generally so healthy that there was not much demand for his services elsewhere.

One of my poor shipmates died, I was told, from his hurts. I rapidly got better. Besides the old gentleman and his son and the doctor, an old lady looked in now and then to see me. She was a very neat, pretty old woman, so cheerful and cheery, always having something pleasant to say, so that she contributed much to raise my spirits. I will say that I was most thankful for all the mercies which had been shown me, and for my preservation from so great a danger.

At last I was pronounced well enough and strong enough to get up and appear in public. A barber, who was going his rounds, came in, and shaved me and cut my hair, and my head and face were all to rights, so that I looked as well as ever, only my ribs hurt me a little, and my limbs felt somewhat stiff.

The old gentleman came to my room when I was ready. 'Take my arm,' said he kindly; 'you will find it rather strange walking at first, and your knees will shake a little.'

I could not refuse his kind offer, though I thought that I could have walked very well by myself. He led me into the large hall, and there, seated by a window at the further end, looking out on the sea, I observed two young women. One was dressed in black, the other in some sober colour or other. They were both at the moment bending down over their knitting, and talking in a low voice to each other, so that they did not observe our entrance.

We had got three-quarters of the way across the room, and the old gentleman was giving me a chair to sit down on, when the noise it made over the floor caused them to look up. There sat one I had so long thought of, whom I had come to search for, Margaret Troall.

She looked at me in a strange, bewildered way, still she knew me, and yet she could not believe her senses. She tried to rise from her chair to come towards me, but something seemed to keep her back. She drew her breath quickly, as if she would have wished to have spoken, but could not. I felt that I ought to speak first.

'They told you I was dead, Miss Margaret,' said I, and I know my voice trembled very much, and I know that had I not leant on the chair I should have fallen. 'They were mistaken; I went to Plymouth only

lately, and found you were no longer there; and when I discovered that
you had gone north, I came here to seek you.'

She recovered herself while I was speaking, and rising from her seat,
came up and gave me her hand. I do not say that there was anything
very extraordinary in the action, but I know that it made me very
happy. Her friends at first looked very much astonished; but a few
words served to explain matters, and then they were doubly glad that
they had had the opportunity of being of so much service to an old
friend of their young relative.

I found that the name of my host, the uncle of Miss Troall, was
David Angus, and that the place where the smack had been wrecked
was in St. Magnus Bay, in the parish of North Morven. My friends
were the holders of one of the largest farms in the district, and lived in
a very comfortable, though what people in the south would call a rough
way. I am not going to talk of all that passed between Margaret and
me. I should not have believed that she had thought so much of me as
she had done, it seemed; but our first meeting had been under peculiar
circumstances. She had seen me mourning deeply for a lost relative,
and she had discovered thus that I had a tender heart, so I may venture
to say, and now my coming all the way north to look for her showed
her that she had made no little impression on it.

Well, all that has passed and gone. I got every day better and
better, and was soon able to walk out with her along the tops of the
high cliffs, and to visit the wild scenes to be found especially in that
part of the island. I especially remember one place we visited, called
the Navis Grind. It is a gap in the cliffs formed by the whole force of
the western ocean rolling against them during a succession of heavy
gales, age after age, till vast fragments of the rock have been forced in
for hundreds of yards over the downs, and now lie like the fragments of
some ruined city scattered over the plain. We delighted in returning to

those scenes of wild grandeur, because they contrasted so strongly with our own quiet happiness.

This was only the second time in my life that I had enjoyed what might be properly called idleness. The first was during my short stay with Aunt Bretta, and then I confess that I often did at times feel weary from not knowing what to do with myself. Now I never felt anything like weariness, I was too happy to spend the greater part of the day in the society of Margaret. Sometimes I used to walk by myself over the downs by the edge of the cliffs, and at others visit the different parts of his farm with my host, and assist him to look after his cattle and horses and sheep, which were scattered far and wide over the peninsula.

I have scarcely mentioned his daughter Minna. She was a fair-haired, smiling, good-natured lassie, who was contented with her lot, because she had sense enough to discover that it was a very happy one.

There was one person, however, who would, I soon with some pain discovered, have been better pleased had I not come to the islands. That was John Angus, my host's son. He did not treat me uncivilly or unkindly, but I saw that it cost him an effort to be as cordial as the rest of his family. He was a good-natured, frank, kind-hearted man, whom under other circumstances I should have hoped to have made my friend. I cannot but think, too, that in time he would have won Margaret's regard, and he was certainly a man to have made any woman happy.

In two weeks or so I was Margaret's acknowledged suitor, or rather, I may say, her affianced husband. I was so happy that I thought sorrow could never again come near me. Now Margaret herself reminded me that I was a Shetlander,—indeed, as I was born at sea, no other people would claim me,—and that I ought to try and find out some of my family. I talked the subject over with Mr. Angus. He remembered many of them, but when he came to consider, every one of my near relations were gone. Some cousins of my father's were the nearest remaining, and then there were several of Aunt Bretta's old friends, the companions of her youth whom she wished me to see. John Angus volunteered to accompany me, and he provided two strong, shaggy little ponies for our journey.

We started away one morning soon after daybreak over the wild tracks, the only substitute for roads through the islands in those days, and crossed into the chief part of the mainland by a causeway so narrow that I could have thrown a biscuit across it. On one side of us was Rowe Sound, and on the other Hagraseter Voe, a long, narrow voe running out of Yell Sound. It would be difficult to describe the wild, and often beautiful scenery through which we passed. Long, deep voes, full of inlets and indentations, with high heathery hills on either side, was the most characteristic feature, and quiet, little inland lochs, with wild-fowl resting on their bosoms, was another, and then high rocky cliffs, the habitation of innumerable sea-birds, and hundreds of green islands and rocks scattered about on every side on the surface of the blue ocean.

John Angus did his best to point out to me the various points of interest we passed. Among the most curious were the Pictie towers, little round edifices built with rough stone, beautifully put together, with passages inside winding up to the top without steps. They were built by a race who inhabited those islands long before the time of which history gives any account. Whence they came, or how they departed, no one knows. Every hamlet throughout Shetland is called a toun. The cottages composing them are very far from attractive-looking edifices, generally built of mud, of one storey, and thatched; with a midden on one side of the door, and a pool of a very doubtful colour and contents on the other. The insides were often large and clean, and tidy enough, and in such 1 found many of my aunt's friends residing.

Wherever I went, I was hospitably received, and I delivered my messages, and rode on. I cannot say that my cousins appeared very highly delighted at seeing me, which was natural enough, considering that till I made my appearance, and announced myself, they had never heard there was such a person in existence. However, Aunt Bretta was remembered by all her contemporaries with affection. I should have enjoyed my visits more had I not been anxious to return to Hillswick.

We were altogether five days away, and in that period, sometimes by means of boats, and sometimes on the backs of ponies, and at others on our own feet, we visited the greater portion of the islands. I often felt that had I been born among them, I should never have desired to leave their quiet shores, and more than once contemplated the probability of spending the remainder of my days there. I spoke my mind on the subject to John Angus.

'Do, Wetherhelm, do,' he answered; 'we shall be glad to have you among us: but you've heard the old notion we islanders have, that he who is saved from drowning by any one of us is certain to work us ill?'

'I've heard of the idea not only as held by the people of Shetland, but by those of many other countries,' I answered. 'Like many other ideas, to my mind, it is not only false, but wrong and wicked. Depend upon it, the idea was invented by those who wanted an excuse for killing the unfortunate people wrecked on their coast in order to obtain their property.'

'That may be,' said Angus; 'still, for my part, I cannot help believing that it is in some respects true. However, sometimes a man may work another harm without intending it. But come along, put your nag into a trot, we have a good many miles of this heavy peat land to get over before we reach home.'

11

It was not till some time afterwards that I knew what John Angus meant by his remarks. He volunteered to take the ponies round to the stable, while I went into the house. It was worth going away for a few days for the pleasure of being received as I was by Margaret. I thought her looking more sweet and lovely than ever. As I said before, I am not going to repeat all that occurred between us. The day was fixed for our marriage, and friends from far and near were invited to it. They came, some by water and others on ponies; the women on pack-saddles, with their head-gear in baskets hung over their arms. Mr. Angus had told me that he hoped, since I was to become his nephew, that I would live on with him and help him in his croft, as there was work enough both for me and his son. John, indeed, had a mind to go and see something of the world, and was proposing a trip to Aberdeen, if not to Edinburgh, before the winter. He would be away, at all events, during the winter, so that my services would be of great value.

This proposal exactly suited my wishes. I was certain that Margaret would be happy with her friends, and I should find plenty of the sort of employment which suited me. I should be out of doors during all the hours of daylight, and I knew that I should be handy in the various occupations in which the family passed their time during the long evenings of winter. Well, then, Margaret and I were married, and the guests who had welcomed me back as a countryman to Shetland, took their departure, and we all settled down into a very regular, happy state of existence. John Angus went away to Scotland, and I took his place as his father's assistant. The winter came round pretty quickly, and though we had fogs and damp sometimes, I did not find the weather nearly so cold as I expected. Even in mid-winter, with a south-westerly wind, it was always quite warm; but when the wind shifted round and came out of the north-east or east, it was cold enough. Still there was

MARRIED.

very little ice, and not often much snow. As I have often remarked when wandering over the globe, every country has its advantages, and those far northern islands have theirs. They have their long days in summer, and bright skies, and fragrant wild-flowers, and fine wild scenery, and, thanks to the hot waters of the Gulf Stream which wash their shores, a tolerably temperate climate all the year round. The winter passed rapidly away. I could often scarcely believe in my happiness, after all the hardships and dangers I had undergone, and I am afraid that I was not sufficiently grateful for it. One thing I felt, that Margaret did not repent the choice she had made. Though I had had rather more education than generally falls to the lot of those of my class, I knew that I was but a rough, untutored seaman, and so I did my utmost to be tender and gentle to my wife, and to study how I best could please her in everything. I did not forget my old friend Miss Rundle,—my wife and I wrote her a long letter between us, full of all sorts of fun; we also took good care to pay the postage. Of course, also, we wrote to Aunt Bretta. She sent back a letter in return, hoping that we would soon come south to see her. We expected John Angus in the spring, but he did not return. He wrote instead, to say that he had got some employment in the south, which suited him for the present, and that he was very happy.

A whole year passed away. During the second winter, I thought that my wife, who had been so long accustomed to the soft air of Devonshire, was suffering from the long continuance of damp fogs. While I was balancing in my mind whether I ought not to take her south, I received another letter from Aunt Bretta. She told me that she was quite sickening to see me and my wife, and that my uncle hoped to be able to find some employment on shore which would suit my taste. When I laid the proposal before my wife, she at once acceded to it. 'I am afraid,' said she, 'that as long as we remain here, we keep poor John away from his family. If we go south, he will return home.' David Angus, and the old lady, and our kind-hearted cousin, were most unwilling to part with us, but we had written to Aunt Bretta to say that we were coming, and we could not again change our plans. About the middle of June we sailed in a smack bound direct for Leith, and once more I found myself on salt water.

CHAPTER IX.

Voyage in the smack—Gale springs up—Washed overboard—Saved on a spar—
  Dreadful fears for my wife's safety—The kind-hearted fisherman—Find the smack
  —Account of her escape—Journey on land—Coach upset—Again preserved—
  Reach home—Old Jerry again—His adventure with the bears.

I WAS walking the deck one night, while my wife was below, and thinking of the events of my past life, when the recollection of my rash oath
came across me like a thunder-clap in summer, when just before the
whole sky overhead has appeared of the purest blue. 'Is my dreadful
fate still to pursue me?' I thought. 'Rather than she should be torn
from me, let me perish with her.' The weather was fine, the wind was
light and fair, and there was not the slightest cause for any apprehension
of danger. Had I been by myself, such an idea would not, I believe,
have crossed my mind; but now that I had so precious a being under
my charge, I was timid as a mother with her first-born child. At last
I went below, and the night passed away in quietness. The next
morning was bright and lovely as ever an early summer has had to
exhibit, and I felt ashamed of my thoughts of the previous evening, as if
I had been ungrateful for the blessings I had received, and mistrustful
of God's merciful providence. Still the ideas I had entertained came
back again during the forenoon, and haunted me at times throughout the
day. Had I been able to speak to my wife on the subject, I doubt not
I should have relieved my mind ; but I was afraid of frightening her and
making her nervous, so I kept them to myself. As the evening drew on,
dark clouds were seen banking up on the horizon. I watched them with
171

an anxiety I had never before experienced at sea, for I had never before
been on the ocean with a freight I prized so much. They continued
rapidly to increase, and before night closed in had formed a thick canopy
overhead, while dark heaving seas came rolling in towards us across the
full width of the German Ocean, and the increasing breeze moaned and
whistled in our rigging. The smack heeled over to the force of the
wind till her lee-bulwarks were under water, but still the master was
unwilling to shorten sail. We were on a lee shore, and he was anxious
to haul off sufficiently to make his passage good for the Firth of Forth.
We might even then have run back for the Moray Firth, where, as the
wind was from the southward of east, we should have got under the lee
of the land ; but then we might have been detained there, very certainly
for many days and perhaps for several weeks, so he resolved, at all
hazards, to keep the sea. Under a close-reefed mainsail and storm-jib,
the little vessel continued her course, looking bravely up to the increasing gale. Still, at times she plunged heavily into the seas, and it often
seemed, as I stood on her deck, as if she would never rise again above
them. I sat, while I could, by my wife in the cabin, to try and comfort
and protect her ; but I could not help rushing on deck every now and
then to ascertain how matters were proceeding. The report, however, I
had to give when I returned below was anything but encouraging. I
had no idea of deceiving people, as some persons do, when danger is
threatening. I am certain that the more a person can contemplate the
possibility of danger, the better able they will be to encounter it when
it comes, if they have employed the meantime in reflection and in considering the best means to meet it.

   We were off the Scotch coast, somewhere between Stonehaven and
Montrose, I fancy, when the gale came down upon us with greater force
than ever, and the old master thought if he could get the try-sail on the
vessel, as we had by this time gained a considerable offing, that he

should be able to heave her to and weather it out till it blew over. As he was about to shift the sails the wind lulled a little, and once more he hoped that he should be able to hold on his course. He forgot that all this time, though he was certainly getting more to the southward, the vessel was also drifting nearer and nearer in-shore. At last the gale, as if it had rested merely to gain strength, breezed up again with greater fury than ever. I was below at the time. 'We must get the try-sail on her, my lads,' I heard the old man sing out. Securing my wife to a sofa in the cabin, I sprang on deck to lend a hand, for I knew that all the strength that could be obtained would be required, and that every moment of delay added to our danger. Many as were the gales I had been in, I had never beheld a more terrific-looking scene than that by which I now found myself surrounded. Vivid flashes of lightning every now and then revealed the dark wall-like waves which rose up with their crests of foam on every side around us, and threatened to engulf the little craft struggling helplessly among them. Still no one stopped a moment to think of all this—the work to be done was to get the main-sail off her and to set the try-sail. I thought at the time that we were much nearer in-shore than the old master fancied. The try-sail was almost set, and we were hauling out the sheet, when I heard the old man sing out, 'Hold on, my lads! hold on! Here comes a sea which will give her a shake.' On it came. I was to leeward. I felt myself torn from the rope to which I held, and my feet lifted off the deck. The wild waves surrounded me. There was a tumult in my ears. With horror and agony I discovered that the sea had carried me overboard. I shrieked out instinctively for help, though I knew that none could be afforded. In vain I struggled to regain the vessel.

My real condition presented itself with terrific clearness to my mind. For my own life I cared not, but I thought of my wife—of her agony and despair when she discovered that I was lost. I would have given

worlds to have got once more on board that little sea-tossed bark. I
was always a good swimmer. Even amid those tossing waves I found
that I could keep my head above water. Still the unequal struggle
could not have lasted long, when at the moment I was losing the dim
outline of the little vessel in the darkness, I found myself thrown against
some floating object. A hope that I might possibly preserve my life
sprung up in my bosom. I grasped the object, and found that it
was part of the mast and top of a large vessel. I clambered upon it
and held fast while I recovered my breath. Though it was violently
tossed about by the seas, which threatened every moment to sweep me
off from it, still I held on. My first thought was to endeavour to
discover how far off was the smack, on board which was all I prized in
life. I could nowhere see her. I have heard of people's hair turning
white in a single night from grief—I felt that mine might have done so
from the agony of mind I endured. Would the smack weather out the
gale? or would my dear wife survive the shock when she discovered
that I had been so suddenly torn from her? 'I have often been
punished, and justly, but this is the most severe punishment of all,' I
thought to myself. A voice whispered in my ear, 'Curse God, and die,'
—the same voice which had whispered the same words into the ear of
the Patriarch Job many ages ago, and has been whispering the like into
the ears of thousands of human beings ever since. 'Oh God, have
mercy on me and support me!' I ejaculated, and the tempter fled from
me.

Scarcely able to breathe from the dense masses of spray surrounding
me, and from the waves which kept continually washing over me, I still
clung on to the wreck. I fancied that the shattered mast was being
floated onward. I do not remember now what reason I had for supposing so. It contributed, at all events, to keep up my hope of being
ultimately rescued. How slowly and painfully the hours passed by!

Often I thought that, from very exhaustion and cold, I must be swept from my hold. At length, as I was looking upwards at the sky to try and discover any break in the clouds which might afford me an indication that the gale was abating, I beheld the first faint streaks of dawn appearing in the eastward. The clouds seemed to lift like a thick curtain to let in the light of day. I looked round towards the land; I could distinguish its dim outline through the darkness which still hung over it. This convinced me that the mast must have drifted much nearer than when I first got hold of it. This fact, however, tended to increase my anxiety for the fate of the smack. What if she has been driven on the rocks, and, as would probably be the case, all on board have perished! 'Oh, why, why was not I allowed to remain with my dear wife, to perish with her, or to be the means of saving her!' I exclaimed, in the agony of my spirit. The intensity of my feelings almost overcame me. As daylight increased, I saw that the summer gale had considerably lessened, and every minute the wind seemed to be going down. I could now clearly make out the shore, the yellow sands, with their fringe of dark rocks, over which the surf was breaking with almost unabated fury. 'What chance of escaping with my life will there be, if I am drifted in among those wild rocks?' I thought to myself. Now there could be no doubt that I was drifting, and rapidly too, towards the shore. With an anxious, piercing gaze, I looked round to the southward to see if I could discover any signs of the smack, half dreading to find her driven in among the rocks, yet still praying and hoping that she might be riding safely at anchor behind some sheltering reef, or within some little harbour on the coast. Not a sign of her could I discover. I looked seaward. Two or three sails were seen, rising and falling in the offing, but too far off to allow me to hope that she could be one of them. On drove the mast; its course was altered, and it was evidently drifting along shore to the southward. I judged that I was not more than three or four hundred fathoms from the breakers. I discovered that by climbing a little further on the mast, I could stand upright without its turning over with me. Finding this, I untied a silk handkerchief I had about my neck, and waved it around my head. I continued waving, hoping that some one would see my signal. I waited anxiously, looking along the shore. At so early an hour few people were out. At last the head of a man appeared above a sand-hill. I waved more vehemently, and shouted, forgetting that my voice could not be heard above the roar of the breakers. Soon I saw him standing on the top of the hill, and looking through a spy-glass at me, and then he waved his hand in return, and, pointing to the southward, ran on. Directly afterwards I saw two or three other people running in the same direction, carrying oars over their shoulders, and a boat-hook. I guessed that they were making for some little harbour or sandy cove, where their boats were drawn up. I prayed that they might come to my aid quickly, for every instant the wreck of the mast drove nearer and nearer to the rocks. Still I cannot say that I felt much doubt about being saved after having already been so mercifully preserved during the night from dangers so terrific. Yet it appeared an age before I saw a boat darting out from an opening in the rocks. Putting her head to the seas, she dashed up towards me. She had not come a minute too soon.

'Stand by, mon! stand by to leap aboard!' I heard a voice sing out, as the bow of the boat came up close to where I was hanging on.

I did not require a second order; at the same time, my limbs were so stiff and benumbed that I could scarcely have obeyed, had not two of the men in the bow of the boat caught me by the collar, and hauled me on board.

'Noo, round wi' her, laddies! round wi' her! we'll hear a' aboot it by and by,' cried the man at the helm.

The boat was at the time scarcely half-a-dozen fathoms from the surf, and any sea rolling in, and breaking sooner than usual, might have rolled her over and over and drowned all hands. With hearty tugs the men who had so bravely rescued me pulled the boat round and out to sea, while the mast was directly afterwards carried among the surf, and hurled round and round, till it was cast in fragments on the rocks. I shuddered when I saw what my fate might have been. There was little time to exchange many words with the fishermen before the boat was pulled into a little sandy cove, and they all, springing out, ran her up high and dry on the beach.

'You maun be weet, laddie,' said the old master of the boat, helping me out of her with the aid of two of the other men. 'Come up to my hoose, and we'll put dry duds on ye, and then you'll tell us how ye came to be floating on that bit of wreck there. She maun hae been a large ship ye belonged to, I'm thinking, and ye were the only one saved? it's sad to think of it.'

Under some circumstances I should have been amused by the eagerness of the old man to hear the account I had to give, at the same time that his kind heart prompted him not to fatigue me by asking questions. I was still more anxious to know if he could give me any account of the smack. As we were going up to the cottage I described her exactly, but he shook his head.

'We were up late last nicht, looking along the shore on account of the gale, and we were not out so early this morning as usual,' was the reply.

Having satisfied the curiosity of my host with an account of my own adventure, I entreated that, as soon as my clothes were dried, I might be allowed to proceed to the southward along the coast, to try and gain tidings of the smack. My hopes revived within me when the fisherman told me that we were not far from the mouth of

the Firth of Tay, and that perhaps the smack might have been driven
in there.

'Still ye should know that there is a danger there which has proved
fatal to many a tall ship,' said the old man. 'It is called the Inchcape
Rock. There's a bell made fast to it, which, whenever a gale is blowing,
tolls by the tossing of the seas as they drive against it. You've heard
tell, maybe, of the pirate, who, in the wantonness of his wickedness,
carried the bell away, and who, although another was placed in its
stead, was lost, with all his companions, on that very rock. Heaven
finds out sinners of high and low degree, at some time or other, however
they may endeavour to escape its vengeance.'

I thought to myself, 'True, indeed, is that. How often have I been
found out and punished for my one great sin!'

Ill and weak as I was, I insisted, as I had had some food on starting,
to proceed along the coast to try and obtain tidings of the smack. If
she had not foundered, she must have been cast on shore or taken shelter
in some harbour at the mouth of the Tay.

'No, no,' said the old man; 'young blood fancies that it can do anything, but I tell ye that ye have no strength to go on now without rest.
I'll send my laddies along the coast, both north and south, and they will
make inquiries and bring back any tidings they can obtain; you will
have news of the vessel more speedily in that way than any other.'

Still I insisted on putting on my own clothes and setting off; but
when I attempted to get up, I found that I could scarcely walk across
the room, much less could I hope to trudge over the links, and rough
rocks and sand which lined the shore along which I wished to proceed.
I was obliged, therefore, to consent to go to bed, and to try and sleep.
At first I thought that would be impossible, but my old sailor habits
triumphed over the anxiety I felt, and the rest I so much needed came
to me.

In less than four hours I awoke. I found myself alone; so I sprang up and put on my clothes, resolved that nothing should stop me from proceeding on my journey. I felt far stronger than I could have expected.

'Stay till my laddies come in, and hear what account they have to give ye,' said the kind-hearted old fisherman, making me sit down once more in the porch in front of his cottage.

The roof was the bow of a small boat, which made a good shelter from the sun, and the supporting-posts the jawbones of a whale which had been stranded on the shore.

That I might have something to distract my mind he gave me a stick that I might fashion it to support my steps as I walked along. When I had cut it to the required length I sprang up, saying I would go on some little way, at all events, begging his son to follow me; when we saw the young man approaching the cottage from the north, I ran forward to meet him.

'Have you heard anything of the smack?' I inquired, in breathless haste.

'No; not a sign of her. There was a big ship lost with all hands— not a soul escaped—in the early part of the night; but often when the big ship goes down the small one swims; ye ken that, mon,' was the answer.

Although he had been out for some hours, he insisted on accompanying me when he found that I had resolved on proceeding, till we should fall in with his brothers. The old man gave me his blessing, and the old wife and the rest of the family parted most kindly with me—they were all so much interested in the account I had given them of myself. As to receiving any remuneration, they would not hear of it.

We toiled on over the links; sometimes I thought that my knees would have given way under me. At last the old weather-beaten tower of Broughty Castle appeared in sight, the ancient guardian to the entrance of the Tay. 'We'll just sit down here till the ferry-boat is ready to cross,' said my companion, throwing himself on the grass bank under the crumbling walls. 'Maybe my brother will be coming over just now, and he will tell us what he has learned.'

I suggested that the smack might have run up to Dundee, but he said that was not in the least likely. If she had come in there she would have brought up off Broughty itself. We made inquiries, before sitting down, of some fishermen who had been on the shore all the morning, and certainly no vessel, they said, answering the description of the smack had come in. At any other time my eye would have dwelt with pleasure on the scenery which is presented by the beautiful estuary of the Tay, but now I could only think of the object of my search. I was leaning back on the grass, hoping to recover strength to proceed, when my companion jumped up and ran down toward the water's edge.

'What news, Sandy! what news do ye bring?'

'The vessel is safe,' was the answer. 'Thank Heaven for its mercy!' I ejaculated; and springing up and running towards the young fisherman, 'Tell me, lad, tell me, how is my wife!'

'The puir young leddy was taken very bad—very bad indeed, when she found that you had gone overboard, and all on board thought that she could not live. No one could give her any comfort, for no one thought you could have escaped. The rest on board, indeed, had soon to think of themselves. The vessel drove past the Inchcape Rock, and all heard the tolling of the bell, and believed that they were going to strike on it.

'While others were bemoaning their fate, and crying out for mercy, and expecting to be drowned, she sat up and seemed to have forgotten the cause of her own grief.

'"Ah," she said with a smile, " what makes you miserable, gives me joy

You fear death. I look forward to it as a happiness, because I shall soon be joined to him who has been torn from me."

'Ay, sir, the bell tolled louder and louder, and each toll that it gave made her heart beat quicker with joy, while it drove the life-blood away from the hearts of those who feared death as the greatest of evils. On drifted the vessel—darkness was around them—still that solemn bell kept tolling and tolling, but yet the expected shock was not felt. The bell tolled on, but the sounds grew fainter and fainter, and the master told them that they had no longer cause to fear, and might thank Heaven for their preservation, for that he knew where they were, and could take them into a port in safety. Well, but of your wife, I know that you will want to hear.'

'Yes! yes!' I exclaimed, 'tell me how is she—where is she!' We were all the time the young fisherman was speaking hurrying down towards the ferry-boat.

'That is just what I was about to tell ye,' he answered, with the deliberate way in which the inhabitants of that part of Scotland of his rank generally speak. 'The young leddy, they told me, no sooner heard that the vessel was in safety, than she gave way to a sorrow which it was pitiful to witness. They tried to comfort her, but she was not to be comforted. She had gone off into a sort of trance when the vessel brought up this morning under St. Ann's Head.

'The master was thinking about putting to sea when I got on board. He and all the people were very much surprised to hear that you had escaped; but the difficulty seemed to be to break the news to your wife. The master promised not to sail till you appeared, and I promised to come and hurry you on.'

'Thank ye, thank ye, my kind friend!' I exclaimed, shaking him by the hand. 'But my wife—tell me about my wife. How did she bear the sudden reaction?'

'It did her all the good in the world,' he answered cheerfully. 'The old master, who is a canny man, went down into the cabin and began to talk of the wonderful things which had occurred to his knowledge at sea—how people had been kept alive floating on a spar for a couple of days, and how others had swam a dozen miles or more, or been washed from the deck of one vessel right aboard another, and fallen overboard, and been picked up floating on a grating, or an oar, by a vessel coming up astern hours afterwards.

'Suddenly the young lady lifted herself up, showing, that though she had appeared to be asleep, she had been listening to every word that had been said.

'"Captain," said she, "in mercy tell me whether you believe that my husband's life has been preserved by any of the means you speak of. Do not deceive me. Do not keep me in doubt."

'"Not for all the world would I deceive you, young leddy," said the master; "I will tell you what I believe to be the truth, that your husband got floated on shore last night, and that he is not a great way off, to prove to you that what I say is true."

'Oh, did not she cry out with joy and thankfulness, and then the old master told me what he had said, and charged me to come on here as fast as I could to bring you on board.'

My two young friends insisted on accompanying me all the way back to the vessel, about three miles along the southern shores of the Firth, and thankful indeed was I for their support. It showed me how an old man must feel when his strength is failing him, and he has a long journey to perform. It taught me always to have more compassion for advancing age than I had before been inclined to feel.

I cannot describe the unspeakable joy it was to my wife and me to meet each other again, after the dreadful anxiety we had both of us experienced, and the dangers we had gone through. I was unwilling to trust her again on the treacherous ocean, even for the short passage round to Leith; but she entreated me not to be so mistrustful of Providence, who had been so merciful to us, and urged me to continue the voyage. I felt at the time that she was right, and that, instead of considering myself as under a curse, I ought to acknowledge that each time I had been shipwrecked, I had received a special mark of God's favour, for my life had been preserved, while so many others of my fellow-creatures had lost theirs. Instead, therefore, of taking her on shore, and going on to St. Andrews, as I had at first proposed doing, I agreed to remain on board the smack. I could not sufficiently thank the two young fishermen for the labour and trouble they had taken for my sake. They laughed when I talked about it.

'Hoot! it's just nothing. We ken by your looks that you would do the same for us, so say no more about it, mon,' was the answer they both gave. I hope they were right in the favourable opinion they had formed of me.

In the afternoon, the weather having completely moderated, we sailed. What a contrast did the next night afford to the previous one! The stars came out, and the moon shone forth, playing brightly on the tranquil waters, just rippled over with a light breeze, which sent us along smoothly on our course. Margaret sat on the deck with me, watching the scene with a delighted eye and thankful heart. Our conversation was far too solemn for repetition.

'Oh, Willand, never let us again doubt God's mercy and kindness towards us. At this hour last night how stormy and dark was the ocean; how full of anguish and misery were our hearts; how utterly hopeless did everything appear; not a gleam burst forth to give us consolation! We were violently torn from each other, it seemed, never to be united again on earth, neither of us knowing what had become of the other; and now see how the face of nature smiles!

12

Once more we are united, and all our prospects appear bright and happy.'

Thus we talked on, and, thankful for the present, did not dream that storms of adversity might yet be in store for us, yet not sent without a gracious and merciful object to try and improve our hearts.

We reached Leith in safety, and as neither of us had before been in Edinburgh, we spent some days there to view that beautiful and interesting city. Such it was even in those days; but though it has lost somewhat in picturesque effect, it has since then been greatly improved.

It may seem strange that a sailor should be afraid of trusting himself at sea; but reason as I might, I could not bring myself to take my wife to the south by water. I therefore prepared to convey her to London by coach, and from thence to Portsmouth. The expense was very great; but I promised her that I would toil hard in whatever occupation I undertook to make it up, and at last she acceded to my wishes. We calculated that we should be about a week or ten days getting to London, for those were times when even the coaches on the great northern road went very leisurely along, and it was not for some time after that they were superseded by the fast London and Edinburgh mail. Times have indeed changed with all of us.

We left Edinburgh one morning at daybreak, and proceeded south to Berwick, where we stopped. Our next stage was York. There we rested the greater part of the day, for my wife seemed very much fatigued, and when I saw how fine the weather continued, I began to repent that I had not gone, as she wished, by sea. I had placed her inside, while I went on the top of the coach. I observed that our fat old coachman, who, although it was summer weather, was muffled up in a greatcoat, with a red comforter up to his eyes, whenever we stopped to change horses went into the bar of the roadside inn and took a pretty stiff glass of brandy and water to keep out the damp, as he told his passengers. At last four rather frisky horses were brought out and harnessed to the coach.

'Steady now, Mr. Currycomb; we have some ugly hills to go up and down,' remarked one of the passengers who had watched his drinking proceedings with some little anxiety.

'Oh, never fear me, sir,' answered the old man, in a thick, husky voice. 'I've driven this road, man and boy, for the last fifty years, and I should think I know how to take a coach along it without anybody telling me how to do it, do you see. If I thinks it's best to trot down a hill, why I'll do it, and no one shall tell me not. That's what I've got to say.'

I have frequently met the same sort of obstinate characters among seamen, the very men who manage to get their ships cast away; but I fancied that they were not to be found among those who live among the civilizing influences of the shore.

For some time we went on pretty well, though now and then the overloaded coach going down a hill rocked to and fro pretty violently. When we stopped the next time, a gentleman who had gone in the inside, because there was no place on the outside, said that he had never been accustomed to travel inside, and that it made him very ill, and asked if any gentleman would be willing to change places with him, and that, as he had already paid his fare, it would not put anybody who would so oblige him to further cost.

I at once said, that as my wife was inside, I should be very happy to be the means of accommodating him, so he mounted on the top of the coach, and I joined Margaret inside. Away we went once more rattling along over the road. The gentleman, I found, whose seat I had got had no idea that the coachman was the worse for liquor, but fancied that the rocking of the coach, which I had observed so palpably from the outside, was only the usual motion, and that he would be free from

it outside. Suddenly I felt that we were going on much faster than
usual.

'What is the matter?' exclaimed Margaret, as clouds of dust arose
on each hand, and we saw people starting aside and looking anxiously
after us as we were whirled along. 'Oh, the horses have run away!'

We heard the passengers hallooing and shouting to the coachman to
stop his horses, to pull up; but he either did not heed them or could
not obey them. On we dashed at a furious rate. We saw by the
appearance of some small, red-brick houses, scattered here and there,
that we were approaching a town. I placed myself by Margaret's side,
and held her tightly down.

On we whirled. Round went the huge vehicle with a swing. There
was a terrific crash. We felt the coach dragged some little way; groans
and shrieks and cries arose around us. The coach stopped. The traces
had been cut, and the horses galloped off. I looked with intense anxiety
at my wife's countenance. She was pale, but she assured me that she
was unhurt. I had held her firmly, so as to break the shock when the
coach went over.

People came to help us out, and my wife was conducted into a house
close at hand, to which the owner invited us. But dreadful indeed was the
scene which met my eyes as I glanced round over the wreck of the coach.
The gentleman who had just changed places with me was lying dead on
the pavement, with three or four other passengers; the old coachman
lay a corpse, mangled horribly by the heels of the horses, over which he
had been thrown, and not one of the passengers had escaped some severe
injury; while the poor guard had his arm broken, and his horn doubled
up under him.

I went into the house, and sat down. 'Wife,' said I, 'you are right;
God watches over us at sea as well as on land, and accidents may occur
on shore as well as on the ocean. Why He has thought fit to preserve

us, while others have been allowed to perish, I know not; I can only take the cup of blessing and be thankful. I will never again attempt to escape out of His hand by endeavouring to avoid a possible danger.'

The gentleman and his wife were very much interested in the account Margaret and I gave of ourselves, and invited us to remain a whole day with them, that she might recover from her fatigue. It is one of the pleasantest things in life to thus receive unexpected kindness from strangers, who can have no thought or hope of recompense. It is satisfactory at the time, and makes one think better of the common human nature which unites us to our fellow-beings. I told our new friend of all the shipwrecks I had suffered.

'Ah! there are as many on shore, depend upon it, as on the ocean,' he answered. 'On shore they are the worst, because they occur generally through our own folly and ignorance and vice. How many a young man has started fairly in life, and yet before many years have passed he has made a complete shipwreck of all the bright promises on which his friends trusted, with himself alone to blame, because he refused to consult or to be guided by the only sure chart and compass which could guide him aright! For what purpose did the wise King of Israel —the wisest of the kings of the earth—write his proverbs, do you think? Not for his own satisfaction or amusement, but because he felt it a sacred duty he owed to posterity to give the result of his own meditations, of his observations, and of his own bitter experience. Yet how few men, comparatively, go to that book of books for counsel, for guidance, and direction. Where can be found more ample directions for getting on in life, as the phrase is, for making money, for becoming great in this world even, than the Book of Solomon affords?'

I agreed with my kind and thoughtful host, and promised to study that work more than I had ever before done. I ought to have said that

I would begin and study it—for, alas! how completely had I before
neglected it.

After this extraordinary incident, I believe that had I been near a
port, I should have again embarked for London; but as it was, we
agreed to continue our journey by land. We reached London in safety.

We did not stay there long. The bustle and noise, and seeming
confusion, after the complete quiet of our Shetland life, was so wearying,
that, having seen some of the chief lions of that great city, we were glad
to set off by the coach for Portsmouth.

Aunt Bretta was delighted to receive us, and my jovial, kind-hearted
uncle welcomed us most cordially. I thought Aunt Bretta would never
have ceased asking questions about dear old Shetland. A stranger
would have supposed from her expressions about it, that there did not
exist a more delightful spot on earth.

Margaret, however, was never weary of replying to all the inquiries
made. I never saw two people suit each other so well as my aunt and
wife,—the one so hearty, full of life and spirits, and brimming over with
the milk of human kindness,—the other so tranquil, so sensible, and
sweet-tempered.

My uncle and I also got on capitally together. I admired his jovial,
frank, hearty, and kind disposition, his thorough uprightness and hatred
of deceit, while he found in me enough good qualities to like, and was
pleased because I admired him and was able to talk with him frankly
and openly on all subjects. That is, I believe, the great secret of
friendship. Mutual esteem and perfect confidence is the only foundation on which it can be built up and made perfect. Both parties to
the bond must feel that they appreciate each other's motives and objects,
and that every allowance will be made for what they say, and the best
possible construction put on their words. When two people meet
between whom such qualifications exist, their friendship is lasting.

My uncle told me, that as he knew I should not wish to be idle, he had obtained a situation for me, which he thought I should like, as suitable to my former habits.

'It is in a private dockyard, where, if you are steady and attentive you will, I am certain, obtain a still more lucrative employment,' he remarked; 'had it been war time I should have tried to obtain an appointment in the Royal Dockyard, because you would then have had protection from the pressgang; but now you need have no fear of that.'

Two days after that, war again broke out with France! It was arranged to our mutual satisfaction that Margaret and I should permanently take up our abode with our relatives. They had a couple of spare rooms, which they had at times let to lodgers, so that we in no way incommoded them.

Never was there a more happy family party. We were not over-refined; we did not set up for people of that sort, it must be remembered, or call ourselves gentlemen and ladies. Nor did our guests. They were, however, always well-behaved, civil people, who would on no account have committed any real solecism in good manners.

Old Jerry Vincent used to look in, as before, very frequently, with a budget of his funny stories, to which other neighbours gladly came to listen. There was invariably much laughter, and no small amount of tea and tobacco consumed, not to speak occasionally of some more potent compound; but my uncle took good care that none of his guests should pass the limits of sobriety, though he had at times some little difficulty in keeping old Jerry in order. I should remark that old Jerry was an exception to the general character of our guests, who were as a rule of a much higher rank in the social scale. I remember especially one of the old man's stories which is worth recording.

'You must know, mates,' said he, 'once upon a time I belonged to a brig of war on the Newfoundland station. It isn't just the place, in my

opinion, that a man would wish to spend his life in. Too much frost
and fog, and wind and rain, to be pleasant. But bad as it was, I
thought there was a worse place to be in, and that was aboard my own
ship. We never know when we are well off. I don't think I was right,
do ye see; but rather, I am very well convinced, that I was a
fool. Young men sometimes don't find that out till it's too late.
Howsomedever, I found another fool as big as myself, which is never
very difficult when you look for him, and he and I agreed to run from
the ship. Now, before I go on with my story, I'll just ask one or two
of you young men, have any of you ever seen the biggest fool in the
world? Well, I thought not; you can't say that you have, and, what's
more, you never will. If you think that you have got hold of him, you
may be sure that you'll fall in with a bigger before long somewhere else.
That is my philosophy, and I am not far wrong, depend on it.

'Well, where was I? Oh, I know. My mate's name—t'other fool,
I mean—was Abraham Coxe. The ship had put into St. John's,
Newfoundland. He and I belonged to the same boat's crew. Soon
after we got there we were sent on shore to water. After some time,
as the rest of our party were rolling the casks down to the beach,
we managed to slip away, and made a run of it for a mile or more,
till we could stow ourselves snug inside the walls of an old cottage.
As soon as it was dark we came out, and set off as hard as we could
go right into the country. We thought some one was following us,
but we were wrong. The officers knew better than we did what sort
of a place we had got into, and calculated that we shouldn't be long
before wishing ourselves back again.

'At night we reached a cottage, where the good people treated us
kindly, for, do ye see, we spun them a long yarn, which hadn't a
word of truth in it, about our being sent away up there to look after
a shipmate who had lost his senses. So, after we had eaten and

drunken and taken a good snooze, we set off again towards the mountains, for we had a notion that we should find our way somehow or other into America. We expected to fall in with another village, but we were mistaken, and by dinner-time we began to feel very peckish. There was no use standing still, so we walked on and on till we got further up among the mountains, and as the sun was hid by clouds, and there was no wind, we very soon lost our way.

'Now, do ye see, to lose your way with a full stomach is not altogether pleasant, but to lose it on an empty one, and not to know where a dinner is to be found, is worse any day than to get three dozen. That's got quickly over, and you know the worst. We had no baccy neither, and the air up there sharpened our teeth till we were ready to bite our tongues out.

' "Well, mate," says I to Abraham Coxe, "I wish that I were safe aboard again. I don't by no manner of means like these short commons."

' " Wait a bit till we have been knocking about for two or three days more, and then cry out, my bo'," says he, for he was a regular Job's comforter, that he was.

'Well, evening was coming on, and as we couldn't find our way out of the mountains, nor get any food either, we thought that we might as well look out for a warm berth to sleep in at night. At last we saw a small hole in a rock, which looked like the mouth of a cave.

' "There will be a comfortable bed-place inside that place, mate," says I, as I poked my head into the hole, while Abraham stood outside. It was almost dark inside, but still there was light enough to make out that there was a good big place further in. I was going along on my hands and knees, when what should I see but several animals like biggish pigs crawling about. I was wondering what they were, when I heard Abraham Coxe sing out ·

' "Quick, Jerry, quick, get out of the cave, for there is a great big bear coming along the valley, and she's close aboard of us!"

' It was all very well for Coxe to say, get out of the cave; but that was more than I could do in a hurry without turning round, when I might have had all the young bears attacking my rump, saving your presence, ladies. Coxe also didn't stop to help me, but scampered off as hard as his legs could carry him. I was going to make the best of my way after him, when I saw a big white bear not three fathoms off, evidently steering for the very place itself.

' There was no use trying to get out, for to a certainty the brute would have grappled me in a moment; so I drew back, thinking to remain concealed. Just then I remembered the beasts I had seen inside, and I guessed that they were the bear's cubs, and that I had taken possession of her abode. It was not a pleasant idea, certainly, but there was no help for it. In another minute the great big she-bear came snuffing up to the hole where I lay. I thought that it was all up with me, and expected every moment to be made into a supper for the bear and her cubs. The little beasts were all the time licking my heels just to have a taste, I thought, of what was to come. The bear began to growl, I fancied because she found me inside; but I believe it was just her way of talking to her cubs. Thinks I to myself, I'll have a fight for it; so I doubled my fists, intending to give her a good lick on the eye before she ate me, when, just as I thought that she was going to make a grab at me, she slued round and began to back into the cave stern foremost.

' "Ho! ho!" says I to myself, "if you goes to make a stern-board, old gal, I'll rake you before you shows your broadside to me again;" so on that I whips out my long knife, which I had tucked away in my belt, with a lanyard round my neck, and drove it with all my force right into her. The more she backed, and the louder she growled, the barder and faster I drove in the knife.   Still she came backing and backing, and I didn't like the prospect at all.   I thought to myself "If she drives me up against the end of the cave, she'll squeeze all the breath out of my body, to a certainty."

'At last, however, when she got to the narrowest part of the hole, she sank down from loss of blood.   I thought she would perhaps begin to move on again, but she didn't.   After she had given a few growls, which grew fainter and fainter, I made sure she was dead.

'As I was pretty nigh famished, thinks I to myself, "I'll have some steaks out of you, old gal, at all events;" so I cut three or four fine steaks out of her rump (saving your pardon, Mrs. Kelson, and ladies all), and precious juicy and nice to look at they were; but how to dress them was the job.   At first I thought that I should have to eat them raw, as I had often done salt beef; but on hunting about on a higher part of the cave, I found a quantity of dry sticks and leaves which had served the bears for a bed, I suppose.   Piling up some of them, I struck a light, and made a fire to dress the steaks, while the young cubs kept rubbing against me, and couldn't make out whether I was their mother or their daddy I believe.   I gave them each a bit of steak, which they seemed to think not bad sucking.

'You see I was inside the cave, though there was just room to look out over the body of the dead bear, but scarcely space enough for me to have squeezed myself out if I had wished it.   I didn't just then wish to go out, for I was very comfortable; I had a dry roof over my head, and company too, and plenty to eat; only I should have liked a glass of grog to wash down the food.

'Well, as I was eating the bear's steak, I thought to myself, "It would have been better for Abraham Coxe if he had stuck to his old shipmate instead of running away at sight of danger."

'I had just finished supper, and was thinking of turning in for the

night, when I heard a loud growl at the mouth of the cave. I made
sure that it was the she-bear come to life again, for I was getting
drowsy, and I began to think what she would say to me for having
stolen her steaks. However, at last I got up and looked out, and there
I saw a great big he-bear walking about in front of the cave, and I
have no doubt scolding his wife for not getting out of his way to let
him in. At last he began to back astern, but he couldn't make her
move.

'"Growl away, my bo'," says I. "If you keep on at that game, I'll
make steaks of you before long."

'I sat as quiet as possible, picking my teeth with the point of my
knife, for the steaks were rather tough, you may guess. The little
bears, playful like, were running about round me, while the old bear
was grumbling away outside, thinking maybe that his wife had taken a
drop too much, and couldn't get up. All of a sudden I heard a great
hullabaloo, and several shots were fired, and down came the old bear as
dead as a door nail in front of the cave.

'Among other voices, I recognised that of Abraham Coxe. "My
poor mate is killed, and eaten by the bears," says he; "but I may as
well have his knife, and his baccy-box and buttons, if they ain't eaten
too."

'"No, I ain't eaten nor dead either, you cowardly rascal, and I hope
a better man nor you may have my traps when I do go," I sings out,
for I was in a towering rage at being deserted.

'At first the people were going to run away, thinking it was my
ghost that was speaking; but when I sang out again, and told them
that I was a living man, some of them took courage, and came and
dragged the two old bears out of the way. At last I crawled out,
followed by the young cubs, to the great astonishment of all who saw
us. To make a long story short, this was the way how the people had

come to my rescue. When Coxe ran away, not knowing where he went, he ran right into the village, which was all the time close to us. When the villagers heard what had happened, they all came out to have a shot at the bears, not expecting to find me alive. They seemed very glad I had escaped, and carried me back in triumph to the village. As it was through our means they got two bears and a number of cubs, they treated us very kindly, and pressed us to stay with them. When, however, we found that we should never reach America by going over the mountains, and as we had no fancy to spend a winter in this out-landish sort of a place, seeing that the summer wasn't very pleasant, we judged it best to go back to our ship and give ourselves up. We got three dozen a-piece, which I can only say we richly deserved, and neither of us ever attempted to desert again. " Let well alone," I used to say. " If I do get away, I shall only find myself before long on board another ship, and worse off than before, probably." '

Jerry's advice was very sound. Many a man deserts to obtain an uncertain good, and finds, when too late, that he has secured a certain ill.

Those truly were pleasant evenings at our quiet little house. I wish that I could recollect all old Jerry's stories I may perhaps call to mind a few more another day, for I think that they are well worthy of repetition.

CHAPTER X.

No happiness could be more complete than ours, and I saw no reason why it should not be permanent. Happy it undoubtedly is that we do not see the dark clouds of adversity gathering in the horizon, yet it would be wiser in men if they would still recollect that, however bright the sky and fine the weather, storms may arise, and thick mists may overshadow them—perhaps sent as punishments, perhaps in mercy to try and purify them. I was actively engaged all day in the duties of my office, and in the evening, when I returned home, I was welcomed by the smiles of my wife, and the cordial kindness of Aunt Bretta. I desired no change—I should have been content to live the same sort of life to the end of my days. I had a few little rubs and annoyances to contend with in my employment, but I did not allow them to vex me, and went on steadily doing my duty, neither turning to the right hand nor to the left.

War with France had again broken out, and England was making every effort to renew the struggle with the numerous foes which her prosperity and greatness had won for her. A difficulty existed then, as now, in manning the navy, and the pressgangs were always hard at work endeavouring to secure by force or stratagem the necessary crews for the ships.

I knew that I was not exempt from the risk of being taken, but as I dressed in shore-going clothes, and as I was not likely to meet any of my old shipmates or other people who knew me to have been a seaman, I had little fear on the subject. Had I been single and without the ties of home, I would gladly have once more gone afloat to serve my country; but how could I be expected to tear myself from all I loved on earth to do duty before the mast among rough and uneducated men, subject to all the rigours of the naval discipline of those days? I talked the subject over with my uncle.

'If the time comes when every man who can handle a rope is wanted, I shall be the first to say " Go,"' said he. ' Till then, my boy, stay at home, do your duty, and look after your wife.'

I was too glad to follow his advice. There was no grass growing in the streets of Portsmouth in those days. The place swarmed with seamen and officers; troops were marching in and out; carriages-and-tour were dashing down from London; bands were playing; the hotels swarmed with visitors come to see their friends off; ships were being commissioned and fitted out with unwonted rapidity; and all was life, activity, and energy. I now and then, on my way home, took a walk up High Street, for the amusement of observing the bustling, laughing, talking, busy throng.

One evening, as I turned to go back, my eye fell on the countenance of a man whose features I felt sure I knew. In an instant I recollected that they were those of Charles Iffley. Forgetting all I had heard to his disparagement, I was going to follow him, when he turned into a cross street among a crowd who were looking on at some itinerant tumblers, and I lost sight of him. I felt very sorry, for I should have been glad to have shaken him again by the hand and invited him to our house. My wife and aunt used constantly to walk out a little way on the common to meet me.

Two days after that, when they met me, they told me that, in the morning, as they were returning home, they had suddenly encountered Charles Iffley. He knew them at once, but did not speak. He stopped for an instant, stared hard at them, and then moved on. When, however, they reached our house door, they observed that he had followed them at a distance and remarked where they had gone in. Just as they had finished their account, the very person we were speaking of appeared at the further end of the road coming towards us. Directly, however, he saw us, he stopped short and looked at me with an astonished and inquiring gaze. He remained long enough, apparently, to ascertain positively who it was. At first he evidently was in doubt. He had heard of my death, and believed that I was dead, I concluded, and that when he saw me alive, and, as he might have suspected, married to the very woman who had refused to become his wife, he at first could not trust his senses.

My impulse was immediately to run forward to meet him, but my wife pressed my arm so tightly that I could not leave her.

'No, no, do not go,' she whispered. 'I do not like his look. He means us mischief.' She must have felt very strongly, I knew, before she could have given way to such an expression. Of course, I yielded to her wish, though it went much against my feelings to turn away from my old associate, ill as I had too much reason to think of him. I could not help agreeing with my wife, as I watched him, that I did not like his look. There was something very evil in his expression as he watched us proceeding towards our home, and I could no longer have any doubt that he recognised me. I never before had seen his countenance wear so malignant an expression, and I feared, not without reason, that even at that moment he was plotting to do us some mischief. A picture I had once seen was forcibly recalled to my memory. It represented Satan watching our first parents in Paradise, and when he is envying them the happiness he can never enjoy, he is considering how he may the most effectually destroy it.

When we got home, we talked the matter over. I did not express my own suspicions to my wife, as they could not fail to agitate her, but I endeavoured rather to make light of it, and to appear as if I hoped, should Charles Iffley feel any desire of revenge, that he would be unable to effect it. I felt regret, also, that I had not hurried after Iffley. Whatever were his feelings, I thought that I might perhaps have turned his heart to better thoughts by talking of bygone days and of our early friendship. 'Well, it may not yet be too late,' I thought to myself; 'I will seek him out and try to persuade him to discard those feelings of jealousy and envy which are now influencing him.' When, however, I mentioned my intentions to Uncle Kelson, he rather laughed at my notion.

'An idle, conceited young puppy. What business has he to interfere with you or yours?' he exclaimed. 'Because a girl, of whom he is utterly unworthy, does not choose to have anything to say to him, is he to set himself up and to look daggers at any man she may happen to marry? Let him alone. Let him go his own gait, as your Aunt Bretta would say. He'll find a rope long enough to hang himself. depend on it.'

My uncle thought he was giving good advice, but even at the time I felt that better is given elsewhere. 'Therefore, if thine enemy hunger, feed him; if he thirst, give him drink: for in so doing thou shalt heap coals of fire on his head. Be not overcome of evil, but overcome evil with good.' I felt that if I could have met with Iffley, I might have heaped coals of fire on his head. I might have softened his heart, just as the contents of a pot are melted by piling up coals, not only around it, but on the very head or top of it. I did not do what I felt and knew was right, and the result of my neglect will be seen.

13

Aunt Bretta was more indignant than any of us with Iffley. 'If he does come to the door, in my opinion, he ought to be turned away!' she exclaimed. 'The idea of a person whom I knew as a little boy, glad to receive a slice of gingerbread, giving himself such airs! I have no notion of it.' This was very severe for Aunt Bretta, whose heart was kindness itself.

On making inquiries of the servant, she discovered that a man exactly answering his description had, while they were out, knocked at the door and asked all sorts of questions.

'She could not mind what exactly,' she said. 'They were about Mr. Wetherholm. Where he had come from? When he had got married? What he was doing? And all sorts of such like things.' After I had heard this account of the servant girl, I could not help feeling somewhat suspicious of Iffley's object. The mere asking them was very natural, and had he come frankly forward to meet us, I should not have entertained any ill thoughts of him; but now, in spite of all my resolution, I could not help dreading that he contemplated doing me some mischief or other. Still I did my best to get rid of such thoughts of an old friend, for they were not pleasant.

When the evening came, I forgot all about the matter. Old Jerry Vincent looked in, and several other friends, among them two former shipmates of Uncle Kelson's, and anecdotes and stories innumerable were told. We got on the subject of smuggling. In those days it was certainly not looked on in its proper light, and a smuggler, if he was bold and daring, was considered a very fine fellow. Most of our guests were Hampshire or Isle of Wight men, and had been personally acquainted with many of the smugglers in their day, and might, perhaps, not have refused to purchase any of the goods they had to offer.

'Some of you may have known Jim Dore?' began Jerry.

One or two nodded.

'I thought so,' said Jerry. 'Well, then, when he began the work he was very young, and there wasn't a bolder or more daring hand in the trade. We were boys together, and a braver fellow or better seaman never stepped. He was a Yarmouth man, born and bred, just inside the Needles there. There was a large family of them. He wasn't always as prudent as he might be, and one day he and the cutter he was in was taken with three hundred tubs on board. Of course he was sent to serve his Majesty. When he found that there was no help for it, he vowed that he would do his duty like a man, and he kept his word.

'He was sent aboard a brig of war employed in looking after smugglers, and though before she had never taken one, now scarcely a month passed that through his means she did not make a prize.

'Once upon a time the brig attacked a large armed smuggler, the crew of which had vowed that they never would be taken alive. There was a desperate fight for more than three hours, and in the end the smugglers kept their word, for they went down with colours flying, under the guns of the brig which was just about to board them. On this occasion, as on every other, Dore behaved so bravely that the captain put him on the quarter-deck, and if he had chosen to follow it, there was the road open to him to become an admiral. But you know there are people who cannot give up habits, so to speak, born and bred with them, as one may say.

'Well, Dore's time of servitude was up for the smuggling affair, and soon after that the brig put into Portsmouth harbour. The next day Dore got leave to go and see his friends, so he hired a wherry, and got ready for a start for Yarmouth. Just as he was shoving off, I saw him and asked him for a cast down there, as I had some friends in those days in the same place. Now, though he was an officer with a cocked hat on his head, and a sword by his side, I knew that he was in no way proud, at all events. He told me to jump into the boat, by all means

On our way down I asked him if he was going to be long away from his ship.

'"Long away, do you say?" he answered, in an indignant tone. "I'll tell you what it is, Vincent, it will be long, I'm thinking, before I go back again. I've been made an officer of, it's true, but I haven't been treated as one or looked on as one, because I wasn't born a gentleman, and slavery in a cocked hat I, for one, will not bear."

'In that way he talked till we got pretty nearly down to Yarmouth. At last he worked himself up into a regular rage, for he was a passionate man, do you see.

'"Give us a knife, some one of you," he sang out.

'I handed him mine. When he got it, he began cutting off the buttons from his coat. Then he unbuckled his sword, and took off his hat. He jumped up, and holding all the things together, as it were in a lump, he hove them away into the sea as far from him as he could, uttering at the same time a loud and deep curse. "There goes the last link of the chain that binds me to slavery!" he exclaimed. "Now, my lads, I'm once more Jim Dore, the bold smuggler."

'The men in the boat thought what he had done was very fine, and so did I in those days, and so we all cheered him over and over again. When he landed at Yarmouth, every one turned out to welcome him as if he had been an admiral just come home after a great victory; and certainly the people did make much of him. Those Yarmouth men are great smugglers, there's no doubt about it. I don't think, however, myself, as I did in those days. Dore was a brave man, and it's a great pity he had not been taught better, and he might have been an ornament to the service he deserted.

'When his leave was up, and he did not return, an officer with a boat's crew was sent to look for him. He got notice of their coming, and got stowed out of the way, for there were plenty of people to help him. He had to keep in hiding for a long time, and often, I dare say, he wished himself back aboard the brig. When the war was over he took to smuggling again, and he soon got command of a large cutter. At last he and some other Yarmouth men went away in her, and from that day to this have never been heard of. It is supposed that the cutter was run down or foundered in a tremendous gale of wind, which sprung up soon after she was last seen.'

One of our friends who came from Poole in Dorsetshire, told us a very good story, when Jerry Vincent and one or two others sang out in chorus, ' Howe! howe! howe! '

I asked what they meant.

'That is what we always say to a Poole man,' answered Jerry. ' Did you never hear tell of the Poole man and the owl? '

I told him that I never had, and asked him for the story.

' Well, you must know that once upon a time there was a homeward-bound Poole man just coming up Channel, and not far off the land, when, the night being somewhat dark, do ye see, an old owl flew by "Howe! howe! howe!" cried the owl.

' The master, who had been dozing aft, thinking all the time, exactly as many another man does, that he was wide awake, just heard the sound as he roused up, and fancied that another skipper was hailing him.

' " From Newfoundland! " he sang out, rubbing his eyes, and dreaming that he saw the strange ship abeam.

' " Howe! howe! howe! " hooted the owl again.

' " With fish," answered the Poole man.

' " Howe! howe! howe! " once more cried the old owl, as he was flying off.

' " Over Poole bar with the next tide, please the pigs," sang out the skipper at the top of his voice, for fear those in the other craft wouldn't otherwise hear him. Nothing would ever persuade him that he hadn't been talking all the time with the skipper of some outward-bound craft.'

'That's all very well, and it is not a bad story, and may be true, or it may not; but you Hampshire men are not all of you so very clever,' answered Mr. Bexley, our Poole friend, who had himself been skipper of a merchantman. 'Have none of you ever heard speak of Botley assizes, eh?'

I asked him what he meant.

'Why,' he answered, 'you know Botley isn't very far from Southampton. Once upon a time a party of young chaps belonging to Botley were returning from a merry-making of some sort, and as it happened, all of them but one were more than three sheets in the wind. For some reason or other, nothing would make this one touch a drop of liquor. As they were walking along they began to jeer him, and at last they declared that he had been guilty of a capital offence, because he had let the glass pass by, and they agreed that they would try him. Well, they came to a place near a wood, where there were a number of trees cut down, and there they all sat round, and the accused was placed in the middle. The most drunk of the party was chosen as judge, and the others were the counsel, some to accuse and the others to defend him.

'The poor fellow tried to get away, but his friends would not let him. He, of course, had nothing to say for himself, except that he did not choose to drink, and the upshot of his trial was that he was condemned to be hung.

'Unfortunately one of them had a rope with him, and without more ado they ran up the culprit to the nearest tree. To be sure, they did intend to put the rope round his waist, but they were too drunk to know exactly what they were about, and by mistake slipped it, Jack Ketch fashion, round his neck. Having done this wise trick, they all ran away, shrieking with laughter at the cleverness of their joke.

They were very much surprised to find, the next morning, that the poor fellow was missing. At last they went out to look for him, and found him hanging where they had left him, but as dead as a church door.

'So, gentlemen, you see that the people in those parts are very clever chaps, and if you take them at their own value, there are none to be found like them in all the world. I have another story for you to prove this.

'One day a poor Jew fell into the Itchen.

'"Oh, shave me! shave me! vil no one shave me?" he sang out; but of all the people standing round there wasn't one who would touch him with his fingers, because they looked on him as a dirty old Jew.

'At last they thought that though he was a Jew it was a shame to let him drown, so half-a-dozen or more of them ran off to get a rake to haul him out. One couldn't find a rake, and another couldn't find a rake; so, long before they came back, the poor Jew was drowned. That is the reason why we say, when a chap is a long time doing a thing that he ought to have done in a hurry, "He's gone for a rake to haul out the Jew."'

'Ay, ay, Mr. Bexley, but you know what the Poole man did when his pig got his head through the bars of the gate?' exclaimed Jerry Vincent, with a good-natured laugh. 'Why, you see, mates, when he found that he couldn't haul it out, to save trouble he cut off the beast's head. Some people in our parts would have sawed through the bars, but we don't pretend to be wise, you know.

'I don't mind telling a story against ourselves. Did any of you ever hear why the Downton people are called "Moonrakers"? They themselves don't mind hearing the story. Once upon a time, some Downton men had sunk some tubs in a big pond, and they were hard at work all

night raking them up. While they were still engaged, who should come
by but a party of custom-house people.

' " What are you doing there, men ?" they asked. " Some mischief,
no doubt."

' " Oh, no ! please, kind gentlemen, we are only trying to rake the moon
out of this pond," answered the Downton men, quite in a simple voice.
You see that the moon was at the time shining brightly down into the
pond.

' " Oh ! is that all ? " said the custom-house people, thinking that they
were a few simpletons escaped out of a madhouse. On went the custom-
house people. After a little time they came back. The smugglers had
just got out their last tub. Some clouds meantime had come over the
moon. " Well, my men, have you got the moon at last ? " said the
custom-house officer.

' " Oh, yes ! there's little doubt about it, for it's no longer there. If
we haven't got it, perhaps you can tell us who has."

' This made the custom-house people feel sure that they were right in
their conjectures ; so on they went, little dreaming of the prize they had
lost.'

We all laughed heartily at Jerry Vincent's and Mr. Bexley's stories.

' I'll tell you a story, for the truth of which I can vouch,' said Uncle
Kelson. ' The circumstance only lately happened. So, strange as it
may seem, there is no doubt about it. You all have heard speak of Sir
Harry Burrard Neale, who commands just now the King's yacht, the
Royal Charlotte. The boatswain of her is a friend of mine, and last
summer he got me a cast down to Weymouth, where I wanted to go to
see the widow of an old shipmate I had promised to look after. We
were just clear of the Needles. There was a light breeze and a smooth
sea, when we made out a small boat standing towards us, seemingly as
if she had come out of Poole harbour or Swanage.

"She seems to me to be a fishing-boat, and as if she wanted to speak us, Sir Harry," said the first lieutenant, who had been spying at her through his glass.

'"So I see," answered the captain. "There seem to be two people in her making signals. It will not delay us much, so heave the ship to, and let us learn what they want."

'This was just like Sir Harry. Many a captain would have stood on and taken no notice of a poor fisherman's boat, even had there been a dozen people waving in her. In a little time the boat came alongside, with a man and a woman in her, and they were certainly the rummest old couple you ever saw in your life.

'A midshipman hailed them, and asked them what they wanted. As well as we could make out, for they spoke very broad Scotch, they said that they wanted their son.

'"Let them come aboard," said Sir Harry kindly, "and we will hear what they have to say."

'With no little difficulty, after a good deal of pulling and hauling, we got the old couple upon deck, and led them aft to Sir Harry.

'"For whom are you inquiring, my good people?" asked the captain.

'"Our bairn, sir—our ain bairn," answered the old lady. "For many a weary week have we been looking for him, and never have our eyes rested on his bonnie face since the black day, near five long years ago, when he was carried away from us. Ah! it was a sair day, sirs."

'"What is your son's name, my good people?" asked Sir Harry.

'"David, sir—Davie Campbell. He was so called after his grandfather, who died in '45, with mony other brave men," answered the old dame.

'"We have a man of that name on board, sir," remarked the first lieutenant to the captain. "He is in the watch below. It will be strange if he should prove to be the man these poor souls are searching for."

' " Let him be called on deck, and we will see if they acknowledge him as their son," said Sir Harry. " There must be many hundred David Campbells in the world, I suspect, so do not raise their hopes too high by letting them know that at all events we know the name on board."

' " David Campbell! David Campbell ! " was passed along the decks, and in a minute a fine active young fellow came tumbling up from below.

' A mother's eye was not to be deceived. She knew him in an instant, and toddled off as fast as her legs would carry her, followed by her husband, to meet him. " He is, he is my ain bairn ! There's none like him ! " she cried ; and not caring a fig for the officers and men standing around,—before even he knew who she was,—she had him clasped in her arms, and was covering his cheeks with kisses, while the old father had got hold of his hand and was tugging away at it just as a man in a hurry does at a bell-rope.

' Now comes the extraordinary part of the story. Campbell had been rather a wildish sort of a chap, and getting into some scrape, had gone on board a tender, at Leith I think it was, and entered the navy. He could not write, and was ashamed to get any one to write for him, so his old father and mother did not know where he was, or whether he was alive or dead.

' At last their hearts grew weary at not hearing tidings of him, and they resolved to set out together to look out for their lost sheep ; for you see they were decent people and well to do in the world, so they had money to bear the expense, which was not slight. They had very little information to guide them. All they knew was, that their son had gone on board one of the King's ships. A mother's deep love and

a father's affection was the only compass by which they could steer
their course. That did not fail them. They went from port to port,
and visited every ship in harbour, and asked every seaman they met
about their son, but nothing could they hear of him. At last, that very
morning, a waggon had brought them to Poole, and seeing a ship in the
offing, which was no other than the *Royal Charlotte*, they had got a
boatman to take them out to us.

'That, now, is what I call a providential circumstance; indeed, from
all I have seen and learned since I came into the world, I am convinced
that there is nothing happens in it by chance. The God of heaven
orders all for the best in kindness to us. Sometimes, it is true, things
do not occur exactly as we could wish, but that does not alter the rule;
for if we could but see the end, we should discover that the very thing
of which we most complain was in reality most for our good.
Remember that, nephew, whenever you get into danger or difficulty;
be sure that you do your duty, and all will come right at last. But I
have not told you the end of my story.

'The Poole boatman was sent on shore, and the traps of the old
couple were handed up on board. Like canny Scotch people, they had
not let their property remain out of their sight, but had brought it with
them. It was delightful to see their pleasure when Sir Harry invited
them to go on to Weymouth, and to live on board as long as the ship
remained there; and he gave orders to have a screen put up for their
accommodation. That, too, was just like him. There is not another
man in the service more considerate or kind to all below him. All, too,
who know him love him; and his Majesty, I believe, trusts him more,
and loves him more, than he does all his courtiers put together.

'Never have I seen a pair of old folks look more happy, as their son
went about showing them round the ship, and when all the officers and
crew spoke kindly to them as they passed.

'The king, too, when he came on board and heard the story, was very much interested, and sent for them to have a talk with them. They did not know who he was, but when they came out of the cabin they said that he was one of the kindest old gentlemen they had ever seen; that he had had a long crack with them all about bonnie Scotland and Scotch people; and that he had asked them a heap of questions about their adventures.

'You should have seen their look of surprise when they heard that it was his gracious Majesty himself.* They wanted to go back to fall down on their knees, and to ask his pardon for talking so freely with him, and it was not till we assured them that the king talked just in the same way with any of the crew, that we could quiet them and make them believe that all was right.

'At last, having assured themselves that their son was well and happy, they returned with contented hearts to Scotland, and many has been the long yarn they have spun, I doubt not, about King George and all the wonders they have seen on their travels.'

Every one was very much interested in my uncle's story. A young man who was present, a friend of mine, belonging to a revenue cutter, observed, 'We were talking of smugglers just now. There is no end to the dodges they are up to.

'Not long ago, soon after I joined the *Lively*, it had come on to blow pretty fresh, and we had had a dirty night of it, when just as morning broke we made out a cutter standing in for the land to the eastward of Weymouth, and about two miles from us. The wind was from the north-west, and it had kicked up a nasty sea, running pretty high, as it well knows how to do in that part of the Channel.

'Our old mate, Mr. Futlock, had the morning watch. It was never

---

* Admiral Sir Harry Burrard Neale was a great-uncle of the author, and the account is given as it was narrated to him many years ago.

his brightest time, for though he did not actually get tipsy, the reaction following the four or five pretty stiff glasses of grog which he drank at night, generally at this time took place. I was in his watch.

' " Youngster," said he to me, " hand me the glass, and let us see if we can make out what that fellow is."

' I brought him the glass, which was kept hung up in beckets within the companion-hatch. I had got my sea-legs aboard pretty well, but I confess that I felt very queer that morning in certain regions, ranging from the top of my head to the soles of my feet, and I doubt not looked very yellow in the cheeks, with every instant an irresistible drawing down of the mouth, and that worst of signs, a most unyoungsterlike disinclination to eat.

' Mr. Futlock took the glass, and with his lack-lustre eye had a long look at the cutter, which was bobbing away into the seas, while she kept her course on a wind as if in no manner of a hurry.

' " She is honest, I believe," he observed, with a wise nod. " Probably a Poole or Exmouth trader; but we must overhaul her notwithstanding. Shake a reef out of the mainsail, my lads."

' This was quickly done, and the sail hoisted up. " Now, keep her away a couple of points more, and we shall about fetch her."

' Our mate's orders being executed, away we went tearing through the foaming, hissing water, now looking, in the morning's pale light, of a dark, melancholy hue. The stranger continued on as steady as before.

' " Oh, there's no use in the world giving ourselves the trouble of boarding her," muttered Mr. Futlock; and he was just going to order the cutter to be kept on a wind, when we saw the stranger haul up his foresail, and let fly his jib sheets, evidently intending to wait our coming.

' " What cutter is that ? " shouted old Futlock.

'"The *Polly* of London, bound for Weymouth," answered a man, who stood at the taffrail, through a speaking-trumpet. "We hove to, sir, that we might tell you we have just run over a large number of tubs away there to the southward."

'"Thank you, thank you," shouted Mr. Futlock in return, as we ran by and were soon out of speaking distance. "I knew that fellow was honest," he observed to me, rubbing his hands at the thought of making some prize money. "Come, rouse aft the main-sheet. We must haul up a little again. Can any one see the tubs?"

'There were plenty of busy eyes looking out for the prize, and it was not long before we discovered them on the weather bow. By keeping our luff we were quickly up to them.

'The commander was by this time called, and now came a difficulty. With the heavy sea there was running, it was a work not free from danger to lower a boat. We first shortened sail; the helm was put down, and the cutter hove to, and then, after several attempts by waiting for a lull, we got the boat with a crew safe in water.

'Mr. Futlock jumped into the boat, and pulled towards the tubs which were first seen, we meantime keeping a bright look-out for any more which might be floating near.

'Not being accustomed to this sort of work, I felt not a little alarmed for the safety of my shipmates, as I saw the boat tumbling about among the white-crested waves.

'Mr. Futlock soon got hold of ten tubs, lashed together, and hauled them into the boat. A little further on he made a prize of ten more. This was no bad beginning. He was returning with them, having in vain searched for others, when we made out another collection just ahead of the cutter. We soon had them all aboard, though the boat was nearly swamped alongside. We hoisted her in at last, and seeing no more tubs, let draw the foresail, and again stood on. When at last we looked about for our communicative friend, he was not visible; but some of the men said they thought they had seen him standing in for the land.

'We cruised about all the morning in the neighbourhood, but not a tub more could we discover. Three days after that we dropped our anchor in Weymouth roads. The commander went on shore to communicate with the officer of the coast-guard on the station.

' "We were looking out for a cutter with a large cargo the other day, but somehow or other we managed to miss her, and she managed to land every tub. We understand that there has not been such a run for years," observed the coast-guard officer.

'Something made our commander fancy that she might have been the very craft we spoke, and which had been so ready with information.

' "A cutter of about fifty tons, with her bulwarks painted yellow inside?" he asked.

' "The very same," answered the lieutenant. "That cunning rascal, Dick Johnstone, was on board of her himself. Hearing that we were on the look-out for his craft, the *Seagull*, he shifted his cargo into her."

' "Then we were cleverly done!" exclaimed our commander, stamping his foot with vexation. "The very fellow old Futlock thought looked so honest that he would not take the trouble to board him. It is the very last time in my life that I will trust to outside appearances."

'All hands of us aboard the cutter felt very foolish when we found that we had lost so good a chance of taking one of the richest prizes we were ever likely to fall in with. However, revenue officers must have all their seven senses wide awake to compass the artful dodges of determined smugglers. After that, we took very good care to be smart about boarding every vessel we fell in with.'

After the conclusion of this yarn we had several other accounts of smugglers and their daring deeds. Some even, it was asserted, had ventured to defend themselves against king's ships, and had fought severe actions, one or two having gone down with their colours flying rather than surrender. On one point all were agreed, that no smugglers had ever become permanently wealthy men. As my uncle observed, they take a great deal of trouble and undergo great risk to obtain a very uncertain advantage.

All the rest of the guests were gone; old Jerry remained behind. We told him what had occurred in the morning, and I asked him if he could find out anything about Charley Iffley; what was his rank, and to what ship he belonged. I begged him, if he could find him, to take a message to him from me, and to assure him that far from bearing him any ill-will, I would gladly welcome him as an old friend.

CΠAPTER XI.

SEVERAL days passed by, and I heard nothing of Iffley. The fears of my dear wife in consequence at length subsided, and she began to see that, after all, she had probably thought worse of my old shipmate than he deserved. We agreed that he must have been somewhat astonished at seeing me alive, and the husband of one whom he had hoped to marry himself, and that chiefly through bashfulness he had not been able to bring himself to come up and address us.

'Bashfulness!' said Aunt Bretta, when she heard this remark; 'I cannot say that I should ever have given Charles Iffley the credit for a superabundance of that quality. However, strange things happen. He may have picked it up at sea, or among his associates on shore; but I doubt it.'

So did I, on reflection. Still, I was glad by any means to calm my wife's apprehensions, which were the more painful because they were so very indefinite. In the evening there was a knock at the door, and old Jerry Vincent walked in.

'Sarvant, ladies; sarvant all,' said he, pulling off his hat to Aunt Bretta and my wife, who handed him a chair.

'Have you heard anything of that young man we told you of?'

14

asked my wife. It was evidently the question she was most anxious
to put.

'Yes, I have, marm, and not much good either,' was the answer.
I've found out that he is aboard the *Royal William;* she's the flag-
ship just now at Spithead. He doesn't often come ashore, and that
made me so long hearing of him.'

'What is he on board? Is he an officer?' asked Aunt Bretta.

'An officer, indeed, whew!' exclaimed Jerry. 'Well, he is a sort of
one, maybe. Not a very high rating, though. He's neither more nor
less than a boatswain's mate. What do you think of that, marm?'

'Charles Iffley a boatswain's mate!' said my wife in a tone of pity.
'I thought he was an officer long ago.'

'Well, marm, I made inquiries on board, and among several people
who knew him on shore, and from what I could learn, he would have
been an officer long ago if he had conducted himself well. He was
placed on the quarter-deck, for you see he has plenty of education, and
knows how to act the gentleman as well as any man. But there are
some men who never get up the tree but what they slip down again, and
never can keep a straight course long together. Charles Iffley is of
that sort. For something or other he did, he got disrated and dismissed the service; but he entered it again, and, from what I am told,
I shouldn't be surprised but what, if his early history isn't known, he'll
work his way up again. The thing that is most against him is his
extravagance. Every farthing he makes in prize-money or pay he
spends on shore, in acting the fine gentleman. People can't, indeed, tell
how he gets all the money he spends. Of course, if it was known on
board the pranks he plays on shore, his leave would be stopped; but
he is so clever that he humbugs the officers, and they think him one of
the most steady and best men. You see there's another thing which
brings him into favour with the captain and first lieutenant; he has a

knack of finding men and getting them to join the ship, by making her out to be the most comfortable ship in the service, and there's no man knows better how to ferret out seamen, and to lead a pressgang down upon a score of them together. I learned all these things from different people, do ye see, but putting this and that together, I made out my story as I tell it to you. To my mind, Charles Iffley is a man I would stand clear of. Depend on't, he's a deep one.'

Jerry Vincent stayed with us some time, and then he said he had an engagement and must go away. As he did so he beckoned me out of the room, and I accompanied him to the door.

'I'll tell you what it is, Mr. Weatherhelm,' said he, 'you have been bred a seaman, and the pressgangs are very hot at work just now. They take everybody who has been at sea, no matter what his present calling—whether he has a wife and family depending on him or not. Now Iffley knows that you have no protection, and he has the power of getting hold of you. From what I hear, he's just the man to use it. If you was his bosom friend, he'd do it; but if he owes you a grudge, depend on it he'll not let you slip out of his gripe. He'd have been down on you before now, but he got a broken head the other night, in attacking the crew of a merchantman just come home from a three years' cruise round the Horn, and had no fancy to be sent off to sea again when they had only just put their foot on shore. However, he is now on his legs again. If you stay here, you'll hear something of him before long; but take my advice, just rig out as an old farmer, or a black-coated preacher, or something as unlike yourself as you can, and take your wife and go and live away somewhere up in the country. It's your only chance. If you stay you'll be nabbed, as sure as my name is Jerry Vincent.'

I thanked the old man very much for his advice, and replied that I had no doubt, on consideration, I should follow it.

'Oh, there's a good lad! Don't be waiting and considering. There's no good comes of that. When a thing is to be done which must be done, go and do it at once.'

'Well, I will, Jerry, I will,' I answered, shaking him by the hand. I waited at the door, and while I watched him down the street I considered what course I would pursue. I was unwilling to tell my wife what he had said, because I knew it would agitate her very much, and I hoped that Jerry thought worse of Iffley than he deserved. Of course, how-ever, I determined to consult Uncle Kelson, and to abide by his advice. It was a serious consideration whether I would, on the mere chance of Iffley's being able to get hold of me, give up my occupation, in which I was succeeding so well, and go and live, for I knew not how long, in comparative poverty, without anything to do. I made an excuse for stepping out of the room to talk to Jerry, and my wife did not appear to suspect that he had had anything more to say about Iffley. As soon as she and my aunt had gone upstairs, I told Uncle Kelson all that I had learned. He looked graver than usual while he listened to the account.

'Well, he must be a scoundrel if he could do it!' he exclaimed at last, clenching his fist. 'Still, such things have been done, but I did hope that no seaman would be guilty of them.' He was silent for some time, and lost in reflection. 'I'll tell you what, Will,' said he at last, 'you must follow old Jerry's advice. It's sound, depend on it. That old man has more wisdom in his little finger than many a man has in the whole of his head. Go to your work to-morrow morn-ing, and I'll look down in the course of the day and see your employer, and explain matters to him frankly. He, I have no doubt, will give you leave of absence for a few weeks, and when you come back you can work double tides. If you stay, you see, you'll be lost to him probably altogether.'

So the matter was arranged. I was rather ashamed, however, at the thought of having to go into hiding, as it were; but still I felt that my wife's mind would be relieved from apprehension when once I was safe away out of Portsmouth. Uncle Kelson had a sister married to a farmer living in the north of Hampshire, and there we resolved to go.

The next day I went to my work as usual, and my uncle came down and had a talk with my employer, and the whole matter was arranged to the satisfaction of all parties.

'Come,' said Uncle Kelson, 'you had better at once take your places by the coach, and start to-morrow. There is no time to be lost.'

We found on getting to the coach-office that all the coaches were full. At that time there was an immense traffic between Portsmouth and London. A postchaise was somewhat beyond our means, but we found a light waggon starting, which took passengers, and Uncle Kelson and I agreed that this would prove a convenient and very pleasant conveyance, as we were in no hurry, and would not object to being some time on the road. It was to start pretty early in the morning. My dear wife was delighted at the thoughts of the journey, and speedily made the necessary preparations. We sent on our trunk by a wheelbarrow, while we followed, accompanied by Uncle Kelson. Even at that early hour the High Street was astir,—indeed, in those busy times, both during day and night, something or other was going forward. We passed several gangs of men-of-war's men. Three or four men evidently just pressed, and who showed a strong disinclination to go and serve their country, were being dragged along by one of the gangs. I could not help pitying the poor fellows; so did my wife.

'Oh, Willand,' said she, 'how thankful I am that you are not among them!'

Our waggon was a very nice one, covered over with a clean white

tilt, and our waggoner, I saw at a glance, was an honest, good-hearted
chaw-bacon. He was dressed in the long white frock, thickly plaited
in front, which has been worn from time immemorial by people of his
calling. Our trunk and bags were put in; we shook hands with
Uncle Kelson, and having taken our seats just inside in the front part,
with plenty of straw for our feet to rest on, the waggoner whipped up
his four sturdy horses, and we began to move on. My dear wife
pressed closer to my side, and we began to breathe more freely; she
thought I was safe from the pressgang. We were just clear of the
fortifications, and were getting into the open country, when I saw the
waggoner turn round once or twice, and look over his shoulder behind
him.

'What can they be after?' I heard him say. A minute more passed.
'Hillo, men, what does ye want here?' he exclaimed suddenly, as half
a dozen or more seamen sprang forward, and seized the horses' heads,
while others leaped up into the waggon.

'We are looking for a deserter,' cried two or three of them. 'Turn
out, my hearty; where are you stowed away?'

I felt, the instant the seamen appeared, that they had come to press
me, but these words revived my hopes of escape.

'There is no one here, my men, besides my wife and me that I know
of,' I observed. 'You have made a mistake, I suspect.'

'Well, we must look,' said the men; 'we are not quite so green as to
take your word for it.'

'You may look as much as you like, measters,' said the waggoner;
'you'll find no one among my goods, unless he's stowed hesself away
unknowest to me.'

The seamen began to poke their cutlasses in between the packages,
and would undoubtedly have run any one through who had been inside
them. While they were thus employed, three or four other men came up.

'What are you about, mates?' exclaimed one of them, whose voice I felt sure I knew. 'The man you want is sitting in the front of the waggon!'

On hearing these words my poor wife uttered a piercing shriek, and fell fainting into my arms. She, too, had recognised the voice, though the speaker had kept out of her sight; it was that of Charles Iffley The seamen instantly sprang on me, and seized me by the arms.

'Hillo, mate, you were going to give us the go-by,' said one of them as they passed a rope round my elbows before I could lift an arm in my defence.

They literally dragged me from my poor wife. She would have fallen, but the waggoner humanely scrambled up into his waggon, and placed her securely at the bottom of it. She was still, I saw, completely insensible. I scarcely regretted that she was so, for I did not at the moment foresee the consequences. The honest carter was in vain expostulating with the seamen for seizing one whom he considered placed under his especial charge, to be delivered safe at the journey's end.

'I don't think as how you have any right to take that gentleman; he's no more a sailor nor I bes,' I heard him say.

'Not a sailor! Why, the man has been at sea all his life till the last year or so,' said Iffley, now coming up, and throwing off all disguise; 'he's, moreover, to my certain knowledge, a deserter from his Majesty's ship *Brilliant*, so attempt to detain him if you dare.'

These words had a great effect on the honest waggoner, who did not attempt to make any further efforts to detain me.

Generally speaking, the most ruffian-like and least scrupulous of the crew were employed in the pressgangs, for they often had very brutal work to perform. The men into whose hands I had fallen were as bad as any I had ever met. They seized me with the greatest ferocity, dragged me out of the waggon. and would not listen to my prayers and entreaties to be allowed to wait till my wife came to her senses; and before even I had time to speak to the waggoner, in spite of all the violent struggles I made to free myself, they hauled me off along the road as if I had been one of the worst of malefactors. In this they were encouraged by Iffley, who seemed to take a malignant pleasure in seeing me ill-treated, though he did not himself attempt to lay hands on me. When I tried to cry out, I found a gag thrust into my mouth, and thus I was rendered speechless as well as in every other way powerless.

My captors hurried me away, and with a feeling amounting to agony, I lost sight of the waggon. At first it occurred to me that Iffley had gone back for the purpose, as I dreaded, of speaking to my wife, and perhaps adding to her misery; but had he entertained such a thought, he had not dared to face her, for I saw him directly afterwards following close behind me, encouraging the other men to hasten along.

Though I made all the resistance of which I was capable, in the hopes that something or other might occur to enable me to free myself, we soon reached the entrance to Portsmouth.

Instead, however, of proceeding down the High Street, Iffley led the way down one of the by-streets to the right. Just as we were passing under the ramparts I looked up, and there I saw walking up and down, as if to enjoy the breeze, a person whom I recognised at a glance as Uncle Kelson. The moment I saw him, hope revived in my breast. I could at all events tell him to go in search of my wife. Perhaps he might even find means to liberate me; but when I tried to sing out, the horrible gag prevented me speaking. I could only utter inarticulate cries and groans.

In vain I shrieked. He did not even turn his head; the sounds were too common. He thought, probably, that it was only some drunken seaman, who had outstayed his leave, dragged back to his ship.

At length, for a moment, he looked round. I struggled more vehemently than before. I fancied that he must recognise me, but, urged by Iffley, my captors dragged me on faster than ever, and turning a corner we were hid from his sight. My strength was now almost exhausted. I could offer but a faint resistance. Hope, too, had abandoned me. Still I tried to make myself heard, on the possibility of some one knowing me and undertaking to carry a message to my uncle and aunt. People stopped and looked, but the same idea occurred to all—my frantic gestures made them believe that I was a miserable drunken sailor.

We reached the water's edge. I was shoved into a boat with several other men who had been captured during the night. They all were sitting stunned, or drunken, or sulky (or some too probably broken-hearted and miserable), at the bottom of the boat, not exchanging a word with each other or with those who had pressed us. I also fell down stunned and unconscious. Who could have discovered any difference between me and my companions in misfortune? When I again opened my eyes, I found that the boat was almost at Spithead. I tried to sit up to look about me, but I could not, and, after a feeble attempt to rise, I again sank back, and once more oblivion of all that had passed stole over my senses. I had a sort of dreamy feeling that I was lifted up on the deck of a big ship, and then handed below and put into a hammock. Then I was aware that some one came and felt my pulse and gave me medicine, but I had no power to think, to recollect the past or to note the present.

At last, by degrees, I found that I was becoming more alive to what was taking place. I felt the movement of the ship. She was heeling over to a strong breeze. Then suddenly the recollection of my wife, of the way I had been torn from her, of the wretchedness I knew she must suffer, of the uncertainty she must feel for my fate, burst like a thunder-clap on me, and almost sent me back into the state from which I was recovering. I groaned in my agony. I wished that death might kindly be sent to relieve me of my misery. But the instant after I felt that such a wish was impious.

I lay quiet for some time, thinking and praying that strength might be given for my support. No, no, I'll try to live, that I may get back to comfort her. What joy it would be once more to return to her! The very contemplation of such an idea revived me. 'Whatever comes, I'll do my duty like a man.'

'That's right, my lad; that's the proper spirit in which to take our misfortunes,' said a voice near me.

Unconsciously, I had spoken aloud. I turned round my head, and saw a gentleman I knew at once was the doctor of the ship.

'I know your story. You have told me a good deal about yourself while you have been lying there,' he remarked, in a kind voice. 'I pity you from my heart, and will do what I can for you.'

'Thank you, sir, thank you,' I answered warmly, and almost melting into tears, for I was very weak. 'Where are we? Where are we going? What ship is this? Is Iffley here?'

'One question at a time, my lad, and you will have a better chance of an answer, as a general rule,' he answered, smiling.

He was a Scotchman, and as warm-hearted, generous a man as the north ever produced, though somewhat peculiar in his manners. To a stranger he appeared slow; but, when time would allow it, he knew the advantage of deliberation.

'First, then, I will tell you that you are on board the *Albion*, and that we have under our convoy a large fleet of merchantmen. We are somewhere to the southward of Cape Finisterre. What you are thinking about is. how you can write home to let your wife know what has become of you. You'll very likely soon have an opportunity.

Let that comfort you.' He said all this that he might break more gradually all that was coming.

'But where are we going, sir?' I asked, in a trembling voice.

'You may perhaps have an opportunity of getting home,' he answered. 'But you see, my lad, we are bound for the East Indies, and shall probably have a somewhat long cruise of it.'

'To the East Indies!' I cried, my voice sinking almost to a whisper. 'When, when, Margaret, may I ever meet you again?'

'Cheer up, my lad, it's a long road which has no turning, ye ken,' cried the kind doctor. 'Remember your resolution to do your duty like a man. You'll be well in a few days, I hope.'

He did not reply to my question about Iffley. Somehow or other, I could not bring myself again to repeat that man's name. I did not forget the command to forgive our enemies, but I felt that flesh and blood—the depravity of human nature—must be struggled with and overcome, before the divine precept could be obeyed.

Once more I was on my feet again, and a man who attended on the sick helped me up on deck. It was a fine day—the sky was blue, the sea was calm, and some thirty ships, with all their canvas set, were grouped close around us. They were huge lumbering tea-chests, as we used to call Indiamen, but they were fine-looking craft for all that. The fresh sea-breeze revived me. Every hour I felt myself growing stronger and better. I looked round for Iffley. I had a nervous dread of meeting him, and yet I felt anxious to ascertain that he was on board.

A person may be on board a big ship like the *Albion* for several days without meeting another, provided they are not on duty together. Such was my case. I had been for two days on deck, an hour or so at a time, without seeing the man who had proved himself so bitterly my enemy. The doctor told me he thought that in a day or two more I

might go to my duty, and that I should be the better for having work
to do.   I looked forward to work with satisfaction, and begged that I
might as soon as possible be struck off the sick list.   He told me that
I should be so on the following day, and that he would speak to the first
lieutenant about me, as he was a very kind man, and would see that I
was not sent aloft till I had sufficiently recovered my strength.   I
thanked him with a hearty blessing for his kindness and consideration.

The very first man on whom my eyes rested when I went on deck
returned fit for duty was Charles Iffley.   He was going along the deck
with his cat-o'-nine-tails in his hand.   I knew by this that he still held
only the rating of boatswain's mate on board.   My heart turned sick at
the sight; in a moment my vivid imagination pictured all I might have
to suffer at his hands.

He saw me, but pretended not to know me, and went on his way as
if I was a stranger.   I was immediately sent for aft, and found that I
had been entered in the ship's books as an able seaman and a deserter
from his Majesty's ship the *Brilliant.*

'What have you to say to this, my man?' said the captain, looking
sternly at me.

'That I am not a deserter, sir,' I answered in a firm voice; and I
then gave him a clear and succinct account of the cutting out expedition
in Santa Cruz harbour, in which I had been engaged, and the way in
which my life had been preserved on that occasion.

The captain, after a moment's consideration, sent a midshipman down
into his cabin for a printed book.   When it was brought to him he
turned over the pages and asked me a few more questions.   'I find that
your account agrees exactly with the description I here have of the
affair, and I believe you.'

I saw Dr. M'Call, who came up at the moment and heard the
captain's words, look evidently pleased.   They exchanged glances, I

thought. At all events, I fancied that I had just and kind-hearted superiors, and that my condition was far better than I might have expected to find it. Still this reflection could not mitigate the great source of my grief—my sudden separation from my wife and my ignorance of her fate. After this I was placed in a watch, and went regularly about my duty. I did my best to perform it, and quickly recovered my strength.

Ours had always been considered a smart ship, and though our captain was a kind man, he sacrificed a great deal to smartness. The most active and bustling men who could make the most show of doing things smartly, often gained more credit than they deserved.

It was one forenoon my watch below when I heard the cry of 'All hands shorten sail!' I had been stationed in the fore-top. I sprang on deck as fast as my strength would allow, but I had not recovered my usual activity. 'Fly aloft, there! fly aloft, you lazy scoundrel, or a rope's end will freshen your way a bit!' I heard a voice cry, close to my ear. It was Iffley's. His countenance showed that he was capable of executing his threats. My blood boiled. I could do nothing. I could say nothing. In a moment I understood the bitter enmity which he had allowed to enter and to rankle in his bosom. I scarcely dared again to look at him. I hurried on. A sudden squall had struck the ship —unexpected after the long calms to which we had been subject. She was heeling over to her lower deck ports. The exertion of all hands was indeed required to shorten sail. I found Iffley following close after me. I sprang up the rigging and quickly reached the fore-top. I could not help seeing his face as he came up. It wore the expression of most malignant hatred. 'Lay out; be smart about it, my lads!' cried the captain of the top, as the foretopsail-yard came rattling down.

In an instant the yard was covered with active forms hurrying out to its extreme ends. I made a spring to get out to the weather-earing.

I had got it in my hand and was hauling on it, when I saw the countenance of Iffley, wearing the same expression as before, close to me. There was now in it a triumphant expression, as if he hoped that his vindictive feelings were about to be gratified. Still not a word did he utter. No one on board would have guessed that we had ever before met. I still kept to my resolution.

The gale came down on us stronger than ever. The officers were urging the men to greater speed. Suddenly I felt the earing in my hand give way, and before I could grasp at the yard to save myself I lost my balance, and to my horror found myself falling into the seething ocean raging beneath me. A strange, hideous, mocking strain of laughter sounded in my ears as I fell, and after that I knew no more till I discovered that I was struggling in the foaming waters.

I had gone down once, but had quickly come up again. I threw myself on my back till I had somewhat recovered my senses, and then turned myself round and kept treading the water while I looked out to see how far I was from the ship.

Away she flew, close-hauled though, with the foam dancing round her, and already at some distance. 'And is this to be my fate?' I thought; 'to die thus a victim to the foul revenge of that man?'

I resolved to struggle for life. I looked round me on every side. The Indiamen were scattered far and wide, none of them were coming up on our track. Still I swam on, but I felt how hopeless was the struggle.

Just then my eye fell on a grating, floating not five fathoms from me, and which had evidently been thrown to me by some one on board, when I was seen to fall from aloft. I exerted all my strength, and at length reached it. The time appeared to be very long. It is impossible, on such occasions, to measure it. Moments appeared minutes —minutes hours. I threw myself on the grating in a position to avoid being washed off it or thrown under it; but it required no slight exertion to hold on. As the dark seas came rolling up, and breaking, with a loud, crashing sound, above my head, I felt as if they must inevitably overwhelm me. Still I did not give up hope.

Unhappy as I had thought myself, I desired life that I might return home once more and ascertain the fate of my wife. I prayed that for this object I might be preserved; that we might once more be united, and once again be happy on earth. Even at that moment, surrounded by the boiling seas, with my ship flying fast away from me, I pictured, with all the vividness of reality, the unspeakable joy of once again being restored to her. I remembered the numberless dangers to which I had been exposed, and the merciful way in which I had been preserved from them.

Not for an instant did I think of Iffley. I forgot that he had been the cause of my present position, and thus I was prevented from harbouring any feeling of revenge against him.

As I was saying, I could not judge how long I was clinging to the grating. Tossed about as I was—now lifted to the summit of a foaming sea—now sinking down into the trough—I kept my eye constantly turning towards my ship.

Suddenly I saw the foretopsail thrown aback—a boat was lowered—my shipmates were coming to my rescue. I felt even then that I was to be saved. I forgot the distance they had to pull and the heavy sea which might both endanger them and hide me from their sight. Still more eagerly did I try to make out the boat, as she laboured among the foaming seas. I caught a glimpse of her as I rose to the top of a wave, but she was not pulling towards me. Those in her could not have seen me.

Then suddenly the horrid thought came across me, that Iffley might have pretended to have seen where I was and to have guided the boat wrongly. Then I blamed myself for thinking even Iffley capable of an act so atrocious. Still, I thought if he had purposely thrown me into the sea, he would be as likely to play the foul trick of which I now suspected him.

Again I sank down into a deep trough of the sea, and could only for a time distinguish the topsails of the ship above the masses of foam which flew around. When I next rose again, there was the boat pulling away from me.

I shrieked out, I raised my voice louder and louder, as if I could by possibility be heard. I might as well have tried to howl down the hurricane in its fiercest mood. This was more trying than all that had gone before.

At length, exhausted by my exertions, I threw myself back on the grating, scarcely attempting to hold on. I was then in the trough of a sea. In another moment I was raised again to the summit of a sea, and, though hopeless, my eyes mechanically turned towards the boat.

Some one on board had seen me—she was pulling towards me. I felt conscious in a moment how wrong I had been to despair. I again exerted all my strength to keep myself on the grating. I saw some one standing up in the bows looking out for me. He pointed to where I floated, that the helmsman might steer the boat aright.

'Hurra! hurra!' A shout reached my ears. I knew that my shipmates had given it to encourage me. A few minutes more, and I found myself hauled into the boat.

The first person on whom my eyes rested was Iffley. He looked, I fancied, conscience-struck and defeated.

'Charley said as how he thought he saw you away to the eastward there; but Tom Potts caught sight of you, and now we know he was right,' said one of the men who were hauling me in.

I was placed in the bottom of the boat, for there was little time in that heavy sea to attend to me, and she pulled back towards the ship. I felt that I was saved. I did not expect to be much the worse for my ducking, and I knew when I got back to the ship that the doctor would look after me. I had now no doubt that Iffley had endeavoured to prevent the boat from coming to my assistance. How bitter must be his hatred to allow me—his shipmate—to die thus horribly, struggling in the sea, when he had the power to save me!

As I was helped up the side, I caught his eye fixed on me, and again I observed that evident look of baffled vengeance which I had before remarked. I felt sure that he would take the first opportunity of giving further proof of his hatred of me. I did not see any means of escaping from it. Had he even spoken to me, I might have expostulated with him; but he kept aloof as if I were a total stranger to him. He carefully avoided even addressing me directly. I felt sure, indeed, that had I spoken to him, he would have stoutly denied all former knowledge of me, and who was to prove it? No one whom I knew on board. I felt as if I were pursued by some monster with supernatural powers, from whom I could not get free.

When I got on board, Dr. M'Call kindly ordered me to go to my hammock, and he came and gave me some medicine. He said that after the illness from which I had so long been suffering, the consequences might be serious if I caught cold from my ducking. However, I turned out the next morning not in the slightest degree the worse for what had occurred. I resolved to be as attentive and exact in my duty as possible; I wished to behave thus, at all events; but I also knew that in that case I should give my enemy less opportunity of injuring me.

Two days after this a man was convicted of stealing on board. He was sentenced to receive fifty lashes. Iffley was one of the boat-

15

swain's mates chosen to inflict the punishment.   The crew were mustered
on deck, and the man was led forward.   He was one of those wretched
men who are both rogues and cowards.

Iffley and the other boatswain's mates stood with their cats, those
dreadful instruments of power, in their hands ready for use.   While
preparations were being made, the miserable wretch looked round on
every side, as if seeking for some one who could save him from the
punishment he was about to receive.   Not a glance of pity did he get
from his messmates.   They knew him too well.   At last he looked
towards Iffley.   I saw them exchange glances.   Iffley, of course, did
not speak, but his looks said something which gave the other courage.

'Captain,' said the man, turning round to our captain, 'you are going
to make the innocent suffer for the guilty.   I wanted to shield a shipmate; but he will be found out at last, I know, and I shall only suffer
without doing any one any good, otherwise I could have borne the
punishment willingly.'

I at the time thought that the man spoke in that whining tone which
a person in spite of himself uses when he is uttering a falsehood, or
saying what has been put into his mouth by another.

'Cast him loose,' said the captain; 'I'll inquire into this.   Bring him
aft here.   Now tell me at once who is the man who has committed this
theft, if you are not guilty of it.'

'I'd rather not say, sir,' replied the culprit.   'I don't like to peach
on another.   He'll be found out before the day is over, and then I shan't
be accused of having told of him.'

'That excuse will not serve your turn, my man,' answered the captain
sternly.   'Unless you can point out the real culprit, you will have to
suffer the punishment awarded you.'

'Oh no, sir, I'd rather not.   Do not be hard on me.   I don't like to
hurt another man, even to save myself,' again whined out the man.

'Let me off, sir, let me off, and the real thief will be found—that he will; you have my word for it.'

'Trice him up again,' said the captain to the boatswain. 'The true thief is about to be punished, I am very certain of that.'

'I'll tell, sir, I'll tell!' shrieked out the wretched man. 'He's one who has been skulking his duty ever since he came on board. I'd rather not speak his name.'

The captain shook his head, and made a sign to the boatswain to proceed.

'Well, if I must tell,' cried out the man, Saull Ley by name, 'the thief is Will Weatherhelm.'

I almost fainted when I heard the accusation, and I am sure that I must have looked as guilty as if I had committed the theft.

A triumphant smile flitted across Iffley's features, and he passed the knotted tails of his cat, as if mechanically, through his fingers, while he cast a glance at me which I too well understood. The captain turned towards me.

'What is this I hear?' he asked. 'Do you acknowledge the theft, Weatherhelm?'

'No, sir; certainly not,' I answered, with as firm a voice as I could command, though I felt conscious that it was faltering as I spoke.

'What proof have you that Weatherhelm committed the theft?' asked the captain of the culprit.

'Because two men, if not more, watched him, and knew that it was him,' was the answer; and now the man spoke in a firmer voice than I had done, and I fancied looked more innocent.

'Produce your witnesses,' said the captain.

The man hesitated for a minute, and his eye ranged with an uneasy glance along the lines of men drawn up on deck, as if anxiously scanning their countenances, for he must have felt that they knew him, and that he was not generally believed. At last his eyes rested on two who were standing together.

'Bill Sykes and Dick Todd saw him, sir; they know all about it. They'll tell you; they'll prove I am innocent.'

The theft had been committed on the purser's stores. Some tobacco and sugar and some other things had been stolen. Now Saull Ley, the accused, had been seen coming out of the store-room on one occasion when the purser's clerk had left the keys in the door for a short time and gone away. The purser, on his return, had missed some tobacco and sugar, and that same evening a small quantity of both those articles had been found in Ley's possession.

'Stand out, Bill Sykes and Dick Todd, and let me hear what you know about this matter.'

Bill Sykes was a landsman, and had soon shown that he was totally unfit for a sailor. Dick Todd had entered as a boy. He was not worth much, and had become a great chum of Sykes'. Still, from the little I had seen of them, I did not think that they would have been guilty of falsely accusing a shipmate. I had therefore little fear of what they could say against me.

I was, however, somewhat startled when they stepped forward, and Sykes, as the eldest, began in a clear way to state that he had seen a man, whom he took to be me, open the door of the purser's room with a key, and, after being absent for a minute or more, return and lock it. He at once knew this was wrong, so he watched what the man he took to be the thief would next do. He said that he met with Todd, and told him as a friend what he had observed. The thief crept along the deck, and the two then saw him go to his bag and deposit something which he took out of his pockets. Both the men acknowledged that they might be mistaken, but that they thought that it was me.

'What have you got to say to this, Weatherhelm?' asked the captain. 'You are accused by the mouths of two witnesses.'

'The accusation is false, sir,' I answered calmly. 'I was not long ago at my bag, and I observed neither tobacco nor sugar in it. If you will send for it, you will find that I speak the truth.'

'Very well. Mr. Marvel, take a couple of hands with you, and bring up Weatherhelm's bag,' said the captain, addressing the mate of the lower deck.

I felt very little anxiety during the time the officer was absent, for I was sure that nothing would be found among my things. He soon returned, bringing the bag. It was placed before the captain.

'Open it,' said he. It was opened on deck in sight of all the officers and ship's company. What was my horror and dismay, to see drawn forth, wrapped up in a shirt, a large lump of tobacco and a paper containing several pounds of sugar! 'Now what have you got to say?' asked the captain, turning to me.

'That I have not the slightest notion how those things came into my bag,' was my prompt answer.

'That is the sort of reply people always give when they are found out,' said the captain. 'It will not serve your turn, I fear.'

'I cannot help it, sir,' I replied, with a feeling of desperation. 'Appearances are certainly against me, sir; I know not by whom those things were put into my bag. I did not put them in, and I did not know that they were there.'

'You said that another man was a witness of this affair,' said the captain, turning to Ley. 'Who is he?'

Ley began to hum and haw and look uncomfortable. 'I'd rather not say, sir,' whined out Ley, 'if it is not necessary.'

'But it is necessary,' thundered out the captain, evidently annoyed at the man's coolness and canting hypocrisy. 'Who is he? or you get the four dozen awarded you.'

I had watched all along the countenance of Iffley. I felt sure that a plot had been formed against me, and that he was its framer and instigator. I saw that he began to grow uneasy at this stage of the proceedings.

'Who is this other man?' repeated the captain.

Ley saw that he must speak out, or that he would still get the punishment he was so anxious to escape. 'There he is; Charles Iffley is the man, sir, who, besides those two, saw Weatherhelm go to his bag and put the stolen things into it.'

'How is this, Iffley? If you saw a man committing a robbery, it was your duty to give notice of it, sir,' exclaimed the captain, in an angry voice, turning towards him.

'I am very sorry, sir,' replied Iffley. 'I am aware of what I ought, strictly speaking, to have done, but I did not like to hurt the character of a shipmate. He always seemed a very respectable man, and I fully believed that I must have been mistaken. It is only now that the things are found in his bag that I can believe him guilty.'

'You are ready to swear to this?' asked the captain.

'Quite ready, sir, certainly,' replied Iffley calmly. 'I add nothing and withhold nothing on the subject.'

Even I was startled by what Iffley said, and the way he said it. I could not help supposing that he believed what he said.

'Have you anything more to say in your defence, Weatherhelm?' said the captain.

'Nothing, sir, except that those men are mistaken. I can only hope that they believe what they say,' I answered, with a firmer voice than I had before been able to command.

'I am very sorry for it, and do not just now altogether believe it,'

I heard Dr. M'Call observe as he walked off. 'You will expect your punishment—six dozen,' said the captain. 'Pipe down.'

Could a painter at that moment have observed Iffley's countenance, it might have served him as a likeness of Satan when he is assured that Eve has fallen. The officers walked aft, the crew dispersed, and I was placed under charge of the master-at-arms.

Two days passed by. How full of agony and wretchedness they were! The pain I was to expect was as nothing compared to the disgrace and degradation. I who had always borne an unsullied name, whose character had always stood high both with my officers and messmates, to be now branded as a thief! How could I ever face those I loved, conscious of the marks of the foul lash on my back? There was no one on board to speak in my favour; no one who had known me before—and how incapable I was of the act imputed to me—except Iffley; and he, I felt too well assured, would do his utmost to destroy me.

The two days passed—no circumstance occurred, as I had hoped it might, to prove that I was innocent—when the boatswain's call summoned all hands on deck to witness punishment. This time I was to be the victim.

The boatswain's mates stood ready. One of them was Iffley. He played eagerly with his cat as I was led forward. 'If come it must,' I ejaculated, 'the Lord have mercy on me—I will bear my punishment as a man.'

CHAPTER XII.

'STRIP!' said the captain.

I prepared to lay my shoulders bare to receive the lash.

'The Indiamen to windward are signalling to us, sir,' shouted the
signal midshipman, turning over the pages of the signal-book. 'An
enemy in sight on the weather-beam.'

'Master-at-arms, take charge of the prisoner; punishment is deferred,'
cried the captain, springing on to the poop.

I was led below. I almost wished that the punishment was over. I
had nerved myself up to bear it, dreadful as it was, without flinching.
Now I knew not for how long it might be postponed, but I had no hopes
of escaping it altogether.

In another minute, the stirring cry of 'Prepare ship for action!' was
passed along the decks. Every one in a moment was full of activity.
The cabin bulkheads were knocked away, fire-screens were put up, the
doors of the magazine were thrown open, and powder and shot were
being handed up on deck.

For some time I was left alone, with a sentry only stationed over me.
I longed to be set free. I trusted that I was not to remain a prisoner
during the action which it was expected was about to take place. I
thought that if I could but send a message to the captain, and entreat

that I might be allowed to do my duty at my gun, he would liberate me while the action lasted.

For a long time, not an officer came near me. At length, to my great satisfaction, I saw Dr. M'Call. He was on his way to see that all proper preparations had been made in the space devoted to his service on the orlop deck for the reception of the wounded.

'Dr. M'Call,' I cried out to him. 'I would not have ventured to have spoken to you, situated as I now am, under any other circumstances, but I have a great favour to ask of you, sir.'

He stopped and listened.

'I need not say that I trust you do not believe me guilty, and I would entreat you to go to the captain and to ask him to allow me to return to my duty during the action. Tell him only what you think of me, and he will, I am sure, give me my freedom till the fight is over. I do not wish to avoid punishment, but it would be a double one to remain manacled here while my shipmates are fighting the enemy.'

'I'll go,' said the doctor, who had quietly listened to all I said. 'I do not believe you guilty. There is little time to lose, though.'

How anxiously I awaited the result of my petition! Every moment I expected to hear the first shot fired, and to find that the action had begun. About three minutes passed. I fancied six times the period had elapsed, when a master's mate and two men came below.

'The captain gives you leave, Weatherhelm, to return to your duty,' said the officer. 'He hopes that you will show you are worthy of the favour.'

'Indeed I will, sir,' I answered as the men knocked the handcuffs off my wrists.

'We've a tough job in hand, depend on that.'

'Thank you, sir, thank you,' I exclaimed, as I sprang to my feet and followed my liberators to the upper deck, where the sentry joined his comrades.

The moment I reached the deck I looked out for the enemy. Just out of gun-shot appeared a seventy-four gun-ship and two frigates. They were firing away at the Indiamen, which were still within range of their guns. The greater number were, however, clustering together, and standing down to leeward of us, so that those nearer the Frenchmen were not idle, and were bravely returning shot for shot.

The three ships came on, the Frenchmen little doubting that we should continue on the same course we were then holding; but our captain was determined to get the weather-gage, and just as their shot came aboard us, he tacked and stood to the northward, which brought the two frigates nearer to us than the line-of-battle ship. One of them bravely stood on till she got close under our guns. The order was given to fire. Our shot took the most deadly effect on her, and she completely heeled over as our whole broadside went crashing in through her decks and sides. Of the three hundred men or more, who an instant before stood up full of life and strength, full fifty must have been struck down, many never to rise again, while her spars and rigging went tumbling down in terrible confusion over her deck.

Again we tacked, and this brought our starboard broadside to bear on the second frigate. While we were especially engaged with the first, she had fired two or three broadsides at us, and as we tacked she managed to rake us, to our no little damage. The success attending our first effort inspirited us to give due effect to the second. Every shot we fired seemed to tell. Besides numbers of men killed and wounded, the foremast of the frigate came toppling down on her deck almost before the smoke which hung around us had cleared away.

Seldom had greater execution been effected in so short a time, but our ship was thoroughly well manned, and every one of us had been well trained at our guns. We knew what we were about, and had strength to do it. Leaving the two frigates almost helpless, we stood on to meet our larger opponent. With her, to all appearance, we were thoroughly well matched. While we had been engaged with the frigates, she had severely handled some of the Indiamen. She had now, however, to look after herself.

Our captain, as soon as we got clear of the frigates, signalled to the Indiamen to go and attack them. This he did in the hope that they would be prevented from repairing damages and be enabled to escape. The Indiamen to leeward, in the most spirited way, instantly began to beat up towards the frigates.

We had not escaped altogether free of harm. Though no material damage had been done to the ship, we had already several men killed and wounded by the shot from our two first antagonists. As we closed with the line-of-battle ship she opened fire on us. We soon found that we had an opponent which would require all our strength and perseverance to overcome, but every man stood to his gun, as British seamen always will stand when well commanded, however great may be the odds against them.

We passed each other on opposite tacks as the line-of-battle ship stood on towards the frigates. As our respective guns were brought to bear, we discharged them into each other's sides. We all cheered loudly and heartily as we saw the result of our fire, but the enemy were not idle. The shot from their broadside came crashing on board us with fearful effect, while the marines in the tops, poop, and forecastle, kept up a heavy fire of musketry. Blocks and spars came tumbling down from aloft; splinters were flying in every direction; round shot were whizzing through the ports and across the decks; the smoke from the guns hung over us in dense masses, obscuring the sky and scarcely enabling us to see from one side of the ship to the other

Many a poor fellow sank to rise no more; numbers were sorely wounded; the heads of some, the arms and legs of others, were shot away; groans and shrieks arose from those who were struck, while the rest of the crew uttered shouts of defiance and anger. All of us were stripped to the waist, begrimed with smoke, and often sprinkled with our own blood or that of our comrades; our handkerchiefs bound round our heads, and our countenances, with the muscles strained to the utmost, exhibiting the fierce passions which animated our hearts.

Yet, though I have attempted to describe the scene, no words can do adequate justice to its savage wildness. I felt, I doubt not, like the rest. In a moment all recollection of the past vanished; I thought only of punishing the foe, of gaining the victory. I saw others killed and wounded near me, but it never occurred to me that at any moment their fate might be mine. As our foremost guns had been fired, they had been instantly run in and loaded, and directly the enemy had passed us, putting down our helm, we luffed up and passed under her stern, raking her fore and aft, to the very great surprise of the Frenchmen, who little expected that we should so quickly again be able to deliver our fire.

The rapidity with which we worked our guns was the chief cause of our success. Instead of tacking, as the enemy fancied we were going to do, we once more filled and ran after him. A loud shout burst from our crew. The Frenchman's fore topmast came tumbling down on deck. We quickly came up after him and gave him a full dose of our larboard broadside.

The two frigates, seeing how their consort had been handled, and that several of the Indiamen were crowding sail towards them, now set all the canvas they could spread in the hope of making their escape, very indifferent to the fate of their big consort, whom they seemed to think was powerful enough to take very good care of herself. She.

meantime, was signalling to them to remain to render her assistance while she brought us up towards them.

We, by this time, had been pretty severely handled. We had fully twenty killed and twice as many wounded, while several of our spars had been shot away, and we were much cut up in sails and rigging. Night, too, was coming on, and it was important to keep our convoy together. We could not tell whether other French ships were near at hand, and if so, not only we, but many of the merchantmen under our charge might have been captured. All these things I thought of afterwards, but not then, depend on it. Flushed with our success, we fully expected that we were going to make all the three Frenchmen strike. The enemy's line-of-battle ship sailed well, and she quickly led us up in chase, so that we were exposed to the fire of her consorts as well as to hers.

Under other circumstances, I believe that our captain was the last man to have left a victory half won; but just as we were once more getting within range of the enemy's guns, we hove to, and he signalled to the convoy to collect together and to continue their course to the southward.

All on board were eager to see what was to happen. We thought that we were going to make sail after the Indiamen, but we had not yet quite done with the enemy. We replied by a loud cheer as the ship's head was once more kept towards them, and then running along their line we delivered another crashing broadside into them. We got something in return, though, and the shot from all the three ships came more thickly about us than ever.

Not far from the gun at which I was serving I saw Saull Ley. Once he had disappeared, and I thought he had been wounded, but when the firing ceased he had come back to his gun. He had evidently attempted the same trick a second time, when we were once more unexpectedly

brought into action, for a couple of men with rope's ends were driving
him back to his station. He had no help for himself but to remain,
though fear had rendered his services of very little avail.

At last the shot he so much dreaded reached him, and I saw him
struck down bleeding on the deck. He shrieked out with terror and
pain when he found himself wounded.

'Oh, help me! help me! I shall die! I shall die! What will become
of me?' he cried out.

'Why, you'll have to go where many a better man has gone before
you,' answered the rest of the crew of his gun, who, on account of his
arrant cowardice, had no feeling of compassion for him. He was, however, lifted from the deck and carried below, to be placed under the
doctor's care.

The enemy, who had laid to for us, seeming to consider that nothing
was to be gained by them if they continued the fight, but that they were
far more likely to have to haul down their flags or to be sunk, once
more filled and stood away from us to the northward. It seemed a
question whether we should follow or not, and I am very certain that
no one felt more regret than did our captain at having to allow the
enemy to escape when he had almost secured the victory.

The property, however, entrusted to his care on board the fleet of
Indiamen was of such vast amount that he could not venture to run the
risk of any disaster. We had gallantly done our duty by beating off
so far superior a force. The enemy was in full flight—we might have
overtaken them—but if we had, and captured them all, we should have
so completely weakened our crew that we could not have ventured to
continue our voyage, and should certainly have had to put into port to
refit. Our helm was accordingly put up, and once more we stood to the
southward after our convoy.

Having to leave the enemy was, I believe, a far greater trial and exertion of moral courage in our captain, than having to follow and attack them once more would have been.

Some officers I have known would have gone after them, and perhaps have risked the loss of the richly-laden merchantmen under their charge. Our crew, to a man, felt this, and not a complaint or a growl was heard at our allowing the enemy to escape.

Darkness soon hid them from our sight. The battle was over, but our work was not. All night long we were busy in repairing damages, and daylight still found us engaged in the same occupation. The magazine was once more closed, the blood-stained decks were washed down, and in the course of the day the ship resumed much of her wonted appearance, though it was no easy work to get rid of the traces of the severe conflict in which we had lately been engaged.

At length the hands were piped below, the watch on deck was set, and the others allowed to turn in and get some of that rest we so much needed. Then it was that the recollection of my painful position returned to me. I was a prisoner released for a time, with a severe punishment hanging over me. Suppose even the captain were to remit my punishment, in consequence of the way in which I knew that I had behaved in the fight, I should still be loaded with disgrace. I should be looked upon as a convicted thief. Such were the feelings with which I went to my hammock. I was just about to turn in, when I heard my name called.

'The doctor has sent for you, Weatherhelm,' said the messenger, who was one of the hospital attendants. 'There is a man dying, and he wants to see you.'

I slipped on my clothes and hurried down to the orlop deck. I found the purser, with the chaplain, standing near the hammock of a seaman. The surgeon came up at the same time. 'I am glad to see you, Weatherhelm,' he said in his usual kind way. 'That poor wretch exonerates you from the charge he made against you, and begged to see you that he might ask your forgiveness.'

I drew near the hammock, and in the features of the dying man I recognised those of Saull Ley.

'Weatherhelm, I'm a great villain, I know I am,' he cried out as soon as he saw me. 'There's a greater, though, and he put me up to it. I would have let you be punished to save my own worthless carcase, and, oh! now I'm suffering greater pain than ever the cat could give me. I stole all the things—I've been telling Mr. Nips. Then we persuaded those two silly lads that it was you, and when they saw me go and put them into your bag, they had no doubt about it, and so Iffley made them believe that they had seen you coming out of the store-room. That's all about it. I've been speaking the truth and nothing but the truth. But you'll forgive me, won't you, Weatherhelm, and let me die easy?'

'I forgive you with all my heart, and I believe that I should have forgiven you even had I suffered the punishment awarded me,' I answered. 'I would ask you but one thing. Why do you fancy that Iffley is desirous to get me falsely accused?'

'Because he hates you, he told me so,' he said. 'He has a long score to wipe off against you, and he vowed if you escaped him this time, he would find means, before long, to be revenged on you.'

'You hear what the man says,' observed Dr. M'Call to the other officers present. 'This is what I suspected, but had not the means of proving. We must not allow that ruffian Iffley to obtain his ends; for ruffian he is, notwithstanding his plausible manners. It's an old story—Weatherhelm would rather it were not told—but there is nothing in it to do him discredit.'

'All I desire, sir, is, that I may be freed from the imputation cast on me, and that, thanks to your consideration in calling witnesses to hear this poor man's dying confession, will, I am sure, be done.'

'Rest assured of that,' remarked the chaplain. 'And now I would say a few words to Saull Ley. You spoke of dying with a quiet conscience if you got forgiveness from the man you might have so cruelly injured, had you not been struck down by the hand of an avenging God; but you have not only forgiveness to seek from man, but from One who is mighty to save, who has the power and the will to wash away all your sins, if you put your entire faith and trust in Him, and repent you heartily of your former life.'

'I cannot, I dare not. He wouldn't listen to such a wretch as me. Don't tell me to go to Him. Find some other means of saving me—isn't there? There must be. Do tell me of it!'

'There is none—none whatever,' answered the chaplain. 'Do not refuse the only means—a sure means—by which even the greatest of sinners may be saved.'

'Oh, go on, sir, go on; tell me all about it,' moaned the unhappy man. 'I've often before now thought of giving up my bad ways. I wish that I had done it long ago.'

The chaplain looked at Dr. M'Call, to learn whether he might continue talking to the wounded man. The doctor signified that he might, but that it would be better if there were fewer persons present.

'Yes; but he must first sign the evidence he has given,' observed the purser, who was of necessity a good man of business. 'Not only must the innocent escape punishment, but the guilty must be punished.'

He accordingly wrote down the statement made by the wounded seaman, and, after reading it to him, put a pen into his hand to sign it. Ley took the pen and hurriedly wrote his name. He did not speak. Suddenly the pen fell from his hand—a shudder came over his frame—without a groan he fell back in his hammock.

'What has happened?' asked the chaplain.

'He has gone to his long account,' answered Dr. M'Call.

16

Alas! how many die like him, talking and thinking about repentance, and saying that they will put their trust in Christ, but never go to Him, never repent!

With a heart truly thankful for the dangers I had escaped and the mercies vouchsafed to me, I returned to my hammock, and slept more soundly than I had done for many a night. The next morning, after breakfast was over, all hands were piped on deck, and the captain sent for me. I found him and all the officers assembled on the quarter-deck.

'I have sent for you, Weatherhelm,' said the captain, 'to tell you that I am very glad you have escaped what would have been a very cruel and unjust punishment. My lads, you know that this man was accused not long ago of a very great crime. I rejoice to say that I have proof, undoubted, that he is entirely innocent. The man who accused him is dead, but he left evidence not only that this man is innocent, but that a most vile attempt has been made to accuse him falsely. I know the man; let him beware that he is not caught in the trap he has laid for another.'

While the captain was speaking, I caught sight of Iffley's countenance. Again I observed on it that expression of hatred and baffled vengeance, and when he himself was so palpably alluded to, there was mixed with it no small amount of craven apprehension. The stern eye of the captain ranged over the countenances of the crew. It rested a moment on him. He quailed before it.

'Pipe down!' cried the captain.

Those of the crew not on duty went below. Many of the more steady men came up to me, and congratulated me on my escape, and I found in a short time that I had numbers of friends on board. Had it not been for the thought of my wife, and of my wish to return home, I should have been happy.

Iffley never came near me. He seemed to dread me far more than I dreaded him. I could not conceive what harm he could possibly do me now that he was known, and must have been aware that he was watched. Still I felt that it would be wiser to be on my guard against him.

When the excitement of the occurrences I have described had passed away, a reaction took place, and I once more began to feel the misery of my position. It seemed like some horrid dream, and sometimes I almost hoped that I should awake and find that I was at home all the time, and that the scenes I was going through were but the effects of a dreadful nightmare.

I frequently found myself reasoning on the subject, but there was a vividness and reality about everything which made me too justly doubt the soundness of my hopes. I had, before I was pressed, more than once been afflicted with a dream so like the present reality, that, as I say, I nearly persuaded myself that I was dreaming now. I had been torn away from my wife without being able to tell her where I was going. I sailed over strange seas without a kit, and without any preparation for the voyage; cast upon strange lands among savages, and had barely escaped with my life; I had wandered about among a variety of extraordinary scenes, and I had found on awaking that scarcely an hour had passed since I fell asleep. But day after day went by, and at length I felt very well assured that I was not dreaming a dream, but living through the sad reality. My great desire was to write home, at least to say where I was, and that I was well; but no opportunity occurred, not a homeward-bound ship did we pass.

We had been several weeks at sea, when one morning two sail were reported in sight from the masthead. They were standing towards us. The idea was that they were two homeward-bound English merchantmen

I accordingly got ready a letter to send home by one of them to my wife.

As they drew near, however, they showed French colours. It was clear, we thought, that they had mistaken us for a French squadron. We accordingly hoisted French colours, and they ran on close under our guns. We then changed our colours for English, and fired a shot across their bows. They were evidently taken by surprise, and did not seem to know what to do. We fired another shot to quicken their imagination. On this they hove to and hauled down their colours.

Directly afterwards a boat came alongside from each of the strangers. The masters of the ships apparently were in them. They came on deck, and inquired what we wanted, and why we fired at them? They spoke tolerably good English, though in the French fashion.

'Why, gentlemen, I am sorry for your sakes to say that war has again broken out between England and France, and that we purpose to make prizes of your ships.'

The poor Frenchmen looked very indignant, and then very unhappy, and stamped and swore and plucked the hair in handfuls from their heads. I thought they would have gone out of their minds, they seemed so miserable and furious; but they were allowed to rage on, and no one interfered with them.

At last our captain observed that it was the fortune of war, and a misfortune to which many brave men were subject; whereon they re-echoed the sentiment, shrugged their shoulders, and in ten minutes were laughing and singing as if everything had turned out exactly as they could have wished it.

The captain ordered two of the midshipmen to go on board the prizes to carry them home. How the sound of the order set my heart beating! I had my letter ready to send. Could I but form one of their crews! I could scarcely venture to ask the favour.

Several men were chosen for each vessel. I understood that their numbers were complete. Again my heart sank within me. My hopes had vanished. I was standing with my letter in my hand, when I saw Dr. M'Call go up to the captain. Directly afterwards I was called up.

'I understand, my man,' said our captain, 'that you have strong reasons for wishing to return home. You shall go in one of the prizes; get your bag ready.'

How I blessed him for his kind words. In ten minutes I was on board the largest prize. She was ship-rigged, called the *Mouche*, and bound from the Isle of France to Bordeaux. Mr. Randolph was the name of the midshipman sent in charge of her.

As I left the side of the *Albion*, I saw Charles Iffley looking out at one of the ports. His features bore more strongly than ever the marks of hatred and anger, and when he saw that I was for a time beyond his reach, he shook his fist at me with impotent rage.

The mates and some of the French crews were sent on board the *Albion*; but two or three blacks and several Frenchmen remained on board the ships to help to navigate them. Still we were all together but very short-handed.

The other prize was the *Nautile*. She was a very handsome ship, and soon gave evidence that her sailing qualities were superior to those of the *Mouche*.

I could scarcely believe my senses when I found myself actually on board a ship homeward bound. I might in a few short weeks once more be united to my wife, instead of being kept away from her as I expected perhaps for years. The sudden turn of fortune almost overcame me.

As I had had some difficulty in believing in the reality of my misery, now I felt it scarcely possible to trust in the reality of my happiness.

Too great for me seemed the joy. Yet I never anticipated for a moment
that any evil could possibly be in store for me at the end of my voyage.
I brought what I thought would be the reality clearly before my eyes.
I pictured to myself my wife in our quiet little home, looking out on the
ever-animated waters of the Solent, and the fleets of men-of-war and
Indiamen and large merchantmen of all sorts brough. up at Spithead.
I thought of her, anxiously waiting to receive news of me; and then
she rose up to my sight, as I thought she would be when she received
notice that I had once more returned safe in limb and health to my
native land. I had no doubt that I should be able to pay for a substitute, and thus be free from the risk of being again pressed and sent
to sea. All before me appeared bright and encouraging.

Mr. Randolph, the officer sent in charge of the *Mouche*, although still
a midshipman, had seen a good deal of service, and was a brave young
man. He had a difficult duty to perform. The *Mouche* turned out a
very slow sailer, and was excessively leaky, so that we always had to
keep three or four hands employed at a time at the pumps. Of course
we made the Frenchmen do this work, at which they grumbled not a
little; but we told them that had their ship not been leaky, they would
not have had to pump, and that they had no reason to complain. They
did not much like our arguments, for they said that if we had not made
prize of their vessel, they should have been quietly continuing their
voyage.

Including the blacks, there were eight Frenchmen on board, while,
with Mr. Randolph, we only mustered seven in all. We had therefore
to keep a very constant look-out over them, lest they should attempt to
take the vessel from us, a trick which more than once had before been
played, and sometimes with success.

I had always thought Mr. Randolph a good-natured, merry, sky-
larking youngster; but the moment he took charge of the prize, he

became a most diligent, careful officer He was always on deck, always on the look-out, at all hours of tne day and night.

I cannot say so much in favour of the officer who had charge of the *Nautile*. He was a mate, and consequently superior in rank to Mr. Randolph. Unfortunately they had had some dispute of long standing, and Mr. Simon, the mate I speak of, never lost an opportunity of showing his enmity and dislike to his younger brother officer. Here we had a practical example of how detrimental to the interest of the service are any disputes between officers.

To return, however, to the time when we first got on board our respective prizes, as they lay hove to close to the *Albion*. The signal to us to make sail to the northward was hoisted from her masthead, and while she stood away after the tea-chests, we shaped a course for England.

How different must our feelings have been to those of the unfortunate Frenchmen, who saw the ships sailing away from them, while they had to go back to be landed they could not tell where, many months elapsing before they would again return to their families!

The trade winds were at this time blowing across our course,—indeed almost ahead, so that we made but very slow progress. At first we kept close enough together, though there was no interchange of civilities between the two crews. When we were within hail, and the *Nautile* was going along with her maintopsail yard on the cap, while we had every sail set, and our yards braced sharp up, her people jeered and laughed at us, and called us slow coaches, and offered to give us a tow, and asked what messages they should take to our wives and families in England. This they only did when the officers were below. We replied that it was no fault of ours, that if they liked to exchange ships, we could say the same to them, but that we would not, for we could tell them that it was not pleasant to be taunted for nothing.

At last Mr. Simon, standing one day on his taffrail, speaking-trumpet in hand, hailed and asked Mr. Randolph if he could not manage to make his ship walk along somewhat faster, for at this rate they would never get to England.

'Greater haste, worst speed, Simon,' answered Mr. Randolph. 'I've been doing my best to make the *Mouche* move faster, but she's a slow fly, and I cannot do it. Besides, she is very leaky, and we have had hard work to keep her afloat.'

'Let her sink, then,' answered Mr. Simon; 'I do not see why she should be delaying us, and giving us a double chance of being retaken by the enemy.'

'While I live and have a man who will stick by me, I'll stick by the ship put under my charge,' replied Mr. Randolph; 'still I must beg you to remain by us. My own people and I will do our best to keep her afloat. When we find we can do so no longer, we will claim your assistance, and get you to take us on board.'

'Oh, is that what you calculate on? We'll see about it,' was Mr. Simon's very unsatisfactory reply.

'We'll trust to you not deserting us,' sung out Mr. Randolph. 'If a gale were to spring up, we should have hard work to keep her afloat; remember that.'

'What's that you say? I can't hear,' answered Mr. Simon, as his ship shot ahead of ours.

'He heard well enough, but does not intend to heed, I fear,' said Mr. Randolph, turning round and walking hurriedly up and down the deck. 'We must trust to our own energies, and my lads will stick by me, I know that.'

Our cargo consisted of sugar, coffee, and rice, and other valuable but bulky articles produced in the East, so that we could not move them to get at the leaks. A very steady man, Thomas Andrews, a quartermaster, was acting as first mate, and he having spoken well of me to Mr. Randolph, I was appointed to do duty as second mate, or, I might say more justly, to take charge of a watch. Mr. Randolph seemed to put a good deal of confidence in me, and he now summoned Andrews and me, and consulted us what it might be best to do towards stopping the leaks.

'It is bad enough now,' he observed, 'but it will be much worse should a gale spring up and cause the ship to labour heavily.'

Andrews and I offered to hunt about to try and find out where the worst leaks existed. We accordingly worked our way down into the bows of the ship in every direction, at no little risk of being suffocated, and at length we assured ourselves from the appearance of the planking, which looked as if the bows had been stove in, that she had run against the butt-end of a piece of timber. It seemed a miracle how the ship could have kept afloat with so large a fracture in her bottom. We reported our discovery to Mr. Randolph, who descended with us to examine the danger.

'Well, if the worst comes to the worst, we can but get on board the *Nautile*,' he observed. 'In the meantime, we'll do our best to keep the old ship afloat.'

Mr. Randolph directed me to take charge of the ship, and to keep an eye on the proceedings of the Frenchmen, while he and Andrews, with two men, descended below with all the planks and carpenter's tools to be found, to try and repair, as far as they could, the damage. Night was coming on, so that it was important to get the work done as speedily as possible. I meantime turned my eye every now and then at our consort, for she was evidently getting further ahead than she was accustomed to do. I hoped, however, that she would soon shorten sail or lay to for us, as she had always done at nightfall. Still she stood on.

Darkness was coming down rapidly on us, and at length I could scarcely distinguish her. I did not like to tell Mr. Randolph, for of course this would only interrupt the work in which he was engaged; but I marked well the point by the compass in which I had last seen the *Nautile*, that we might know where to look for her in the morning.

Three hours passed away before Mr. Randolph and Andrews returned on deck. They said that they had been able to patch up the leak far better than they expected, and that, if the weather held moderate, we might hope to carry the ship into Plymouth.

The night passed by much as usual. The French prisoners had hitherto behaved very well, and seemed so inclined to be peaceable and orderly that insensibly our vigilance over them relaxed. It was my morning watch on deck. I looked out anxiously for the *Nautile* when daylight dawned. Brighter and brighter grew the day, but in vain I rubbed my eyes. Not a sign of her was to be seen.

Mr. Simon had, then, cruelly and shamefully deserted us. Complaints, and more than complaints, both loud and deep, were uttered. He knew our condition,—he knew that we were any moment liable to founder,— and still he had made sail and left us merely to get home a few days sooner, or to run some little less risk himself of recapture. It is very seldom that I have heard of conduct so selfish in the navy, or, indeed, in the merchant service.

I do not want to make out that seamen are better than other men, but I maintain that they are certainly not worse, and that in many respects they are as honest and free from vice as any other class of men. One thing was very certain, we could not hope to overtake him. We must therefore take care of ourselves as best we could. The leak had been partially stopped, and if we continued to enjoy fine weather, we might get into port very well; and, as Andrews observed, 'The prize is not always to the strong, nor the race to the swift.' Our consort might run his head into the very dangers he was so anxious to avoid.

We went on very well for two or three days longer, and then I could not help remarking that there was a considerable change in the manner of the Frenchmen. They were far less obedient and civil than they had been, and when ordered to perform any duty, they went about it in a sulky, disagreeable manner.

Mr. Randolph, I thought, did not observe the change, but I mentioned the subject to Andrews.

'I'll keep my eye on the fellows,' said he. 'They'll find it rather difficult to catch a weasel asleep.'

A few days after this we fell in with a westerly breeze, which increased rapidly into a strong gale, and away we ran before it much faster than the old *Mouche* had yet been made to fly.

Unfortunately the sea got up, and the ship began to labour very much. The consequence was, as we had expected, the leak we had patched up once more burst open, and it became necessary to keep all hands, watch and watch, at the pumps. Mr. Randolph took his spell like the rest of us, and no one seemed to work with a more hearty goodwill.

I watched with some anxiety to see what the Frenchmen would do. First one of them fell down while working at the pumps, and when we picked him up he said that he was so ill he could not labour any more, but must go to his hammock. Then another followed his example, and then a third, and a fourth, till only one remained besides the three blacks, who went on working away as merrily as ever.

The fifth Frenchman seemed suddenly to get into very good humour, and to exert himself as much as any of us. Had the gale continued, I believe that we should all of us really have been knocked up, but happily we very quickly ran out of it, and once more we had smooth water and a fair breeze.

While the sea was still running high, the only Frenchman who remained on deck, as he was coming aft, slipped and fell. Two of the blacks only were near him. They picked him up, while he cried out with pain, asserting that he had either broken his arm or put it out of joint. He insisted on being carried to his hammock, and when Mr. Randolph offered to try and doctor him, he shrieked out and declared that he could not bear the pain of being touched. At last we were obliged to let him alone, and then we had all our five prisoners laid up and apparently useless.

It thus became more important than ever to try once more to stop the leak. Mr. Randolph and Andrews accordingly set about it as they had done the first time, taking with them two hands. This left only two others, besides me, on deck, and the three blacks. Negroes have, I have always fancied, very little command over their countenances, and if a person is accustomed to watch them, he will always be able to discover, almost as easily as he would among a party of children, whether there is anything in the wind. Now, as I saw the negroes moving about the decks, I felt very sure from the roll of their eyes and the way in which every now and then they exhibited their teeth, that they had a grand secret among them. I stepped aft, and telling the man at the helm to be on his guard, I called Sam Jones, the only other man left on deck, and sent him down into the cabin to collect all the arms he could find, to load the pistols and muskets, and to place them just inside the companion hatch, so that I could get at them in a moment.

'Now,' said I to Jones, 'just go forward as if you were thinking of nothing particular, and then slip quietly down below and tell Mr. Randolph that I think there's something wrong, that he had better be on his guard and return on deck as quickly as possible. Do you jump up again without a moment's delay. Get a handspike or anything you can lay hold of, and keep guard over the fore hatchway, and see that neither the blacks nor any of the Frenchmen go down there.'

'But the Frenchmen, they can't do any harm; they are all sick in bed,' observed Jones.

'Don't be too certain of their sickness,' I observed. 'They may be sick, but it is just possible that they are shamming, and it is well to be on the safe side.'

Without further delay, Jones went forward to do as I directed him. I meanwhile stood by the companion hatch, ready to hand a musket up to Thompson, the man at the helm, should occasion arise to require it. The Frenchmen, I ought to have said, all slept together in a part of the hold which was planked off for their accommodation. I kept watching the blacks narrowly. I saw their eyes turned every now and then towards the main hatchway. I was convinced that no time was to be lost if bloodshed was to be prevented.

'A heavy squall coming on,' I shouted out. 'Hands aloft and furl topsails! Here, Sambo, Julius, Quasha, aloft with you quickly and furl the maintopsail.' They pretended not to hear me, but once more looked down the hatchway. 'Do you hear? Up with you, you scoundrels!' I shouted out at the top of my voice, loud enough, I thought, at all events, for Jones to hear me. At that moment the heads of three Frenchmen appeared above the combing of the main hatchway

CHAPTER XIII.

THE moment I saw the heads of the Frenchmen, I handed out a musket
from the companion-hatch, and gave it to Thompson, while I took one
myself and levelled it at them. 'Ah, my friends, understand that I
will fire at the first man of you who steps on deck!' I sang out.
'Return to your beds, if you are sick, but on deck you must not
venture.'

Thompson imitated my example, and we both stood with our muskets
levelled and ready to put our threats into execution. At first the
Frenchmen popped down again very quickly, but gaining courage, they
all five put their heads up again at the same moment.

Looking round and seeing only Thompson and me on deck, they
sprang up as if they were about to make a desperate rush towards us,
thinking of course that they could easily overcome two men.

Telling Thompson to aim at the blacks in the rigging to keep them
there, I covered the foremost Frenchman with my musket. I could
have killed him on the spot, but I was most unwilling to shed blood
except in the very last necessity. Once more I sang out. He continued
advancing.

'I have given you ample warning!' I cried out. My finger was
on the trigger.

At that moment Mr. Randolph, followed by Andrews and the other men, sprang on deck, and seeing the state of affairs, each of them grasping a handspike, they ran towards the Frenchmen.

The latter soon saw that their opportunity was lost. The negroes, for the sake of being more out of the way, as they fancied, of Thompson's musket, had climbed as high as they could up the rigging, so that he was able to hold another Frenchman in check.

The Frenchman nearest to me, seeing my resolute bearing, and having no fancy for throwing his life away even for the sake of his companions, very wisely backed against them, and they seeing Mr. Randolph and his party advancing from forward, to avoid getting their heads broken, leaped precipitately down the hatchway, whence they had but just before emerged.

Leaving Thompson to keep the blacks aloft with his musket, I sprang to the hatchway and sang out, 'We do not want to do you any harm, but if you attempt any trick, for our own sakes we must shoot every one of you!' I said this because I saw one of them striking away over a tinder-box, with the intention, I had little doubt, of trying to set the ship on fire.

Mr Randolph highly applauded me for what I had done. On looking below and seeing what the Frenchmen were about, he and Andrews, with Jones and another man, leaped down among them, and seizing the first they could lay hands on, lifted him up crop and heels to me The move so much astonished his companions, that they did not come to his assistance; and another being treated in the same way, we had their forces divided, and very speedily brought them to terms. We first lashed the hands of the two we had on deck behind them, and made them sit down with their backs against the bulwarks on the starboard side, and then we got up the other three one by one, and placed them, bound in the same way, on the opposite side. Next we called down the blacks, and arranged them round the mainmast.

'Now, my friends, by all the laws of war you ought to be shot!' said Mr. Randolph. 'We treated you very kindly; we gave you of the best of everything on board, and in return you have attempted to knock us on the head, and to take the ship from us. However, it was natural that you should wish to recover what was once your own, so that if you will promise, on the honour of Frenchmen, not to make another attempt of the sort, we will allow you your freedom during the day-time, on certain conditions. Three of you must remain forward, and never come abaft the foremast unless I call you; and two must never go before the mizzen-mast; at night we must shut you all up. I warn you, also, that as surely as any one of you attempts to infringe these regulations, I will shoot him. We are very good friends; I do not bear you the slightest enmity, but our own safety demands this.'

Our prisoners shrugged their shoulders. '*C'est la fortune de la guerre*,' was the only answer they at first made. They most of them understood pretty clearly what Mr. Randolph had said; besides, one, who understood English the best, interpreted to the rest.

Mr. Randolph waited a little time. 'Do you agree to my terms?' he asked.

'*Oui, monsieur*; *oui, oui*,' was answered by all of them simultaneously.

'If I grant you your freedom at once, will you give me your honour to act as I desire?' asked Mr. Randolph. 'I do not wish you to do so while you sit there bound like slaves.'

The idea seemed to take their fancy amazingly, and as soon as we had unlashed their arms, by Mr. Randolph's orders, they got up, and all together, putting their hands on their breasts, swore solemnly not again to attempt to retake the ship. It is impossible to describe their manner, or the air with which they uttered the words.

They did not seem, however, much to like being kept separate from each other, but Mr. Randolph very wisely would not abate in any way the regulations he had formed. He allowed one of them at a time to go into the caboose to cook, for they did not at all approve of our style of cooking, and one of them, who spoke English, remarked that it was only fit for bears and wolves. We laughed, and observed, in return, that people have different tastes, and that we had no fancy for the kickshaws and trifles which satisfied them. (*Quelque chose* and *troufles*, perhaps I ought to have written.)

When a Frenchman is asked what he will have for dinner, he begins by saying *quelque chose au troufles*, and then goes on to enumerate all sorts of things, just as an Englishman replies, a mutton-chop or beef-steak, and finally orders turtle-soup, salmon, and a venison pasty ; not that I can own to having ever been guilty of such a proceeding.

After we had settled with the Frenchmen, we allowed the blacks to come down, and ordering them into the waist, told them to keep there on pain of being shot, and on no account to communicate with any one else. They, grinning, pointed to our muskets, and assured us that while we kept those in our hands they would most implicitly obey us.

These matters being arranged, we each of us stuck a brace of pistols in our belts, and hung cutlasses to our sides, while a musket was placed so that the man at the wheel could get hold of it in a moment. The rest of the arms and powder were locked up in the after-cabin.

These precautions were, I am convinced, not greater than were necessary. When the Frenchmen saw that we had taken them, and that we were wide awake, they did not dream of breaking their word ; but had we exhibited any carelessness, or any undue confidence in them, the honour they had pledged would not, I suspect, have resisted the temptation which they would have felt again to try and take the ship from us.

As it was, all went on very quietly. We soon got once more into the

way of joking and talking with the Frenchmen, and apparently were on
as good terms as ever, but Mr. Randolph every now and then gave us
a hint to be on our guard.

'Don't trust them, my men,' said he. 'The more they laugh, and
chatter, and smile, the more they are inclined for mischief, depend on
that.'

He was right, and I think, considering his youth, that he deserved
great credit for his discretion and judgment; for I believe that many an
older man might have been deceived by the plausibility of their manners
and their apparent cordiality.

Fortunately we had very fine weather, and a fair wind, and in about
a week after the occurrence I have described we struck soundings in
the chops of the Channel. Our difficulties and dangers, however, were
not over; we had to keep a stricter watch than ever on our prisoners,
for they could tell by the colour of the water that we were near home,
and that if they did not at once regain their liberty they must give up
all hopes of so doing. We had likewise to keep a constant look-out for
strange sails. The enemy's privateers abounded, we knew, in the mouth
of the Channel, though their men-of-war were not so fond at the time
of showing themselves in those latitudes where they were very likely to
be picked up by British cruisers.

With the few hands we had on board, we could scarcely hope to
make a successful resistance against any armed vessel; still, when Mr.
Randolph asked us if we would stick by him should we fall in with an
enemy, we promised to do our best.

'Never fear, then,' said he; 'though we might not be able to beat
them off, we'll try and frighten them away. As we cannot expect the
Frenchmen to help us, we'll make their clothes serve some purpose at all
events.'

We had discovered some chests of clothes in the ship, and most of the prisoners had more than one suit ; these we instantly set to work to fill with straw, and in a short time we had manufactured a crew of forty men at least. We rigged out some as officers, and put spy-glasses in their hands, and, knocking out the flints of some of the muskets, we put them into the hands of others, and stuck them about the ship. We then loaded all the guns and ran them out, and got ready also all the remainder of the firearms.

' Had the *Nautile* stuck by us we might have put a very good face on the matter, whatever craft we might have fallen in with, if she had done as we have,' Mr. Randolph observed to me as I stood at the helm.

' It is a pity, sir; but I hope we may still run the gauntlet of our enemies and get safe into port,' I answered; and earnestly, indeed, did I pray that such might be our lot.

As I drew nearer home, still more intense had become my anxiety to ascertain the fate of my beloved wife. I will not here dwell on the subject. Sometimes the thought of all she must have suffered on my account and on her own became almost insupportable. I felt that it was wiser not to dwell on it, and yet I could not cast it from me. My only, my great resource was prayer—great and supporting it was. Let any one, placed as I was, try it, and they will find that I in no way overrate it. Whenever I felt the miserable depressing feeling coming on, I fled instantly to that great source of comfort, of all true happiness, and it never failed me.

However, as I say, I will not dwell on that subject now. I may be inclined thus to write, but all who read may not be in a proper frame of mind to reflect on the matter, and thus I may perchance do more harm than good.

As I was saying, we had been keeping a bright look-out, even before we struck soundings, both day and night. If the wind should hold fair, in two or three days we might hope to be in Plymouth Sound.

All hands were talking of home, of those they expected to meet, and of the delights of a run on shore. The night was very fine, but towards morning a thin mist settled down over the sea, and though it did not obscure the bright stars which glittered overhead, it prevented us from seeing to any great distance around. However, we every now and then hove the lead, and we were convinced that we were in the fairway up Channel.

At length, when daylight slowly broke, the mist assumed a white, silvery appearance, the smooth water close alongside could clearly be perceived, and the mist was seen as it were skirmishing round us, broken away, it seemed, by our coming against it, and then it grew thicker and thicker, till the eye could no longer penetrate through it. We might have been, for what we could tell, in the centre of an enemy's fleet. I made the remark to Mr. Randolph.

'Should such be the case, the mist will prove our best friend,' he answered. 'I only wish that it may continue till we get abreast of Plymouth; it may help us to run the gauntlet of our enemies.'

We glided steadily and swiftly on for about an hour or more after this, with everything set alow and aloft, and studden sails rigged out on either side, there being a light air from the westward.

Suddenly, I felt a puff of wind from the northward just fan my left cheek as I stood at the helm. Again it came, and I had to keep the ship away to prevent her being taken aback. We, however, got a pull at the lee braces, and again kept her on her course without taking in the studden sails; again the wind came from the nor'ard of west, and most reluctantly we had to take in all our studden sails, one after the other, and to brace the yards up on the larboard tack. Scarcely had we done so when the breeze increased still more.

I was looking to leeward trying to pierce the mist, when, as if by magic, a wide rent was made in it. Upward it lifted, rolling away rapidly on either side, and revealing in the space thus made clear, a long, low craft floating in the water, without a stitch of canvas set on her short stumps of masts. I pointed her out to Mr. Randolph.

'I am afraid that she is mischievous, sir,' said I. 'There's a wicked look about her which does not at all please me. She is more like a French privateer than any other craft I know of.'

'She is not a big one, at all events,' he answered. 'We ought to be able to tackle her, and our dummies may do us good service by keeping her at a respectful distance. However, she may be a Jersey or a Guernsey-man, they have many lugger privateers. What do you think, Andrews?'

'She may be a Jersey-man, but, to my mind, that craft was built and fitted out in France, whoever now owns her,' answered Andrews. 'Weatherhelm ought to know, he has served aboard some of them.'

'I am afraid she is French, sir,' said I, after I had taken a steady look at her. 'And whatever she is, there is up sail and after us. If the fellow has a quickish pair of heels, he'll very soon cut us off.'

While I was speaking, the square-headed sails of the lugger were run up on her short, stumpy masts. Above them quickly appeared their topsails, almost as big as the lower sails, and away she came bowling after us, at a rate which gave us not the slightest hope of escape, if she should prove an enemy, unless some bigger friend might appear to assist us.

Now we more than ever felt the desertion of the *Nautile*. Had she remained with us, we two together might have been able to give a very good account of so small an enemy,—indeed, we should probably not have been attacked. Our only resource was, however, to put as bold a face on the matter as we could. The Frenchmen had not yet come on deck, so Mr. Randolph ordered them to be kept down below that they might not make any signs to the enemy. He took the helm, and ordered us to stand to our guns. Each of us had a musket by our sides, and he ordered us first to let fly a volley, and then, without a moment's delay, to fire a broadside.

We hoped thus to prevent the enemy from discovering the smallness of our numbers, and we trusted that we might by chance knock away some of his spars and prevent him from following us. I could not help admiring the gallant way in which the little craft dashed on towards us. It looked as if we might have run over her, and sent her to the bottom without the slightest difficulty.

'Be ready, my men,' shouted Mr. Randolph, as she got within musket-shot of us. Leaving the helm, he sprang on the taffrail, and, cap in hand, waved the lugger off, pointing to his guns as if he was about to fire.

We had meantime hoisted the English ensign to our peak. The lugger paid not the slightest heed to his signals, but stood on edging up to us. Again he waved. A musket-ball came whizzing by and very nearly knocked him over. Had it been sent from a rifle his moments would have been numbered. I never saw a cooler or braver young man.

'Give it them, then, my lads, and with a will,' he shouted. 'They think, perhaps, we are not in earnest.'

We each of us took steady aim, and, as the men were exposed on the decks, we believed that we had knocked several of them over. Some of us had a couple of muskets, and as we fired one after the other as rapidly as we could, we hoped that we had given the enemy a respectful idea of our numbers. Mr. Randolph had three muskets, and as soon as he had fired them he began to reload, tending the wheel at the same time.

'Now give them a taste of the big guns!' he shouted out. With a shout we let fly our whole broadside, but the way in which of necessity we run the guns in again to reload might have betrayed us.

We bad hoped that after the hot reception we had given the lugger she would have sheered off, but not a bit of it. On she came as boldly as at first, and before we had time to run one of our guns out again she had come alongside, and hove her grappling-irons aboard us.

To hope to defend ourselves was useless, so retreating aft we rallied round Mr. Randolph, while we allowed the enemy, who swarmed in numbers up the side, to expend their rage on our dummies. They seemed highly amused at our trick, for loud shouts of laughter broke from them when they discovered the enemy to whom they had been opposed. As we made no further resistance, they did not attempt to injure us. Their officer came aft and put out his hand to Mr. Randolph.

'You are a brave young man,' said he, in very fair English. 'You have defended your ship nobly, and had I not before perfectly known the number of people you had on board, and your means of defence, you would have deceived me, and I should have sheered off.'

Mr. Randolph took the hand offered to him, and thanking the captain of the French privateer (for such he was) for the good opinion he entertained of him, inquired how he came to know anything about us.

'I took your consort, the *Nautile*, three days ago, and have ever since been on the look-out for you,' was the answer. 'They told me on board when to expect you, and how many you were in crew. When, therefore, I saw the figures you had dressed up, I watched them narrowly, and seeing that they did not move, suspected a trick. But what have you done with my countrymen? You have several as prisoners.'

Mr. Randolph assured him that they were safe, and that we had shut them up that they might be out of harm's way, and might not interfere with the defence of the ship.

Altogether, the French captain was so delighted with his success in capturing us and the rich prizes he had obtained (for we found that he had already taken several other vessels besides the *Nautile*), that he promised we might depend upon being treated with every courtesy. He then went below and released the other Frenchmen, who were so overjoyed at their escape from the English prison in which they expected in a few days to be lodged, that they rushed into the arms of their countrymen, and such a scene of hugging, and kissing, and shouting, and jabbering I never before beheld. We could not tell what they might say of us, and we were afraid that the tide which had been in our favour might turn, but they apparently gave a fair report of the way we had treated them, and our captors were as friendly as before.

No longer time than was necessary was lost. We Englishmen were transferred to the lugger, and a few more Frenchmen were sent on board the ship, and together we stood away before the wind for St. Malo, on the French coast.

I need not say that, independently of having to go to a French prison, how wretched I was at finding in a moment all the hopes I had entertained of once more returning home completely blasted. I could have sat down and wept bitterly, but tears would not come to my eyes. I thought my heart would indeed break.

Mr. Randolph had been invited into the captain's cabin, and was treated with every courtesy. Some of the men had gone forward, but I felt no inclination to leave the deck. I sat down on a gun-carriage, turning my eyes in the direction of the shore on which I had hoped so soon to land, and which now I might not visit for many a day. I cannot picture my wretchedness. I only hope that none of my readers may feel the same. I rested my head upon my hands in a vain endeavour to drive away thought. It was truly a dark moment of my existence.

I felt even as if I could not pray. I had sat thus for some time, when I felt a hand pressed on my shoulder.

'Willand, is it you—you indeed, lad?' said a voice, in a kindly tone which I felt I ought to know.

I looked up. Before me stood a fine, sailor-like looking fellow. I scanned his countenance narrowly, and then springing to my feet put out my hand. 'La Motte, my dear fellow, it is you yourself, I am sure of it!' I exclaimed. 'Where did you come from? How did you find yourself on board here?'

'I have been to, and come from, all parts of the world since we parted, and I'll tell you all about that another time,' he answered. 'And as to being on board here, I am a prisoner like yourself. The craft I belonged to, of which I was first mate, was captured two days ago and sent into St. Malo. I have no greater reason to be happy than you have. However, the Frenchmen treat us very civilly on board, and that is a satisfaction; we might have been much worse off.'

We might indeed, for very often the French privateers treated their prisoners with great cruelty, robbing them of their money and clothes, and half starving them. They were then sent on shore, and thrust into some wretched, dirty prison, where they were allowed to linger out their days till the end of the war. Such we had expected to be our fate.

The Frenchmen believed that the English did not treat their prisoners any better. They had a story written by one of their countrymen, a French officer, who had broken his parole and got back to France, to the effect that French prisoners were fed in England on horse-flesh and beans. He declared that on one occasion the inspecting officer of prisons rode into a court-yard of a prison, where he left his horse, and that as soon as he had disappeared, the famished prisoners set upon it, and tearing the horse to pieces, devoured it and the saddle

also; and that when the officer got back, he found only the stirrup-irons
and the bit in the horse's mouth.

Whatever we may think of the digestibility of the morsels carried off
by the hungry prisoners, the tale seems to have been eagerly swallowed
by the countrymen of the narrator.

La Motte endeavoured to cheer me up, by talking of old times and
of our adventures in the Mediterranean and elsewhere,—indeed, I felt
his presence a very great comfort. He was of a most cheerful, happy
disposition, and allowed nothing to put him out.

'I was on my way home from the West Indies in a fine brig, the *Ann*,
and I had a little venture on board of my own, with which I hoped
to make a good addition to my fortune, and perhaps, before long, to
settle down and marry. Well, it's all gone; but what's the use of
sighing? What has happened to me has happened to a thousand other
better men much less able to bear it. So I say to myself, "Better luck
next time." I never can abide those people who sigh, and moan, and
groan if any mishap overtakes them, as if they were the only unfortunate people in the world. To everybody they meet they tell their
woes, as if nothing else was of so much consequence. You are not one
of those, Weatherhelm, I know, nor am I. Everything comes right in
the mill at last, if we will but wait patiently till the mill turns round.'

La Motte rattled on in this way till he talked me into better spirits
again. At all events, he prevented me from dwelling on my misfortunes.

'Now, in reality, we ought to consider ourselves very fortunate,' he
continued. 'We might have been captured by a set of ruffianly fellows,
who would have robbed us and ill-treated us in every way. Instead of
that, the crew are the best sort of privateer's men I ever fell in with.
The captain and first mate are very good, kind-hearted men. They have
both of them been made prisoners themselves, and have spent a year or
more in England. They tell me that they love the English, for that

they were treated with the greatest kindness all the time they were in England, and that they wish to repay that kindness, though I must say they take an odd way to show their love by fitting out a vessel to go and rob them on the high seas; but I suppose that is their profession, and they cannot help it.'

While La Motte was speaking, a fine-looking man came up, and, taking him by the arm, addressed him as his *bon ami*, and told him that dinner was ready.

La Motte thanked him, and then told him that I was an old shipmate, and hoped that he would extend the same kindness to me that he had done to him.

My new friend was, I found, the mate of the privateer. He said certainly, and begged that I would at once come down and join them at dinner. At first I was inclined to refuse, as I thought Mr. Randolph would consider me presuming if I was to go and sit down at table with him; but La Motte, finding that he was a sensible, good-natured young officer, undertook to explain matters to him.

We found Mr. Randolph and the captain already seated at the table. La Motte, in a few words, explained that I was an old friend and shipmate of his, and that if I was not, I ought to be an officer, and hoped that he would not be offended.

Mr. Randolph laughed, and said certainly not, and I soon felt at my ease.

The Frenchmen were in high glee at the number of prizes they had taken, and, as they had a fair wind, they fully expected in a couple of days, at furthest, to be safe within the harbour of St. Malo. I knew from sad experience that there is many a slip between the cup and the lip, and I hoped that we might yet, before we reached the looked-for harbour, fall in with a man-of-war or a bigger privateer and be recaptured; of course I did not give expression to my wishes, but on such a chance my only hope rested of reaching home.

After dinner I went on deck again, and continued pacing up and down, anxiously scanning the horizon in the hope of discovering some sail coming in pursuit of us. Though I was aware that my presence on deck could not in any way bring about this result, still I could not tear myself away again till night closed down upon us.

La Motte then insisted on my coming below. 'I told the Frenchmen something of your story,' said he; 'if I had not done so, they would have thought you discourteous, and your conduct somewhat strange. However, they now enter into your feelings and pity you heartily.'

'I am indeed obliged to you, La Motte,' said I. 'But somehow or other I do not like to have myself talked about. My feelings appear to me to be too sacred to be mentioned except to a friend.'

'That is very natural and right,' he answered. 'But, believe me, Weatherhelm, I did what was for the best, and I am certain you will benefit by it.'

At last I turned in for the night, and, wearied out with anxiety, fell asleep. I was conscious that I was on board the privateer, but I dreamed that we were chased and overtaken by a ship of war, and that just as her boat was boarding us we blew up. Then I found myself, with many of my companions, floating about in the water, without any ship in sight or means of escape.

At length I awoke, and the recollection of all that had occurred came pressing down on my heart like a heavy weight. Feeling that the cool, fresh air might revive me, I dressed and went on deck. It was bitterly cold, with a sharp northerly breeze blowing, the sky was of one uniform grey, while the water, which rose and fell without breaking, was of a dull leaden hue.

No prospect could have been more cheerless and uninviting. The

Mouche, under all sail, was bowling on ahead, (I suspected that the French crew would have no little difficulty in keeping her afloat) while the lugger was acting the part of a whipper-in. I cast my eyes round the horizon. Away to the eastward they encountered a sail just rising above the water. I watched her for some time, till I was convinced that she was a large ship, and standing towards us.

At length she attracted the attention of the second mate, who was the officer of the watch. He began to eye her somewhat anxiously, and in a short time he sent down and called up the first mate. They looked at their own sails, and then at the stranger, and then at the *Mouche*, as if consulting what was to be done, and then finally called up the captain. They evidently could not at all satisfy themselves as to the character of the approaching ship.

I anxiously scanned their countenances; as I observed them falling, so my own hopes rose, that the sail in sight might prove an English ship of war. I tried in vain to conceal my own anxiety by walking up and down the deck, as I had done the day before.

The French officers seemed at length to have decided on some plan which satisfied them. The *Mouche* had already made all the sail she could carry; she had royals set and studden sails out on either side, while the lugger followed, under her ordinary canvas, in her wake. While I was walking up and down, the first mate joined me.

'Ah, my friend!' said he, in very good English, 'you hope the vessel in sight is a countryman. That is very natural. We hope that if she is, we shall escape her. We intend to do our best to get away, be assured of that. If, however, we are taken, you will remember that all Frenchmen are not savages, and that we were kind to you when you were our prisoners.'

'Indeed we all shall,' I replied. 'I hope, indeed, whenever Frenchmen fall into the hands of the English, that my countrymen will always treat them with kindness and consideration.'

'That is good; that is the right thing,' said the mate. 'If go to war we must, we need not make it more barbarous than it must be of necessity.'

I was surprised to find these expressions proceeding from the mouth of a privateer's man. However, I believe that there were not many people of his class like him. I certainly hoped that I might have an opportunity of showing him that I meant what I said, and that we should very soon again change our relative positions.

Mr. Randolph, and La Motte, and the rest of the English prisoners, soon afterwards came on deck, and eagerly watched with me the progress of the stranger. There seemed to us very little doubt that she would cut us off before we could possibly reach St. Malo.

As the day drew on, however, the weather gave signs of changing. The wind, which had been blowing steadily from the northward, chopped round to the north-west, and then to the westward, growing stronger and stronger, and very quickly kicking up an ugly sea, while thick rain began to fall, increasing every instant in density.

We Englishmen looked at each other, and as the rain fell thicker, so did our countenances fall lower and lower. The change of wind placed the lugger and her prize to windward, and the stranger far away to leeward, the thick rain almost shutting her out from sight.

The Frenchmen rubbed their hands, and blessed the wind and the rain, and commiserated us on our prospects of being carried to France. All we could hope was, that it would clear up again before the evening, and that the wind would shift back into its old quarter.

We waited in vain for the change. Hour after hour passed by. The wind blew great guns and small arms, and the rain came down in dense masses, which completely shut out the stranger from our sight. I thought that probably the Frenchmen would alter their course, but we stood steadily on, only keeping up a little to be well to windward of our port, in case the wind should veer round more to the north-west. Evening at length came. It grew darker and darker; and with heavy hearts we prisoners had to abandon all hopes of rescue.

The night passed away, while it was blowing and raining all the time till near the morning. As soon as it was daylight I hurried on deck. The horizon was clear. With what eagerness I looked around; not a sail was in sight! The English ship, if such she was, finding herself so far to leeward, had probably abandoned all hope of overtaking us.

At length the coast of France hove in sight. We looked at it as likely to prove our home for many a weary day. It was past noon when we anchored in the harbour of St. Malo, and I could not be surprised at the exultation of the Frenchmen, when they found themselves surrounded by no less than five prizes, which they had taken in the course of two or three weeks.

Their friends in numbers came off to welcome them, and brought all sorts of wines and spirits, and provisions from the shore, far more indeed than the crew could by possibility consume. The wine and spirits, however, seemed to be most welcome, and the crew, having an abundance of wherewithal to carouse, sat down to make themselves happy. Never have I heard a set of human beings jabber away at the rate they did; they laughed, and sang, and pledged each other without cessation.

La Motte, who was listening to them, told me that they were boasting of all the deeds they had done, or would do, or had heard of being done, till they were satisfied that their nation was not only the greatest, the richest, the wisest, the most happy in the world, but that none ever had or would come up to her.

Just before dark, the captain took Mr. Randolph on shore; but he observed that he could not take us there, and that we must wait on board till the following morning.

The first mate came up to La Motte and me, and observed that he should have to go on shore likewise. 'If you go, remember that you will have to be shut up in a prison, and that you will not find very pleasant,' he remarked significantly. He looked aft as he spoke, when we observed hanging on at the stern one of the boats belonging to the prize. 'Wise men know how to take a hint. All I can say is, that I feel most kindly disposed towards you; and if you land in France, I will do my best to ameliorate your condition, but that will be but little, remember.'

We thanked him cordially for his kindness, and then he called the only two sober men of the crew, and ordered them to pull him on shore in another boat. Of course there was not the slightest doubt as to what he meant. The means of escape were offered us. The only question remaining was how to make use of them. The boat hanging on astern was about 25 feet long. I had often examined her on board the *Mouche*. She was in good condition, and not a bad sea-boat, I judged from her appearance. Her sails and oars were in her, and I had little doubt that our good friend the mate had had them put into her on purpose to aid us. Thus far, all was well, but we had many difficulties still to contend with. Our next care was to ascertain who would accompany us in our adventure.

There were altogether fifteen prisoners remaining on board besides ourselves. I knew that I could depend on Andrews, and so I could on Jones. They both eagerly jumped at our proposal, and expressed themselves ready to run all risks for the sake of reaching England. Their only regret was, that Mr. Randolph was not on board to accompany us. We concluded that the captain had been compelled to take him on shore, as English officers were always looked on as great prizes by the French, and he might have got into trouble had he escaped.

We went quietly round among all the prisoners, and invited them one by one to join us, with the exception of three or four, who had accepted the invitations of the Frenchmen to drink with them, and had now as little sense remaining in their heads as their hosts.

When La Motte and I went up to them to see what could be done, they could only exclaim, holding up their glasses, 'Come here, old fellows! The Frenchmen's liquor is good, and they are jolly cocks, and we never wish for better companions. Come now, take a glass, you'll not taste finer anywhere.'

When we declined joining them, they jeered and laughed at us, and called us milksops, so that we soon saw that they would in all probability betray us if we attempted to induce them to join us.

Two men, who were sober, declined, saying that they would rather go to a French prison than trust themselves in a small open boat in mid-winter in the Channel. As they were somewhat sickly, perhaps they were right in their decision. They promised, however, to help us as far as they were able, and vowed that they would rather die than betray us.

The carouse of the Frenchmen continued. First, they made long speeches about liberty, equality, and fraternity, and then they sang till they were hoarse, and then they began hugging each other and shrieking, and lastly, they got up and danced and skipped and frisked about, till tripping up their heels they toppled down on deck, and lay sprawling about unable to move. Now and then one tried to rise, but all he could do was to reach a bottle, and to pour a little more liquor down his throat, which soon finished him off completely, and he, like the rest, lay utterly senseless and inanimate.

It was now night, and time to make our preparations. The priva-

18

teer's-men's friends had brought on board a large supply of provisions. These we set to work to collect, and we calculated that we should have enough to last us for several days. But without water we could not venture to sea. There was none on deck, so we had to grope about below to find it. Great indeed was our satisfaction, therefore, when we suddenly came upon two breakers, each holding nine or ten gallons, and full of water. We soon had them up on deck, and rolled them to the side, ready to be lowered into the boat. We now hauled her up alongside, and got everything we had collected stowed away in her.

'But we must not go without a compass,' said La Motte, 'I remember seeing one in the captain's cabin. I am sure that he would let us have it. Perhaps he has left it out on purpose.'

Such we had every reason to believe was the case, for in a minute La Motte returned bringing a well-fitted boat compass, which was just suited for our purpose. We also got hold of a lantern and a quantity of candles, and we threw as many greatcoats and blankets into the boat as we could collect, for it was bitterly cold, and we had reason to dread its effects more than anything else.

We should have started at once, but La Motte told us that he had overheard some of the Frenchmen talking of a guard-boat which came round the harbour once, at all events, during the night, somewhere about ten o'clock, and that it would be wiser in us to wait till she had gone by. Accordingly we veered our boat astern, and agreed to wait till then.

We all went below and lay down, hoping to get a little sleep and rest before it was time to start. La Motte volunteered to remain on deck till the guard-boat came round, and as he spoke French like a Frenchman, he said that he should lead the officers to suppose that all the prisoners had gone on shore, and that might prevent them from keeping any strict watch on the lugger. He told me also that he was very anxious on another account. He had observed a fort which we should have to pass close by on our starboard-hand on going out. The sentry was certain to hail us, and unless we could give the password and countersign, he would, as in duty bound, fire at us, and then give notice of our escape. In all probability, boats would be sent in pursuit of us, and we should be recaptured. This suggestion came like a blow, sufficient to upset all our hopes of escaping.

'Well,' observed La Motte, 'there is only one thing to be done. I must find out the watchword and countersign. There is some risk, but it must be run.'

There was a small boat, a dinghy, belonging to the lugger, which was sometimes carried aft, but she was now placed inside the long-boat on deck. She was so light that two men could easily lift her. La Motte said he must have her in the water, and that he would go on shore and steal up to where any sentinels were stationed, and that he would listen when the patrols came round to relieve them. He should thus be certain to obtain the information he required. Dangerous as I thought the adventure, of course I would not hinder him from going, as, could I have spoken French, I would have gone myself. Accordingly I helped him to get the dinghy into the water, which we did without any noise.

'Now, Weatherhelm, my dear fellow,' said he, 'go and lie down and wait patiently till I come back; a little sleep will do you good—you want it.'

'I thanked him cordially, and wrung his hand as he stepped into the punt, for my heart misgave me that I should never see him again. As to going to sleep, that was, I felt, out of the question; I could scarcely bring myself to lie down. I watched the little boat with intense anxiety as he pulled away towards the shore. I felt much for him, but I must confess that for my own sake I was still more anxious for his success

I was indeed enduring a bitter trial. May none of those who read my history have to go through the same! The thought of being a second time disappointed in my hopes of returning home, and of learning the fate of my beloved wife, was more than I could bear. My movements showed the agitation of my mind. Sometimes I sat down on a gun; then I rose and walked the deck; then I went below and threw myself on a locker in the cabin; but I was quickly on deck again looking out for La Motte. Then I recollected that he was not at all likely to return so soon, so I once more went below to try and warm my chilled limbs.

Another fear assailed me. I was afraid that if we delayed, some of the drunken Frenchmen might recover from their stupor and find out our project. All of a sudden another idea occurred to me,—if we got the watchword, could we not carry the lugger and all her senseless crew away together? We might handcuff them all without the slightest difficulty. I own that for the moment I forgot how ungrateful such an act would be to her captain and mate, who had treated us so kindly. While I was thinking on the subject, Andrews woke up and looked about him.

'Is it time yet for us to be off?' he asked, in a whisper.

'No, not yet. But I say, Andrews, are you ready to carry a bold project into execution?' I asked in a low voice. I then told him what I had thought of. He jumped at the idea.

'With all my heart!' he answered. 'Nothing I should like better. I hate these Frenchmen, and as for the drunken rascals on board, we can soon settle them; if they are likely to be troublesome, as soon as we get clear of the harbour, we may heave them all overboard.'

'What are you thinking about?' I exclaimed, horrified at the cold-blooded way in which he spoke of murdering so many of our fellow-creatures. Suddenly, the proposal I had made burst on me in its true light. Of what black ingratitude should we have been guilty in depriving the men who had trusted us, of their property; and then, had we followed the suggestion offered by Andrews, of destroying in cold blood a number of our fellow-men, who at all events had committed no crime against us!

'No, Andrews, no!' I answered, after a little reflection; 'I would rather remain a prisoner than run away with the lugger, even if we could accomplish the undertaking; much less would I injure any of the poor fellows remaining on board. Just consider, what should we say if a set of Frenchmen treated us in that way?'

'Anything is lawful in war,' he answered, not agreeing with my notion. 'The Frenchmen should have kept a better look-out after us.'

'You forget that the captain and mate left us intentionally with the means of escape at our disposal, and which they clearly pointed out to us. I am sorry that I even thought of carrying off the lugger, and much more that I mentioned it to you.'

At length I brought Andrews round to see the proposal in the light I did, and he promised not to mention it to any one else. Thus conversing, the time passed by much more rapidly than it had done when I was left to my own thoughts. I felt sure it must be getting late. I looked at my watch; it was nearly ten o'clock, the hour at which La Motte had told me the guard-boat made her rounds. I became very anxious about him; I felt almost sure that he must have been seized, and if so he ran a great risk of being considered a spy, in which case he would have been immediately shot. We, however, could do nothing; we must sit still and wait. There is no greater trial for men than this. If we had had any work to do, we could have borne it much better. It wanted but ten minutes to ten.

'Some accident must have befallen your old shipmate,' said Andrews; 'if he does not come back, we must make the attempt without him. I

marked well the entrance of the harbour. If we muffle our oars, and
keep close under the fort, we may slip out without being observed.
Are you inclined to make the attempt?'

'Certainly,' I answered; 'I would run any risk to be free. Ah!
what is that? I saw something moving on the water. It is the guard-
boat coming. What shall we reply?'

'We had better slip down below, and let them hail us till they are
hoarse,' replied Andrews. 'But no; that is not the guard-boat; it
is the dinghy.'

In another instant La Motte was alongside. He sprang on board.
'I have it!' he exclaimed; 'but I have had a sharp run for it, and was
very nearly taken. Even now I am not certain that I am not pursued.
I have been thinking of an explanation to give for being on shore, if
I am found out. I must pass for a Frenchman belonging to the lugger.
Do you two go below, and pretend to be drunk, or asleep, like the rest.
There will be no fear then. I will call you as soon as the guard-
boat has gone away. We must all then be ready to start in a moment.'

Andrews and I immediately followed La Motte's directions, and
going below threw ourselves on the lockers. I heard La Motte's
measured tread overhead, as if he was walking the deck as officer of the
watch. I listened for every sound. Presently I heard him reply in a
clear, sharp voice, apparently to a hail given from a boat at a little
distance. There could be no doubt that it was the guard-boat. The
answer satisfied the officers. Another minute elapsed, and La Motte
sprang down below. 'It is all right, Weatherhelm,' he whispered;
'the guard-boat is away, and now is our time to be off. Call up the
other men.'

It was quickly done, and all those who had resolved to venture on the
undertaking were speedily on deck. We hauled up the boat, and
silently took our seats on the thwarts. I pulled the after oar; La

Motte steered and acted as captain; indeed, had it not been for him, we could not have made the attempt. It was a hazardous affair, for we might have to encounter another guard-boat, and we had to pass among a number of vessels on our way to the mouth of the harbour.

'If we are seen, I hope that we may be mistaken for the guard-boat,' said La Motte, as we were preparing to shove off. 'Now, my lads, shove off, and try and row as much like Frenchmen as you can.'

The advice was not unnecessary, for the steady, measured pull of English men-of-war's men would have inevitably betrayed us. The night was dark, but not sufficiently so to prevent us from distinguishing the outline of the harbour. Away we pulled, rapidly but with irregular strokes. We had to pass close to several privateers, but their crews were either on shore or drunk, and no notice was taken of us.

More than once it occurred to me, that although we should not have wished to run off with the vessel of the people who had treated us so well, yet that we might be able successfully to cut out one of the other craft brought up nearer the mouth of the harbour; but I reflected that the experiment would be too hazardous. Should we fail, we should in all probability lose our lives; as it was, we might well be contented with the advantages we possessed. We had a good boat, though she was small, an ample supply of provisions, fine weather, and a fair wind from the southward.

We were about half-way down the harbour, when the sound of oars reached our ears. A large ship was near us; we paddled softly in, and lay close alongside under the shelter of her dark shadow. Not a sound was heard aboard her; every one was asleep. The noise of oars drew near; I trembled, lest some of her crew might be returning on board, and if they discovered us, all would be lost. We listened breathlessly; the sound of the oars passed by; it was the guard-boat going her rounds. Had we continued pulling a minute longer, we should have been discovered. I looked up as we lay on our oars; the sky was clear the stars were twinkling brightly overhead; there seemed every probability of the fine weather continuing. In a couple of days at most we might hope once more to tread our native shores, and be free to go where we might wish.

I need scarcely repeat all the anxious thoughts which crowded on my mind; the joy, the happiness unspeakable I anticipated. I would not, I dared not, dwell on the reverse. The sound of the oars was lost in the distance. La Motte gave a sign to us to shove off, and letting our oars glide into the water, we again continued our course. Our hearts beat quick as we approached the fort. The sharp tones of the sentry's challenge rung on our ears as he saw us passing. 'Liberté!' answered La Motte promptly; another question was asked. 'Victoire!' he replied. 'We are ordered out by the captain of the port with a despatch to a vessel in the offing, I know no more.'

'*C'est bien!* you may pass,' said an officer, whom the sentry's voice had summoned from the guard-room.

We pulled on as before; away we glided; now we hoisted our sail. Gradually the fort was concealed by the darkness from our sight. We were free:

CHAPTER XIV.

Happy prospect of reaching England—Weather changes—Heavy gale—Expect to be lost—Days and nights of suffering—Our greatest comfort—A ship in sight—Disappointed again—Another ship appears—Our hopes and fears—A snow-storm —Get on board an emigrant ship—Carried far away from home—Death of ship-mates.

ONCE clear of the harbour, without any sail in sight, we all gladly loosened our tongues. In spite of the cold of a winter's night, our spirits rose, and all hands laughed and chatted, and talked of what they would do when they got on shore. We had no necessity to look at our compass, for the stars enabled us to steer a course for the northward.

With the wind as it was, we thought that we should probably make the land somewhere about the Dorsetshire coast, should we not in the meantime fall in with any homeward-bound ship.

From the position of St. Malo on the coast of France, far down in the deep bay or bight in which is found the islands of Jersey and Guernsey, it will be seen that we had a long voyage before us to perform in an open boat of so small a size and in the middle of winter. However, not one of us thought about that. By daylight we had made such progress that we were completely out of sight of land. A difference of opinion now arose among us. La Motte very naturally wished to put into Guernsey. It was his own country; he knew it well, and he undertook to pilot us in there. Most of the men were anxious, as the breeze was fair, to stand on at once for the coast of England.

'Now, mates,' said he, 'just listen to what I have to say. If the wind continues fair, and we do not fall in with an enemy's cruiser, all well and good, we may hit some harbour, or we may beach the boat with safety, and get on shore; but now just look at the other side of the question. We may be picked up by an enemy, and as we are in a French boat with the name of her port on her stern, we shall be sent back from whence we have come, and be much worse off than if we had remained aboard the lugger. That's one thing which may occur; or the wind may change, and a gale spring up, and instead of making the English coast in a couple or three days, as you expect, we may be swamped, or be knocked about for a week or ten days, and perhaps after all be driven back on to the coast of France. Now, what I say is this? Here is Guernsey on our starboard bow. We may be there by to-morrow morning at farthest. I've friends who'll treat you kindly. You'd have time to look about you, and you'll have no fear of being pressed; whereas if you land in England, after all, before you get to your homes you may find yourselves in the hands of a pressgang, and once more aboard a man-of-war.'

I thought that there was so much reason in what La Motte urged, that, anxious as I was to be in England, I could not help siding with him. All the rest of the men were, however, dead against us. They had talked so much of the delights of being on shore, that, in spite of all risks, they were unwilling that any delay should occur.

'No, no; hurrah for Old England!' they cried. 'As long as the breeze holds, let us stand on. We are not likely to fall in with an enemy. If we see a stranger which looks suspicious, we'll douse sail, and let her pass by. The weather, too, promises to be fine. Why think of evils which may never occur?'

Perhaps La Motte and I did not resist as much as we might have done. At all events, we yielded to the wishes of the rest, and stood on

The day passed away pleasantly enough. The sun came out and shone brightly, and for the time of the year it was tolerably warm; so that we all kept our spirits up, and, congratulating ourselves on our good fortune, did not think of coming disaster.

As is usual on such occasions, we soon got to telling the various adventures we had met with in our past lives. I have not here time to describe them, but I remember one remarkable thing was, that nearly all had been wrecked just as often as I had. Instead of looking at such disasters as punishments, they all agreed that they ought to consider themselves very fortunate in escaping, instead of losing their lives, as had so many of their shipmates. I could not help thinking the same thing, and I now began to be more convinced than ever that I was mistaken in my youthful idea that a curse hung over me. When I came to consider the matter, I perceived that I had brought on myself nearly all the misfortunes which had happened to me, or they could be very clearly traced to ordinary causes, which had affected in most instances others as well as myself. I talked the subject over with La Motte, who was a right-thinking man, and not without some wit.

'I perfectly agree with you, Weatherhelm,' said he. 'It is, in my opinion, far better to be wrecked a dozen times than drowned once, especially if you escape the twelfth time, and live happy ever afterwards. I hope sincerely that your disasters have now come to an end. You seem to have suffered a good many since we parted.'

'I have enjoyed some very great blessings, too,' I answered. 'I am sure I ought not to complain.'

'That is just the sentiment I like to hear,' he observed. 'People think that they are to have all the plums and suet, and none of the hard dough, which makes up the pudding of life. We ought to be contented to take the two together—the sweets and the bitter, the rough and the smooth. That is what I have done, and I have saved myself a great deal of disappointment by not expecting more than I was likely to get.'

I have often thought since of La Motte's practical philosophy.

We had every one of us soon need of all the courage and resignation we possessed. The wind, which had been steady all the day, began towards the afternoon to chop about. First it flew round to the north-east, and blew pretty hard, and we none of us liked the look of the weather. Still we hoped that it might not grow worse. We took a reef in the mainsail, and brought the boat close up to the wind.

Before long, however, it came on to blow still harder, and the sea got up very much, and the spray came flying over us, and now and then a sea broke on board, and we had to keep a couple of hands baling to prevent the boat from filling. Night was coming on : we close-reefed the mainsail, and took a reef in the foresail, and continued our course close-hauled. By degrees the wind shifted round to the north-north-east, and though close-hauled as we lay, we were fully four points off our course, and if it held on that way, it seemed a chance even if we should fetch the coast of Cornwall. Night was coming on, but there was no improvement in the weather.

Having taken a cheerless supper, for our spirits had sunk very low, we sat still in our places without speaking. The rain came down on us and wetted us through and chilled us to the bones, and the weather grew thicker and thicker. Sometimes we could scarcely see a yard ahead, and we ran a great risk of being run down by a vessel, or of running into one. Still we could do nothing further to help our-selves.

Away we flew into the pitchy darkness, the seas hissing and roaring around us, the boat tumbling and tossing about, now in the trough of a sea, now on the summit, surrounded by dense masses of foam, which seemed at times completely to wrap us up—the wind howling, and the rain coming down in torrents, sufficient of itself to swamp the boat.

Either La Motte or Andrews or I sat at the helm, and very nice steering it required to keep the boat from swamping. We lighted the binnacle lamp to enable us to keep as near as we could to our proper course. We had also our lantern ready to show as a signal in case we were able to make out any vessel approaching us.

I had been in many perils, as I have described, but none of them seemed greater than those I went through on that night. Often I thought that the boat could not possibly swim another minute. Often she was almost gunwale under before we could luff up in time to ease her. Now a huge black sea came roaring up, which I thought must come down and swamp us; but it broke just before it reached the boat and merely sent the foam flying over our heads. Thus hour after hour passed slowly away. Some of the men began to grumble, and to blame themselves for their folly in leaving the privateer.

Andrews declared that it would have been better if we had cut out a vessel, as at all events we should have been on board a craft fit to combat the gale. La Motte, with more justice, remarked, that it was a pity they had not consented to follow his suggestion, and to run for Guernsey while we could have done so.

'But why not run there now?' asked some one.

'Because the whole island is surrounded by rocks, and it would be next to a miracle if we escaped running on them,' he answered. 'Our only course now is to stand on. Perhaps the wind will once more shift, and we may be able, after all, to keep our course for England.'

Never have I felt the hours draw on so slowly as they did during that dreadful night. Still no new hour brought any change for the better. I thought the morning never would come. As for sleep, that was out of the question, nor did any of us feel an inclination for food. I believe that not one of the party ever expected to see the sun rise again to cheer our hearts.

Yet, in spite of our apprehensions, the little boat behaved beautifully. Each sea, as it came roaring up, she surmounted like a wild fowl, and though down she plunged into the trough, it was but to rise again in triumph to the summit.

At length the rain ceased, but it blew as hard as ever. I was looking eastward, when a pale, thin line appeared in the sky, just above the horizon. It grew broader and broader, and brighter and brighter, and we know it was dawn. Those who had thought that they should never again see the sun rise, now felt that they ought not to have desponded. First, more cold, silvery lines appeared in the sky, and then yellow lines, which warmed into orange, and pink, and red; and a small portion of the sun himself broke forth between the clouds, and sent a bright beam of glittering gold across the dancing waves, but quickly again he was hidden above the leaden canopy which hung over us.

Few of us had ever passed a more trying night, and we all felt grateful for the mercy which had been shown us, and, as if by common agreement, we all with one accord offered up our thanks to Heaven, and prayed that we might yet further be preserved through the dangers which surrounded us. Wild and careless as sailors too often are, there are times when they exhibit a true and unaffected piety, and when they are not ashamed of exhibiting their feelings to their fellow-men. This was one of those occasions.

We were all aware that we had passed through a night of great peril, and we knew that we had, in all probability, many more dangers to go through, in which all our knowledge, and strength, and bravery could avail us nothing. Our weakness and helplessness was thus forcibly brought home to us—our own utter insufficiency to help ourselves. It is this feeling, which every seaman must at times have to experience, which has so beneficial an effect on him in turning his heart to God, in making him, in spite of himself, acknowledge the super-intending care of the Creator.

As daylight came on, we looked round the horizon, more especially to the southward, but not a sail was in sight. We felt sure that, at all events, we were not pursued. Had the wind continued from the south-ward, we might have fallen in with some homeward-bound ship, but it was not likely that we should now meet with one. Having assured ourselves that no change was likely to take place immediately in our prospects, we served out our frugal breakfast.

La Motte and I agreed that it would be wiser at once to put ourselves on short allowance, for we could not tell how long we might be kept out. To this all the rest cheerfully assented. I had for some time been watching the sky to the eastward. When the sun rose, the wind went down, but I did not like a wide break in the clouds which suddenly appeared. The rent I had observed grew larger and larger, till the whole eastern sky was bright and clear. I felt too sure that it be-tokened an easterly gale. I pointed out what I had observed to La Motte. He was of my opinion.

We were not mistaken. Down it came before long, strong and bitterly cold, tearing up the surface of the sea, and sending the foam flying like vast snowdrifts before it. We were almost frozen with the cold and wet. We wrapped ourselves up as best we could in our blankets and greatcoats, but even with this aid we were well-nigh perished. We had no means of lighting a fire and warming up any-thing by which we might restore circulation. The gale increased. Away the boat flew before it, out to sea, away from land, away from all help.

Bitter was our disappointment. How could we hope to get back? how obtain relief? Our condition was bad indeed. Some of the men

had been expressing a wish to endeavour to reach Guernsey. They
now, with reproaches on themselves, acknowledged their folly in not
having, when at the proper time, accepted La Motte's offer to take
them there. Fiercer and fiercer blew the easterly gale, every cloud
disappeared, but yet the sky was not bright, nor did the rays of the
sun give any warmth. A gauze-like veil overspread the sky, while we
were surrounded by a thin mist of spray, which together completely
prevented the sun's beams from reaching us.

Our utmost exertions were required to keep the boat before the sea,
and to bale out the water which continually washed into her. Those of
us who were not thus actively employed sat with our greatcoats and
blankets huddled up round us, the pictures of misery. Want of sleep
and warm food made us feel the cold still more severely, and, in spite
of our wraps, we were chilled to the very bones. Our teeth chattered
and our limbs shook as if we had been afflicted with the ague. We
could no longer keep up our spirits by conversation. What possible
grounds had we for hope. All we could expect was to run on till the
boat was swamped, or till one after the other of us dropped off and died
from cold, starvation, and exhaustion.

La Motte struggled on bravely to prevent himself from giving in,
while at the same time he exerted himself to keep up the spirits of the
rest. His example inspired me to arouse myself, and I endeavoured to
aid him in encouraging our companions.

'Hurrah, my lads!' he suddenly shouted. 'As long as there's life
there's hope—remember that. Death's door is not open yet. Don't be
knocking to get in before you are invited. What are we afraid of?
We have a tight boat under us, and provisions enough to last us for
several days to come. We had got a long way to the nor'ard before
this easterly gale sprung up, and we can't be so very far off the Land's
End or the Scilly Islands. This sort of gale never lasts long. It will

blow itself out in a day or two, and then we may haul up and stand in for the land. Many men have been in a far worse state than that we are in, and have got well out of it. Why should we fancy that we are going to be lost? Cheer up, I say. Can any of you sing? Andrews, you can. Come, out with a song, lad. You shake your head. Come, I'll help you.' And, with a voice which sounded full and clear amid the hissing roar of the gale, La Motte struck up a cheering, merry song, well calculated to arouse even the most apathetic from the lethargy into which they were sinking.

Andrews, inspired by the strains, followed his example, as did several other of the men, and away we flew over the waves, singing cheerfully, with, as it were, the jaws of death gaping wide on either side to catch us.

Now La Motte sang a more solemn strain; it was a psalm. All of us joined heartily in it. We prayed that God would protect us amid the dangers which surrounded us, and then we expressed our full confidence in His mercy and goodness. That did us more good than the lighter songs. It was certainly more in accordance with our feelings; yet, perhaps, La Motte took the best means for arousing the people from the lethargy which was overpowering them.

It has often struck me that people, when they are singing psalms, are too apt to forget that they are praying, or praising God, or returning thanks for mercies received. They seem to forget the meaning of the words, and to think only of the music. They do not sing sufficiently with their hearts. That was not the case with us in that storm-driven boat. The music was, I daresay, very imperfect, but never did men enter more heartily into the spirit of the psalm than did we on that occasion.

Andrews and another man belonged to Cornwall, and had in their youth been accustomed to sing psalms in the congregations of their

19

people, as had two or three of the other men, though for many a long
year of their sea life the custom had been sadly neglected. Now, when
they felt conscious that they might never have an opportunity of again
singing while alive, they joined with their whole heart and soul in the
work. Thus the day passed away.

The night was approaching. We had reason to dread it as much as
we had the previous one, except that the sky being clear, there was more
light to enable us to avoid any danger in our course. We took a frugal
supper and a cup of cold water, all we dared consume of our scanty
stores. Drowsiness now began to overcome most of us. I felt myself
capable of keeping awake better than any of the rest, for I saw that
even La Motte was giving way. I therefore urged him to let me take
the helm while he lay down. To this he consented. Andrews and I
wrapped him up in a blanket, and in an instant he was fast asleep
showing how much self-command he must have exercised to keep awake
at his post.

In the meantime, while two men continued baling and one kept a
look-out ahead, the rest stretched their limbs as well as they could along
the thwarts of the boat and went to sleep. My fear was that they
might not be able again to arouse themselves. Strange, indeed, were my
feelings as I sat in the stern of the boat while she flew hissing along over
the foaming waves and plunging into the dark unknown. I looked up
into the clear sky, glittering with innumerable stars, and my mind
wandered from the present world to the wonders of eternity, which the
scene I gazed on seemed to picture forth. I forcibly felt the insufficiency of this world to satisfy to the full the aspirations of man's
soul; and the reality of the life to come, and all that that life will have to
show, impressed itself more vividly on my mind than it had ever before
done. The glories of the eternal future put to flight all fears for the
present perishable body.

Still, I did not neglect my duty to my companions. I did my best to keep my mates of the watch awake. I watched the seas as they came rolling up on either side, so that I might keep the boat steadily before the wind. Thus the first watch passed by. I had not the heart to call La Motte. I told the other three men to arouse up their companions, and I resolved to keep awake for a couple of hours more. An hour after this it might have been, as I turned my head over my right shoulder, I caught sight of a huge towering mass close aboard, as it seemed.

It was a large ship. On she came. I felt sure that our last moments had arrived. There was no use shouting. The other men looked up. Terror kept them dumb. Had we indeed strained our voices till they cracked, no one would have heard us on board the ship. The dark pyramid of canvas seemed to reach up to the very clouds as she flew along, careering before the gale.

In another moment I thought we should have been run down, and struggling under her vast keel, but my eye had deceived me. She dashed on; but instead of her stem striking us, her broadside appeared on our starboard hand. She was a line-of-battle ship of the largest class. Then, indeed, we found our voices and shouted, and perhaps the sentries or look-outs might have heard us; but away she rushed, like some monstrous phantom of a dream, and, mighty as she was, she quickly disappeared in the darkness ahead. Our companions, who had been awoke by our shouting, lifted up their heads, but as the ship passed by, lay them down again, probably under the belief that what they had seen was merely the effect of their imagination.

La Motte remained awake. 'What is the hour?' he asked. I told him. He therefore insisted on my taking his place, though I saw that he had some difficulty in unbending his limbs from the position they had assumed while he was sleeping. In an instant I was asleep. It was daylight when I was once more aroused to take the helm. I found that there was a sail in sight, just rising above the horizon in the northeast, but we could not tell in what direction she was standing.

The morning passed as had the former one. Our attention was kept awake by watching the progress of the strange sail. Her topsails rose above the horizon, then her courses appeared, and it became very clear that she was sailing on a parallel course with us. At the distance we were from her, we could not have been distinguished from the white crest of a rising wave, so that we knew it was useless to hope for any assistance from her. Trying, indeed, it was to watch her gliding by us. Sometimes, when she rose on the top of a sea, and rolled from side to side as she ran before the wind, we could see her copper glancing brightly in the sunbeams, and could almost count her ports; yet we ourselves, we knew, could scarcely have been seen, even had any on board been looking out for us. On she went, her crew rejoicing in the fair breeze which was carrying them on to their destined port, while we were grieving at being driven away from ours.

' " It's an ill wind that blows no one good," remember that, mates,' said La Motte. ' We may get the fair breeze before long.'

Scarcely had the stranger disappeared in the western horizon when another sail rose in the east out of the water. We watched her even with greater eagerness than before. We fancied that we could not again be doomed to disappointment.

' She is more, I think, to the southward than the other ship,' said Andrews. ' She'll pass not far to the nor'ard of us, and can't help seeing us.'

I watched the new-comer attentively, but could not agree with Andrews. She appeared to me to be following exactly in the track of the former vessel. I earnestly hoped that I might be wrong in my opinion. The ship came on, rapidly overtaking us. We ought to have found cause for satisfaction when we thus had evidence that we could not be driving fast to the eastward, and that when we came to haul up we should still find ourselves at no great distance from the Cornish coast.

We waited, anxiously watching the ship; but all differences of opinion were soon settled when she appeared abeam, fully as far off as the former one. As our hopes had risen to a high pitch, so they now fell proportionately low. I began to fear that despondency would seize on all hands. The ship came up on our quarter; then she got abeam of us. We could see her as clearly as we had seen the former one. Some of our people shouted and waved their hats and caps. No answering signal was made. Again they shouted and shrieked out till they were hoarse. Their cries and their signals were equally vain. Those on board could probably scarcely have seen the boat even had they been looking for her, and of course our shouts would not have reached one-tenth part of the distance. The ship glided quickly on. She passed us altogether, and, like her predecessor, disappeared in the western horizon. As she was leaving us, some of the men lost all command of their feelings and broke forth into imprecations loud and deep, and abused the ship and all on board her, as if they were to blame for not having seen us. I saw that in their present state of mind there would be no use finding fault with them, so I tried to cheer them up.

'Never mind, mates,' said I. 'We should not have been much better off if we had got on board those ships. They are outward-bound, and must have carried us wherever they are going, and perhaps we might have had to go half way round the world before we could get home again. Let us wait till we sight a ship bound up Channel, and then if we miss her we may have reason to complain.'

The remarks I made seemed to have some effect, for I heard no more complaints for some time. The day wore on and no other vessel passed

us. A change in the weather began to take place as the evening drew
on. The wind lessened considerably during the afternoon, and as night
approached it dropped into a perfect calm. Still there was a good deal
of sea, and we had more difficulty than ever in keeping the boat from
being swamped. We got the oars out, but we found that we had lost
so much strength that we could scarcely use them. However, we
managed to pull the boat's head round, and once more endeavoured to
keep a course towards the north-east.

Yet exert ourselves as we might, we found that we could only just
keep the boat's head to the sea, and that we were utterly unable to
move her through the water. Gradually the sea went down, and at last
most of the men declared that they neither would nor could pull any
longer, and that we should gain nothing by it, as very likely the wind
would shift again to its old quarter, and drive us back once more all the
distance we had thus made good.

La Motte and I endeavoured to cheer them up, but all our attempts
were vain. We saw ourselves that they were too likely to be right, and
indeed we could not help sharing in their despondency. I scarcely know
how the night passed. It did pass, however, and so did another day.
It was a perfect calm; we did not move. All our oars were laid in,
and the men threw themselves along the thwarts, and declared that they
should sleep there till some vessel should pass near enough to take us on
board.

Our stock of food had diminished very much, and I feared, on examining it, that we should scarcely have enough to carry us to the English
coast, even should a breeze spring up from the southward to help us
along. No one now took much count of time. I fell asleep during the
night, and so did La Motte, and I believe that no look-out was kept.
We might have been run over without our making an attempt to save
our lives.

Another day broke at last. There was a light wind, but it was from the south-east. We hoisted our sail, though we had scarcely sufficient strength to get it up. However, we made but little progress. I had fallen asleep, when I was aroused by the voices of my companions shouting as loudly as their strength would allow. The tones sounded strangely hollow and weak. I was scarcely aware that my own voice was much like theirs.

I looked up to see what had produced these shouts. A large ship was bearing down towards us from the eastward. We had our whole sail set, and as the sun shone on it, I hoped that we might now possibly be seen. I was not so sanguine as some of the men had suddenly become on seeing the ship. I knew that too often a very slack look-out is kept on board many ships, and even then only just ahead to see that no vessel is in the way or likely to get there. The topsails and more than half the courses of the stranger had already appeared above the horizon. We rose them rapidly. By the time that we could see her hull, I judged from the cut of her sails that she was certainly not an English ship.

'She is very like a French vessel,' observed La Motte after watching her earnestly for some time. 'Still she does not look like a ship of war, that is one comfort.' It was very certain, at all events, that she was standing directly for us, and that there was no chance of our missing her.

'Now, mates, just make up your minds what we shall do,' said La Motte; 'shall we go on board her whatever she is, or wherever she is going, or shall we remain in the boat and still endeavour to make the English coast?'

'Let us get clear of the boat!' exclaimed all the men; 'we may be knocking about here for some days to come, till we are all starved.'

'But we may obtain provisions from the ship sufficient to last us for

a week, or more, perhaps,' observed La Motte; 'she is evidently outward-bound, and many a long day may pass before we get back to
England.'

'Better that than being swamped or dying by inches,' was the
answer.

Finally, we discovered that all the men, including Andrews, had
made up their minds to be quit of the boat at all events. La Motte
told me that he knew how anxious I was to return home, and that he
was ready, if I wished it, to remain with me in the boat, and to endeavour
to make the shore.

Sincerely I thanked him for this mark of his friendship and kindness.
I debated in my mind whether I ought to accept his offer. In my
anxiety to reach home, I would have risked everything; still I thought
that I ought not to expose the life of another person for my sake. How
I might have decided, I scarcely know. I suspect that I should have
accepted his offer, but the matter was pretty well settled for us.

Clouds had been gathering for some time in the sky, and while we
were speaking, thin flakes of snow began to fall, and continued increasing
in density, so that we could scarcely see the approaching ship. We
could not ascertain whether we had been seen by those on board before
the snowstorm came on, and, if not, there was too great a probability
that she would pass us. At all events, she was now completely hidden
from our view.

We calculated that if she kept on the exact course she was on when
last seen, we should be rather to the southward of her. We therefore
got out our oars, and endeavoured to pull up to her. Every one, however, was so weak, that it was with difficulty we could urge the boat
through the water. Our last morsel of food had been consumed that
morning; indeed, for the two previous days we had taken barely enough
to support life.

We looked about—we could not see the ship—we shouted at the top of our voices—all was silent—we pulled on—again we shouted, or rather shrieked out. A hail came from the eastward. It sounded loud and clear compared to the hollow tones of our voices Presently the dark hull and wide-spreading sails of a ship broke on our sight through the veil of falling snow, and directly afterwards we dropped alongside her.

She hailed us in German. I understood a little of the language, but La Motte spoke it perfectly. Great indeed was our satisfaction to find from this that she belonged to a friendly power. She appeared to have a great number of passengers on board, for they crowded the sides and gangway to look at us, and very miserable objects, I daresay, we appeared.

Thinking probably that we were afraid of them, they told us that the ship was the *Nieuwland,* belonging to Bremen, bound for Baltimore, in the United States, and that the people we saw were Hanoverian emigrants.

When we told them in return that we were Englishmen escaping from a French privateer which had captured us, they warmly pressed us to come on board. When, however, we tried to get up to climb up the sides, we found that we could scarcely stand on our legs, much less help ourselves on deck. Three or four of our companions were so weak and ill that they could not rise even from the bottom of the boat, and it was sad to see them, as they lay on their backs, stretching out their hands for help to those who were looking down on them over the ship's side.

Certainly we all must have presented a perfect picture of woe and misery—half-frozen and famished—pale, haggard, shivering, with our beards unshaven, and our hair hanging lank and wet over our faces, our lips blue, our eyes bloodshot, our clothes dripping with moisture. Our condition was bad enough to excite the compassion of any one.

The master and seamen of the ship and the emigrants evidently felt for us, by the exclamations we heard them utter. They quickly fitted slings, which were lowered to hoist us up, and the seamen came into the boat to help us. One after the other we were conveyed on board, and at once carried below. Not one of us could have stood, had it been to save our lives.

I felt grateful for the looks of pity which were cast on us as we were lifted along the deck, while many of the emigrants volunteered to give up their berths. I remember how delightful I felt it to find myself stripped of my damp clothing, lying between dry blankets, with a bottle of hot water at my feet and another on my chest, while kind-hearted people were rubbing my limbs to restore circulation. It was some time, however, before anything like the proper amount of heat came back to my chilled frame. Then some warm drink was given me, and I fell into a deep slumber.

I believe that I slept nearly twenty-four hours on a stretch without once waking. At last, when I opened my eyes, daylight was streaming down on me through the open hatchway. The doctor came and felt my pulse. He spoke a little English, and told me to keep up my spirits, and that I should do very well. Then some broth was brought me by one of the emigrants, and after I had taken it I felt very much better. I inquired after my companions.

'They are not all in as good case as you are,' said the doctor. 'Two poor fellows have died, and a third, I fear, will not be long with us.'

'Which of them have gone?' I asked. 'I trust the officer, La Motte, is doing well.'

'He is weak, and suffers much, but still I have hopes that he may recover,' was the answer.

I was very sad on hearing this, yet I felt what cause I had to be thankful that I had escaped with my life, and was not likely to suffer in my health, as was the case with some of my companions.

With returning strength, however, came more forcibly on me the consciousness of the postponement once more of all my hopes of happiness. I had risked everything; I had gone through the most trying hardships to reach home, and now I found myself being carried away far from that home, without any immediate prospect of reaching it. I turned round in my berth and burst into tears.

The kind-hearted German who was attending on me inquired, in his broken English, what was the matter. I felt that it would be a relief to me, and would gratify him, if I were to tell him my history. He was much interested in it, and warmly sympathized with me. He did not consider my tears unmanly. I do not think they were, either. I was weak and ill, too. Perhaps otherwise, as is the English custom, I should have kept my feelings and my history to myself. Yet I think that English habit of hiding our thoughts and feelings, shows a want of confidence in the sympathy and kind feeling of our fellow-men which is altogether wrong. Nothing could surpass the kindness and sympathy of my German friends, especially of Karl Smitz, the young man who attended on me.

We had a fair breeze and fine weather, so that in three days I was able to get out of my berth. My first visit was to La Motte. He was unable to move. With fear and trembling I looked at him, for he seemed to me sadly changed from what he had been when we left the lugger: I had not seen myself, and I was not aware how haggard and ill I even then appeared.

He told me that he only felt weak and bruised, and that he had hopes he should soon be well. I found that three of our late companions had been committed to the deep, and that a fourth was in a dying state. This made me feel still more anxious about La Motte. From our old friendship, now cemented by the hardships we had gone through together, I could not help regarding him with the affection of a brother. I sat by the side of his berth till the doctor came and told me I must go on deck, as fresh air was now the only medicine I required.

The captain welcomed me on deck when I appeared in the kindest way, and said that he was glad to find even one of his guests on the fair road to recovery. He, it appeared, had heard my story, and he came up to me and told me that he had no doubt I was anxious to get to England, and that if we fell in with any homeward-bound ship, he would put me on board her. I told this to La Motte when I went below, and he said that if he had strength even to move he would accompany me.

Two days after this I was sitting on a gun-carriage enjoying the fresh breeze, when there was a movement on deck among the crew and passengers, and I saw four men coming up the main hatchway, bearing between them what I saw at once was a human form, wrapped up in a fold of canvas. It was placed on a plank near a port at the opposite side of the ship. A union-jack was thrown over it, and I guessed from that circumstance that the dead man was another of my companions. I called to Karl Smitz, who was passing.

'Ah! they did not know that you were on deck, or they would have told you before the poor fellow was brought up,' he observed. 'Yes, he was another of those we saved out of the boat. We are now going to bury him as we would wish to be buried ourselves.'

Soon after this the captain came into the waist with a Lutheran prayer-book, from which, with an impressive voice, he read some prayers. Then both the seamen and emigrants—men, women, and children—stood round and burst forth into a hymn most sweet and melodious; first it was sad in the extreme, and then it rose by degrees to tones of joy, as it pictured the spirit of the departed borne by angels into Abraham's bosom; while another prayer was being uttered, the body of my shipmate was launched into the deep. Thus four of us had been taken and six remained.

I was long very anxious for La Motte; he, however, slowly recovered, and in about a fortnight was able to come on deck. By that time Andrews and the other men had recovered, and were able to do duty. We are all of us anxious to be of use, for no honest seaman, or any other true man for that matter, likes to eat the bread of idleness. The ship was rather weak-handed, and the captain was very glad of our services.

La Motte and I consulted together, and we agreed that we ought to make him some recompense for the trouble and expense he had been at, and all the care he had taken of us. The other men agreed to what we proposed. We accordingly, when he was on deck one day, went up to him and told him how grateful we felt for his kindness, and begged him to accept our boat. He smiled at our warmth.

'No, indeed, my good men, I can accept nothing from you,' he answered; 'I have only done what is the duty of every seaman to do when he finds his fellow-men tossed about on the ocean in distress. What was your lot may be mine another day; and I should expect others to do for me what I have done for you.'

'Well, sir,' said La Motte, 'we feel the truth of what you say. Unhappily, some seamen do not act as you have done; and there are wretches who will pass a ship in distress, and never attempt to relieve her. However, what I am going to say is this; our clothes are in a very bad condition, and if you will supply us, we will consider them as payment for the boat.'

This proposal pleased our kind captain, and he forthwith gave us a suit of clothes, and a warm cap, a pair of shoes, and a couple of shirts, out of his slop-chest. We were thus all of us able to put on a decent and comfortable appearance. I am very certain no good action ever goes unrewarded in one way or another, though, perhaps, through our blindness, we do not always find it out.

A few days after this a terrific gale sprung up. All hands were roused up in the middle watch to reef topsails. We Englishmen, hearing the cry and roar of the tempest which had suddenly struck the ship, sprang on deck. The crew were aloft in vain struggling with the bulging topsails. At that moment the foretopsail, with a report like thunder, blew out of the bolt-ropes, carrying with it two men off the lee yardarm. The poor fellows were sent far away to leeward into the boiling sea.

Any attempt to help them was utterly hopeless; we heard their despairing shrieks, and for an instant saw their agonized countenances as the ship swept by them, and all trace of them was lost. We hurried on to the main-topsail-yard just in time to save the people there from sharing the fate of their messmates. The courses were furled, the main-topsail closely reefed, and the ship flew onward on her course.

CHAPTER XV.

THE good ship *Nieuwland* made rapid progress. Though I was flying away from home and all I longed to be with, yet anything was better than moving slowly. If we did not fall in with any ship in which I might return, I felt that the sooner I got to the end of the voyage, the sooner I might be starting back again. The gale continued for several days; the wind at length dropped and then came ahead, blowing stronger than ever. It was now necessary to heave the ship to.

In performing the operation, a heavy sea struck her bows, and two more of the crew were washed overboard. Happily the emigrants were below, or many would probably have shared the same fate.

I had now what I much required, abundance of work as a seaman. When it is well for a person to fly from his own thoughts, there is nothing like useful occupation to help him along; nothing is so bad as to allow oneself to dwell on one's misfortunes. The best advice I can give to a man when he is unhappy, is to go and help others. He will find plenty of people requiring his aid, and numbers far more unhappy than himself.

The ship had suffered a good deal during the gale, and we began to be apprehensive for her safety should the weather continue bad; but it soon cleared up, and we had every hopes of reaching our port in a week or ten days at the farthest. The day after the fair weather set in, a sail was reported ahead. As we drew near each other, we saw that she was in a very shattered condition. She was a brig, we perceived, but only one mast was standing. Her bowsprit was carried away, and her foremast was gone by the board.

Our captain made a signal to ask what assistance was required. The answer was, 'Some spars for our foremast and bowsprit, and some hands who may be willing to return to England to help navigate the ship. We have lost five overboard.'

Our kind captain called us all aft. 'Here is an opportunity for those who may desire it to return home,' said he. 'The brig is in no very good plight, as you see; but many a vessel in a worse condition has made a safe voyage. I will not advise you either way. I shall be very sorry to lose you, but you are at liberty to go.'

We thanked him very much for this additional proof of his love of justice and fair dealing, and La Motte and I consulted together what we would do. I at all events was ready to run every risk for the sake of returning home. I also felt that we might be the means of saving the brig and the people on board her.

La Motte agreed to accompany me; so we told the captain that we would go. Andrews and another man said that they would accompany us. Our captain therefore signalled that he would afford all the help asked for, and told the people in the brig in the meantime to send a boat on board us. As we passed under the counter of the brig, previous to heaving to, a man standing on her taffrail hailed us through his speaking-trumpet:

'We cannot do what you ask; we have not a boat that can swim, and we have only four hands remaining on board.'

It struck me as I looked at the man that I knew his figure, and even the tone of his voice; but where I had seen him I could not tell. While the ship was being hove to, we went round to bid farewell to the numerous friends we had found on board. Had we been brothers, we could not have been treated more kindly, and to no one was our gratitude more due than to the honest Bremen captain.

The boat was ready; we stepped into her, with a couple of spars towing astern. The captain took his seat in the stern-sheets.

'I'll go on board and see my brother skipper,' said he. 'Now, my sons, farewell. I shall not forget you, and you will not forget me, I hope. We may never meet together again in this world, or we may; but I hope that we shall all be steering the same course to that world which will last for ever and ever. Don't ever forget that world, my sons. Whatever you do, wherever you go, always keep it in view. It is of more value than gold or much fine gold. Get, I say, on that course, and do not let any one ever tempt you to alter it. In fair weather or foul, steadily steer for it, and you will be sure to make it at last.'

We all listened attentively to the good man's words; he spoke with so much earnestness, and had given us so strong a proof of his practical Christianity, that we could not but feel that they merited our respect. The captain of the brig—the same man who had hailed us with the speaking-trumpet—stood at the gangway to receive us when we pulled alongside.

I rubbed my eyes as I looked at him. I rubbed and rubbed again. There stood, scarcely altered, it appeared to me, a man I had believed long since swallowed up by the hungry waves, Captain Tooke, once the master of the *Fate*, the brig in which I had been wrecked off the Scilly Islands. If it was not him,—saved by some wonderful means,—I felt sure that it was a brother or near relative; for if he was not my old captain, no two people could be more alike. The sea had gone down completely, so that we without difficulty boarded the brig. Her master thanked the Bremen captain very warmly for the assistance he had brought him, and welcomed us.

20

'You are brave lads for coming on board such a wreck of a craft as mine is,' said he, looking at us, and putting out his hand to La Motte. 'However, if we are mercifully favoured by fine weather, we will get her all ataunto before long.

We told him that if the ship was sound in hull, we had no fears about the matter; we should soon get her to rights.

'That's the spirit I liked to see,' he answered, and then turning to the Bremen captain, he continued, 'Tell me, my friend, how much am I to pay you for these spars? Ask your own price. They are invaluable to me.'

'Nothing,' was the answer. 'I had several to spare, and none nave been lost during the voyage. Well, if you press the point, you may pay the value over to these men when you reach your own country. They have lost their all from being taken prisoners, and will require something to take them to their homes.'

'That I will, with all my heart,' answered the captain of the brig.

While he was speaking, I kept looking at him. Though his features were the same, his way of expressing himself was so different to that of Captain Tooke, that I felt I must be mistaken.

Farewells were said between the two captains, and once more the Bremen captain shook hands with us all round. The emigrants cheered as the ship bore up round us, and away she went to the west, while we lay as near the wind as our dismasted state would allow us.

I was anxious to settle the question as to the identity of the captain, so I asked one of the men what his name was. He somewhat startled me by answering 'Tooke.' He, however, could tell me nothing about his past history; so I went up to the captain himself, and asked him if he had not been on board the *Fate* when she was wrecked?

'Yes,' he replied; 'I was the sole survivor of all on board that unfortunate craft.'

'No, sir, you were not,' I answered, and I told him how a number of us had got away in the boat, and how all, with the exception of old Cole, Iffley, and I, had been lost, and how the old mate had died, and we were the only ones left. He told me that when the mast went overboard, he had clung to it, and that the tide had carried it out into mid-channel. When morning broke, he found himself close to a vessel hove to. The wind then began to fall, and the sea to go down, and in a short time they sent a boat and picked him up. He by that time was very much exhausted, and could scarcely have held out another quarter of an hour.

He himself had been all his life utterly careless about religion; but while he was hanging on to the mast amid the raging ocean, he had been led to think of the future, towards which he felt that he was probably hastening, and he could not help discerning the finger of God in thus bringing him directly up to the only vessel within many miles of him. When he got on board, however, he was struck by the utter want of respect shown by the master and all the crew for anything like religion. He and they were scoffers and blasphemers and professed infidels. He said that he was so horrified and shocked at all he heard, that he trembled lest he might have become like them.

From that time forward he prayed that he might be enlightened and reformed, and he felt truly a new heart put into him. He had never since gone back. He had met with many misfortunes and hardships. He had been frequently shipwrecked; had lost all his property; had been taken prisoner by the enemy; had been compelled to serve as mate instead of master; and had scarcely ever been able to visit his family on shore. Still he went on, trusting in God's mercy, and feeling sure that whatever happened to him was for the best.

'And, sir,' said I, when he had finished his account of himself, 'I heartily agree with you. I have often fainted and often doubted, but I have always come back to the same opinion, that what is, is best—that is, that whatever God does is best for us.'

This conversation, by the bye, did not take place at once. We first set to work to get the ship to rights. We got sheers up, and, the weather being calm, we without difficulty got the new mast stepped, and another bowsprit rigged. The mast was only a jury-mast, but we set it up well with stays, and it carried sail fairly.

While we were working away, I observed the countenance of one of the men who was doing duty as mate, he being the most experienced of the three survivors of the crew.

'I am certain that you must be an old shipmate of mine,' said I as we were hauling away together. 'Is not your name Flood, and were you not on board the *Kite* schooner when we were attacked by pirates?'

'The very same, lad,' said he. 'And you—I remember you, too, very well now—you are Will Weatherhelm.'

'The same; and is it not extraordinary that thus, in the middle of the Atlantic, I should meet with two men whom I have not heard of for years, and one of whom I thought was dead?'

'Not more extraordinary than that those two men should have become thoroughly changed characters,' he answered. 'I was a careless reprobate, Weatherhelm, when you knew me, and now I have learned to think and to pray, and to strive to do well.'

It certainly was surprising to me to hear John Flood speak as he did, for, unhappily, in those days there were not many seamen who could say the same for themselves. But, poor fellows, their opportunities were few of hearing anything about religion, and I believe men will be judged according to the advantages they may have possessed. Let those take heed, therefore, who have them, that they do not throw them away.

Flood gave me an account of the way the brig—the *Fair Rosamond* was her name—met with her accident. It was indeed providential that she and all on board had not perished. She had sailed from Port Royal, in Jamaica, bound for Liverpool, with several other vessels, under convoy of a frigate. The first part of the voyage was favourable, but the *Fair Rosamond* was very deeply laden with sugar and rum and other West India produce, and being then out of trim, she proved herself a very dull sailer.

To avoid the risk of capture, the convoy had steered a more northerly course than is usual, and had not kept east till nearly in the latitude of Newfoundland.

'We were constantly lagging behind, and the frigate had to come and whip us up so often that we completely lost our character in the fleet,' continued Flood. 'We did our best to keep up with the rest of the convoy, by setting every stitch of canvas we could carry; but nothing would do, and we should have had to heave part of the cargo overboard to have enabled her to keep up with the rest. At length we were overtaken by a gale of wind, and we had to heave to. We thought that the rest of the fleet were doing the same near us. It was night. When morning broke not a sail was to be seen. We were more likely to fall into the hands of the enemy, but still we could take our own time, and we thought that we were less likely to meet with an accident than when, blow high or low, we had to press her with canvas. However, we were mistaken. We had been driven a long way to the nor'ard of the Gulf Stream, and the weather was cold and bad, when one night, just as I had come on deck to keep the middle watch, and had gone to the wheel, I looked up and thought I saw a great white glittering cloud right ahead of us. I sang out, and the first mate, who was officer of the watch, crying, "Hard a-lee!" ran forward. I put down the helm, but scarcely had I done so before I saw what I knew to be a huge iceberg rising up directly ahead of us. I fully believed that our last moments were come.

It appeared to me as if the ship was running into a cavern in the side of some vast mountain of marble. I held my breath. If my hair ever stood on end, I believe that it did on that occasion. My eyeballs seemed starting from their sockets. I felt the blood leave my cheeks and rush round my heart, as if it would burst. A terrific crash came. There were despairing shrieks and cries. I thought the brig was lost. The bowsprit was carried away; the foremast came toppling down, and at the same time a sea struck the ship, and swept over the decks. I held on by the wheel. The captain rushed on deck just as the sea had passed over us. I felt the brig rebound as it were from the iceberg, and I found that we were drifting away from it. The two men who were below came on deck at the same time the captain did. We shouted to our companions. We looked about aboard and around us, on either side where the wreck of the foremast was still hanging on to the channels, but no voice replied—not a glimpse of them could be seen. We four were left alone on that stormy ice-surrounded sea, with a shattered, almost unmanageable ship. We did not fear. Our captain was a host in himself. We could not get the wreck of the mast on board, so we had to cut it away. Happily the wind came round from the nor'ard, and by rigging a stay from the head of the mainmast to the stump of the bowsprit, we were able to set a sail and to get the brig's head round. We had been knocking about ten days when you fell in with us. Two vessels passed us, and must have seen our condition, but they did not alter their course. All who sail the ocean are not good Samaritans, like your friend the Bremen captain.'

Such was the brief account Flood gave me of their disaster. I have always designated the good man of whom he spoke as the Bremen captain, for I could not pronounce his name, and did not write it down. I hope we shall meet in heaven.

I must hurry on with my adventures. Once more I indulged in the hope of being speedily restored to my wife and home. The weather was fine, and, considering her crippled state, the brig made fair way. In some respects we were better off than on board the Bremen ship, for we had ample and good provisions and plenty of room, and as our supply of clothes was small, Captain Tooke distributed among us those belonging to the poor fellows who had been lost.

I had one night turned in, after keeping the first watch, under the belief that all was going well. I was roused up with the so often heard cry, 'All hands shorten sail!' I hurried on deck to find the brig plunging into a heavy sea, which was straining every timber in her. A fierce north-easter was blowing. To attempt to face it was impossible, and it was not without difficulty that we got the brig's head round from it. Away we went before the wind, and away from England and my home. By the captain's computation we were only three hundred miles or so to the northward of the Bermudas. The brig had for some time been in a leaky state, and we had frequently to turn to at the pumps, but, with fine weather, we had had no fear of keeping her clear. Now, however, the case was altered, and Captain Tooke resolved to run for the Bermudas.

It is no easy matter to hit a small spot in the middle of the ocean, after dark and blowing weather, when no observation has lately been taken. We had to keep a bright look-out not to miss the islands. I felt especially anxious about the matter. Should we run past them, we might, after all, be compelled to put into an American port to repair the ship, and my return home might be still further postponed.

The morning came; the day wore on. No land was in sight. My heart sank within me. Over and over again I went to the main-top-mast-head to look out for the group of rocks I so anxiously desired to see.

At length, just on the starboard bow, I caught sight of a blue mound rising out of the water. I hurried below to tell the captain. In a couple of hours we were safely at anchor within St. George's harbour.

I was in hopes that the brig would be quickly repaired, and that we should be allowed to proceed on our voyage. However, as it turned out, an agent of the owner's resided there. He ordered the brig to be surveyed. The surveyor was connected with the chief shipbuilder of the place. He pronounced her unfit to proceed on her voyage without a thorough repair. The cargo was consequently discharged, and the crew were paid off. Captain Tooke regretted this exceedingly, but could not help it. He said that he should have been perfectly ready to take the brig home, with a new mast and a little caulking in her upper works, which could be got at simply by heeling her over. However, he had to submit.

He not only paid us our wages, but the wages which were due to the poor fellows who were lost, and also the value of the spars which had been given to him by the Bremen captain. Thus I found myself possessed of more money than I had had in my pocket since I had been pressed. The question was now, how I could most speedily reach England. I took counsel with La Motte. He observed, that the longest way round is often the shortest way there; and that, perhaps, by going to some port in the United States, we might more quickly get to Europe, as there was no vessel in harbour bound there at that time.

Just as we had arrived at this determination, a homeward-bound West Indiaman, which had parted from her convoy, put into the harbour. She had lost several men by yellow fever, and her captain, who came on shore, was very glad to ship us the moment we offered. He took all the men who had been paid off from the *Fair Rosamond*.

Once more we were under weigh for Old England. The *Jane* was a fine ship, belonging to London. She was in good repair, and well found, and with the fresh hands taken on board, well manned. We had no reason to dread gales of wind or disasters of any sort. The wind came fair, and we had a fine run till we were not far off the chops of the Channel, when it fell a dead calm. There we lay for a couple of days, well-nigh rolling our masts out, when a light breeze sprung up from the eastward. Though it was against us, anything was better than a calm. Oh, how I longed to be at home! Again almost in sight of England, I could not help every moment conjuring up pictures of the scenes that home might present. Sometimes they were bright and happy, but then they would become so sad and painful that I grew sick at heart by their contemplation. 'At all events,' I said to myself, 'all my doubts will soon be at an end. I shall know what has occurred.'

Such thoughts were passing through my mind, when the look-out from the masthead reported several sail in sight, coming down before the wind. The report caused considerable excitement on board. They might be friends, but they might be enemies; and if so, there was too great a probability of our finding ourselves entering a French port as prisoners, instead of returning home as we had expected. Our captain resolved to stand on close-hauled, till he could ascertain whether they looked suspicious, and if so, to keep away to the northward. As they drew nearer, we did not doubt from the breadth of canvas they showed that they were men-of-war. In a short time we got near enough to them to exchange signals, when we made out that they were British ships. The headmost one, a frigate, signalled to us to heave to, an order our captain very unwillingly obeyed.

'Perhaps she only wants to send some message home, but I doubt it. Lads, look out for yourselves,' said he.

I knew too well to what his remark referred. We, as ordered, hove to, and a lieutenant and midshipman with a boat's crew strongly armed came aboard us.

'Turn the hands up, captain,' said the lieutenant briskly. The order was obeyed, and we all had to appear on deck. 'You are strongly manned, captain,' observed the officer, running his eye over us. 'You can easily manage to get into port with half the number of hands you now have.'

'Could not work my ship without all the hands I have,' answered the captain gruffly.

'There is nothing like trying,' observed the lieutenant. 'Let me see your papers. Ah, I observe you entered some of these men when part of your voyage was accomplished. You can do very well without them, at all events. They none of them have protection. No, I see that clearly. Come, lads, get your bags up; I can take no excuses. Our ships must have men; I know nothing more about the matter. Be smart now.'

I endeavoured in vain to expostulate. I entreated the officer to allow me to proceed in the ship. He replied that it was his duty to take me. He could not stop to argue about duty. I must go. I knew that he was right; but, oh, how grievous was this new trial to bear! I thought that I should have been beside myself.

La Motte was doing duty as mate of the ship, and he escaped. All I could do was to tell him where to find my wife, and to entreat him to lose no time in visiting her, and in assuring her of my safety. He promised faithfully to fulfil my wishes, and with a heavy, almost breaking heart, I stepped into the man-of-war's boat.

I felt inclined to curse the country which could allow of such a system. Happily, I did not. I knew that it arose from the ignorance of those in authority as to how to get seamen for the king's ships, and not from cruelty or heartlessness. It may seem surprising to those who live in happier times that no better plan could be thought of.

I found myself conveyed on board the *Nymph*, a thirty-six twelve-pounder gun frigate, commanded by Captain Edward Pellew. When questioned, I did not deny that I had before served on board a man-of-war, and having given an account of my adventures, I was rated at once as an able seaman. I went about my duty, and did it to the best of my power, but it was mechanically, without any spirit or heartiness.

Month after month passed away. I felt as if I was in a trance. I could not think. I tried to forget the past; I dared not meditate on the future. How I lived through that time I scarcely know. I never laughed or smiled, I scarcely spoke to any one; even the active duties of the ship did not arouse me.

CHAPTER XVI.

On board the *Nymph*—A hot engagement—Escape of the enemy—I am transferred to the *Pelican*—Action off the Isle of Bas—I fancy myself with a wooden leg—We put into Plymouth—Writing under difficulties—A sad disappointment—We sail —A chase—Trying time—Action between the *Venus* and *Sémillante*—In search of the enemy.

CAPTAIN EDWARD PELLEW, who commanded the *Nymph*, was, I was told, one of the smartest officers in the British navy.

'Where there is anything to do, he'll do it; and if there is nothing to do, he'll find something,' was the opinion expressed of him on board.

He had during the last war been first lieutenant of the *Apollo*, Captain Pownoll.

'I belonged to her at the time,' said my messmate Dick Hagger. 'We were in company with the *Cleopatra*, Captain Murray, who, one morning, sent us in chase of a cutter seen in the north-west quarter. About half-past ten, when we had got nearly within gunshot of the cutter, we saw a large ship standing out from the land. That she was an enemy, there was no doubt; so Captain Pownoll at once did his best to close her. The wind was about north-east, and the stranger, standing to the nor'ard on the starboard tack, was enabled to cross our bows. Soon afterwards she tacked to the eastward, and we also hove about until, she being on our weather quarter, we again tacked, as did also the stranger. We exchanged broadsides with her in passing, when we once more tacked and brought her to close action about noon. It was the hottest fight I had ever then been engaged in. We tossed our guns in and out, determined to win. It was sharp work; numbers of our men were falling, several killed and many wounded. Among the former was our brave captain, who was shot down about an hour after the action commenced, when our first lieutenant, Edward Pellew, who was now our captain, took command of the ship. You may be sure that he continued the fight bravely, cheering us on. What we might have thought about the matter had another man been in his place, I don't know; but we knew him, and felt sure that he would keep it up as long as we had a stick standing or a shot in the locker.

'We were now edging away off the wind towards Ostend. It was soon seen that it was the intention of the enemy to run ashore. We had by this time made her out to be the *Stanislaus*, a French thirty-two gun frigate, though she was only carrying at the time, so we afterwards found out, twenty-six long twelve-pounders, so that she was no match for us.

'Our young commander now did his best to prevent the *Stanislaus* from running ashore by crossing and recrossing her bows; but on heaving the lead, we found that we were in little more than twenty feet of water, and that if we stood on, we ourselves must be aground before long.

'The master and other officers now came up to Mr. Pellew, and strongly advised him to wear ship. You may be sure we were very sorry when we had to bring the *Apollo* to the wind, with her head off shore; and a few minutes afterwards the *Stanislaus* took the ground, when her foremast and main-topmast fell over the side. Still greater was our disappointment when we heard that Ostend was neutral ground, and that we should be violating what was called the neutrality of the port by renewing the engagement. I am not certain that our commander would not have run all risks, had not the enemy fired a gun to leeward to claim the protection of the Dutch. It is but right to say

that the French fought well, for besides our captain. we had five poor
fellows killed and twenty wounded.   Our rigging was cut to pieces, and
we had three feet of water in the hold.   The French loss was much
more severe.

'Mr. Pellew got his promotion to the rank of commander for this
action.   I next served with him on board the *Pelican*, a fourteen-gun
brig to which he was soon afterwards appointed.   We were off the Isle
of Bas, towards the end of April 1782, I mind, when we made out
several vessels at anchor in the roads.

'Our commander at once resolved to attack them, and for this purpose
stood inshore, when we saw two privateers—a brig and a schooner,
each of equal force to the *Pelican*—spring their broadsides towards the
entrance of the roads, to prevent us entering.   Our commander was
not the man to be stopped by threats of that sort.   Standing on, we
opened a brisk fire on the two privateers, and soon drove them, as well
as a third which appeared inside, on shore, close under the shelter of
some heavy batteries, whose guns at once began blazing away at us.
We were struck several times, and two of our men were wounded, but no
one was killed.   It was about as pretty and well-executed an affair as
I ever saw, and we were all right glad to hear that our commander
had obtained his post rank for it.   So you see, Will, we've got a man to
be proud of.'

I agreed with Hagger, but yet my heart was too sore to feel any
satisfaction at knowing this, and I would a thousand times rather
have been on shore with my dear wife; and who, under my circumstances,
would not?   Still I might hope by some means or other to be able
to rejoin her.   The frigate, I found, had been fitted out at Portsmouth,
and to Portsmouth she would in all probability return.   I would
thankfully have received a wound sufficiently severe to have sent me to
hospital   Then, if I once got home, discharged from the ship, I deter-

mined to take very good care not again to be pressed. It would be hard indeed if Charles Iffley should discover me. In the meantime, I resolved, as I had done before, to perform my duty.

I prayed, for my wife's sake, should we go into action, that my life might be preserved. For myself, just then, I cared very little what might become of me.

I remember, however, laughing as I thought, if my right leg were to be shot away, how Uncle Kelson and I should go stumping about Southsea Common together,—he had lost his left leg,—now our heads almost knocking against each other, now going off at tangents. I pictured to myself the curious figure we should cut.

Hagger thought, as he looked at me, that I had gone daft.

'What is the matter, Will?' he asked. I told him.

'Don't let such fancies get hold of your mind, man,' he answered. 'You'll keep your two legs and get safely on shore one of these days, when we have well trounced the mounseers. Ever bear in mind that "there's a sweet little cherub who sits up aloft, to take care of the life of poor Jack."

'He'll take care of both your legs for your wife's sake, as I doubt not it would be better for you to keep them on.'

After cruising up and down the Channel for some time, we put into Plymouth, where we found the *Venus* frigate. Commander Israel Pellew, our captain's brother, came on board to keep his brother company, he having no command at the time.

No leave was granted, and very little communication held with the shore. I was unable to obtain a sheet of paper and a pen, the officers only having writing materials. I would willingly have given a guinea for a sheet of paper, a pen, and some ink; but it was not until we had been at anchor some time that I got a sheet from the purser's steward, with a wretched pen and a small bottle of ink, for which I paid him five shillings. I was thankful to get it at that price, and immediately hurried down to write a letter to my wife. Bitterly to my disappointment, before I had finished it, I heard the boatswain's shrill call summoning all hands on deck to heave up the anchor and make sail. Placing the half-finished letter in my bag, which I had brought from the *Jane*, I followed my shipmates.

We sailed in company with the *Venus*, Captain Faulknor, and stood down Channel in search of French cruisers. My earnest prayer was, that we might put into Spithead, whence I should have an opportunity of sending my letter on shore, even though I should be unable to get leave to go myself. As a pressed man, I knew that I should have a difficulty in obtaining that.

The *Venus* had been hurriedly fitted out. She had no marines on board, while she was twenty seamen short of her complement. She was rated as a thirty-two gun frigate, mounting twenty-four long twelve-pounders on the main-deck, with six eighteen-pounder carronades and eight long six-pounders on her quarter-deck and forecastle, which gave her a total of thirty-eight guns. Thus, except her carronades, her guns were of light calibre. We were somewhere about a hundred leagues north-west of Cape Finisterre when a sail was seen to the south-east. Captain Pellew, as senior officer, ordered Captain Faulknor (the *Venus* being much the nearer) to chase. We at the same time made out another sail to the eastward. Hoping that she might be an enemy, we immediately steered for her. She proved, however, to be an English frigate bound out with despatches to the West Indies. As her captain could not go out of his way to look after the Frenchman, we bore up alone to follow the *Venus*, hoping to get up in time to take part in the engagement, should she be fortunate enough to bring the stranger to action. We could calculate pretty accurately whereabouts to find our consort, when about noon the next day it came on calm for some hours, and though we set all sail, the ship made but little progress through the water.

Late in the evening, the sound of rapid firing reached our ears, and we knew that the *Venus* must be engaged, but whether or not with a ship of superior force, it was impossible to decide. It greatly tried our patience to hear the sound of the battle and yet not be able to take part in it. Even I was aroused, and for a time forgot my own troubles. The midshipmen went aloft to the mastheads, but still they were unable to catch sight of the combatants. The fast-coming gloom concealed the clouds of smoke which might have risen above the horizon and shown their position.

The officers walked the deck with hurried strides, their glasses in their hands, every now and then turning them in the direction from which the sound came, though they knew they were not likely to see anything.

The men stood about whistling for a wind until it seemed as if their cheeks would crack.

At last the breeze came; the order was given to trim sails. Never did men fly to their stations with more alacrity.

The days were long, and as night came down at last on the world of waters, we could hear the firing more distinctly than ever, but still we could not see the flashes of the guns.

Next morning a sail was sighted to the south-east. She was standing towards us, but alone.

'She may be the *Venus*, or she may be an enemy which has captured her, and is now coming on to fight us,' I observed to Dick Hagger.

He laughed heartily. 'No, no, Will,' he answered. 'Depend upon it, the *Venus*, if she is taken, which I don't believe, would have too much knocked about an enemy to leave her any stomach for fighting another English ship.'

21

'But suppose she is not the ship with which the *Venus* engaged, but a fresh frigate standing out to fight us.'

'I only hope she may be; we'll soon show her that she has caught a Tartar. Depend on't, we'll not part company till we've taken her.'

The matter was soon set at rest, when, the stranger nearing us, we observed her crippled state, and recognised her as our consort.

'She's had a pretty tough fight of it,' said Hagger as we gazed at her. Her foretop-gallant main and cross-jack yard were shot away, her yards, rigging, and sails sadly cut up, but what injuries her hull had received we could not make out.

On closing with each other, both ships hove to, and our third lieutenant, Mr. Pellowe, whose name curiously enough was very like that of our captain (we used to call the one the Owe, the other the Ew), went on board, accompanied by Commander Israel Pellew. I was one of the boat's crew. We found, on getting up to her, that no small number of shot had struck her hull, some going through her sides, others her bulwarks, besides which she had received other damages.

Her people told us that they had had an action, which had lasted the best part of three hours, with a French frigate of forty guns, the *Sémillante;* and that, though they had suffered sharply, the Frenchman had been much more knocked about.

After engaging her for two hours, they had got up to within half a cable's length of her, when, trimming their sails as well as they were able, they ranged up alongside with double-shotted guns and gave her a broadside.

Having shot ahead, they were going about to repeat their fire, when they discovered to leeward a large ship under French colours. The *Sémillante,* recognising the stranger, bore up to join her, when their captain, seeing that he should have no chance of victory, considering the way their ship had suffered, and that they might be taken, hauled close to the wind, and, making all the sail they could carry, stood away from their new enemy.

If it had not been for that, they declared they would have taken the *Sémillante*, and of this there seemed little doubt. They had had two seamen killed, and the master and nineteen seamen wounded.

We afterwards learned that the enemy had had twelve killed and twenty wounded.

Considering the disparity of force, the action was a gallant one, and we more than ever regretted that we had been prevented taking part in it; for we should, we felt sure, have captured one or both of the French ships.

As soon as the shot-holes in the *Venus* had been stopped and her rigging repaired, we made sail together in search of the enemy, we hoping to have an opportunity of tackling the fresh ship, while our consort attacked her old opponent.

CHAPTER XVII.

WE continued our course under all sail to the eastward, and next evening
caught sight of two sail, which we took to be French, standing up
Channel.

We made chase, but lost sight of them in the night. Next morning,
however, there they were, hull down, right ahead. We continued the
pursuit along the French coast, but had the disappointment of seeing
them at last take refuge in Cherbourg harbour. Knowing that they
were not likely to come out again, we stood across channel, the *Venus*
running into Plymouth to land her wounded men and repair damages,
while we stood on for Falmouth.

Again I was disappointed in not being able to despatch my letter, for
after we knew where the *Venus* was bound for, no communication was
held with her.

I had got the letter written and addressed, but had not closed it, as I
wished to add a few more words at latest. For safety's sake, I kept it
in my bag, as it might have got wetted and soiled in my pocket. Until
we were off Falmouth, I did not know that we were to stand in. I was
then too much engaged in shortening sail to get out my letter. When
I was at last able to go below, I hurried to my bag, intending to add a
postscript, but what was my dismay to be unable to find it.

I felt again and again, and then turned out all my things, but could nowhere discover the missing epistle. I hastened to try and obtain another sheet of paper from the purser's steward, but he was just then too much engaged to attend to me, and directly after I got it my watch was called and I had to return on deck.

The moment my watch was over, I went below and, as well as I could, began writing. It was no easy matter in the dim light and hubbub going on around me. I finished it, however, telling my dear wife all that had occurred, how miserable I was at being separated from her, and my hopes, while I remained in the Channel cruiser, of being allowed to get on shore some day, even though we might be together but for a few short hours. The letter was closed and wafered; I rushed on deck with it, but only to find that the last boat from the shore had shoved off, and the next instant the hands were turned up to make sail.

I felt more inclined than I had ever done since my childhood to burst into tears. I think I should have done so from very vexation and disappointment, had I not been obliged to hurry to my station, putting my letter in my pocket as I did so.

It was trying, every one will allow, for all this time my dear wife could not tell what had become of me. My other friends might think me dead, but I knew that she would never believe that to be the case until she had strong evidence of the fact. Even if she had, I felt sure nothing would ever induce her to marry again.

The wind was fair up Channel. Arriving nearly abreast of the Start Point, we ran out to the southward, the captain hoping to fall in with one of the two French frigates which a short time before we and the *Venus* had chased into Cherbourg. One of the two was, as I before said, the *Sémillante*, the other was the *Cleopatra*.

On the morning of the 18th of June, just as day broke, the Start bearing east by north, distant five or six leagues, we discovered a sail in the south-east quarter, and immediately afterwards bore up in chase, carrying all the canvas we could set.   As we approached the stranger, we felt nearly sure that she was the very French frigate we were in search of.   She was under all sail, some of us thought, for the purpose of getting away.

'We shall have another long chase, and if that there craft has a fast pair of heels, she'll get into Cherbourg and make us look foolish,' said Dick Hagger as we watched her.

We stood on, and soon had the satisfaction of discovering that we were sailing faster than the stranger.   The captain and several of the other officers were examining her through their glasses.

In a short time they formed the opinion that she was no other than the *Cleopatra* which had before got away from us, and such we after-wards found to be the case.

A shout rose from our deck when we observed her haul up her foresail and lower her topgallant sails, showing that she had made up her mind to fight us.

In about two hours and a half, we got so near that we heard some one from her quarter-deck hail us.

Captain Pellew, on this, not making out distinctly what was said, shouted, 'Ahoy! ahoy!' when our crew gave three cheers, and right hearty ones they were, and shouted, 'Long live King George.'

As yet, not a shot had been fired, and it might have been supposed that we were two friendly ships meeting.   On hearing our cheer, the French captain—his name we afterwards heard was Mullon—came on to the gangway, and waving his hat, exclaimed, '*Vive la Nation!*' on which his crew tried to give three cheers, as we had done; but it was a very poor imitation, I can vouch for it.

They had no one to lead them off, and they uttered shrieks rather than cheers, which, when we gave them, came out with a hearty ringing sound.

We saw the French captain talking to his crew, and waving a cap of liberty which he held in his hand. He then gave it to one of the men, who ran up the rigging and screwed it to the masthead.

'We'll soon bring that precious cap of yours down, my boys,' cried Dick.

We were all this time at our guns, stripped to the waist, ready and eager to begin the game; and if the Frenchmen behaved as they seemed inclined to do, it would be, we felt sure, pretty sharp work.

The French captain now coming to the gangway, waved his hat. Our captain did the same, and passed the word along the deck that we were not to fire until we saw him raise his hat to his head.

Eagerly watching for the signal, we stood on, gradually nearing the French frigate, both of us running before the wind, until our foremost larboard guns could be brought to bear on the starboard quarter of the *Cleopatra.*

The captain raised his hat. Almost before it was on his head, the foremost gun was fired, the others being rapidly discharged in succession.

We were not to have the game all on our own side, for the French ship at once returned the compliment, and her shot came crashing on board of us.

We now, being within rather less than hailing distance of each other, kept blazing away as fast as we could run our guns in and out.

We were doing considerable damage to the Frenchman, we could see, but we were suffering not a little ourselves. Two of our midshipmen had fallen, killed while steadily going about their duty. Soon afterwards I saw another poor young fellow knocked over. Then the boatswain, in the act of raising his whistle to his mouth, had his head shot away; and some of the men declared that they heard it sounding notwithstanding, as it flew overboard. I saw three or four of our jollies—as we called the marines—drop while firing away from the forecastle. A round shot also striking our mainmast, I every instant expected to see it fall.

Though badly wounded, it was not cut through, however, and the carpenter and his crew set to work immediately to fish it.

We had been engaged some twenty minutes or so, when we saw the *Cleopatra* haul up some eight points from the wind.

We followed her closely, having no intention of allowing her to escape, if such was the expectation of her commander.

After blazing away some little time longer, down came her mizen-mast; directly afterwards her wheel was shot away. She was thus rendered unmanageable, though for some time her crew endeavoured to keep her on her course by trimming sails; but our shot soon cutting away her braces, she played round off, and came stem on towards us, her jibboom passing between our fore and main masts, pressing so hard against the already wounded mainmast that I expected every instant to see it fall, especially as we had lost the main and spring stays. It was a question which would first go, our mainmast or the Frenchman's jibboom.

Fortunately for us, the latter was carried away, and our mainmast stood. The moment our captain saw the stem of the *Cleopatra* strike us, supposing that the French were about to board, he shouted out, 'Boarders, repel boarders!' But the Frenchmen hadn't the heart to do it, and instead of their boarding us, we boarded them.

One party, led by our first lieutenant, rushed on the enemy's forecastle; while another division, headed by the master, got through his main-deck ports.

Although the *Cleopatra's* jibboom had given way, her larboard main-topmast studding-sail boom-iron had hooked on to the leech rope of our main-topsail, and was producing so powerful a strain on the mast that it seemed as if it could not possibly stand a minute longer. Seeing this, a brave fellow named Burgess, a maintop man, sprang aloft, and, in spite of the bullets aimed at him by some of the French marines stationed aft, cut the leech rope from the end of the main-yard.

Our third lieutenant had in the meantime cut away our best bower anchor, which had hooked on to the enemy's ship.

I was one of those who had got through the main-deck ports. Following our gallant master, we fought our way aft, the Frenchmen for some time defending themselves bravely; but they could not resist the impetuosity of our charge, our cutlasses slashing and hewing, and our pistols going off within a few inches of their heads. At last many of them began to cry for quarter.

Although they numbered eighty more men than we did, most of them, throwing down their weapons, leapt below, tumbling head over heels upon each other. The rest fled aft, and seeing we had won the day, made no further resistance. Remarking that the Frenchman's flag was still flying, I sprang aft to the halyards, and down I hauled it, cheering lustily as I did so, the cheer being taken up by the remaining crew of the *Nymph*.

The *Cleopatra* was ours. Never did I witness a more fearful sight. The decks fore and aft were slippery with gore, and covered with the dead and dying. During the short time we had been engaged, upwards of sixty had been struck down who, not an hour before, full of health and spirits, had attempted to reply to our cheer. Among them, on one side of the quarter-deck, lay the gallant Captain Mullon, surrounded by a mass of gore, for a round shot had torn open his back and carried away the greater part of his left hip. In one hand he was holding a paper, at which, strange as it may seem, he was biting away and endeavouring to swallow. I, with two other men, went up to him to ascertain what he was about. In the very act his hand fell, his jaw dropped, and there was the paper sticking in his mouth. He was dead. It evidently, however, was not the paper he intended to destroy, but, as it turned out, was his commission; for in his right pocket was found the list of coast signals used by the French, which, with his last gasp, he was thus endeavouring to prevent falling into the hands of the British.

Without loss of time one hundred and fifty prisoners were removed on board the *Nymph*, and just as the last had stepped on board the ships separated.

The third lieutenant, who had been sent on board with a prize crew, at once set to work to repair the damages which the *Cleopatra* had received, while all hands in the *Nymph* were actively employed in the same way. When we came to look at our watches, we found that we had dished up the enemy in just fifty minutes from the time the first shot had been fired at her until her flag was hauled down.

'Pretty quick work,' said Dick Hagger to me as we were working together repairing the rigging. 'I told you the captain would be sharp about it; he always is at all he undertakes.'

On making up the butcher's bill, however, as the purser called it, we found that although the Frenchmen out of three hundred and twenty men and boys had lost sixty-three, we, out of our two hundred and forty, had had no less than twenty-three killed and twenty severely wounded, making fifty in all. Of these, the gentlemen belonging to the midshipmen's berth had suffered most severely, for four of them had been killed and two wounded. Of the senior officers, none had been killed; but the second lieutenant had been wounded, as was the lieutenant of marines, with six of his men.

As soon as sail could be got on the two frigates, we, to my great joy, steered a course for the Isle of Wight. I now felt more thankful than ever that I had escaped, as there seemed every probability that I should be able to see my dear wife, or at all events communicate with her. As soon as I went below, though I could with difficulty keep my eyes from closing, I opened my letter and added a few lines describing the action, and then placed it in my pocket, ready to send off on the first opportunity.

In spite of the poor fellows suffering below, and the number of shipmates we had lost, we felt very happy as with a fair breeze we sailed in through the Needles, our well-won prize following in our wake.

Never did those high-pointed rocks look more white and glittering, or the downs more green and beautiful, while the blue sea sparkling in the sunlight seemed to share our joy. The people on the shore, as we passed the little town of Yarmouth, waved to us, and threw up their hats, and the flags from many a flagstaff flew out to the breeze.

As soon as we brought up at Spithead, I eagerly looked out for a boat going to the shore, by which to send my letter, hoping to have it delivered at once, instead of letting it go through the post office; but, as it was late in the evening, no shore boats came off, and I had to wait all the night, thinking how little my dear wife supposed I was so near her.

I turned out at daybreak, before the hammocks were piped up, that I might take a look at the spot where I thought she was living. Suddenly a sickness came over me. What if she should have been taken ill when I was so rudely torn from her! Perhaps she had never recovered, and was even now numbered among the dead. I could scarcely refrain from jumping overboard and trying to swim to Southsea beach. It seemed so near, and yet I knew that I could not do it. Then I thought I would go boldly up to the first lieutenant and tell him how teacherously I had been carried off,—snatched, as it were, from the arms of my young wife,—and ask him to give me leave for a few hours, promising faithfully to come back at the time he might name.

Then I reflected that the ship was short-handed, that we had the prisoners to guard, and that until she had been brought up safe in Portsmouth harbour, every man would be required for duty.

'It would be useless to ask him,' I groaned out. 'He'll remember I'm a pressed man, and would not trust me. It is too common for men to break their word and desert, indifferent to what others may suffer in consequence. No,' I thought, 'I'll try to send my letter first, and then wait with all the patience I can muster until I can get an answer.'

Before long the hands were turned up, and we all set about our usual duties, washing down decks and giving them a double allowance of holystoning, to try and get out more of the blood stains before visitors should come on board.

Scarcely was this work over than the order was given to get up the anchor and make sail, as, tide and wind being favourable, we were to run into harbour.

My heart bounded at the thought, I sprang with eagerness to my station, the ship gathered way and, followed by our prize, we stood towards the well-known entrance of Portsmouth harbour.

CHAPTER XVIII.

The ship made snug—Visitors come on board—Jerry Vincent—News of my wife, and home—How my uncle became indignant—Jerry wishes me to take French leave—I refuse, I ask for and obtain permission to go ashore—Meeting with Uncle Kelson—Jerry prepares my wife for the interview—Tempted to desert—A happy time—Jerry's recollections—On board the *Arethusa*—Yarns—A ghost story—A slippery deck—The pirates' heads.

THE *Nymph* under all plain sail, our prize following in our wake, glided on past Southsea Castle—the yellow beach, the green expanse of the common, the lines of houses and cottages beyond the Postdown hills rising in the distance, the batteries of Gosport and Portsmouth ahead, the masts of numberless vessels of all sizes seen beyond them.

I waited at my station in the foretop for the order to shorten sail. I cast many a glance towards the shore, where she whom I loved best on earth was, I fancied, gazing at the two ships with thousands of other spectators, little supposing that I was on board one of them. As we entered the harbour, we heard with joyous hearts the order given to shorten sail. The boatswain's pipe sounded shrilly; the topmen flew aloft. Never did a ship's crew pull and haul, and run out on the yards, with greater alacrity to furl the canvas.

The water was covered with boats, the people standing up and waving and cheering. It was no easy matter to steer clear of them as we stood up the harbour. When rounding to off the dockyard, the anchor was dropped, the cable running out like lightning, as if eager to do its duty and help to bring us safe home. The prize then passing us, brought up close under our stern.

Scarcely was the cable stoppered, and the ship made snug, than hundreds of boats pulled up alongside, those on board anxious to hear all about the victory we had gained.

Among the first was a somewhat battered-looking wherry, with a little wizened old man and a boy pulling. The former, catching sight of me as I stretched my neck through a port, throwing in his oar, uttered a shout of astonishment, and then, with the agility of a monkey, quickly clambered up the side by a rope I hove to him.

'What! Will, Will, is it you yourself?' exclaimed Jerry Vincent, wringing my hand and gazing into my face. 'We all thought you were far away in the East Indies, and Mistress Kelson made up her mind that you'd never come back from that hot region where they fry beefsteaks on the capstan-head.'

'But my wife—my wife! is she well? Oh, tell me, Mr. Vincent,' I exclaimed, interrupting him. 'She expected me to come back.'

'She's well enough, if not so hearty as we'd be wishing ; for, to say the truth, the roses don't bloom in her cheeks as they used to do.'

I cannot describe the joy and relief this reply brought to my heart. The gratitude which I felt made me give old Jerry a hug, which well-nigh pressed the breath out of his body.

'Why, Will, my boy, you are taking me for Mrs. Weatherhelm,' he exclaimed, bursting into a fit of laughter. 'You'll soon see her, and then you can hug her as long as you like, if you can get leave to go on shore; if not, I'll go and bring her here as quick as I can pull back to the point and toddle away over to Southsea.'

'Oh, no, no; I wouldn't have her here on any account,' I answered as I thought of the disreputable characters who in shoals would soon be crowding the decks, and who were even now waiting in the boats until they were allowed to come on board.

'Tell me, Jerry, about my uncle and Aunt Bretta; how are they both?

'Hearty, though the old gentleman did take on when you were carried away by the pressgang. If ever I saw him inclined to run a muck, it was then. We had a hard matter, I can tell you, to prevent him from posting off to London to see the First Lord of the Admiralty, to grapple him by the throat if he did not send an order down at once to have you liberated. I don't know, indeed, what he'd have done; but at last we persuaded him that if he made up his mind to proceed to such extremities, the First Lord would either laugh in his face or order the porters to kick him down stairs. He in time came to that conclusion himself, and so quieted down, observing that you would do your duty and bear yourself like a man.'

'I must try and get leave from the first lieutenant. He could not refuse me, when I tell him I was torn away from my wife, and I will promise to be back again at any time he may name.'

'You may try it, Will, but I'm not so sure about the matter. If he doesn't, why, I'd advise you to take French leave and slip into my wherry as soon as it's dark. I'll have a bit of canvas to cover you up, and pull you ashore in a jiffey. You can land at the yard of a friend of mine, not far from the point, and disguise yourself in shore-going toggery. Every one knows me, and I'll get you through the gates; and if I'm accused of helping you off, I'll stand the consequences. It can only be a few months in gaol, and though I'd rather have my liberty, I can make myself happy wherever I am.'

'No, Jerry, I would not let you run that risk for my sake on any account; nor would I run it myself, much as I love my liberty and my wife,' I answered. 'You stay here and I'll go and ask the first lieutenant at once; if he refuses me now, he'll be sure to give me leave another day.'

'Well go Will,—go,' said Jerry. 'I'm much afraid that your first lieutenant, unless he is very much unlike others I have known, won't care a rap about your wife's feelings or yours. He'll just tell you it's the same tale half the ship's company have to tell. and if your wife wants to see you, she may come aboard like the rest of the women.'

Without waiting to hear more of what Jerry might say, I hurried aft, and found the first lieutenant issuing his orders.

'What is it you want, my man?' he asked as I approached him, hat in hand.

'Please, sir, I've got a young wife ashore at Southsea, and I was torn away from her by a pressgang. May I have leave to go and see her, and I promise to be back at any time you may name.'

'A pressed man!—no, no, my fine fellow, no pressed men can be allowed out of the ship. They may take it into their heads not to return at all,' he answered, turning away.

'Pardon me, sir,' I said, 'but I give you my word of honour that I will come back as soon as you order me.'

He glanced round with a look of astonishment, muttering, 'Your word of honour! Who are you, my man?'

'I am a Shetlander, sir. I have been brought up to keep my word. Though I was pressed, I have done my duty. It was I, sir, who hauled down the flag of the *Cleopatra* when we took her.'

While he was speaking, a midshipman brought him a letter. He opened it, and glancing over the few lines it contained, his eye brightened. I stood watching, resolved not to be defeated.

As soon as he had folded the letter and put it into his pocket, I again stepped up.

'May I go, sir?' I said.

'Well,' he answered, smiling, 'you hauled down the Frenchman's flag. I am to have my reward, and you shall have yours. You may go ashore, but you must be back in three days. All the crew will be required for putting the ship to rights, to take the mainmast out of her and replace it by a new one,' and he ordered one of the clerks to put down my name as having leave.

I found afterwards that the letter I saw him read contained an intimation that he was forthwith to be made a commander.

In a few days the news was received that the great Earl of Chatham had presented our captain and his brother to King George, who had been pleased to knight our captain, and to make Commander Pellew a post captain.

No one else, that I know of, obtained any honours or rewards, though each man and boy received his share of prize-money, and with that we had no cause to complain.

However, to go back to the moment when the first lieutenant gave me leave. 'Thank you, sir! thank you!' I exclaimed, with difficulty stopping myself from tossing up my hat for joy.

As soon as the words were out of his mouth, I rushed below, and, taking the things I wanted out of my bag, I tumbled into Jerry's wherry.

The old man pulled as fast as he and his boy could lay their backs to the oars.

'Stop, stop, my lad! wait for me!' he exclaimed as I jumped ashore and was preparing to run to Southsea. 'You'll frighten your wife and send her into "high strikes" if you pounce down upon her as you seem inclined to do. Wait till I go ahead and tell her to be looking out for you. You won't lose much time, and prevent a great deal of mischief, though I can't move along quite at the rate of ten knots an hour, as you seem inclined to do.'

I at once saw the wisdom of Jerry's advice, and waited, though somewhat impatiently, until he and his boy had secured the boat.

'Come along, Will, my lad,' he said at length, stepping ashore; 'I'll show you what my old legs can do,' and off he set.

22

We soon crossed the High Street, and made our way through the gate leading out of the town on to Southsea Common.

The village of Southsea was but a small, insignificant place in those days. We had not gone far when we caught sight of a person with a wooden leg stumping along at a good rate some way ahead. Although his back was towards us, I at once felt sure that he was Uncle Kelson.

'All right!' cried Jerry, 'that's Mr. Kelson. He always carries a press of sail. It couldn't have been better. I'll go on and make him heave to, and just tell him to guess who's come back; but I don't think there's much fear of his getting the "high strikes" even though he was to set eyes on you all of a sudden.'

I brought up for a moment so as to let Jerry get ahead of me.

'Heave to, cap'en! heave to! I ain't a thundering big enemy from whom you've any cause to run,' I heard him shouting out. 'Just look round, and maybe you'll see somebody you won't be sorry to see, I've a notion.'

My uncle, hearing Jerry's voice, turned his head, and instantly catching sight of me, came running along with both his arms outstretched, his countenance beaming all over like a landscape lighted up by sunshine. I was somewhat fearful lest he should fall, but I caught him, and we shook hands for a minute at least, his voice almost choking as he exclaimed, 'I am glad! I am glad! Bless my heart, how glad I am! And your wife, Will? You'll soon make her all to rights. Not that she is ill, but that she's been pining for you, poor lass; but no wonder: it's a way the women have. Glad I hadn't a wife until I was able to live on shore and look after her. Come along! come along!' and he took my arm, almost again falling in his eagerness to get over the ground, which here and there was soft and sandy, and full of holes in other places.

'Please, Mr. Kelson, as I was atelling of your nevvy, it won't do just
to come down on the lass like a thunder-clap, or it may send her over
on her beam ends,' said Jerry as he ranged up alongside, puffing and
blowing with his exertions. 'Just you stop and talk to him when we
get near the house, and let me go ahead and I'll break the matter gently,
like a soft summer shower, so that they'll be all to rights and ready for
him when he comes.'

Jerry, I guessed, wanted to undertake the matter himself, suspecting
that my uncle would, notwithstanding his good intentions, blurt out the
truth too suddenly.

I therefore answered for him, that we would wait till Jerry had gone
to the house and summoned us, though I had to exert no small amount
of resolution to stop short of the door when we got in sight of it.

Jerry ran on at first, but went more deliberately as he approached the
door, when, knocking, he was admitted.

He must be spinning a tremendous long yarn, I thought, for it seemed
to me as if he had kept us half an hour, though I believe it was only
two or three minutes, when at length he appeared and beckoned.

'Come along, Will! come along, my boy!' cried my uncle, keeping
hold of my arm; but, no longer able to restrain my impatience, I sprang
forward and, brushing past old Jerry, rushed into the house.

There was my Margaret, with Aunt Bretta by her side to support her;
but she needed no support except my arm. After a little time, though
still clinging with her arms round my neck, she allowed me to embrace
my good aunt. My uncle soon joined us, and Old Jerry poked his head
in at the door, saying with a knowing nod, 'All right, I see there's been
no "high strikes." I shall be one too many if I stop. Good-day,
ladies; good-day, friends all. I'll look in to-morrow, or maybe the next
evening; but I shall have plenty of work in the harbour, taking off
people to see the prize and the ship which captured her.'

'Stop, Jerry, stop!' cried my uncle; 'have a glass of grog before
you go?'

'No, thankee, cap'en,' answered Jerry. 'I must keep a clear head on
my shoulders. If I once takes a taste, maybe I shall want another as I
pass the Blue Posteses.'

Uncle Kelson did not press the point, and the old man took his
departure.

Of course it required a long time to tell all that had happened to me,
but I need not describe those happy days on shore. My dear wife
would scarcely allow me for a moment to be out of her sight. She once
asked the question, 'Must you go back?'

'I have given my word that I would,' I answered. I knew full well
what her heart wished, though she had too much regard for my honour
even to hint at the possibility of my breaking my word.

Aunt Bretta and Uncle Kelson were of the same way of thinking; but
old Jerry, who paid us a visit the second evening according to his promise, looked at the matter in a very different light.

'Now, Will, I've been thinking over this here business of yours every
day since I first clapped eyes on you, and I've made up my mind that
as they had no right to press you aboard that 'ere frigate, you have
every right to make yourself scarce. I've got the whole affair cut and
dry. There's a friend of mine who is as true as steel. He's got a
light cart, and we intend to bundle you in soon after dark, and drive
away, maybe to Chichester, and maybe to some country place where
you can lie snug till the frigate has sailed, and the hue and cry after
you is over.

'It's all as smooth as oil. There'll only be one man less aboard, as
there would be if a shot was to take your head off; so it can't make any
odds to the captain and officers. And let me tell you, you'll have a
different set over you; for Mr. Morris the first lieutenant, has got his

promotion, Mr. Lake is too badly wounded to allow him to return on board for some time, and the captain is sure to get a better ship; so you don't know what double-fisted fellows you'll get in their places.

'Follow my advice, Will; escape from all the tyranny and floggings, for what you can tell, that are in store for you. Run, and be a free man.'

'No, no, Mr. Vincent; the advice you give is well meant, but I dare not even ask my husband to do as you propose,' answered Margaret in a firm voice, though she looked very sad as she spoke. 'He would not be a happy man if he broke his word, and he has given that word to return. Even I can say, "Go back to your duty."'

'So do I,' said Uncle Kelson, ' though, if he had not given his word, I don't know what I might have advised.'

'We can all pray for him,' said Aunt Bretta, 'and I trust that we shall see him again before long, when he is free and can with a clean conscience remain with us.'

'I thank you, Jerry, for your good wishes,' I put in. 'It cannot be, you see. I wish I could get away from the ship; but until I am paid off, and properly discharged, though I was pressed, I am bound to remain; so if you care for me, do not say anything more on the subject.'

'Well, well, if it must be, so it must,' answered Jerry with a deep sigh. 'Some people's notions ain't like other people's notions, that's all I've got to say; and now I think it's time for me to be tripping my anchor.'

'No, no, not until you have wetted your whistle,' said Uncle Kelson, beginning to mix a glass of grog.

The old man's eyes glistened as he resumed his seat, replacing his hat under the chair; and putting his hand out to take the tumbler which my uncle pushed towards him across the table, and sipping it slowly, he looked up and said:

'I forgot to tell you that Sir Edward Pellew, as we must now call

him since he got the sword laid across his shoulders by the king, has
been appointed to the command of the *Arethusa*, a fine new frigate
which will make a name for herself, if I mistake not, as the old one did.
You remember her, cap'en, don't you? It was her they writ the song
about,' and he began singing :

> " Come all ye jolly sailors bold
> Whose hearts are cast in honour's mould,
> While English glory I unfold :
> Huzza ! to the *Arethusa* ;
> She is a frigate tight and brave
> As ever stemmed the dashing wave,
> Her men are staunch to their fav'rite launch,
> And when the foe shall meet our fire,
> Sooner than strike, we'll all expire
> On board of the *Arethusa !*

> " 'Twas with the spring fleet she went out,
> The English Channel to cruise about.
> When four French sail, in show so stout,
> Bore down on the *Arethusa*.
> The famed *Belle Poule* straight ahead did lie,
> The *Arethusa* seemed to fly,
> Not a sheet or a tack or a brace did she slack,
> Though the Frenchman laughed and thought it stuff,
> But they knew not the handful of men how tough
> On board of the *Arethusa !*

> " On deck five hundred men did dance,
> The stoutest they could find in France ;
> We with two hundred did advance,
> On board of the *Arethusa !*
> Our captain hail'd the Frenchman, ' Ho!'
> The Frenchman then cried out ' Hullo !'
> ' Bear down, d'ye see, to our Admiral's lee.'
> ' No, no,' says the Frenchman ; ' that can't be.'
> ' Then I must lug you along with me,'
> Says the saucy *Arethusa !*

> " The fight was off the Frenchman's land,
> We forced them back upon their strand,
> For we fought till not a stick would stand
> Of the gallant *Arethusa*.

And now we've driven the foe ashore,
Never to fight with Britons more,
Let each fill a glass to his fav'rite lass,
A health to our captain and officers true,
And all who belong to the jovial crew
On board of the *Arethusa !*"

'I mind,' continued Jerry after another sip at his grog, 'that she carried thirty-two guns, and was commanded by Captain Marshall. It was in the year 1778, just before the last war broke out. We hadn't come to loggerheads with the mounseers, though we knew pretty well that it wouldn't be long before we were that. We and two other frigates sailed down Channel with a fleet of twenty sail of the line under Admiral Keppel.

'When off the Lizard, on the 17th of June, we made out two frigates and a schooner to the southward. On seeing them, and guessing that they were French, the Admiral ordered us and the *Milford* to go in chase. The strangers separated, the *Milford* frigate and *Hector*, a seventy-four, following the other ship, which turned out to be the *Licorne*, and took her; while the *Albert* cutter pursued the schooner, and captured her by boarding after a sharp struggle. We meantime alone followed the other stranger, which was the French forty-gun frigate *Belle Poule.*

'On getting within hailing distance, our captain, in the politest manner possible, invited the French captain to sail back with him to the English fleet.

'"No, no," answered the French skipper, "that it cannot be, seeing I am bound elsewhere."

'"Then, mounseer, I must obey orders and make you come with me," says our captain just as politely as before, and without further ado he ordered the crew of the foremost main-deck gun to fire a shot across the French ship's bows. It was the first shot fired during the war

We in return got the Frenchman's whole broadside crashing aboard us.

'We then began pounding away at each other as close as we could get. It seemed wonderful to me that we were not both of us blown out of the water. Our men were falling pretty thickly, some killed and many more wounded, while our sails and rigging were getting much cut up.

'You see the enemy had twenty guns on a side to our sixteen, but we tossed ours in and out so sharply that we made up for the difference. For two mortal hours we kept blazing away, getting almost as much as we gave, till scarcely a stick could stand aboard us; but our captain was not the man to give in, and while he could he kept at it. At last, our rigging and canvas being cut to pieces, and our masts ready to fall, so that we could not make sail, the *Belle Poule* having had enough of it, shot ahead, and succeeded in getting under the land where we were unable to follow her.

'The song says that we drove her ashore; but though we did not exactly do that, we knocked her well about, and she had forty-eight men and officers killed and fifty wounded. As it was, as I have said, the first action in the old war, it was more talked about than many others. We lost our captain, not from his being killed, but from his getting a bigger ship, and Captain Everitt was appointed in his stead.

'The old *Arethusa*, after this, continued a Channel cruiser. We had pretty sharp work at different times, chasing the enemy, and capturing their merchantmen, and cutting out vessels from their harbours; but we had no action like the one the song was wrote about.

'At last, in the March of the next year, when some fifty leagues or more off Brest, we made out a French frigate inshore of us. Instead of standing bravely out to fight the saucy *Arethusa*, she squared away her yards and ran for that port. We made all sail in chase, hoping to come up with her before she could get into harbour. We were gaining on her, and were expecting that we should have another fight like that with the *Belle Poule*, when, as we came in sight of the outer roads of Brest, what should we see but a thumping seventy-four, which, guessing what we were, slipping her cable, stood out under all sail to catch us.

'We might have tackled the seventy-four alone, with a good breeze; but we well knew that if we did not up stick and cut, we should either be knocked to pieces or be sent to the bottom; so our captain, as in duty bound, ordered us to brace up the yards and try to make the best of our way out of danger. We might have done so had there been a strong breeze blowing, but we could not beat the ship off shore as fast as we wanted.

'Night came down upon us, and a very dark night it was. We could not see the land, but we knew it was under our lee, when presently thump goes the ship ashore. Our captain did his best to get her off, but all our attempts were of no use. The saucy *Arethusa* was hard and fast on the rocks.

'The word was given to lower the boats. I was one of the first cutter's crew. We had got her into the water, and the master, as good a seaman as ever stepped, came with us, and two young midshipmites.

'"We'll not be made prisoners if we can help it, lads," said the master. "Here, lower down these two casks of bread, and this breaker of water."

'We had no time to get more, and we hoped the other boats would follow our example, but they would have to be sharp about it. We got round from under the lee of the ship, against which the surf was already breaking heavily, and pulled away to the windward out to sea. You may be sure we pulled as men do who are pulling for their lives and liberty. If we had been a minute later, we shouldn't have done it. No other boats that we could see followed us. Next morning we were twenty miles off shore.

'We felt very downcast at the thoughts that we had lost our little frigate, but were thankful to have got away from a French prison. We learned afterwards that the captain, fearing for the lives of his people, sent the other boats at once to the shore, and establishing a communication, managed to land the whole crew, who were forthwith made prisoners. It was fortunate that we had the biscuit and water, or we should have been starved to death; for it was a week or more before we fell in with an English homeward-bound West Indiaman, when we had not a gill of liquid left, and not a biscuit apiece. I learned the value of water at that time, but I have always held to the opinion that a little good rum mixed with it adds greatly to its taste,' and Jerry winked at my uncle with one eye, and with the other looked at his tumbler, which was empty.

Uncle Kelson mixed him another glass.

'Ladies both,' he said, looking round at my aunt and Margaret, 'here's to your health, and may Will be with you a free man before many months are over. Maybe you haven't heard of the ghost we had on board the old *Cornwall*, some years before the time I am speaking of? If you haven't, I'll tell you about it. Did you ever have a ghost aboard any ship you sailed in cap'en? Maybe not. They don't seem to show themselves now-a-days, as they used to do.

'Dick Carcass was the boatswain of the old *Cornwall* when I served aboard her. He was a tall spare man with high shoulders and a peculiar walk, so that it was impossible to mistake him meet him where you might. He was also a prime seaman, and had a mouth that could whistle the winds out of conceit. If he did use a rope's end on the backs of the boys sometimes, it was all for their own good. We were bound out one winter time to Halifax, Nova Scotia. It isn't the pleasantest time of the year to be sailing across the North Atlantic. We had had a pretty long passage, with westerly gales, which kept all hands employed.

The boatswain was seldom off deck, and a rough life he had of it.

'At last, what with the hard work he had to do, and having been in hospital too before we sailed, he fell sick, and one night the doctor came out of his cabin and told us he was dead. Now our captain was a kind-hearted man; and as he expected to be in port in two or three days, instead of sewing the boatswain up in a hammock and lowering him overboard, he gave notice that he should keep him to give him decent Christian burial on shore, and let the parson pray over him, for, d'ye see, we had none aboard. To pay him every respect, a sentry was placed at the door of his cabin in the cockpit. He had been dead three or four days, and we had expected to get into port in two or three at the furthest; so as the wind continued foul, and might hold in the same quarter a week longer, the captain, thinking the bo'sun wouldn't keep much longer, at last determined to have him buried the next morning. That night I had just gone below, and was passing close to the sentry, when he asked me if I couldn't make his lantern burn brighter. He was a chum of mine, d'ye see. I took it down from the hook where it was hanging, and was trying to snuff it, when all of a sudden the door of Mr. Carcass's cabin opened with a bang like a clap of thunder, and, as I'm a living man, I heard the bo'sun's voice, for you may be sure I knew it well, shout out:

'"Sentry, give us a light, will ye!"

'Somehow or other—maybe I nipped the wick too hard—the candle went out, and down fell the lantern. I did not stop to pick it up, nor did the sentry who got the start of me, and off we set, scampering away like rats with a terrier at their tails, till we gained the upper step of the cockpit ladder. We then stopped and listened. There were steps thundering along the deck. They came to the very foot of the ladder. Presently we heard something mounting them slowly. The sentry moved on. So did I, but looking round I saw as surely as 1 sit here, the head of old Dick Carcass's ghost rising slowly above the deck.

'We did not stop to see more of him, but walked away for'ard. Again we stopped, when there he was, standing on the deck—eight feet high he looked at least—rubbing his eyes, which glared out at us like balls of fire.

'We made for the foreladder, and there thought to get out of its way by moving aft as fast as our legs could carry us. Presently, as I looked over my shoulder, I saw the ghost come up the ladder on to the forecastle. The men there saw him too, for they scuttled away on either side, and left him to walk alone. For five minutes or more he kept pacing up and down the deck, just as he was accustomed to do when he was alive. By this time the men were crowding aft, the sentry among them, when the lieutenant of the watch, thinking maybe there was going to be a mutiny, or something of that sort, sings out and axes what we were about.

' "Sir," answers the sentry, who was bold enough now; "there's the ghost of Mr. Carcass a walking the fo'cas'l."

' "The ghost of Mr. Carcass be hanged! he is quiet enough in his cabin, poor man. What are all you fools thinking about?" says the lieutenant. "Be off for'ard with you."

' "He is there, sir! he is there! It is the bo'sun's ghost," we all sung out, one after the other, none of us feeling inclined to go near him.

' "Blockheads!" cried the lieutenant, beginning to get angry.

' "It is him, sir; it is him," cried others. "He's got on the hat and monkey jacket he always wears."

'The lieutenant now became very angry, and ordering us out of the way, boldly steps forward. When, however, he gets abreast of the barge, he stops, for there he sees as clearly as we did the bo'sun's tall figure pacing the deck, with his hands behind his back, looking for all the world just as he had done when he was alive.

'Now the lieutenant was as brave a man as ever stepped, but he did not like it, that was clear; still he felt that go on he must, and so on he went until he got up to the foremast, and then he sings out slowly, as if his words did not come up readily to his mouth:

'"Mr. Car—car—car—cass, is that you?"

'"Sir!" said the ghost, turning round and coming aft.

'"Mr. Car—car—car—cass, is that you?" again sings out the lieutenant.

'"Sir!" answers the boatswain, and he came nearer.

'The lieutenant stepped back, so did we, all the whole watch tumbling over on each other. Still facing for'ard, the gallant lieutenant kept retreating, and the ghost kept coming on slowly, as ghosts always do, I'm told, though I can't say as I've had much experience with those sort of gentry. At last the ghost sings out :

'"Pardon me, Mr. Pringle, what's the matter? have all the people gone mad?"

'"Who are you?" asked the lieutenant.

'"I am Richard Carcass, bo'sun of this here ship, to the best of my knowledge, and was never anybody else, sir."

'"What! aint you dead?" says the lieutenant.

'"Not that I knows on," answers the ghost. "I was alive when it struck eight bells in the middle watch, and its now only just gone two. I take it it is the morning watch, for I heard it strike just before that stupid sentry put out his light, and for some reason or other I couldn't make out, took to his heels."

'"Why, the doctor said you were dead," says the lieutenant.

'"The doctor, then, doesn't know a dead bo'sun from a live one," answered Mr. Carcass.

' " Well, I wish you'd let him see you, and hear what he's got to say on the subject; " and he ordered the midshipman of the watch to call the doctor, who came on deck, grumbling not a little at being roused out from his berth. When he saw the bo'sun he seemed mighty pleased, and taking him by the hand told us all that he was as alive as ever he was, and advised him to turn in again and get some sleep, as the night was cold, and he was on the sick list.

' Well, ladies, that was the only ghost I ever saw. He was not dead either, but had been in a sort of trance, and when he heard two bells strike, not knowing how many days had passed since he had gone to sleep, he called for a light, but not getting it, he dressed in the dark and came on deck, thinking he ought to be there.'

Jerry spun other yarns before he took his leave. He was once, he declared, on board a trader bound out from Ireland to the West Indies with butter and cheese, 'The *Jane and Mary*, that was her name,' he continued. 'We were off the coast of St. Domingo, almost becalmed, when we made out a couple of suspicious-looking craft sweeping off towards us. That they were pirates we had no doubt. At that time those sort of gentry used to cut the throats of every man on board if there was the slightest resistance.

' Our skipper, Captain Dillon, was a determined fellow, and had proved himself a good seaman during the passage.

' " Lads," he sang out, " do you wish to be taken and hove overboard to feed the sharks, or will you try to save the ship if those scoundrels come up to us? I'll promise you we'll beat them if they venture aboard."

' We all answered that we were ready to stick by him, for I believe there was not one of us that did not think we should be dead men before the day was an hour older. The mates promised also to fight to the last.

'"Be smart then, my lads, get up some of the cargo from the hold." We soon had a dozen butter casks hoisted up, knocked in their ends, and payed the decks, and sides, and ropes, and every part of the ship over with the butter. We chucked our shoes below, and got the cutlasses, boarding pikes, and pistols ready. In a few minutes the deck was so slippery, that a man, unless without his shoes, could not stand upon it. We were all ready, with our cutlasses at our sides and the pikes handy, to give the scoundrels a warm reception. Meantime the *Jane and Mary* did her best, as far as the breeze would help her, to keep moving through the water.

'The pirates crept up, and kept firing away at us, one on one quarter and one on the other.

'We answered them with the few guns we carried, though each of them had nearly twice as many as we had, while their decks were crowded with men. Presently they ranged up alongside, and both boarded together, a score or more villanous-looking rascals leaping down on our decks, expecting to gain an easy victory; but they never made a greater mistake in their lives, and it was the last most of them had the chance of making. The moment their feet touched our deck, over they fell flat on their faces, while we with our cutlasses, rushing in among them, killed every mother's son of their number. Others following, shouting, shrieking, and swearing, met the same fate; when the rest of the pirates, seeing what was happening, though not knowing the cause, but fancying, I suppose, that we had bewitched them, sheered off, and the breeze freshening we stood away, leaving the two feluccas far astern. Forty men lay dead on our decks, and not one of us was hurt.

'"Heave the carcases overboard, and swab up the decks," cried our skipper, as coolly as if nothing had happened.

'We had a pretty job to clean the ship afterwards, but we didn't mind the trouble, seeing that we had saved our lives, and the skipper was well content to lose the dozen casks of butter which had served us so good a turn.

'That skipper of ours had no small amount of humour in his composition, though it was somewhat of a grim character. Before we hove the bodies overboard, he ordered us to cut off the heads of those who had fallen, forty in number, and to pickle them in the empty butter casks, lest, as he said, his account of the transaction might be disbelieved by the good people of Jamaica.

'We arrived safely in Kingston harbour, where the merchants and a lot of other persons came on board. Many of our visitors, when they heard the skipper describe the way we had beaten off the pirates, looked incredulous.

'"Seeing is believing," says he, and he ordered the casks which had been kept on deck to be opened. It was mightily amusing to watch the way our visitors looked at each other, when our skipper forthwith produced the gory heads, among which was that of the captain of one of the piratical craft and that of the first mate of the other.

'Some of them started back with horror, as well they might, for the heads looked dreadful enough as they were pulled out in succession.

'"There's the whole score," says the skipper, as we arranged them along each side of the quarter-deck. "Now, gentlemen, what have you got to say about my veracity?"

'After that, you may be sure the captain's word was never doubted. The heads were then hove overboard, and it was said that Old Tom, the big shark which used to cruise about between Port Royal and Kingston, got the best part of them for his supper. I'm pretty sure he did, because for many a day after that he was not seen, and some thought he had died of indigestion by swallowing those pirates' heads. Howsomdever, he wasn't dead after all, as poor Bob Rattan, an old messmate of mine, found out to his cost. Just about two months had gone by, and Bob one evening was trying to swim from his ship to the shore, when Old Tom caught him by the leg and hauled him to the bottom. His head was washed ashore three days afterwards, bitten clean off, a certain proof that Old Tom had swallowed the pirates' heads, and not finding them agree with him, had left poor Bob's alone.

'Taking in a cargo of sugar we sailed homewards; but I can tell you, till we were well clear of the West Indies we didn't feel comfortable, lest we should fall in again with the pirates, when, as we had no butter aboard to grease our decks, the chances were, we knew, that in revenge they would have cut all our throats and sent the ship to the bottom.

'You see, ladies, that a man may go through no end of dangers, and yet come scot free out of them. So I hope will our friend here, and have many a yarn to spin, and that I may be present to hear them, although I don't think he'll beat mine; and now, as it's getting late, I'll wish you good evening;' and Jerry, taking his hat from under the chair, shook hands with all round.

'You won't take my advice then, Will?' he whispered, as he came to me. 'Well, well, it's a pity. Good night, lad, good night. I'll see you aboard the *Nymph*;' and he hurried away across the common towards the beach where he had left his boat, intending to pass the night under her, as was his general custom in the summer

CHAPTER XIX.

THE time for which I had obtained leave came soon, far too soon, to an end. It seemed as if I had been but a few hours with my dear wife, and now I must part again from her for an indefinite period, how long I could not tell. I knew that while I had health and strength, no sum could obtain my discharge. Men were wanted for the service, and every effort was made to get them, while strict watch was kept on those who had been obtained. Pressgangs were sent on shore every day all along the coast where there was a chance of picking up men. Agents even visited the mines, and people who had been working under ground all their lives, were suddenly transferred to the deck of a man-of-war, and very fine seamen they made too, for they were hardy, intelligent fellows, and liked the change, and no wonder.

Captain Nelson, and other officers, had thus picked up from the Cornish mines a number of prime seamen. However, as I was saying, the time came for me to part from my wife and my kind uncle and aunt. I would not let Margaret accompany me on board, though she wanted to do so, for the reason I have before stated. She and Uncle Kelson, however, came with me down to the Point, where Jerry had promised to be on the look-out to take me on board. Even there the scene was such as it must have pained any right-minded woman to witness.

Drunken seamen and marines, and women, and Jews, and crimps, all crowded together so that it was difficult to get through the surging mass of human beings, many of them fighting and wrangling and swearing, while the Jews were trying to sell their trumpery wares to such of the poor ignorant sailors as had any money left in their pockets, and the more sober of the men were endeavouring to lift their tipsy shipmates into the boats.

I led Margaret back up the street; 'Go home with uncle, dearest,' I said, 'I cannot be happy with you in this fearful crowd. The sooner you are out of Portsmouth the better.'

Uncle Kelson took her arm, and led her along the street, while I hurried back to the Point, for I had not many minutes to spare, as I would not have been a moment behind-hand on any account.

I remember seeing an old Irish woman with a pipe in her mouth, seated on one of several casks placed close together in the middle of the Point. I fought my way through the crowd, and seeing Jerry's wherry, jumped into her, begging him at once to shove off as I was late. He and his boy pulled away; but scarcely had we got half a dozen fathoms from the Point when there was a dreadful explosion. Flames burst up from the midst of the crowd, arms and legs and human bodies were lifted into the air, while others were shot out into the water or on board the boats, while fearful shrieks and screams rose from the scene of the catastrophe. Almost immediately afterwards not a single person could be seen standing on the Point, but many lay there dead, or fearfully mangled. Boats full of people were pulling away from the spot, and the rest of the crowd were flying up towards the street.

It turned out that the old Irishwoman I had noticed seated on the cask, not dreaming that it contained gunpowder, had shaken out the ashes from her pipe on it. How the casks of powder came to be left there is more than I can say. All I know is, that great carelessness prevailed in all departments of the navy in those days, and it's only a wonder that more accidents did not occur.

Numbers of persons were killed by the explosion, others were dreadfully mutilated, and scarcely a scrap of the old woman herself could be discovered. I felt grateful to Heaven that my dear wife and uncle had escaped. Had they come on with me, we should have been close to the spot and among the sufferers. I could not go back, though Jerry wanted to do so, as I had to be on board by noon, and there were but a few minutes to get alongside the ship.

I reported myself to the first lieutenant as having come on board.

'Very well,' he said, and just then it struck eight bells. I had not been long on board when I heard it reported that the *Nymph* was to go into dock, and that the crew would be turned over to other ships wanting hands. It was but too true, and I found that Dick Hagger, I, and others were to be transferred to the *Culloden*, 74, forming one of the Channel fleet, under Earl Howe, and then commanded by Captain Schomberg. She was soon ready for sea, and we went out to Spithead, where the ships were rapidly collecting. I had never seen so many men-of-war together, for there were thirty-four sail of the line, eight frigates, and smaller vessels.

No leave was granted, so I could not get on shore, for we were to be ready to start at a moment's notice, directly intelligence should arrive from the numerous cruisers off the French coast that the Brest fleet had put to sea.

We had a mixed crew, and a bad lot many of them were—jailbirds, smugglers, who were good, however, as far as seamanship was concerned, long-shore men, and Lord Mayor's men, picked up from the London streets, the only difference between the two last being that the latter had tails to their coats,—one slip of the tailor made them both akin,—and we dubbed them K.H.B., or king's hard bargains. Then we had a lot of ordinary seamen, and very ordinary they were. We A.B.'s were in the minority by a long chalk. Lastly came the marines; they were mostly steady men, and, as they had been at sea before, were better sailors than the ordinary seamen, besides which they knew their duty and did it. Without them I am very sure the crew could never have been kept under.

Flogging was the order of the day; scarcely a morning passed but we had two or three triced up, and the boatswain's mates swore that they had never worn out so many cats-o'-nine-tails before.

I don't know that it was the officers' fault, for they knew no better way of maintaining discipline. It was because some hundreds of men, few of whom had ever served on board a man-of-war, were brought together.

I had been on board some days when I caught sight of a face I knew too well; it was that of Charles Iffley. I was certain it was him, though when I inquired I found that he had entered under the name of Charles Trickett.

I saw him start when he first recognised me, but he kept out of my way, and I had no wish to speak to him. His presence, I feared, boded me no good. Whether his feelings of revenge were satisfied, I could not tell; but if not, I was very sure that he would wreak them on my head if he could.

During the early spring, merchant vessels of all sizes, but mostly large ones, kept coming in until nearly a hundred were assembled, when the whole fleet, including men-of-war, amounted to one hundred and forty-eight sail,—three being of a hundred guns, four of ninety-eight, while a large number were seventy-fours. The merchantmen were bound out either to the West Indies or Newfoundland, and some of the men-of-war were intended to convoy them.

At last, on the 2d of May, a frigate came in with the news that the Brest fleet had put to sea. We immediately made sail from St. Helen's and stood down Channel.

Besides looking out for the French fleet, which Lord Howe had determined to attack, we had to see the merchantmen clear of the Channel, and besides that to try and intercept a French convoy coming from America, said to consist of three hundred and fifty sail, laden with provisions and stores, the produce of the West Indian islands, of which the French Republic stood greatly in need.

On arriving off the Lizard, eight of the large ships and six of the frigates were detached to see the merchantmen clear of the latitude of Cape Finisterre, while the Channel fleet, thus reduced to twenty-six sail of the line, besides seven frigates and smaller vessels, stood for Ushant. Before long the frigates made the signal that the French fleet were at sea.

We after this kept cruising up and down looking for them, though our Admiral knew that many of the ships were far larger than ours, but our numbers were equal.

To describe all that took place is more than I can do. I know that it was on the 28th of May that the Admiral heard through some prizes which had been taken that the French fleet of which he was in search were close to us.

Soon after sunrise we made them out bearing down towards us with topgallant sails set. The signal was at once thrown out by the Admiral to prepare for battle. It was a fine sight to see them coming down upon us; but though there was a strong breeze blowing and a heavy sea on, they did not near us as fast as we had expected, and we were ordered to go to dinner. It was the last many a fine fellow on board some of the ships was to take, but I do not believe that any one, on account of the thoughts of the coming battle, ate a worse meal than usual.

Greatly to our disappointment, a short time after we returned on deck, the French fleet were seen making off, but our spirits revived when Lord Howe threw out the signal for a general chase, followed, almost immediately afterwards, by another to engage the enemy's ships as soon as we should arrive up with them. Only our leading ships were, however, able to do so, and we saw them blazing away at the Frenchmen till night closed in on us.

The *Audacious* got most fighting, and being terribly knocked about, was nearly taken by the enemy. She gave as much as she received, and so battered the *Révolutionnaire* that the French ship had to be taken in tow by one of her own frigates.

Next day we had some more fighting, much in the same fashion as on the first, but more severe, several of our ships having lost their topmasts and yards, and two or three of the French being completely disabled.

Thus we kept manœuvring for two days, till, to our great disappointment, we lost sight of the French fleet during the night of the last of May. We had been standing to the westward, when at daybreak on the first of June, latitude 47° 48' north, longitude 18° 30' west, the wind a moderate breeze, south by west, and the sea tolerably smooth, we descried the French fleet, carrying a press of sail about six miles off on our starboard or lee bow, and steering in a line of battle on the larboard tack. At 5 A.M. our ships by signal bore up together and steered north-west. At about 7 A.M., we having again hauled to the wind on the larboard tack, plainly saw the French fleet, consisting of twenty-six sail of the line, the whole, with the exception of one or two, complete in their masts and rigging.

Shortly after this we saw the welcome signal flying, ordering us to breakfast, and as soon as it was over, the still more welcome one to bear down on the enemy. The next signal thrown out was for each ship to steer for and independently engage the ship opposite to her in the

enemy's line, the *Cæsar* leading the van. The *Bellerophon*, or Billy
Ruffian, as she used to be called, followed her ; next came the *Leviathan*.
We were about the thirteenth in line. The ships of both fleets were
carrying single-reefed topsails. Of those of the French, some were
lying to, and others backing and filling to preserve their stations. We
were steering about north-west, with a fresh breeze south by west, and
going little more than five knots an hour.

We were standing on, every ship keeping regularly in line, when what
was the disgust of the true men on board the Culloden to hear the
captain give the order to back the fore and main topsails, three other
ships having done the same, though we were not even yet within range
of the enemy's guns. We soon, however, saw the Admiral speaking
with his signals, and ordering us to make more sail. Our brave old
chief was at the same time setting top-gallant sails, and letting fall his
foresail in order that the *Queen Charlotte* might be first through the
enemy's line. In a short time that noble ship was engaged single-
handed with three of the enemy, for neither the *Gibraltar* nor the
Brunswick were near enough to aid her. She was opposed to one
French hundred and twenty gun ship, and two of eighty guns. In
a short time, down came her fore-topmast, followed shortly afterwards
by her main-topmast, while so damaged were her lower yards and
rigging, that she was almost unmanageable. Notwithstanding this,
she kept blazing away, till she beat off the two eighty gun ships,
which made their escape, and had now only the biggest opposed to her.

The action had now become general, a few of our ships had cut
their way through the French line, and engaged the enemy to leeward ;
the remainder hauled up to windward and opened their fire, some at
a long, others at a more effectual distance. I am sorry to say the
Culloden was among the former. Perhaps our captain thought, with
his undisciplined crew, that it would be hazardous to venture along

side an enemy's ship. He was wrong if he thought so. Bad as our fellows were, we had enough good men to load and fire the guns and the others were able at all events to haul them in and run them out again. It was impossible to see what was taking place. Each captain had to act for himself, and the greater number were doing their duty nobly. The *Brunswick* for some time was hooked by her anchors alongside a French ship, which she almost knocked to pieces. Another, coming up to rescue her friend, received so tremendous a fire that her three masts were speedily cut away by the board.

One ship after another of the French struck, and several were almost dismasted. Of these, four were recovered by the French Admiral, who now stood away to the northward, leaving Earl Howe in possession of six line-of-battle ships which had been captured. The victory was an important one, for although many of our ships had suffered severely, we had not lost one, while besides the six we had taken from the French, we had fearfully knocked about a large number of others.

The old Earl, as far as I know, made no complaint of the way in which some of the ships had disobeyed his orders and kept out of action. We in the *Culloden*, who knew what ought to have been done, felt ashamed of ourselves, that's all I can say.

As soon as the worst damages could be repaired, the whole fleet made sail and stood up Channel, steering for Spithead, where we arrived early on the morning of the 13th, and brought up with our six prizes.

I felt very little of the enthusiasm which animated most of the thousands of visitors who came off to see us; but many were mourners, anxious to obtain information of the loved ones they had lost, and others to see their wounded relatives and friends groaning in pain below. My great desire was to let my wife know that I had escaped, and I was very thankful when Jerry Vincent came alongside, and I was able to despatch a letter by him, he promising to deliver it immediately, and to tell her that I looked well and hearty.

A few days afterwards the King and Queen came down to Portsmouth, and went on board the *Queen Charlotte*, to present the old Admiral—for he was then seventy years of age—with a diamond-hilted sword, and to hang a gold chain round his neck. They then dined with him, and returned on shore in the evening. One of the vice-admirals was made Lord Graves, and the other Viscount Bridport. The rear-admirals were created baronets, and the first-lieutenant of every line of battle ship in the action was made a commander. The rest got empty thanks, and a small share of prize money, which was spent by the greater number of the men the first time they got ashore, so that the grog-sellers, lodging-house keepers, and Jews, benefited chiefly by that. The ships which had suffered went into Portsmouth harbour to refit; but as the *Culloden* had no honourable wounds to show, we were kept at Spithead, and no leave was granted.

The men grumbled and growled, complaining that they were ill-treated, and that it was not their fault that they had not taken a more active part in the battle. The captain and officers best knew the reason why, and they also were out of sorts, for they heard it whispered that they had shown the white feather. They consequently, being out of temper, bullied us, and we were kept at work, exercising at the guns, and making and shortening sail.

Our former captain being removed, Captain Thomas Trowbridge, well known as a good officer, took command of the ship, and we put to sea for a cruise.

The state of the crew, however, had become too bad to be amended in a hurry. Discontent of all sorts prevailed on board.

As we lay at Spithead, one day Hagger came to me and said:

'Will, I don't like the look of things, there's something going to happen. The men complain that the provisions are bad, and we don't get fresh meat and vegetables from shore as we ought, and there's no leave given, and flogging goes on just as it did before, and that our present captain is as severe as the last. There's a knot of them got together, and they are plotting something. That fellow, Charles Trickett, is at the bottom of it, though he takes good care not to be too forward. They have won a good many men over, and they tried to win me, but I'm not going to run my head into a noose to make bad worse.'

'I know all you tell me,' I replied, 'except that I was not aware there was any plotting going on. No one has spoken to me, and Trickett is the last person to do so, though he would be ready to get me into a scrape if he could. I don't think they would be mad enough to attempt anything when they must know what would be the upshot. The leaders will be taken, and either flogged round the fleet, or hung at the yard-arm. I'm glad that you've kept clear, Dick.'

Next day a man I had seldom spoken to came up while I was writing a letter to my wife, and asked me to put my name to a paper which he said wanted a witness, and he could not find any man just then who could sign his name. He was one of the Lord Mayor's men, but notwithstanding by this time had become a pretty smart hand. He had been a pickpocket or something of that sort in the streets of London, and always spoke of himself as being a gentleman, and was fond of using fine language.

'You'll render me an essential service, Weatherhelm, if you'll just do as I request. Here is the paper,' and he produced a large sheet folded up. 'You'll see me write my name, and you'll just write yours as a witness under it. There's the word "witness," you see, in pencil, you need not cover it up.'

He wrote down his own name as Reginald Berkeley, and I attached my signature.

'Thank you extremely,' he said, taking up the paper before I had time, notwithstanding what he said, to write down the word 'witness,' which I knew ought to be in ink. 'That is all I require. It may, I hope, be the means of bringing me a nice little income of a thousand a year or so, to which I am entitled if I obtain my rights, as my solicitor tells me I am sure to do. I'll not forget you, Will, depend upon it. You shall come and stay with me at a snug little box I own down at Richmond,—that is to say, as soon as I come into possession of it, for I have not, properly speaking, got it yet,—or if you want a few pounds at any time, they are at your service. Thank you, thank you, go on with your letter. I must apologize for interrupting you;' and putting the paper in his pocket, he walked away.

I thought no more about the matter, and having finished and closed my letter, went on deck to get it sent on shore, as I knew my wife would be anxiously expecting to hear from me.

A short time after this another fellow, very much the same sort of man as Berkeley, as he called himself, addressed me, and invited me to come forward and take a glass of grog with him.

' I've got a little store of liquor of my own, and I like to share it with honest fellows like you, Weatherhelm,' he said. ' You and I haven't had much talk together, but I have heard of you from Hagger and others, and seen what a prime seaman you are.'

' I'm much obliged to you, Pratt,' I answered, for that was his name, ' but I am not over fond of spirits, and never take a glass except when they are served out, and even then I had as soon, on most occasions, go without it as have it.'

'I dare say you are right,' answered Pratt, 'there's nothing like keeping a cool head on your shoulders; we want cool heads now to guide us. You see we have been barbarously treated, and I am sure you will agree that we ought to get our rights, if we are worthy of being called men. I am told that some of the best hands in the ship have made up their minds on the subject, and they have asked me to join them; but I want to know what your opinion is, for I do not suppose, as you are a fellow of spirit, that you'll be hanging back.'

I guessed what he was driving at, and was cautious in what I said. I advised him not to join any mad attempt to gain by force what he called our rights, saying that I had made up my mind to have nothing to do with anything of the sort. On this I endeavoured to get clear of him, but he stuck to me, and managed somehow or other to lead me among a knot of men who were all talking eagerly together. Several of them spoke to me, and one of the party began to go on much in the same strain that Pratt had done. As he held me fast by the arm, I could not get away from him without using violence, and that I did not want to use. The men were talking away, many of them together, speaking of their grievances, and complaining of the treatment they had received. Some swore that they had been flogged unjustly for things they had never done, others complained of their leave being stopped, some of the badness of their provisions, others of the tyranny of the officers, and the hard work they had to do. I made no observation, for I did not wish to have myself mixed up with them.

There was some truth in what they said, but a great deal of exaggeration, and I observed that the King's Hard Bargains were the very men to make most to do of what they suffered. Except that I had escaped a flogging, and being an able seaman never had to perform what is called dirty work, I had to suffer as much as any of them.

All this time, neither Trickett, or rather Charles Iffley, nor the fellow who called himself Reginald Berkeley, had appeared among us.

They came at last, as if sauntering by, and joining in, asked the men what they were talking about. Several again went over the list of their grievances.

' It's not to be borne!' cried Iffley.

' I should think not!' exclaimed Berkeley; ' I've heard tell of a crew taking the ship from their officers, and sailing away, either to live the life of free rovers of the ocean, or to carry her into some foreign port where they have sold her for a large sum of money, and divided the profits among themselves. I don't say this is what we should do, or what we should be compelled to do, if things don't mend.'

Soon after Berkeley had spoken, half-a-dozen of the most ruffianly fellows in the ship, two of whom boasted of the murders they had committed,—others had been smugglers or pirates for what I know,—came among us, and proposed that we should begin work that very night.

' Now is our opportunity,' they said. ' The captain is on shore, so are many of the officers, including the lieutenant of marines.'

I soon found that matters had proceeded much farther than I had supposed, and that Berkeley and Pratt had spoken to me merely to try and get me to join them, their plans being already formed. Still, what those plans were I could not tell, or I ought, I considered, to go aft and tell the first lieutenant. If I went now, he would think that I had got hold of some cock-and-bull story, and very likely take no notice, while, should the mutineers suspect me, I might have been knocked on the head and have been hove overboard by them in revenge.

I told Hagger, however, what I feared. He acknowledged that he had been spoken to on the subject, but did not think it would be wise, without more certain information, to take any steps in the matter.

The long evening drew on, the hammocks were piped down as usual, and the watch below pretended to turn in; but I observed that they merely kicked off their shoes, and slipped under the blankets all standing.

It had just gone four bells in the first watch, when every man turned out of his hammock. The watch on deck came springing down below and immediately unshipped the ladders. While some were engaged in lashing up the hammocks, others rushed aft and secured the warrant and petty officers.

Another more daring band made their way down to the magazine, took out a quantity of ammunition, and as many muskets and tomahawks as they could lay hands on. They then set to work to form a barricade across the deck between the bits with the hammocks, and shifted the two second guns from forward, which they loaded with grape and canister, and pointed them towards the hatchway. Hunting about, I found Dick Hagger, and he agreed with me that we should try to get on deck; but the ladders being unshipped, we had no means of doing so, and several of the men, seeing what we were about, swore that they would cut us down if we made the attempt. There were several others who also wished to escape, and observing what we had been trying to do, came and joined us. I saw a few marines among the mutineers, but the larger body of the 'jollies,' on turning out of their hammocks, retreated aft with their sergeants and corporals; but as the guns were pointed at them, they could do nothing.

The whole lower part of the ship was thus in possession of the mutineers, together with the magazine, stores, and water, though they could not prevent the officers from getting away or sending on shore to give information of what had occurred.

All night long things continued in this state. No one slept. Councils were held among the men, who swore that until their grievances were redressed they would not give in, and they would rather, if force were

used, blow the ship up, and go to the bottom. There was nothing to
prevent them doing this except their unwillingness to destroy themselves. There were some daring spirits among them, but the greater
part had cowardly hearts. They thus fortunately took half measures.
They might have destroyed all the officers, overpowered the marines,
and carried the ship off. They knew well enough, however, that there
was not a man among them capable of navigating her, and that there
was a great chance that they would run her ashore before they got
away from St. Helen's. They were sure also that there was not an officer
who would have taken charge of her, even if they had held a pistol to
his head to try and compel him to navigate the ship.

CHAPTER XX.

I HAVE spent many a trying night, waiting anxiously for day, but this was as trying as any. It was, if I recollect rightly, the 3d or 4th of December. When at length the morning broke, the mutineers seemed as determined as ever. At last it was proposed to let the warrant and petty officers go on deck. On hearing this, Hagger and I with a few others crept along to the after hatchway, pretending that our object was merely to ship the ladder to allow the officers to reach the upper deck. The officers hurried up as fast as they could, glad to get away out of the power of the mutineers. Several of the men followed them, and Hagger and I had got our feet on the ladder, when we were seized hold of and dragged back, and the ladder was again unshipped.

Ten or twelve of the men had made themselves most active, and were looked upon as the ringleaders of the conspiracy, Berkeley and Pratt being among the number; but Iffley, if he had really been at the bottom of the affair, pretended to be led by the others. Whenever he spoke, he counselled mild measures, though he managed, some way or other, that they should not be adopted.

Having command of the store-rooms, the mutineers served out among

24

those below as many provisions as were required.   Dividing themselves
into two watches, one stood guard with fifty or sixty muskets, and the
guns pointed aft, while the rest either slept or sat on deck and smoked.

There were hot discussions as to what should be done, and occasionally
there were quarrels, for enough grog was served out to excite the men s
spirits; but the ringleaders took care that they should get no more, for if
once drunkenness began, they were aware that they would very speedily
be overpowered.   In the course of the afternoon, the first lieutenant
hailed down the after-hatchway, saying that three admirals whom we all
knew had come on board to hear what grievances we had to complain of,
and to endeavour to redress them.

On hearing this, the ringleaders went aft, each man armed with a
musket, a tomahawk or cutlass by his side, looking as brazen-faced and
impudent as could be, trusting to the numbers at their backs.

Among the officers who addressed us were Lord Bridport and Admiral
Cornwallis.   Lord Bridport inquired, in a kind way, what the mutineers
had to complain of, and pointed out the folly and wickedness of their
proceedings.   ' What would become of our country if other ships were
to follow your bad example, my lads?' he asked.   'The honour and glory
of England, of which you are so justly proud, would be humbled in the
dust, and we should have the Frenchmen coming over to England with
their guillotine and their Republican notions, and the ruin of all we
hold dear would be the consequence.   But I am not afraid of that.   I
know English seamen too well to suppose for a moment that others
would imitate you.   They may have grievances to complain of, but would
disdain to adopt the mode you have of showing your dissatisfaction.'

Admiral Cornwallis spoke in a more indignant strain.   ' I am ashamed
of you, lads,' he exclaimed ; 'you call yourselves British seamen, and yet
upset all discipline, and act the part of rascally buccaneers who turn
against their officers the moment they have anything to complain of.'

He said a good deal more in the same strain, but the men would scarcely listen to him. Some of them shouted out together what they wanted, but even on those points they were not all agreed.

'Are you going to return to your duty, lads?' asked Admiral Bridport at last.

'No, we are not,' shouted several of the men. 'We don't return to our duty until we get our rights.'

On this the admirals walked away, and we saw them shortly afterwards, through the ports, leaving the ship for Portsmouth.

The second night went by much as the first had done. The mutineers, numbering about two hundred and fifty men, retained possession of the lower deck, and would allow no one to come down, and none of the better disposed men whom they doubted to go up. Hagger and I, with others, were thus kept prisoners. They had opposed to them the commissioned, warrant, and petty officers, all the marines except six, who, silly fellows, had been persuaded to join them, and about thirty seamen who had managed to escape on deck. They might thus quickly have been subdued by force, but then the lives of many on both sides must have been sacrificed; and if once blood had been shed, the mutineers, knowing that they fought with ropes round their necks, would have struggled desperately to the last, and would very likely have blown the ship up when they found all hope had gone. At length the watch off duty lay down on deck to sleep, for they had used all the hammocks to form a barricade. Hagger and I followed their example, hoping that next morning they would come to a better state of mind; but we were mistaken, and all day they held out, just as they had done before, and so they did the next and the next.

At last two or three of the petty officers, who were the least obnoxious, came and asked them to allow water and provisions to be got up, saying 'that if those below were badly off in one way, they themselves were worse off in another, as neither had come off from the shore, and they were pretty well starving.'

Though some of the ringleaders would have prevented this if they could, the greater part of the men were ready enough to let those on deck have the provisions, and accordingly they set to work and sent up whatever was wanted.

Though they did this, they seemed as resolved as ever to resist. The heavy guns and small arms were kept loaded, and some of the ring-leaders talked as big as ever, but I saw that the greater number were getting heartily weary of their confinement and their state of uncertainty. The authorities must have well known that this would be the case. At last, on the morning of the 11th, word was received that Captain Pakenham (with whom a good many of the men had served) wanted to speak to them.

Coming to the hatchway, he addressed the men in firm but gentle terms. I forget exactly what he said, but I know it at once had a good effect with many of them, notwithstanding that the ringleaders tried to persuade them to hold out longer.

I was trying to persuade some of my shipmates to listen to what Captain Pakenham was saying, and to return to their duty, when Berkeley and Pratt, seizing hold of me, swore that they would shoot me through the head if I uttered another word, and dragged me forward.

At the same moment Hagger, who had been nearer the hatchway, with some of the better-disposed men, getting hold of the ladders, suddenly shipped them, and sprang up on deck, followed by nearly the whole of the rest of the crew, who were glad of the opportunity of escaping, as they hoped, from the consequences they had brought upon themselves. Only nine besides myself remained below, including Trickett and the two men I have spoken of.

Captain Pakenham at once asked the men who had escaped, if they were prepared to return to their duty, and in one voice they declared that they were. He had before taken his measures, and the marines, who were drawn up ready to act, coming down the ladder, made a rush forward.

Three or four of the more desperate of the ringleaders sprang to the guns, with the intention of firing them; but before they had time to do so, the marines, forcing their way over the barricade, seized every man they could find, I being among the number.

As two of them got hold of me, I assured them that I had been prevented from the first by force from going on deck, and that I had not joined the mutineers. They laughed at my assertion, and I was dragged along the deck and brought before Captain Pakenham.

Though he had spoken mildly enough to the other men, he was stern when addressing us, and being speedily handcuffed, we were committed to the charge of the lieutenant-at-arms, and placed under a guard of marines.

I begged Captain Pakenham to listen to me, asserting as before that I had never joined the mutineers, and called upon Hagger and the others to bear witness to the truth of what I said.

Hagger, stepping out from among the men drawn up on either side of the deck, declared that what I said was the truth; that we had both tried to escape from the first, but had been prevented; and that, as the officers knew, I was among the best-conducted men in the ship.

'All you have to say will be heard at the trial, which will, depend upon it, be held in a few days,' answered Captain Pakenham. 'You were found among the ringleaders, who refused, when summoned at the last, to come up and return to their duty; you must therefore, meantime, abide by the consequences.'

No words can describe the grief and dismay I felt, not on my own account, but lest my wife and uncle and aunt should hear what had happened.   They would be confident that I was innocent, but at the same time they would know the risk I ran of being inculpated with the guilty.   How could I prove that I had taken no part in the mutiny?   I had been below all the time, and except on the evidence of Hagger, I could not prove that I had made any attempt to escape.   His evidence, indeed, might not be of any value, as he had been with me, and had himself remained below.   I had been found with the ringleaders, and very probably two such utter scoundrels as were Berkeley and Pratt would not, unless it could benefit themselves, be induced to confess that they had kept me back by force.

I entreated to be supplied with paper and pen and ink, that I might write to Uncle Kelson to tell him what had happened, and beg him to break the news to Margaret, as also to ask him if he could procure legal advice; but the boon was refused me, and I was told that before the trial I should not be allowed to hold communication with anybody.

The prisoners in vain tried to keep up their spirits.   Most of them soon broke down altogether, and sat with their heads bent, resting on their manacled hands, except two desperate fellows who had long faced death in every form, and were not afraid of him now, though they well knew what the punishment of their crime must be.   Men were hung for lesser crimes than theirs, and the maintenance of discipline being the great object of the authorities, they were not likely to be let off.

So great was the agony of my mind that I thought I should go mad. At last I dropped into a dreamy state, my great wish being that the day of the trial should come on.   Had I been called to suffer alone I should not have complained, but it was the thought of the trouble, the distress and sorrow it would be to Margaret and my uncle and aunt, to hear that I had died an ignominious death at the yard-arm, assured though they might be of my innocence, which caused me the greatest grief.

At last, on the 15th of December, several admirals and captains assembled to hold a court-martial on board the *Culloden*, and we ten men, accused of mutiny, were brought up for trial. It was quickly proved that four of our number had been captured while attempting to fire the guns behind the barricade, and that the whole of us had been found below when the rest of the ship's company had returned to their duty. We were asked singly what we could say for ourselves.

Trickett was the first who spoke. He pleaded that he had been led away by others, that he did not know their object, and had no idea that matters would have proceeded to extremities. 'I wished to see my shipmates righted, but I should have advised them, had they allowed me, to employ only legal means. As a proof that I was not one of the ringleaders, permit me to present this paper which came into my possession, and which, as you will see, does not contain my name.'

As he spoke, he produced a paper, and presented it to the President, who, after glancing over it, read it aloud. It began, I remember, ' We, the undersigned, bind ourselves to hold fast to each other, and to take all the means in our power to obtain our rights, and have our grievances redressed; we resolve that no consideration shall hinder us, and that if our petition is not listened to, we will take possession of the ship, and carry her over to the French.' The paper wound up with terrible oaths, calling God to witness that nothing should make them give up their object.

'I see by the names attached to this precious document,' said the President, 'that they are all those of the prisoners on trial, with the exception of that of the man who handed it in, which doesn't appear,' and he slowly read out the names. Among the last was that of Pratt, then came that of Reginald Berkeley, and lastly, to my horror and dismay, was my own.

'I never signed that paper!' I exclaimed; 'nothing should have induced me to put my hand to it.'

'Can you swear that your name is not Willand Wetherholm, and that this is not your signature?' asked the President, and the paper was shown me.

'That is my name, and that is my signature, but I didn't put it to any document of that sort. I was writing a letter to my wife, just before the mutiny broke out, when the man whose name appears above mine, came and asked me to put my name as a witness to his signature, stating that it was required for legal purposes, in order to enable him to obtain a property to which he was entitled.'

'A likely story,' observed one of the members of the court. 'Reginald Berkeley, as you call yourself, is this man's story correct? Did you ask him to witness your signature for such a purpose as he states?'

I saw Iffley and Berkeley exchange glances.

'I don't remember the circumstance, my lord,' he answered with the greatest effrontery. 'I know that the paper was passed round for signature, and that I put my name to it; and I suppose Wetherholm put his, knowing what was written above it.'

When again allowed to speak, I once more acknowledged that the signature was mine, but that through carelessness, not having looked at the document, which was doubled back, I had simply acceded to Berkeley's request to sign as a witness.

'The word "witness" was written in pencil at the time, and I was about to write over it in ink when I was interrupted,' I said.

The President examined the paper through his spectacles, but declared that he could see no traces of any pencil marks. It was passed round to two or three other officers, who agreed with his lordship.

At last it was handed to Captain Pakenham, who, holding it up against the light, produced a magnifying glass from his pocket, through which he examined the paper.

'I see traces of pencil marks. Yes; and the letters " w—i—t," then there is a blank, and "ss," though an attempt has been made to rub it out, and probably the person who tried to do so fancied that he had succeeded. Sergeant, examine that man's pockets,' and he pointed to Iffley.

The sergeant, after fumbling about, produced a piece of india-rubber.

'I thought so,' observed the Captain. 'There has been some knavery at work. This is greatly in the man's favour.'

I breathed more freely at this than I had for many a day. He then turned to Dick Hagger, and told him to make his statement.

Dick, pulling his hair, at once stepped forward, and in a clear voice began: 'My lords, and cap'ens, and gentlemen, I'll speak the truth and nothing but the truth. I hated the notion of this here mutiny directly I got an inkling of it, and so did my messmate Will Weatherhelm, and we had made up our minds, if it was likely to come to anything, to get away aft and tell the commander or first lieutenant; but when we was agoing, quite unbeknown to us, before we had time to get on deck, the mutiny broke out, the ladders were unshipped, an' we was kept prisoners. We were both of us marked men, and when we again tried to join the officers we was held back. Every one who has ever served with Weatherhelm knows him to be a good seaman, and an orderly, well-conducted chap, who wouldn't, for to get a pocketful of gold, have become a rascally mutineer.' The warrant and petty officers who were called, gave both Hagger and me good characters, and his evidence appeared to weigh greatly in my favour; still I could see that most of the members of the court-martial considered it necessary to make an example of the whole of those who had been captured, and one after the other the ringleaders were condemned to death. Berkeley and Pratt fell on their knees on hearing their sentence, and implored for mercy.

'It was through the treachery of that man that Wetherholm's signature was obtained,' said Captain Pakenham, pointing to the former; 'I am not inclined to grant him it.'

The other members of the court were of his opinion.

Charles Iffley, though he had been the chief instigator of the mutiny, was pardoned, in consequence of his having produced the paper with the signature of the ringleaders.   My fate still hung in the balance, for Captain Pakenham alone seemed to consider me innocent.   I saw my judges conferring together.   How my heart bounded with joy when the President at length acquitted me !

Iffley cast a glance of disappointed spite towards me as he heard this, and walked away.   I was again a free man.   My first act, after returning thanks to Heaven from the bottom of my heart for my merciful deliverance, was to obtain a sheet of paper, and write an account of what had happened and my happy acquittal to Uncle Kelson, and beg him to break the matter to my wife, for I was afraid that she would be overmuch agitated should I address her directly.

Several boats were returning to the shore, and I, without difficulty, got a man I knew to take it.   The first to come up and congratulate me was Dick Hagger.

'I was sure, Will, that they couldn't bring you in guilty.   It would have been against all right and reason; and if they had, why, I would have gone up and axed to be hung too, and told them you was no more a mutineer than I was!'

Many other shipmates came up, and expressed themselves much in the same way.   No one, however, spoke to Iffley, for they well knew that he was at the bottom of the whole affair, and deserved hanging more than any of the rest.   He was from that day forward shunned by all in the ship, for even the men who had mutinied would not trust him.

This made him more morose and ill-tempered than ever, and I could not help suspecting that if he had an opportunity, he would still try to do me an injury.   Discipline was now perfectly restored, but the ship was still not a happy one.   No liberty was allowed, and we were kept hard at work exercising the guns and reefing sails. When I asked for leave to go on shore, I was refused.

'If we grant it to one, we must to another,' was the answer.

So I had to stop on board, and as Dick observed, 'grin and bear it.'

Thus nearly a month went by. The condemned men had been sent on board various ships for safe keeping, there to remain until the day they were doomed to die. On the 13th of January, early in the morning, they were brought on board the *Culloden*, heavily handcuffed, and looking the picture of misery and despair. At the same time boats from every ship in the fleet came alongside to witness the execution.

The wretched men, still with their irons on, were now conducted to the upper deck. Ropes were rove through the main, fore, and mizzen-yard arms. The whole eight were thus standing, with the chaplains by their sides, giving them the last consolations of religion, when our captain appeared with a paper in his hand. It was a pardon for the three youngest. The other five looked up with imploring glances, and an expression of hope lighted up their countenances, but there was no pardon for them. The three having been led on one side by the marines who had them in charge, the preparations for the execution of the other five were continued. They were shortly finished. The gun, the signal for their execution, was fired, and in another instant they were all run up in sight of the whole fleet, and of the crews of the boats who were compelled to witness their punishment. It was an awful sight. I felt that but for God's great mercy I might have been among the hapless men who were struggling now in mid air. I sickened as I gazed at them, and hid my eyes with my hands, as did many another stout-hearted fellow.

After a time they were lowered down. The doctor pronounced them dead, and they were placed in shells and taken on shore to be buried. The ropes were unrove, the hands were piped down, and the boats returned to their respective ships. The fearful drama was over.

CHAPTER XXI.

THE *Culloden* having gained a bad name for herself, in consequence of the late event and her behaviour on the 1st of June, her officers and crew were distributed among several ships; I, with Dick Hagger and other men, being sent on board the *Mars*, seventy-four, one of the squadron under Vice-Admiral the Honourable William Cornwallis, whose flag was flying on board the *Royal Sovereign*, of one hundred guns. The other ships were the *Triumph*, *Sir Erasmus Gower*, the *Brunswick*, and *Bellerophon*, seventy-fours, the *Phaeton* and *Pallas* frigates, and the *Kingfisher*, an eighteen-gun brig.

We sailed at the end of May from Spithead, for a cruise off Ushant. On the 8th of June we made the land about the Penmarcks on the French coast, and soon after the *Triumph* threw out the signal of six sail east by north.

We immediately gave chase. After some time, one of the frigates, with the little *Kingfisher* and the *Triumph*, being considerably ahead, commenced firing at the enemy, while we were crowding all sail to get up with them, the admiral having made the signal to close.

Before we had done so, however, the admiral ordered us and the *Bellerophon* to chase two French frigates to the south-west, one of which had a large ship in tow. This, after a short time, they abandoned to us, and we took possession of her. We stood so close in that the batteries at Belle Isle opened upon us, and shoaling our water, the signal for danger was made.

Thereupon Admiral Cornwallis recalled us, and we stood off the land with the prizes we had taken, and eight others, captured by the frigates, laden with wine and brandy. A good many small vessels, however, escaped us by plying to windward under the land, to gain the anchorage in Palais Roads.

The next day it was calm, so that the enemy could not, even if they had had a mind to do so, come out and attack us, and in the evening a breeze springing up, we took the prizes in tow, and stood away for the Channel.

Sighting Scilly, Admiral Cornwallis ordered the *Kingfisher* to convoy the prizes into port, while we stood back to the southward and eastward to look after the French squadron. Several days had passed when the *Phaeton*, our look-out frigate, made the signal of a French fleet in sight; but as nothing was said about the enemy being of superior force, and as she did not haul her wind and return to us, Admiral Cornwallis must have concluded, as did our captain, that the signal had reference to the number rather than to the apparent strength of the French ships, and we accordingly stood on nearer than we should otherwise have done. It was not indeed until an hour afterwards that we got a sufficiently clear sight of the French fleet to make out that it consisted of one very large one hundred and twenty gun ship, eleven seventy-fours, and the same number of frigates, besides smaller craft. Dick Hagger, who had been sent aloft, told me that he had counted thirty at least.

'Never mind! If we can't out-sail them, we'll fight them, and show the mounseers that "hearts of oak are our ships, British tars are our men"' he exclaimed with a gay laugh, humming the tune

All hands on board our ship were in the same humour, and so were the crews of the rest of the squadron. We knew that we could trust our stout old admiral, for if he was at times somewhat grumpy, he was as gallant a man and as good an officer as any in the service. I heard it said, many years after, that when some of the Government gentlemen offered to make a lord of him, he declined, saying, ' It won't cure the gout.'

The admiral now threw out the signal to the squadron to haul to the wind on the starboard tack under all sail, and form in line ahead, the *Brunswick* leading, and we in the *Mars* being last. Thus we stood on for about three hours, when we saw the French fleet on the same tack separate into two divisions, one of which tacked and stood to the northward, evidently to take advantage of the land wind, while the other continued its course to the southward. Of course it was the object of our admiral to escape if possible; for, fire-eater as he was, he had no wish to expose his ships to the risk of being surrounded and sunk, as he knew well enough might be the case should the French get up with us.

After this we twice tacked, and then we saw the French north division tack to the southward, when the wind shifted to the northward, and this enabled that division to weather on us, and the south division to lie well up for our squadron.

The first division now bore east by north about eight or nine miles, and the south division south-east, distant about ten miles on our larboard quarter. Night soon came on, and we could not tell but that before it was over we might have the French ships close aboard, and thundering away at us.

' Well, if they do come,' cried Dick, ' we'll give them as good as we take, although we may have three to fight; but what's the odds if we work our guns three times as fast as they do ? '

To our surprise the watch was piped down as usual, for the admiral knew better than we did, that the enemy could not be up with us until the morning while the wind held as it then did.

We slept like tops, not troubling our heads much about the battle we might have to fight before another day was over, but I doubt whether many of the officers turned in.

The middle watch got their sleep like the first. After that the hammocks were piped up, and every preparation made for battle. Two of our ships, the *Bellerophon* and *Brunswick*, which were always looked upon as fast sailers, had, somehow or other, got out of trim, and during the night had to cut away their anchors and launches, and to start a portion of their water and provisions. The old 'Billy Ruffian,' however, do all they could, would not move along, and they were compelled to heave overboard her four poop carronades with their carriages, and a large quantity of shot. Notwithstanding this, and that they were carrying every stitch of canvas they could set, we and the other ships had to shorten sail occasionally to keep in line with them. It may be supposed that we had been keeping a bright look-out for the French fleet, and when daylight broke we saw it coming up very fast, formed in three divisions.

The weather division, consisting of three ships of the line, and five frigates, was nearly abreast of our ships. In the centre division we counted five ships of the line and four frigates, and in the lee division four sail of the line, five frigates, two brigs, and two cutters. These were somewhat fearful odds, but notwithstanding, as far as I could judge, the hearts of none on board our ship, and we were the most exposed, quailed for a moment. We had made up our minds to a desperate fight, but we had confidence in our old admiral, and we knew that if any man could rescue us, he would do it.

Stripped to the waist, we stood at our quarters, waiting the order to fire, and resolved to fight to the last. At that moment I did not think

of my wife, or home, or anything else, but just the work we had in hand.
At such times it does not do to think. We all knew that it was our
business to run our guns in as fast as possible and fire when ordered.
We watched the approach of the French ships, eager for the moment
when we should begin the fight.

A seventy-four was the van ship of the weather division, and a frigate
led the centre division. We had had our breakfast and returned to our
guns, when the seventy-four opened her fire upon our ship, the *Mars*.
We immediately hoisted our colours, as did the rest of our squadron,
and returned it with our stern-chasers. Directly afterwards the French
frigate ran up on our larboard and lee quarter, and yawing rapidly,
fired into us. This sort of work continued for nearly half an hour.
Several of our men by that time had been struck down, though none that
I could see were killed, while our standing and running rigging was
already a good deal cut up. We had been blazing away for some time,
and the enemy's shot were coming pretty quickly aboard, when I heard
a crash, and looking up saw that our main-yard was badly wounded.
Now for the first time I began to fear that we should get crippled, and,
being surrounded by the enemy, should be unable to fight our way out
from among them.

Two other ships, the *Triumph* and *Bellerophon*, were now warmly
engaged, and soon afterwards the remainder of the squadron began
firing their stern or quarter guns as they could bring them to bear on
the enemy. The *Brunswick*, it should be understood, was leading, then
came the *Royal Sovereign*, next the *Bellerophon* and *Triumph*, we being, as
I before said, the sternmost. We now saw the *Royal Sovereign* making
signals to the two ships to go ahead, while she, shortening sail, took her
station next in line to the *Brunswick*.

We had kept up so hot a fire on the first ship which had attacked us,
that we had at length knocked away her main-top-gallant mast and had

done considerable damage to her rigging. To our great satisfaction, we saw her sheer off and drop astern.

'Hurrah! there's one done for,' cried Dick Hagger.

'So there is, my boy, but one down another came on,' remarked a wag among the crew of our gun, pointing as he spoke to a French seventy-four, which, crowding all sail, was approaching to open directly afterwards a brisk cannonade on our larboard quarter.

'Never mind, lads, we will treat her as we did t'other, and maybe we'll capture both of them,' cried Dick.

I did not see there was much chance of that, considering that the whole French fleet was at hand to support the crippled ships. Had we been more nearly matched we might have done it.

We were now getting pretty severely mauled. First one and then another got up under our quarter, and blazed away at us. More men were wounded, and our fore-top-sail yard was badly damaged, in addition to our main-top-sail yard, while we had to cut away the stern galleries the better to train our guns, run through the after ports. The other ships—especially the *Triumph, Sir Erasmus Gower*—were keeping up a tremendous fire from their stern-ports. Notwithstanding this, the French were getting closer and closer.

Four hours thus passed away. While we were thus engaged, it must be remembered we were pressing on with all sail, so that we kept ahead of the enemy. While our sticks stood we had no fear of making our escape, but we well knew that at any moment a shot might carry away one of our masts, and then, too probably, our brave chief would have to leave us to our fate for the sake of the safety of the rest of the squadron, not that we supposed for an instant that he would do so until compelled by the most dire necessity. Strange to say, I had not the slightest fear of being shot, but I did dread the thought of being captured and shut up in a French prison, to be treated as we heard that English prisoners

25

were treated by the French Republicans. The wretches who had cut off the heads of their king and beautiful queen, and had guillotined thousands of innocent persons, until the very streets of Paris ran with blood, were not very likely to be over kind to the English they got into their power. As yet, to be sure, they had not made many prisoners, but those they had made we heard were treated barbarously.

The expectation of what we should receive should we be defeated did not make us fight with the less determination. Still, as day wore on, the French ships in greater numbers crowded up astern, and the chances that we should escape seemed to diminish. Not a man, however, quitted his gun. We should have a tremendously hard fight before we were taken—of that we were certain; and many said, and believed it too, that Sir Charles would let the ship sink under his feet rather than strike our flag. Matters seemed getting worse and worse. We saw the *Royal Sovereign* throw out signals to us to alter our course to starboard, and get away from the ships most annoying us.

Immediately afterwards we saw her keep away in our direction, accompanied by the *Triumph*. We cheered lustily as she opened her powerful broadside upon the enemy, when we running down were brought into close order of battle, thus being saved from the mauling we were getting.

Our two friends did not arrive a moment too soon; for just then four of the French van ships had borne up, hoping to secure us. On seeing the approach of a three-decker, they again hauled their wind.

While this work had been going on, the *Phaeton* frigate, which had been sent by the admiral in the morning to a distance of some miles, was seen approaching, making the signal of a strange sail west-north-west, soon afterwards for four sail, and finally she let fly her top-gallant-sheets, and fired two guns in quick succession, which we all well knew was the signal for a fleet, probably that of Lord Bridport.

This cheered up our hearts, as may be supposed, for we fancied that the tables would soon be turned, and that instead of being chased, we should be chasing the Frenchmen, with the prospect of a stand-up fight, ending in the capture of a part, if not the whole of their fleet.

No one thought at the time that the *Phaeton* was carrying out a *ruse de guerre*, which had shortly before been arranged by Admiral Cornwallis.

In the afternoon, about three o'clock, we saw the *Phaeton* making private signals to the supposed fleet; and then using the tabular signals with which the French were well acquainted, she communicated to our admiral the fact that the fleet seen were friends.

About an hour and a half afterwards, she signalled that they were ships of the line. She then hoisted the Dutch ensign, as if replying to a signal made by the admiral in the distance to Admiral Cornwallis, ordering him to join company.

Shortly afterwards she shortened sail, then wore, and stood back towards us. We had been all day retreating, most of the time warmly engaged with our overpowering enemy, when soon after 6 P.M. the French ships suddenly ceased firing; and shortly afterwards, their admirals making signals to them, they shortened sail and stood to the eastward. By sunset they were nearly hull down in the north-east, while we sailed on, rejoicing in having escaped from as dangerous a position as squadron was ever placed in. I don't know if I have succeeded in explaining the position of our ships sufficiently well to be understood by shore-going persons. So close were the French ships upon us, that had they not given up the chase when they did, it would have been scarcely possible for us and the *Triumph*, which, if she had not suffered as much as we had, was too much cut up to have afforded us any assistance, to have effected our escape. I am very certain that our old admiral would not have deserted us, nor was it likely that the

other two ships would have done so. We should all, therefore, after a
desperate fight, either have gone down, been blown up, or captured.
As it was, our brave admiral's masterly retreat excited general admira-
tion. Every seaman on board was well able to judge of our danger,
and of the way in which we had been rescued. Had he not so gallantly
bore up to save us in the *Mars*, our ship must inevitably have been taken.
He might, as some officers would have done, have left us to our fate,
for the sake of preserving the rest of the squadron; but he had no notion
of doing anything of the sort, and gallantly determined that if he could
help it, not a single one of his squadron should fall into the hands of
the enemy. In his despatch, giving an account of the transaction, he
spoke in the handsomest way of the behaviour of the officers and ships'
companies engaged, saying very little of the manner in which he had
come to our rescue. He and all of us got the thanks of both Houses of
Parliament for what had been done, and all will acknowledge that he
richly deserved them. As soon as we lost sight of the French fleet, we
steered a course for Plymouth, to carry the intelligence that it was at
sea. From the way the stern of our ship had been knocked about, we
were compelled to remain for some time at Hamoaze to refit, and were
therefore unable to sail with the fleet under Lord Bridport, which went
out to look for the French fleet from which we had effected our escape.
He came up with the enemy off Isle-groix; and after a tough fight, in
which a good many officers and men were killed and wounded, three
French ships were captured. One of them was the *Alexander*, but she
was so knocked about by the *Queen Charlotte*, that she was worth little.
The two others, the *Tigre* and *Formidable*, were fine new seventy-fours.
The former was allowed to retain her name, but we already having a
Formidable in the service, her name was changed to the *Belle-Isle*, near
which the action was fought.

We and the *Triumph* were at once ordered up to Hamoaze to get our damages repaired. We were much injured aloft, and when I looked at the stern of our ship, she had the appearance of having received a dreadful pounding. The *Triumph* had suffered still more, as from her position in the line she had to keep up the heaviest stern fire. In order to train her guns, the stern galleries, bulk-heads, and every part of the stern of the ward-room, except the timbers, had been cut away, and it was said that from her three stern batteries—namely, her first deck, her second deck, and quarter deck—she had expended in single shots five thousand pounds of powder.

I now hoped that I might be able to get leave in sufficient time to reach Southsea, and spend a few days with my wife, and I resolved to make bold and ask for it as soon as I could see the commander. Meantime, the moment I was off duty I hurried below and began a letter to my wife. While thus engaged, all hands were piped on deck.

'What can it be for?' exclaimed Dick. 'We are not going to sea, I suppose, in this state?'

On reaching the deck, we found numerous boats alongside, and besides them also several lieutenants not belonging to our ship. As soon as we were mustered, our commander addressed us. He said that as the *Mars* would be some time refitting, the Admiralty had ordered part of our crew to be drafted on board a line-of-battle ship and two frigates requiring hands, the *Thunderer*, *Arethusa*, and *Galatea*. He did not ask for volunteers, but said that those whose names were called over must get their bags at once and go off in the boats waiting alongside to receive them. I don't know what my shipmates felt, but I hoped earnestly that I should not be among those selected. I listened almost breathlessly as the names were called over, and as they did so, the men were sent down for their bags. A hundred and fifty or more had been chosen, about two hundred were wanted. At last, what was my dismay on hearing my own name called! It was vain, I knew, to expostulate;

I had to submit. Before going below, I stopped to speak to Hagger. Taking out the almost finished letter, I begged him to add a postscript, saying how I had been sent off, but that I trusted I might return before long. Scarcely were the words out of my mouth when his name was called.

'It can't be helped, Will,' he said; 'bear up, lad, I'm thankful I'm going with you. You must try and finish your letter, and send it off when we get aboard the ship we're ordered to join.'

I made no reply, my heart was too full to speak. I wanted to do my duty, but this disappointment was almost more than I could bear.

'Move on, be smart now, lads!' I heard one of the officers sing out, 'there's not a moment to lose.'

Dick and I hurried below, shouldered our bags and returned on deck, when we found that we were both to go on board the *Galatea* frigate, commanded by Captain Keats. The boats immediately shoved off, and away we pulled down the Sound.

CHAPTER XXII.

I fail to send a letter to my wife—We sail with transports and emigrants for Quiberon —Early success of the expedition—Action between the Royalists and Republicans —I accompany a midshipman to Fort Penthièvre with an important message—I witness some strange scenes—A rough night—Surprised by the Republicans— Attack and capture of the fort—We escape—Conduct of the Royalists—Steadiness of the British marines—Advance of the army under General Hoche—The fleet rescue the party—Return of the expedition.

THE *Galatea*, we found, formed one of a squadron under the command of Commodore Sir John Warren. It consisted of the *Robust*, *Thunderer*, and *Standard*, seventy-fours; the frigates *Pomone*, on board which the commodore's flag was flying, the *Anson*, *Artois*, *Arethusa*, *Concorde*, and our frigate the *Galatea*, convoying fifty sail of transports with about two thousand five hundred French Royalists. The expedition was bound for Quiberon, the inhabitants of which district had remained faithful to their king, and it was hoped that from thence the Republicans could be attacked, and a large part of the country gained over to the royal cause.

The *Galatea* was a smart frigate, and now that she was well manned was likely to make a name for herself. On being sent below to stow away my bag, I managed to sign my name in pencil to my letter, by placing it on a gun, and to add a few lines describing what had happened, and then I hurried on deck, but the boatswain's pipe was already shrilly sounding, and his voice shouting, 'All hands up anchor!'

The commodore's frigate was letting fall her topsails, and the other ships were following her example. The capstan went merrily round, the anchor was away, the sails were sheeted home, and we stood out of Plymouth Sound, steering for the southward.

My poor wife would have to wait some time now before she could hear from me, or know indeed where I was.   There was nobody on board the *Mars* to whom I could have entrusted the duty of writing to her.   I had to bear it, therefore, as I had to bear many another trial.   Hope still supported me.   As far as we could learn, we were not likely to be long away.   Lord Bridport had driven the French fleet into harbour and was watching them, although we, of course, might on our return fall in with an enemy and have a fight.

The weather was fine and the wind fair, but we had plenty to do in keeping the transports together.   There were many of them very slow sailers, merchant vessels hired for the purpose, some of them brigs of a hundred and fifty to two hundred tons, which must have afforded very miserable accommodation to the unfortunate emigrants.   The troops were under the command of a royalist officer, the Comte de Puisaye, who had as his lieutenants the Comtes d'Hervilly and de Sombreuil.

On the 25th of June we entered the capacious bay of Quiberon, which affords one of the most secure anchorages on the French coast.   On one side is the Peninsula of Quiberon, which extends out some way from the mainland, and seaward are two small, well-cultivated islands, so that it is completely protected from westerly and south-westerly gales.   The next day was spent in preparations for landing, and to allow the laggards to come up; and on the 27th, at daybreak, the troops, conveyed in a large flotilla of boats, escorted by six of the squadron, pulled for the village of Carnac, where they landed.   A small body of about two hundred Republicans attempted to oppose them, but were quickly driven back, leaving several dead on the field, while the Royalists did not lose a man.

This slight success encouraged the royalist inhabitants, who came down to the number of sixteen thousand, eager to receive the arms and ammunition which we landed from the ships for their use.

The troops were at once cantoned among the inhabitants, who gladly supplied them with everything they required. The French officers and soldiers we put on shore were in high spirits, laughing and joking, and seemed confident of success, and the people who came down to help to unload the boats were equally merry, declaring that they had only to attack the Republicans to compel them to lay down their arms.

Some days passed by, during which the Royalists on shore were drilling and preparing for action. At length an expedition was planned to attack the Peninsula of Quiberon. Two thousand Royalists, and five hundred emigrants, supported by three hundred British marines, were disembarked. They at once marched towards the Fort of Penthièvre, situated on a commanding eminence on the northern extremity of the peninsula, which was invested at the same time on the other side by the Comte d'Hervilly.

Without much fighting, its garrison of six hundred men soon surrendered. We immediately set to work to land stores and provisions for the supply of the royalist troops.

A day or two after this, the Comte led a body of five thousand men, including two hundred British marines, against the right flank of the army of General Hoche, which was strongly posted on the heights of St. Barbe. At the same time, for their support, five launches, each armed with a twenty-four pounder carronade, manned from the ships of war, were sent in and stationed close to the beach. I was in one of them, and could see what was going forward.

We watched the small body of red-coats and the motley dressed Royalists marching on to the attack. At first they advanced with considerable firmness, but being met by a withering fire from the heights, and being ill-disciplined, they began to beat a hasty retreat. The marines were compelled, of course, to retire too, but they did so with their faces to the foe, defending the fugitives as well as they could.

On this, Captain Keats, who commanded the boats, ordered us to open fire, and we began to blaze away at the Republicans in a fashion which

considerably retarded them in their pursuit of the retreating force. So
well directed were our shot on their flanks, that beyond a certain line
they were unable to advance.

Both the marines and Royalists got back to the beach, though not
without considerable loss. Among the badly wounded was their brave
leader, who was conveyed on board our frigate, and placed under the
care of our surgeon. Though he suffered much from his wound, his
thoughts were still with his friends ashore.

It was, I think, about two days afterwards, being anxious to communicate with his friend the Comte de Sombreuil, at Fort Penthièvre,
which was under the command of the Comte de Puisaye, he requested
that a messenger might be sent on shore with a letter. Captain Keats
accordingly ordered Mr. Harvey, one of the senior midshipmen, to take
the letter, and allowed him to select a man to accompany him. He
chose me, I having served with him already in two ships, and being well
known to him.

We at once, shoving off in the second gig under charge of another
midshipman, pulled for the beach nearest the fort, towards which, as
soon as we landed, we made our way. We remarked six transports,
laden, as we were told, with provisions and stores of all sorts, come to an
anchor as close to the fort as they could bring up.

As we stepped on shore, Mr. Harvey directed the gig to return without
delay to the frigate. ‘ I don't like the look of the weather,’ he observed.
‘and depend upon it, before nightfall, it will come on to blow hard.’

We were to remain at the fort until the following morning, when the
boat was to come in again and take us off.

Mr. Harvey delivered his despatch to the young Comte, who received
him very graciously, and gave him the best accommodation he could for the
night, while I, that I might be ready to attend to his wants, was allowed
to sleep on a sofa in a little ante-room outside of the one he occupied.

Mr. Harvey told me that the Count was greatly out of spirits in consequence of the numerous desertions which had taken place from the fort. Various causes were at work. Some of the garrison were Republicans at heart, and others, hopeless of the success of the Royalists, were afraid of the consequences should they remain. One or two plots had been discovered, but the conspirators had been seized, and it was hoped that those who had been won over would be deterred from carrying out their plans.

Notwithstanding these forebodings of evil, the officers met, as I suppose was their custom, at an early supper. I looked in with some of the attendants to see what was going forward. The table was covered with all sorts of good things, such as French cooks know well how to prepare. Wine flowed freely, and conversation seemed to be carried on with great animation. Speeches were made, and compliments paid to Mr. Harvey, who spoke very good French, for which reason he had been selected to convey the letter to the Count. The major commanding the marines, a captain, and two lieutenants, were also present, but as none of them spoke French, Mr. Harvey had to reply for the whole party.

After supper the marine officers went to their quarters, which happened to be on the side of the fort nearest the sea, in rooms prepared for them.

I remember we had to run across an open space, and were nearly wetted through by the tremendous rain which poured down upon us. It was blowing very hard too, the wind howled and shrieked among the buildings of the fort, while the windows and doors rattled till I thought that they would be forced in.

'I was afraid, Wetherholm, that we were going to have a dirty night of it,' observed Mr. Harvey. 'I hope the gig got back safely, but I doubt very much whether she will be able to return for us to-morrow if this weather continues. However, it may only be a summer gale, though from the appearance of things it might be mid-winter.'

I looked out; the sky seemed as black as ink, and the night was so
dark that had it not been for the light in the window above the door we
had to make for, we could not have found our way.

Mr. Harvey, of course, wore his sword, and, as was customary for the
men sent on shore, I had my cutlass slung to my side and a brace of
pistols; for, as we were before the enemy, we might at any moment be
called upon to fight.

I having hung up Mr. Harvey's coat to dry, and his sword against the
wall, went to the ante-room, and taking off my wet jacket lay down on
the sofa, all standing. At sea, I should not have been two minutes in
my hammock before I had fallen asleep, but the howling and shrieking
wind sounded very different on shore, and seemed to make its way
through every chink and crevice, producing all sorts of strange sounds,
a mingling of moanings, shriekings, whistlings, and howlings. Frequently
the building itself would shake, until I fancied that it was about to come
down upon our heads. Notwithstanding this, I was just dozing off,
when I was aroused by still stranger sounds. I listened; I felt sure they
could not be caused by the wind. They were human voices. I could
distinguish shrieks and shouts and cries. Almost at the same instant
there came the sharp report of pistols.

I sprang into Mr. Harvey's room to awaken him. Fortunately he had
a light burning on the table.

'There's something fearful happening, sir,' I said, as he started up,
looking very much astonished. I got down his coat and sword, which I
helped him to put on.

'The treachery the Count spoke of is at work, I fear, but I hope the
conspirators will quickly be put down. We must go to the help of our
friends if we can manage to find them,' he said, while he was quickly
slipping into his clothes.

We hurried down stairs; the rest of the people in the house were rushing out, but, as far as I could discover, they were hurrying off, away from the direction of the firing and shouts.

Presently I could hear the cry of ' Vive la République,' then came a sharp rattle of musketry, some of the bullets pinging against the walls above our heads.

' Come on, Wetherholm, I· think I can find out where the Count is quartered; we may be in time to help him.'

As we were about to leave the house, the cry of ' Vive la République' again echoed from all parts of the fort in front of us, the shouting and shrieking continuing, mingled with cries and groans and fierce exclamations, with the constant report of pistols. Still Mr. Harvey was pushing on, when through the darkness we could distinguish a number of persons flying towards the rear of the fort.

At length we made out others following them, the flash from their pistols showing that they had swords in their hands. They fortunately turned away from where we were standing.

' There can be no doubt that the fort has been surprised, and that it will go hard with the Count and his soldiers,' said Mr. Harvey. ' I should like to have assisted him in defending his post, but perhaps the best thing I can do is to bring up the marines to his support. I think we may find their quarters, though I am not very certain about the direction.'

I agreed with Mr. Harvey, for I saw that it would be madness to rush among a number of people fighting, when we could not distinguish between friends and foes.

We accordingly made our way across the fort to where we believed we should find the major of marines. Mr. Harvey thought we ought to keep more to the left, but I felt certain that if we turned to the right we should reach the building.

' Who goes there?' I heard a voice shout out.

It was that of the sentry stationed in front of the building used for the marine barracks, and finding who we were, he told us that the men were mustering in the court-yard. Hurrying forward, we there found the major ready to lead them out.

On Mr. Harvey telling him the state of things in front, he directed us to proceed to the quarters of the Comte de Puisaye, to say that he would endeavour to drive back the Republicans and to hold the fort until the Count should come up with all the troops he could collect.

Mr. Harvey and I accordingly hastened forward on the errand. As we went on, we heard several of the fugitives passing us. One, from the clatter of his scabbard, was evidently an officer. Mr. Harvey stopped him, and told him that the English marines were ready to hold their ground, and that we were going to the General's quarters, begging him, if he knew the way, to conduct us.

This information seemed somewhat to restore his confidence; but he expressed his fears that unless assistance could be brought immediately to the Comte de Sombreuil, he would be overwhelmed. He was, he believed, defending the building in which he was quartered with several of the leading officers, but that many who were in their houses, as well as all those on guard, had been shot by traitorous soldiers who had revolted. He himself had had a narrow escape from a party of assassins, among whom he distinguished the voices of some of his own men; but he had cut down several of them, and then, favoured by the darkness, had effected his escape. We owed our safety to the brave defence made at this time by the Comte de Sombreuil, who was thus preventing the Republicans from advancing farther across the fort.

Conducted by the officer, whose name I forget, we at length reached the quarters of the Comte de Puisaye. He was issuing orders to the officers who were coming and going, to collect the troops under his immediate command.

As they came in they were formed up into various companies. Being imperfectly disciplined, they were much longer assembling than they ought to have been, and I greatly feared that the fort would be lost before the troops were ready to march.

Mr. Harvey waited until he believed that they would follow in another minute or two, and then set off with me, intending to return to where we had left the marines.

As we got near his quarters, we heard a rapid firing, returned evidently by a large number of men, for, as they fired their pieces, they shouted again and again, 'Vive la République!' When, however, they discovered that these were English troops in their front, they did not venture to rush upon the bayonets they would have had to encounter.

Mr. Harvey, after some difficulty, found Major Stubbs, who commanded the marines, and told him what the General proposed doing.

' He must come pretty quickly, or we shall be overpowered,' he answered. 'If it was daylight we should know what we were about, but in this pitchy darkness, with the rain clattering down upon us, the wind howling in our ears, and hosts of enemies pouring in on the other side of the fort, we may get separated and cut to pieces, and I will not sacrifice my men if I can help it.'

The bullets came whistling past our heads, and it seemed to me that the men were dropping fast, but as one marine fell the others closed up their ranks and bravely held their ground. What would become of them and us I did not know; but at last the officer to whom Mr. Harvey had spoken, found us, and informed him that the Comte de Puisaye, seeing the hopelessness of endeavouring to regain the fort, had determined to retreat with his troops, and to save the lives of as many of the Royalist inhabitants as he could collect, advising Major Stubbs to draw off his men, and at the same time saying he should be obliged to him if he would cover his retreat.

The darkness and the howling of the storm prevented the movements of the marines being discovered. The stout old major passed the order along the line, and his men, facing about, made their retreat towards the rear of the fort, which was gained before the enemy attempted to pursue them.

I don't know what the major said, but I suspect it was not complimentary to the Comte de Puisaye.

We remained with the marines, who had, as far as I could make out, lost a large number of men. What had become of the young Comte de Sombreuil and the other French officers, we could not tell; but probably, as the firing had ceased from the building in which they had been defending themselves, they had all been put to death.

Major Stubbs halted for some time, during which a number of inhabitants of the houses and cottages in the neighbourhood came in entreating his protection.

At length, escorting them, we again advanced towards the south-east point of the peninsula, which afforded the easiest landing-place, and which, from the nature of the ground, could be defended should the Republicans advance in force to attack us. We found that the Comte de Puisaye, with upwards of a thousand of his troops, and more than double that number of Royalists, had arrived there before us. The Comte had received intelligence of the attack on the fort and its capture, and believing that De Sombreuil and his companions inside had at once been cut to pieces, had considered it useless to go to his assistance.

He had, therefore, mustering his troops, formed an escort to the fugitive Royalists, and immediately commenced his march to the point.

Mr. Harvey expressed his fear that, in consequence of the gale, the ships would be unable to get up to embark the people, and advised him to make preparation for a determined resistance should the Republicans follow and attack him.

Scarcely had the troops been drawn up in position, to make the best defence possible, and to protect the landing-place, than several terror-stricken fugitives arrived, bringing the alarming intelligence that the Republicans, in great force, under Hoche, were advancing.   The darkness, increased by the gloomy state of the weather, continued much longer than usual, and prevented us from ascertaining the truth of these statements. The unfortunate people were in the greatest alarm, for they well knew the barbarous treatment the Royalists had received throughout the country from the Republicans. As their comparatively small force could not hope to hold out long should they be attacked by the overwhelming army of General Hoche, they fully expected to be massacred to a man.   In vain they turned their eyes seaward; no ships could be seen through the gloom coming to their relief, nor were there any boats on the shore.   The wind, however, was falling, and daybreak was close at hand.   I felt sure, also, that the marines, who were posted in a position which would certainly first be attacked, would hold their ground.   This gave confidence to the Royalist troops.

I was standing near Mr. Harvey, who was looking seaward.   One after another, the fugitives who had escaped from the massacre came in, bringing further intelligence of the nearer approach of the Republicans. One of them, an officer, told Mr. Harvey that the Comte De Sombreuil, the Bishop of Doll, and other emigrants of distinction, after holding out in their quarters until all their ammunition had been expended, and many of them killed, had capitulated to the Republicans on the condition that they should be allowed to retire on board the English ships.

'This is better news than I expected,' observed Mr. Harvey; 'I feared that the Count and all his companions had been killed. I wish I could believe that the Republicans are likely to keep their word.'

A short time after this, while I was standing close to Mr. Harvey on an elevated spot overlooking the bay, the dawn broke. He gave a shout
26

of satisfaction as we saw dimly through the gloom, or rather the grey light of early morning, the whole squadron beating up. On they came.

As the wind fell they shook out the reefs in their topsails. There was no time to spare if they were to save the lives of the unfortunate people gathered on the shore.

The *Galatea* was leading. In fine style she came on and dropped her anchor with a spring on her cable, so as to bring her broadside to bear in the direction by which the Republicans would approach.

The other ships of the squadron brought up in succession, and directly afterwards a large flotilla of boats was seen approaching the beach.

To account for the opportune arrival of the squadron at this moment, I may state what I afterwards heard, that directly the fort was captured, the Comte de Puisaye had sent off a boat, though she ran a great risk of being swamped, to the commodore, who had, immediately the gale abated, got under weigh.

The leading columns of the Republicans appeared in the distance, just as the *Galatea's* guns had been brought to bear on the shore.

A few shots made the enemy beat a hasty retreat, and allowed us to embark the troops and fugitive Royalists without molestation.

The boats were under the command of Captain Keats, and by his good management nearly four thousand people were embarked without a casualty, leaving behind, however, for the benefit of the Republicans, ten thousand stand of arms, ammunition of all sorts, and clothing for an army of forty thousand men.

CHAPTER XXIII.

A few particulars of the expedition—I learn to be patient—A strange sail—Cheated of a prize—We destroy a French frigate—Chase a brig—Becalmed at an awkward time—Our captain plans a cutting-out expedition—Success of our efforts—Dick Hagger and I with others are put on board a prize under Mr. Harvey—Sail for England.

WE were now kept actively engaged, but my readers would not be interested were I to give a detailed account of the various incidents of the unfortunate expedition to Quiberon. After taking possession of two islands commanding the bay, we were despatched, in company with the *Standard*, sixty-four, to summon the Governor of Belle Isle to deliver up the island for the use of the French king.

The boat proceeded to the shore with a flag of truce, carrying a long letter from the captain of the *Standard*. A very short reply was received, we heard, from the Republican general, who declared that, as he was well supplied with provisions and artillery, we might come when we liked, and he should be ready for us.

I know that we sailed away and left him alone. Soon after this we were joined by the *Jason* frigate, escorting a fleet of transports, containing four thousand British troops, under command of Major-General Doyle, who was accompanied by the Comte d'Artois and several other French noblemen. The troops were landed on the Isle d'Yeu with provisions, stores, and clothing, and there they remained doing nothing, for nothing could be done. The Republicans, under their clever, daring chiefs, had completely gained the upper hand, and the Royalist cause was lost. We meantime had to enjoy the luxuries of salt pork and mouldy biscuit, either blockading the enemy's ports or looking out for their cruisers or merchantmen.

Thus we continued week after week, month after month, until my heart grew sick at the long delay.   We had occasional opportunities of writing home, and I always availed myself of them, but I got very few letters in return, though my wife wrote frequently.   The packet was often carried on to the Mediterranean, or to other more distant parts of the world.

At last, while cruising with three other frigates and an eighteen-gun brig, the *Sylph*, off the mouth of the river Gironde, we one morning made out a French frigate in the south-south-west, standing in towards the entrance of the river, the wind being at the time north-north-west.   Our frigate and the *Sylph* were close in with the land, while our consorts were considerably astern of us.   We immediately crowded all sail to cut off the French frigate from the mouth of the river, while our captain ordered several signals to be made, intended to deceive her and induce her to suppose that we were also French.   Dick Hagger and I were on the forecastle.

'She'll take the bait, I hope,' he observed, glancing up at the strange bunting which was being run up at the fore royal masthead and quickly lowered.   'See, she's answering.   Well, it may be all ship-shape, but I don't like telling lies, even to an enemy.   Hurrah! I suppose the signals were to tell her to come to an anchor, for see, she is shortening sail.'

Presently the French frigate rounded to and brought up.   It was just what we wanted, for if she had stood on, she might have run up the river and escaped us.   All we now had to do was to get up alongside her, and we trusted to our guns to make her ours.   We carried on, therefore, as we had been doing to reach her.

This probably made her suspect that all was not right, for in a few minutes, letting fall her topsails, she stood away to the southward.

'She has cut her cable, and is off again,' cried Dick; 'however, she can't get up the river, that's one comfort, and we shall have her before long.'

The French ship was now under all the canvas she could spread, standing to the southward. We had the lead going, for we were running through a narrow channel, with a lighthouse on one side on some rocks, and a sandbank on the other. We had a pilot on board, however, who knew the coast, and our captain was a man of firm nerve. The men in the chains were singing out all the time. For my part, I know I was very glad when we cleared the danger, and once more ran off before the wind, followed by the commodore in the *Pomone* and the *Anson* frigate. Meanwhile the commodore sent off the *Artois* frigate and *Sylph* brig to examine two suspicious ships seen away to the south-west. Night was approaching, and just before darkness came down on the ocean, we were not more than two miles astern of the chase. We could still see her dimly through the gloom ahead, and we hoped to keep sight of her during the night. Suddenly, however, about nine o'clock, a heavy squall struck us, accompanied by thunder and lightning, with tremendous showers of rain. The order was given to shorten sail. We flew aloft; there was no time to be lost. The thunder rattled, almost deafening us, and the lightning flashed in our eyes. Between the flashes it was so dark that we had to feel our way on the yards, for as to seeing six inches from our noses, that was out of the question. For nearly an hour it blew fearfully hard, and when we came down from aloft and looked ahead, we could nowhere see the chase, nor were either of our consorts visible astern. We, however, continued standing to the southward as before. What had become of the other ships we could not tell.

'The weather seems to be clearing,' observed Dick; 'if we keep a sharp look-out, the chances are we catch sight of the chase again.'

The third lieutenant, who was forward peering out with his hands on either side of his eyes, asked if any of us could see her.

'Yes, there she is!' cried Dick immediately afterwards, 'away a little on the starboard bow.'

The lieutenant, looking again to assure himself that Dick was right, sung out to the captain. Immediately the order was given to make all sail. We were, during this time, scarcely more than a mile from the shore, but the wind held fair, and there were no rocks to bring us up. Thus we stood on until daybreak, when we found that we were about the same distance from the chase as we had been at sunset, while, looking round, we discovered the frigate and brig, hull down, in the north-west.

As the other vessels were so far off, we now fully expected that the Frenchman would make a stand-up fight of it, and that before many minutes were over we should be blazing away at her, for, as far as we could judge, she was as big if not bigger than our ship. All this time, however, she had neither hoisted ensign nor pennant. This seemed strange, as there was no doubt about her being a Government ship. For some time she stood on, edging away towards the land. 'Perhaps there is danger ahead, and the Frenchmen hope to lead us upon it,' I observed to Dick.

'We are all right as to that,' he answered. 'Our master knows the coast too well to run the ship ashore. I only wish we could see the enemy haul her wind to, and wait for us.'

'She is going to haul her wind, see!' I exclaimed, as I saw the French frigate brace up her yards.

'Yes, she is, but she's putting her head towards the land; I do think she's going to run ashore.'

That such was the case there appeared every probability; still there was room enough for her to come about, and as we eagerly watched her, I hoped she would do so.

She stood on and on, and presently what was my amazement to see her mizzen-mast go by the board!

'The Frenchman must have cut it away,' cried Dick. 'I was right, then.'

So he was; of that there could be no doubt. Soon afterwards down came her main-mast. On she went, however, until we saw that she was ashore, and then her foremast followed the other masts, and the sea catching her, drove her broadside on to the beach, where she heeled over away from us, so that it was difficult to see what her crew were about. As the seas kept striking her, it seemed that her people must be in considerable danger.

Our men bestowed no small amount of abuse on the French for trying to deprive us of the frigate, when they could not keep her for themselves.

Our captain ordered three guns to be fired at her as we passed within a quarter of a mile of the shore; but though some of hers might have been brought to bear on us, not one was discharged. We then stood off and hove to. The boats were lowered and manned, our first lieutenant going in command of them, with directions to effect the destruction of the frigate. The heavy surf breaking against her bottom, and sweeping round towards the side turned to the shore, made it difficult and dangerous work to attempt boarding her.

The tide was now falling, and a considerable number of the French crew seeing us coming, in spite of the risk of being swept away, plunged into the water, and partly by swimming and partly by wading, managed to reach the beach. None of them made any attempt to defend the ship, nor did we molest the poor fellows who were making for the land.

At length we managed to get up to the ship, when the captain and several of his officers surrendered themselves as prisoners. We also took off a few Portuguese seamen, who had been taken out of two captured Brazil ships. We were soon joined by the boats of the *Artois* and the *Sylph*, which had in the meantime approached. The former was now standing off the shore, while the *Sylph* came close in to protect the boats should the French seamen venture to attack us.

Having put the prisoners on board the *Artois* and *Galatea*, we returned once more to effect the destruction of the frigate. The rollers, however, went tumbling in on shore with so much fury that the boats would probably have been lost had we made the attempt. We therefore had to wait patiently until the rising tide should enable us with less hazard to get up to the ship. Meantime we took the *Sylph* in tow, and carried her to within seven hundred yards of the shore, where, dropping her anchor, she got a spring on it, and began firing away at the frigate, so as to riddle her bottom and prevent the possibility of her floating off at high water. At last we once more pulled in, the tide allowing us to approach close to the beach, when Mr. Harvey, in whose boat I was, went on shore with a flag of truce to tell the French seamen, who were gathering in considerable numbers on the sand-hills, that we were about to destroy their ship, and to advise them to keep out of the way. I was very glad when my young officer came back to the boat.

They did not attend to the warning they received, but as soon as we pulled for the ship they came down, threatening us in considerable numbers. On this the *Sylph* opened her fire, and soon sent them to the right about. We now boarded the ship, which I should have said was the *Andromaque*, and having searched every part of her to ascertain that none of her crew or any prisoners she might have taken remained on board, we set her on fire fore and aft, so effectually that even had the Frenchmen returned and attempted to put out the flames they would have found it impossible to do so. She burned rapidly, and as we pulled away towards the *Sylph* the flames were bursting out through all the ports. The *Sylph* then got under weigh, and, taking the boats in tow, stood off the land and rejoined the frigates.

We had not got far when a tremendous roar was heard, and we could see the whole after-part of the ship blown into fragments, some flying seawards, others towards the land, many rising high into the air.

We gave a cheer of satisfaction, for since we could not carry off the frigate as a prize, the next best thing was to prevent her doing any farther harm to our commerce.

This exploit performed, we separated from our consorts, and after cruising about for some time, we one morning, when about twenty miles off the land, just at daybreak, saw, inside of us, a large brig, which, from the squareness of her yards, we knew to be a vessel of war. The wind was from the southward, and she was close-hauled. We instantly made all sail, and stood after her, hoping to get her within range of our guns before she could run on shore, or seek for safety in port.

She at once kept way, and was evidently steering for a harbour, though I forget its name, which lay some short distance to the northward. She soon showed that she was a fast craft, for though the *Galatea* sailed well, she maintained her distance. At length, getting her within range of our long guns, we made sure of capturing her. Two shots struck her, but did not produce any serious damage.

'Never mind, she'll be ours in a few minutes,' observed Dick, as he stood near me at our gun. We expected in a few minutes to send a broadside into her.

Just then our topsails flapped loudly against the masts, and we lay becalmed. The brig almost immediately got out some long sweeps, and with her boats towing ahead, quickly crept away from us. I thought our captain would have ordered out the boats to attack her, but I suppose that he thought it was not worth risking the lives of the men by boarding a vessel with a crew so strong as she probably possessed. Thus we lay for some hours, rolling our sides into the smooth, shining waters. I heard some of the officers say that they could see through their glasses several other craft at anchor in a small bay protected by a fort. As evening approached a breeze sprang up, and making sail, we stood off the land. As soon as it was dark, however, the ship was put about, and we stood back again for some distance, when we hove to, and the

boats were lowered.   The captain then announced that he intended to
send four boats in, under the command of the first lieutenant; the
third lieutenant taking charge of one, Mr. Harvey of another, and the
boatswain of a fourth.   Dick and I were in Mr. Harvey's boat.   The
object was to cut out the brig we had chased into port, as well as any
other vessels we could get hold of.   It was just the sort of work sailors
are fond of, though at the same time often as dangerous as any they can
engage in.   They like it all the better, however, for the danger.

The brig was to be the first attacked, and we hoped to surprise her,
as probably some of her officers and crew were ashore.   If we could
take her, we had little doubt about cutting out one or two of the others
which had been seen at anchor.

The night was very dark, and just suited for our purpose.   The first
lieutenant took the lead in one of the gigs.   The two cutters and pinnace
followed close astern, to prevent the risk of separating.   In perfect
silence we pulled away from the frigate with muffled oars.   As yet we
could see no light to guide us, but we expected to catch sight of some
of those on shore as we drew nearer.   To get up to the anchorage we
had a point to round.   There was the risk, should any sentry be posted
there, that we should be discovered.   The lieutenant accordingly gave it
as wide a berth as he could.   Once round it, we could see the masts of
the brig against the sky, but there was no light visible, nor was any
movement perceptible on board her.   We pulled on steadily, hoping to
get up to her without being discovered.   We fancied that the Frenchmen must be keeping a bad look-out.   On and on we glided, like spirits
of evil bent on mischief, when, as we were within a cable's length of the
brig, suddenly a flame of fire burst from her ports, with the loud reports
of six heavy guns, followed by the rattle of musketry.

'On, lads, on!' cried our commanding officer; and the boats casting
off from each other, we pulled away as hard as we could.

The first lieutenant and Mr. Harvey in our boat, pulled for her bows, one on either side, while the other boats were to board on her quarters. Our boat was to go round to the starboard side, which was the inner one. The instant we hooked on, we clambered up, Mr. Harvey gallantly leading, Dick and I being close to him. We reached the deck without opposition, for the Frenchmen were all over on the other bow, attempting to beat back the lieutenant and his people, so that we took them completely by surprise, and were cutting and slashing at them before they knew we were on deck. They quickly turned, however, to defend themselves, and this allowed the lieutenant and the gig's crew to clamber on board. United, we drove them back from the forecastle. Some, to save themselves, tumbled down the fore-hatchway, but others, unable to get down, retreated aft. Here they joined the rest of the crew, who were fighting desperately with the third lieutenant and boatswain's party, but were being driven slowly back.

The uproar we made, the flash of the pistols, the clash of our cutlasses, the shouts and shrieks of the combatants, served to arouse the garrison in the fort and the crews of the other vessels. The guns in the fort had not opened upon us, probably because the Frenchmen were afraid of hitting their friends, not knowing whether we had captured the brig or been driven back.

The Frenchmen, as they generally do, fought bravely, but they could not withstand the desperate onslaught we made. Attacked as they were on both sides, they were unable to retreat, and those who had been aft leapt down the hatchways, crying out for quarter. Mr. Harvey told them that if they made further resistance they would be shot. He then called his boat's crew away, as had been arranged, to cut the cable, and began to tow the brig out of harbour, while the crew of another boat flew aloft to loose the sails. The canvas was let fall and rapidly sheeted home. The moment we began to move the fort opened fire. One of the

first shot struck our boat, which at once commenced to fill. Strange to
say, not a man among us was hit. We on this dropped alongside the
brig and scrambled on board, just as the boat sank beneath our feet. On
this the lieutenant, seeing that the brig had got good way on her, calling
his own boat's crew and that of the pinnace, shoved off, with the intention
of taking one of the other vessels, leaving the third lieutenant and Mr.
Harvey to carry out the brig. The shot from the fort came pitching
about us, and we were hulled several times. One shot struck the taffrail,
and as the splinters flew inboard, the third lieutenant, who was at the
helm, fell. I at once ran to help him, while Mr. Harvey took his place.
He was badly wounded, I feared ; but on recovering he desired to be left
on deck, observing that should he be taken below, the French prisoners
might, he feared, get hold of him, and hold him as a hostage, until we
promised to liberate them, or restore the brig.

Soon after this we got out of range of the guns from the fort. Looking astern, we could see the flashes of pistols, and could hear the rattle of
musketry, as if a sharp fight were going on. It was very evident that
the first lieutenant was engaged in warm work. Possibly we thought
he might have caught a tartar and been getting the worst of it. Mr.
Harvey proposed going back to his assistance, but the lieutenant feared
that if we did so, we should run a great risk of getting the brig ashore,
and might probably be captured. We therefore stood on until we were
clear of the harbour. Just as we were rounding the point, and looking
aft, I made out a vessel under weigh.

'Hurrah, Mr. Lloyd has made a prize of another vessel,' I shouted.

Some of the men doubted this, and declared that she was coming in
chase of us. I could not deny that such might possibly be the case, but
presently the fort opened upon her, which proved, as we supposed, that
she was another prize. We accordingly hove to, out of range of the
guns of the fort, to wait for her ; still some of the men fancied that she

might be after all, as they had at first supposed, an armed vessel coming out to try and retake us. To guard against this, Mr. Harvey ordered us to load the guns. We found plenty of powder and shot, so that we felt sure, if she was an enemy, of beating her off. The breeze freshened as she got clear of the harbour and stood towards us. We were at our guns, ready to fire should she prove an enemy. All doubt was banished when, on approaching, a British cheer was raised from her deck, to which we replied, and making sail, we stood on together.

In about half an hour we were up to the frigate, when both prizes hove to to windward of her, that we might send our prisoners as well as our wounded men on board. Besides the third lieutenant, we had had only two hurt in capturing our prize, the *Aimable;* but the first lieutenant, in capturing the other, the *Flore*, had had two men killed and three wounded, besides the boatswain and himself slightly. Not only had the crew of the *Flore* resisted toughly, but boats had come off from the shore and attempted to retake her, after her cable had been cut. The *Flore* had, however, escaped with fewer shot in her hull than we had received.

During the night we ran off shore, and as soon as it was daylight the carpenters came on board to repair our damages. The captain had meantime directed Mr. Harvey to take charge of the *Aimable*, and to carry her into Plymouth.

'I have applied for you, Wetherholm and Hagger, to form part of my crew,' he said, on returning on board. 'I know you are anxious to get home, as it will be some time probably before the frigate herself returns to port.'

I thanked him heartily, and Hagger, I, and the other men, sent for our bags. As soon as all the arrangements had been completed, we made sail and stood for the British Channel. The *Flore*, which sailed in our company, had been placed under charge of the second master. We had been directed to keep close together so that we might afford each other support. The wind being light, we did not lose sight of the frigate until just at sundown, when we saw her making sail, apparently in chase of some vessel, to the southward. Our brig was a letter of marque, and had a valuable cargo on board, so that she was worth preserving, and would give us, we hoped, a nice little sum of prize-money.

For long I had not been in such good spirits, as I hoped soon to be able to get home and to see my beloved wife, even if I could not manage to obtain my discharge, for which I intended to try. When it was my watch below, I could scarcely sleep for thinking of the happiness which I believed was in store for me.

We had kept two Frenchmen, one to act as cook, the other, who spoke a little English,—having been for some time a prisoner in England,—as steward. They were both good-natured, merry fellows. The cook's name was Pierre le Grande, the other we called Jacques Little. He was a small, dapper little Frenchman, and played the violin. He would have fiddled all day long, for he preferred it to anything else; but he could not get any one to dance to him except Le Grande, who, as soon as he had washed up his pots and kettles, came on deck, and began capering about to Jacques' tunes in the most curious fashion possible.

The rest of us had plenty to do in getting the brig into order, and occasionally taking a spell at the pumps, for she leaked more than was pleasant. We tried to discover where the water came in, but could not succeed. However, as the leak was not serious it did not trouble us much.

As we were so small a crew, we were divided into only two watches. Mr Harvey had one and gave me charge of the other, at which I felt pleased, for it showed that he placed confidence in me. I understood navigation, which none of the other men did, and I had a right to consider myself a good seaman.

CHAPTER XXIV.

We are chased by a large vessel—Overtaken by a storm—A stern chase—The stranger is dismasted—We are in a dangerous position—Loss of our crew—The gale moderates—The brig gives signs of sinking—We set about building a raft—An unexpected appearance—Jacques and his fiddle—The raft completed and launched—The first night—Dick and I compare notes—Troubled sleep—A dreadful reality—My companions swept overboard—Clinging on for life.

Two days had passed by since we left the frigate. It was my middle watch below, and I fancied that the greater part of it had passed by when I heard Mr. Harvey's voice shouting, ' All hands on deck, and make sail.'

I was on my feet in a moment, and looking astern as I came up, I saw through the gloom of night a large vessel to the southward, apparently standing to the eastward, while a smaller one, which I took to be the *Flore*, had hauled her wind, and was steering west.

' She is taking care of number one,' observed Dick to me, as we together went aloft to loose the top-gallant sails, for, like a careful officer, being short-handed, Mr. Harvey had furled them at sun-down. We then rigged out studden sail booms, hoping, should the stranger not have perceived us, to get a good distance before daylight. Soon after the first streaks of dawn appeared in the eastern sky, we saw her alter her course in pursuit of us. We had, however, got a good start, and, unless the wind fell, we might still hope to escape her.

At first it was doubtful whether she would follow us or the *Flore*. If she should follow her, we should be safe, as she would have little chance of capturing us both. As the day drew on the wind increased, and at length it became evident that the stranger intended to try and take us.

'She may, after all, be an English frigate,' said Dick to me.

'Mr. Harvey doesn't suppose so, or he wouldn't be so anxious to escape her,' I answered. 'He thinks it best to be on the safe side and run no risk in the matter.'

We were all at our stations, including the cook and steward, who were told to stand by and pull and haul as they might be ordered.

I asked the latter whether he thought the ship in chase of us was English or French.

He shrugged his shoulders, observing that he was not much of a sailor, and could not tell one ship from another unless he saw her flag.

Mr. Harvey stood with his glass in his hand, every now and then giving a look through it astern. Then he glanced up at the sails. The top-gallant masts were bending like willow wands. Every instant the wind was increasing, and the sea was getting up; still he was unwilling to shorten sail while there was a possibility of escaping.

At last, after taking another look through his telescope, he shut it up, observing to me, 'She's French! there's no doubt about it. We'll hold on as long as we can, she hasn't caught us yet.'

Scarcely two minutes after this there came a crash. Away went both our top-gallant masts, and as I looked aloft, I was afraid that the top masts would follow. Still the wreck must be cleared. Dick and I sprang up the main rigging, and I hurried aloft to clear the main-top-gallant mast, while two others, imitating our example, ascended the fore rigging. The brig was now plunging her bows into the fast-rising seas. It was a difficult and dangerous work we had undertaken, but getting out our knives, we succeeded in cutting away the rigging, and the masts and yards with their canvas fell overboard.

'That's one way of shortening sail,' said Dick as we came on deck. 'To my mind, the sooner we get a couple of reefs in the top sails the better.'

This was indeed very evident. Mr. Harvey taking the helm, the rest of us went aloft and performed the operation. We were too much occupied to look at the frigate. When we came down off the yards, we saw that she had shortened sail, but not before she also had carried away her fore-top-gallant mast. We were still going as rapidly as before through the water, but the increase of wind gave the advantage to the larger ship, which kept drawing closer.

I have not spoken of time. The day was passing, and Mr. Harvey ordered the steward and cook to bring us some food on deck, for no one could be spared below to obtain it. Already it was some hours past noon. If we could keep ahead until darkness came down, we might still manage to escape by altering our course, as soon as we had lost sight of the frigate. At length, however, we saw her yaw. She had got us within range of her guns. She fired, and two shot came whizzing past us. On this Mr. Harvey ordered us to run out two long guns, brass six-pounders, through the stern ports, and to fire in return.

We blazed away as fast as we could run them in and load, but it was a difficult matter to take aim with the heavy sea on through which we were plunging. We managed, however, to pitch two or three of our shot on board, but what damage we caused we could not tell.

Again the frigate yawed and fired all her foremost guns. One of the shot came crashing into the mainmast, and two others hulled us. I sprang towards the mast to ascertain the extent of damage it had received. It seemed a wonder, with so large a piece cut out of it, that it could stand, and I expected every moment to see it go. Still, should the wind not increase, I thought it might be preserved, and Mr. Harvey calling all the hands not engaged at the guns to bring as many spars as could be collected, we began fishing it. We were thus engaged when two more shot pitched on board, carrying away part of the bulwarks and capsizing one of the guns.

27

Another followed, bringing one of our men to the deck with his head shattered to pieces. Our position was becoming desperate. Presently two more shot struck us between wind and water. Several of the men, who had before shown no lack of courage, cried out that we had better strike before we were sent to the bottom.

'Not while our masts stand,' answered Mr. Harvey firmly.

We had had but slight experience in fishing masts, so I had little confidence in its strength. Mr. Harvey then called me aft to work one of the guns.

I again pitched a shot into the frigate. My great hope was that I might knock away one of her spars, and give us a better chance of escaping. The wind had been drawing round to the westward of south. We still kept before it. Presently the frigate braced up her yards, intending apparently to fire her whole broadside at us. As she did so, the wind suddenly increased. Over she heeled. She was almost concealed from sight by the clouds of spray and dense masses of rain which came suddenly down like a sheet from the sky.

Even before Mr. Harvey could give the word we were letting fly everything. The brig rushed on through the foaming seas. When I looked aft, I could just distinguish the dark hull of the frigate rolling helplessly from side to side, her masts gone by the board.

On we flew, soon losing sight of her altogether. Though our masts were standing, our canvas, except the fore-top sail, was blown to ribbons. The storm showed no signs of abating, for although there was a short lull, the wind again blew as hard as ever. The thunder roared, the lightning flashed from the clouds, and the night became pitchy dark. The seas increased, and, as they came rolling up, threatened to poop us.

How long the gale might last it was impossible to say. Before it had abated we might have run on the Irish coast. It would be wiser to heave the brig to while there was time; but the question was whether the main-mast would stand. The fore-top sail was closely reefed, the helm was put down; but as the vessel was coming up to the wind, a sea struck us, a tremendous crash followed, the main-mast, as we had feared, went at the place where it had been wounded, and, falling overboard, was dashed with violence against the side, which it threatened every moment to stave in.

Mr. Harvey, seizing an axe and calling on us to follow and assist in clearing away the wreck before more damage was done, sprang forward. At any moment the sea, striking the vessel, might sweep us off the deck. With the energy almost of despair, we worked away with axes and knives, and at length saw the mast drop clear of the side. While we were still endeavouring to clear away the wreck of the mast, Mr. Harvey had sent one of the crew below to search for some more axes, as we had only three among us. Just at this juncture he came on deck, exclaiming, in a voice of alarm, 'The water is rushing in like a mill sluice!'

'Then we must pump it out,' cried Mr. Harvey, 'or try and stop it if we can. Man the pumps!'

We had two each, worked by a couple of hands, and we began labouring away, knowing that our lives might depend upon our exertions.

The brig lay to more easily than I should have supposed possible, though we were still exposed to the danger of an overwhelming sea breaking on board us. We got the hatches, however, battened down, and kept a look-out, ready to catch hold of the stanchions or stump of the main-mast, to save ourselves, should we see it coming.

As soon as the pumps had been manned, Mr. Harvey himself went below, accompanied by Dick and another hand, carrying a lantern to try and ascertain where the water was coming in, with the greatest rapidity.

It appeared to me that he was a long time absent. He said nothing when he at last came up, by which I guessed that he had been unable to discover the leak. 'As long as there is life there's hope, lads,' he said:

'we must labour on to the last;' and he took the place of a man who had knocked off at the pumps. He worked away as hard as any man on board. After some time I begged that I might relieve him, and he went and secured himself to a stanchion on the weather side. I at last was obliged to cry 'Spell ho!' and let another man take my place.

I had just got up to where Mr. Harvey was seated on deck, and having taken hold of the same stanchion, remarked that the brig remained hove to better than I should have expected.

'Yes,' he observed; 'the foremast is stepped much further aft than in English vessels, but I wish that we had been able to get up preventer stays; it would have made the mast more secure.'

Scarcely had he uttered the words than a tremendous sea came rolling up and burst over the vessel.

'Hold on for your lives, lads!' shouted Mr. Harvey.

Down came the sea, sweeping over the deck. I thought the brig would never rise again. At the same instant I heard a loud crash. Covered as I was with water, I could, however, see nothing for several seconds; I supposed, indeed, that the brig was sinking. I thought of my wife, my uncle and aunt, and our cosy little home at Southsea, and of many an event in my life. The water roared in my ears, mingled with fearful shrieks. Chaos seemed round me. Minutes, almost hours, seemed to go by, and I continued to hear the roar of the seas, the crashing of timbers, and the cries of my fellow-men.

It must have been only a few seconds when the brig rose once more, and looking along the deck I saw that our remaining mast had gone as had the bowsprit, while, besides Mr. Harvey, I could distinguish but one man alone on the deck, holding on to the stump of the mainmast. At first I thought that Mr. Harvey might have been killed, but he was only stunned, and speedily recovered. He got on his feet and looked about him, as if considering what was to be done.

' We're in a bad state, Wetherholm, but, as I before said, while there' life there's hope. We must try to keep the brig afloat until the morning and perhaps, as we are in the track of vessels coming in and out of the Channel, we may be seen and taken off. Where are the rest of the men?

' I am afraid, sir, they are washed overboard, except the man we see there; who he is I can't make out.'

' Call him,' said Mr. Harvey.

' Come aft here ! ' I shouted.

' Ay, ay ! ' answered a voice which, to my great satisfaction, I recognised as that of Dick Hagger. He did not, however, move, but I saw that he was engaged in casting himself loose. He at length staggered aft to where we were holding on.

' Did you call me, sir ? ' he asked.

' Yes, my man. Where are the rest of the people ? ' said Mr. Harvey.

' That's more than I can tell, sir,' answered Dick. ' I saw the sea coming, and was making myself fast, when I got a lick on the head which knocked the senses out of me.' After saying this, he looked forward, and for the first time seemed to be aware that we three, as far as we could tell, were the only persons left on board.

The blast which had carried away the foremast seemed to be the last of the gale. The wind dropped almost immediately, and though the seas came rolling up and tumbled the hapless brig about, no others of the height of the former one broke over us. Our young officer was quickly himself again, and summoned Hagger and me to the pumps.

We all worked away, knowing that our lives might depend upon our exertions. Though we did not gain on the water, still the brig remained buoyant. This encouraged us to hope that we might keep her afloat until we could be taken off. It was heavy work. Dick and I tried to save our officer, who had less physical strength than we had, as much as possible.

Hour after hour we laboured on, the brig rolling fearfully in the trough of the sea, and ever and anon the water rushed over us, while we held fast to save ourselves from being carried away. At length we could judge by the movement of the vessel that the sea was going down, as we had expected it would do since there was no longer any wind to agitate it.

At length daylight broke, but when we looked out over the tumbling, lead-coloured ocean, not a sail could we discern. We sounded the well, and found eight feet of water. Our boats had all been destroyed,—indeed, had one remained, she would even now scarcely have lived.

'We may keep the brig afloat some hours longer, but that is uncertain,' said Mr. Harvey, after he had ceased pumping to recover strength. 'We must get a raft built without delay, as the only means of saving our lives. At present we could scarcely hold on to it, but as the sea is going down, we will wait to launch it overboard till the brig gives signs of being about to founder.'

We agreed with him. He told us to take off the main hatch, and get up some spars which we knew were stowed below. While we were thus occupied, my head was turned aft. The companion hatch was drawn back, and, greatly to our surprise, there appeared the head of Jacques Little. He was rubbing his eyes, looking more asleep than awake.

'*Ma foi!*' he exclaimed, gazing forward with an expression of horror on his countenance, 'vat hav happened?'

'Come along here and lend a hand, you skulking fellow!' cried Dick. 'Where have you been all this time?'

'Sleep, I suppose, in de cabin,' answered Jacques 'Vere are all de rest?'

'Gone overboard,' said Dick. 'Come along, there's no time for jabbering.'

'Vat an Le Grande?' exclaimed Jacques. '*Oh! comme je suis fâché!* Dat is bad, very bad.'

Jacques had evidently been taking a glass or two of cognac to con
sole himself, and even now was scarcely recovered from its effects. We
made him, however, help us, and once aroused, he was active enough.
Between whiles, as we worked at the raft, we took a spell at the pumps.
At last Mr. Harvey told us that our time would be best spent on the
raft. We sent Jacques to collect all the rope he could find, as well as to
bring up some carpenter's tools and nails. Having lashed the spars together, we fixed the top of the main hatch to it, and then brought up the
doors from the cabin, and such portions of the bulk-heads as could be
most easily knocked away. We thus in a short time put together a raft,
capable of carrying four persons, provided the sea was not very rough.
Most of the bulwarks on the starboard or leeside had been knocked
away; it was therefore an easy task to clear a space sufficient to launch
the raft overboard. We hauled it along to the side, ready to shove into
the water directly the brig should give signs of settling. Still she might
float for an hour or two longer.

Dick, while searching for the spars, had found a spare royal, which,
after being diminished in size, would serve as a sail should the wind be
sufficiently light to enable us to set one. We put aside one of the smaller
spars to fit as a mast, with sufficient rope for sheets and halyards.

Mr. Harvey gave an anxious look round, but not a sail appeared above
the horizon. He then ordered Jacques to go below and bring up all the
provisions he could get at, and a couple of beakers of water. Fortunately there were two, both full, kept outside the cabin for the use of the
pantry. We soon had these hoisted up, and Jacques speedily returned
with a couple of baskets, in which he had stowed some biscuits, several
bottles of wine, some preserved fruits, and a few sausages.

'Come, lads, we are not likely to be ill provisioned,' said Mr. Harvey,
making the remark probably to keep up our spirits.

Once more he sounded the well while we were giving the finishing

strokes to our raft. He did not say the depth of water in the hold, but
observed, in a calm tone, 'Now we'll get our raft overboard.' We had
secured stays with tackles to the outer side, so as to prevent it dipping
into the water. By all four working together, and two easing away the
tackles, we lowered it without accident. We had found some spare oars,
and had secured a couple of long poles to enable us to shove it off from
the side. There were also beckets fixed to it, and lashings, with which to
secure ourselves as well as the casks and baskets of provisions.

'Be smart, lads, leap on to the raft!' cried Mr. Harvey.

Dick and I obeyed, and he lowered us down the baskets, but Jacques,
instead of following our example, darted aft and disappeared down the
companion hatchway.

'Come back, you mad fellow!' exclaimed Mr. Harvey, still standing
on the deck, wishing to be the last man to leave the brig.

'You had better come, sir,' I could not help saying; for I feared, from
the depth the brig already was in the water, that she might at any moment
take her last plunge.

We were not kept long in suspense. Again Jacques appeared, carrying his fiddle and fiddlestick in one hand, and a bottle of cognac in the
other, and, making a spring, leapt on the raft. Mr. Harvey leapt after
him.

'Cast off,' he cried, 'quick, quick!'

We let go the ropes which held the raft to the brig, and, seizing the
poles, shoved away with all our might; then taking the paddles in hand,
we exerted ourselves to the utmost to get as far as we could away from
the sinking vessel.

We were not a moment too soon, for almost immediately afterwards
she settled forward, and her stern lifting, down she glided beneath the
ocean, and we were left floating on the still troubled waters. Yet
we had cause to be thankful that we had saved our lives. We were

far better off than many poor fellows have been under similar circumstances; for we had provisions, the sea was becoming calmer and calmer,
and the weather promised to be fine. We could scarcely, we thought,
escape being seen by some vessel either outward or homeward bound.
There was too much sea on to permit us, without danger, to set the sail,
but we got the mast stepped and stayed up in readiness. The wind was
still blowing from the southward, and we hoped it would continue to
come from that direction, as we might thus make the Irish coast, or if
not, run up St. George's Channel, where we should be in the track of
numerous vessels.

The day was now drawing to a close, and we prepared to spend our
first night on the raft. Mr. Harvey settled that we should keep watch
and watch, he with Jacques in one and Dick and I in the other. The
weather did not look altogether satisfactory; but as the sea had gone
down, we hoped that we should enjoy a quiet night, and get some sleep,
which we all needed.

Jacques seemed in better spirits than the rest of us; he either did not
understand our dangerous position, or was too light-hearted to let it
trouble him.

'Why should we be dull, Messieurs,' he said, 'when we can sing and
play?' And he forthwith took his fiddle, which he had stuck up in one of
the baskets, and began scraping away a merry air, which, jarring on our
feelings, had a different effect to what he had expected. Still he scraped
on, every now and then trolling forth snatches of French songs. At
last, Mr. Harvey told him to put up his fiddle for the present, and to lie
down and go to sleep.

'I shall want you to look out by and by, when I keep my watch,' he
said; 'and meantime you, Wetherholm and Hagger, take charge of the
raft, and I hope in a short time to be able to let you lie down.'

Saying this, Mr. Harvey laid down on a small platform which we had built for the purpose of enabling two of us at a time to be free of the wash of the water. Dick and I kept our places, lashed to the raft with our paddles in our hands. Our young officer was asleep almost immediately he placed his head upon the piece of timber which ran across the platform and served to support the mast.

'What do you think of matters, Will?' asked Dick, after a long silence. 'If it comes on to blow, will this raft hold together?'

'I fear not,' I answered; 'at all events, we should find it a hard job to keep alive on it if the sea were to get up, for it would wash over and over us, and although we might hold on, our provisions would be carried away. I hope, however, before another day is over that we shall be picked up by some homeward-bound craft; but don't let such thoughts trouble you, Dick. Having done our best, all we can do is to pray that we may be preserved.'

'I don't let them trouble me,' answered Dick, 'but still they will come into my head. I've fought for my king and country, and have done my duty, and am prepared for the worst.'

'You should trust rather to One who died for sinners,' I felt myself bound to say. 'He will save our souls though our bodies perish.'

'I have never been much of a scholar, but I know that,' answered Dick, 'and I believe that our officer knows it too. If he didn't, he would not be as sound asleep as he is now.'

I was very glad to hear Dick say this, for although we were at present much better off than we might have been, I was fully alive to our precarious situation. Even should the weather prove fine, we might not reach the shore for many a day, and our provisions and water would not hold out long, while, should it come on to blow, they might be lost, and we should be starved, even if the raft should hold together and we had strength to cling on to it.

Dick and I occasionally exchanged remarks after this, but still the time went on very slowly. Neither of us had the heart to call up Mr Harvey; but about midnight, as far as I could judge, he started up, and calling Jacques, told Dick and me to lie down. We did so thankfully securing ourselves with lashings one on either side of the mast. Before I closed my eyes, I observed that not a star was twinkling in the sky which seemed overcast down to the horizon. Though there was not much wind, there was rather more than there had been, and there was still too much sea on to allow us to set sail.

I was never much given to dreaming, but on this occasion, though I closed my eyes and was really asleep, I fancied all sorts of dreadful things. Now the raft appeared to be sinking down to the depths of the ocean, now it rose to the top of a tremendous sea, to sink once more amid the tumbling waters. I heard strange cries and shrieks, and then the howling of a gale as if in the rigging of a ship. I thought I was once more on board the brig, and saw the sea which had swept away my shipmates come rolling up towards us. Again the shrieks which I had heard sounded in my ears, and I felt the wild waters rushing over me. I started up to find that it was a dreadful reality. The portion of the raft to which I was clinging was almost submerged. The larger part appeared broken up. I looked round for my companions. The night was pitchy dark, I could see no one. I called to them. there was no reply. I felt across to where Dick had been—he was gone!

'Dick Hagger, Mr. Harvey, Jacques, where are you?' I shouted.

Dick's voice replied, 'Heave a rope and haul us in.' I felt about for one, but not a line could I find, except the lashings attached to the raft.

'Where are you?' I again cried out.

'Here, with Mr. Harvey; I tried to save him,' was the answer.

Alas, how helpless I felt! With frantic haste I endeavoured to draw out some of the lashings, in the hopes of forming a line long enough to reach Dick, but my efforts were in vain. The raft was tossing wildly

about.   It was with the greatest difficulty I could cling on to it, pressing
my knees round one of the cross timbers.   I heard once more the cry:

'Good-bye, Will, God help you!' and then I knew that Dick and the
young officer he was trying to save had sunk beneath the waves.

Again and again I shouted, but no voice replied.   Though thus left
alone, I still desired to live, and continued clinging to the shattered raft,
tossed about by the foaming seas.   Frequently the water rushed over
me; it was difficult to keep my head above it long enough to regain my
breath before another wave came rolling in.   It seemed to me an age that
I was thus clinging on in pitchy darkness, but I believe the catastrophe
really occurred only a short time before daylight.   In what direction the
wind was blowing I could not tell.   When the raft rose to the top of a
sea I endeavoured to look round.   No sail was in sight, nor could I distinguish the land.   I felt that I could not hold out many hours longer.
One of the baskets still remained lashed to the raft, but its contents had
been washed out, and the casks of water had been carried away.   Hour
after hour passed by.   There was less sea running, and the wind had
somewhat gone down.   The thoughts of my wife still kept me up, and
made me resolve to struggle to the last for life, but I was growing weaker
and weaker.   At length I fell off into a kind of stupor, though I still
retained sufficient sense to cling to the raft.

CHAPTER XXV.

How long I had remained thus I could not tell, when I was aroused by
hearing a man's voice, and looking up, saw a boat close to me, beyond
her a ship hove to.   One of the crew sprang on to the raft, and casting
off the lashings, he and others leaning over the bow of the boat, dragged
me on board.   After this I knew nothing until I found myself in a
hammock on board a large merchantman.   A surgeon soon afterwards
came to me.

'You will do well enough now, my man,' he said to me in a kind voice;
'but you were almost gone when we picked you up.'

I inquired what ship I was on board.

'The *Solway Castle*, homeward-bound East Indiaman,' he answered.

This was indeed satisfactory news, as I should now, I trusted, be able
to get back to my dear wife without the necessity of asking leave.   I
might indeed almost consider myself a free man, for I did not feel that it
would be my duty to return to the *Galatea*, considering that the prize I

had been put on board had gone down. After the doctor had left me, the sick bay attendant brought me a basin of soup which wonderfully revived me, and in shorter time than the doctor said he expected I could not help acknowledging that I was almost myself again.

I felt very sad as I thought of the loss of young Mr. Harvey and my old friend Dick Hagger; still the hopes of so soon being at home again made me think less of them than I might otherwise have done, and contributed greatly to restore my strength. I was treated in the kindest way by the doctor, and many others on board, who, having heard my history, commiserated my hitherto hard fate. A fair breeze carried us up Channel. When I was able to go on deck I kept a look-out, half expecting to see an enemy's ship bear down on us, although, unless she should be a powerful frigate or line-of-battle ship, she would have had a hard job to capture the *Solway Castle*, which was well armed, and carried a numerous crew. Still I could not help recollecting the old saying, 'There's many a slip between the cup and the lip.' The truth was, I had not yet recovered my full strength, and the doctor remarked that I required tonics to set me up and drive gloomy thoughts out of my head. We kept well over to the English coast to avoid the risk of falling in with French cruisers. We had got abreast of Portland when a strange sail was made out to the southward, which, as she was seen edging in towards the land, it was supposed without doubt was an enemy. The passengers, of whom there were a good number returning after a long absence from India, began to look very blue.

'Never fear, ladies and gentlemen,' I heard the captain observe, 'we'll show the Frenchman that we're not afraid of him, and the chances are, make him afraid of us.' Saying this, he ordered the studden sails we had carried to be taken in, and the royals to be set, and then bringing the ship on a wind, boldly stood out towards the stranger. The effect was as desired. The stranger, hauling her wind, stood away to the southward, taking us probably for a line-of-battle ship, which the stout old ' tea chest ' resembled at a distance. By yawing and towing a sail overboard, we stopped our way, until the captain thought the object had been answered, when once more, squaring away the yards, we continued our course up the Channel.

As we passed the Isle of Wight, I cast many a look at its picturesque shores, hoping that a pilot boat might put off at the Needles, and that I might have the opportunity of returning in her, but none boarded us until we were near the Downs, when, unfortunately, I was below, and before I could get on deck the boat was away. However, I consoled myself with the reflection that in another day or two we should be safe in the Thames, and I resolved not to lose a moment in starting for Portsmouth as soon as I stepped on shore. I thought that I might borrow some money from my friend the doctor, or some of the passengers, who would, I believed, willingly have lent it me, or if not, I made up my mind to walk the whole distance, and beg for a crust of bread and a drink of water should there be no other means of obtaining food. My spirits rose as the lofty cliffs of Dover hove in sight, and rounding the North Foreland, we at length, the wind shifting, stood majestically up the Thames. When off the Medway, the wind fell, and the tide being against us, we had to come to an anchor. We had not been there long when a man-of-war's boat came alongside. I observed that all her crew were armed, and that she had a lieutenant and midshipman in her, both roughish-looking characters. They at once stepped on board with an independent, swaggering air. The lieutenant desired the captain to muster all hands. My heart sank as I heard the order. I was on the point of stowing myself away, for as I did not belong to the ship, I hoped to escape Before I had time to do so, however, the midshipman, a big whiskered fellow, more like a boatswain's mate than an officer, with two men, came below and ordered me up with the rest. The captain was very indignant

at the behaviour of the lieutenant and the midshipman, declaring that his
crew were protected, and had engaged to sail in another of the Company's
ships after they had had a short leave on shore.

'Well and good for those who are protected, but those who are not
must accompany me,' answered the lieutenant. 'We want hands to man
our men-of-war who protect you merchantmen, and hands we must get
by hook or by crook.' Having called over the names, he selected twenty
of the best men who had no protection. I was in hopes I should escape,
when the midshipman pointed me out.

The lieutenant inquired if I belonged to the ship. I had to acknowledge
the truth, when, refusing to hear anything I had to say, though I pleaded
nard to be allowed to go free, he ordered me with the rest into the boat
alongside. Having got all the men he could obtain, the lieutenant
steered for Sheerness, and took us alongside a large ship lying off the
dockyard, where she had evidently been fitting out. She looked to me, as
we approached her, very much like an Indiaman, and such I found she
had been. She was, in truth, the *Glatton*, of one thousand two hundred
and fifty-six tons, which had a short time before been purchased, with
several other ships, from the East India Company by the British Government. She was commanded, I found, by Captain Henry Trollope, and
carried fifty-six guns, twenty-eight long eighteen pounders on the upper
deck, and twenty-eight carronades, sixty-eight pounders, on the lower
deck. Her crew consisted in all of three hundred and twenty men and
boys, our arrival almost making up the complement. The ship's company was superior to that of most ships in those days, although somewhat
scanty considering the heavy guns we had to work.

We were welcomed on board, and I heard the lieutenant remark that
he had made a good haul of prime hands. It was a wonder, men taken
as we had been, could submit to the severe discipline of a man-of-war,
but all knew that they had no help for it. They had to run the risk of

being flogged or perhaps hung as mutineers if they took any steps to show their discontent, or to grin and bear it.

Most of them, as I did myself, preferred the latter alternative. I had never before seen such enormous guns as were our sixty-eight pounder carronades, larger than any yet used in the service,—indeed, their muzzles were almost of equal diameter with the ports, so that they could only be pointed right abeam. We had neither bow nor stern chasers, which was also a great drawback. Some of the men, when looking at the guns, declared that they should never be able to fight them; however, in that they were mistaken. Practice makes perfect, and we were kept exercising them for several hours every day.

The ship was nearly ready for sea, and soon after I was taken on board we sailed from Sheerness, for the purpose of reinforcing the North Sea Fleet under Admiral Duncan. In four or five days, during which we were kept continually exercising the guns, we arrived in Yarmouth Roads. Scarcely had we dropped anchor than we were ordered off again to join a squadron of two sail of the line and some frigates, commanded by Captain Savage of the *Albion*, sixty-four, supposed to be cruising off Helvoetsluis.

Next morning, long before daylight,—it had gone about two bells in the middle watch,—we made the coast of Flanders, and through the gloom discovered four large ships under the land. The wind, which had hitherto been fresh, now fell, and we lay becalmed for some hours in sight of Goree steeple, which bore south by east. We and the strangers all this time did not change our relative positions. That they were enemies we had no doubt, but of what force we could not make out. As the day wore on, a breeze sprang up from the north-west; at the same time we saw two other good-sized ships join the four already in view. We instantly made all sail, and stood towards the strangers, making signals as soon as we got near enough for them to distinguish our bunting. No

28

reply being made, we were satisfied that they were an enemy's squadron
There were four frigates and two ship corvettes, while a large brig corvette
and an armed cutter were seen beating up to join them from leeward.

'We're in a pretty mess. If all those fellows get round us, they'll blow
us out of the water, and send us to the bottom,' I heard one of the sailors
who had been pressed out of the Indiaman observe.

'Our captain doesn't think so, my boy,' answered an old hand.
'Depend upon it, he intends trying what the mounseers will think of our
big guns.'

The order was now given to clear for action, and we stood on with a light
breeze in our favour towards the enemy. The wind freshening, the four
frigates, in close line of battle, stood to the north-east. Shortly afterwards
they shortened sail, backing their mizzen-top sails occasionally to keep in
their stations. We were nearing them fast. Up went the glorious flag of
Old England, the St. George's ensign, just as we arrived abreast of the
three rearmost ships, the two corvettes and the smallest of the frigates.
Our captain ordered us, however, not to fire a shot until we had got up
to the largest, which he believed from her size to be the commodore's, and
intended to attack.

'I wonder what we are going to be after?' I heard the man from the
Indiaman inquire. 'We seem to be mighty good friends; perhaps, after
all, those ships are English.'

'Wait a bit, my bo, you'll see,' answered the old hand, 'our captain
knows what he's about. If we can knock the big one to pieces, the others
will very soon give in.'

The ship next ahead of the commodore had now fallen to leeward, so
that the latter formed the second in the line. Not a word was spoken.
I should have said that as we had not men sufficient for our guns, for
both broadsides at the same time, we were divided into gangs, one of
which, having loaded and run out the gun, was directed to leave it to be

pointed and fired by the others, picked hands, and we were then to run over and do the same to the gun on the other side. We thus hoped to make amends for the smallness of our numbers.

The ship we were about to attack was evidently much larger than the *Glatton*, upwards of three hundred tons as it was afterwards proved, but that did not daunt our gallant captain. We continued standing on until we ranged close up alongside her, when our captain hailed and desired her commander to surrender to his Britannic Majesty's ship. No verbal reply was made, but instead, the French colours and a broad pendant were hoisted, showing that the ship we were about to engage was, as we had supposed, that of the commodore. Scarcely had the colours been displayed, than she opened her fire, her example being followed by the other French ships. We waited to reply until we were within twenty yards of her. Then we did reply with a vengeance, pouring in our tremendous broadside. The shrieks and cries which rose showed the fearful execution it had committed.

Still the French commodore continued firing, and we ran on, keeping about the same distance as before, exchanging broadsides. Meantime the van ship of the enemy tacked, evidently expecting to be followed by the rest of the squadron, and thereby drive us upon the Brill shoal, which was close to leeward. The van ship soon after arrived within hail of us on our weather beam, and received our larboard guns, which well-nigh knocked in her sides, while the groans and shrieks which arose from her showed that she had suffered equally with her commodore. Anxious to escape a second dose of the same quality of pills, she passed on to the southward, while we cheered lustily at seeing her beaten. We had not much time for cheering; we were still engaged with the commodore on our lee bow, while the second largest frigate lay upon our lee quarter, blazing away at us. Just then our pilot shouted out, ' If we do not tack, in five minutes we shall be on the shoal!'

'Never mind,' answered the captain; 'when the French commodore strikes the ground, put the helm a-lee.'

Just as he spoke, the French ship tacked, evidently to avoid the shoal, and while she was in stays, we poured in another heavy raking fire which well-nigh crippled her.   Meantime the other French ships had gone about.

'Helm's a-lee!' I heard shouted out, but as our sails and rigging were by this time terribly cut about, it seemed as if we should be unable to get the ship round.   The wind, however, at last filled our sails, and round she came.   We, as well as the Frenchmen, were now all standing on the starboard tack.   The three largest frigates had fallen to leeward, and could do us but little damage, but the three smaller ones kept up a harassing long-shot fire, to which we, on account of the distance, could offer but a very slight return.   All our topmasts being wounded, and the wind freshening, it became necessary to take a reef in the topsails.   In spite of the risk we ran, the moment the order was issued we swarmed aloft, though we well knew that at any moment the masts might fall, while the enemy's shot came flying among us.

The frigates and the two corvettes to leeward, seeing us cease firing, stood up, hoping to find us disabled; but springing below, we were soon again at our guns, and gave them such a dose, knocking away several of their yards, that they soon stood off again to join the other ships, which had already had enough of it.   I forgot to say that latterly we had had the brig and the cutter close under our stern, and as we had no guns with which to reply to the smart fire they opened, we could only fire at them with musketry.   After a few volleys, however, they beat a retreat, and as night closed down upon us, all firing ceased on both sides.   The Frenchmen had fired high, and our sails and rigging were too much cut up to enable us to follow them.   Strange as it may appear, scarcely a dozen shot had struck the hull, and in consequence, notwithstanding the tremendous fire to which we had been exposed, we had not had a single man killed, and two only, the captain and corporal of marines, wounded. The former, however, poor man, died of his wounds shortly afterwards. During the night every effort was made to get the ship into a condition to renew the action. At daybreak we saw the French squadron draw up in a close head and stern line. By eight o'clock, having knotted and spliced our rigging, bent new sails, and otherwise refitted the ship, we stood down to offer battle to the enemy, but they had swallowed enough of our sixty-eight pounders, and about noon they bore away for Flushing. We followed until there was no hope of coming up with them, when our ship's head was turned northward, and we steered for Yarmouth Roads, to get the severe damages we had received more effectually repaired than we could at sea.

I afterwards heard that the large French frigate we had engaged was the *Brutus*, which had been a seventy-four cut down, and now mounted from forty-six to fifty guns. We saw men and stages over the sides of the French ships stopping shot-holes, and we heard that one of them had sunk in harbour.

I was in hopes that we should go back to Sheerness to refit, and that I might thus have an opportunity of getting home. I had done my duty during the action, so had every one else. The wind freshening during the night, the hands were ordered up aloft to shorten sail.

'Be smart, my lads,' I heard the officer of the watch sing out, 'or we may have the masts over the sides.'

I was on the main-top-sail yard-arm to leeward, when, just as I was about to take hold of the ear-ring, the ship gave a lurch, the foot rope, which must have been damaged, gave way, and before I could secure myself, I was jerked off into the sea. It was better than falling on deck, where I should have been killed, to a certainty. I sang out, but no one heard me, and to my horror, I saw the ship surging on through the dark ness, and I was soon left far astern. I shouted again and again, but the flapping of the sails, the rattling of the blocks, and the howling of the wind drowned my voice.

At the same time the main-top-gallant mast with its sail and yard was carried away. I saw what had happened, and I feared that two poor fellows who had been handing the sail must have been killed. Their fate made me for the moment forget my own perilous condition. When I saw that I had no hope of regaining the ship, I threw myself on my back to recover my breath, and then looked about, as I rose to the top of a sea, to ascertain if there was anything floating near at hand on which I might secure myself. Though I could see nothing, I did not give way to despair, but resolved to struggle to the last for life. Having rested, I swam on until a dark object appeared before me. It was a boat, which, though filled with water, would, I hoped, support me. I clambered into her, and after resting, examined her condition. She was, as far as I could ascertain, uninjured. I had my hat on, secured by a lanyard, and immediately set to work to bale her out with it. I succeeded better than I could have expected, for though the sea occasionally washed into her, I managed by degrees to gain upon the water. At length I found that her gunwale floated three or four inches above the surface. This encouraged me to go on, and before daybreak she was almost clear. When dawn broke I looked out, but no land was in sight, nor was a sail to be seen. I was without food or water, but I hoped to be able to endure hunger and thirst for some hours without suffering materially.

The day went on, the hot summer's sun beat down upon my head, and dried my clothes. Several sail passed in the distance, but none came near me. There was nothing in the boat with which I could form even a paddle. I looked round again and again, thinking it possible that I might find some spar which might serve cut in two as a mast and yard. I would then, I thought, try to steer the boat to land, with the help of one of the thwarts, which I would wrench out to make a rudder, using my clothes tacked together as a sail.

Such ideas served to amuse my mind, but no spar could I see. Another night came on, and, overcome by hunger, thirst, and weariness, I lay down in the bottom of the boat to sleep. At length I awoke. Some time must have passed since I lay down. I felt so low, that I scarcely expected to live through another day should I not be picked up. I looked about anxiously to ascertain if any sail was near; none was visible, and I once more sank back in a state of stupor. I knew nothing more until I found myself in the fore peak of a small vessel, a man sitting by the side of the bunk in which I lay feeding me with broth. In a few hours I had recovered sufficiently to speak. I asked the seaman who had been attending me, what vessel I was on board.

'The *Fidelity*, collier, bound round from Newcastle to Plymouth,' he answered. 'We picked you up at daybreak. The captain and mate thought you were gone, but I saw there was life in you, and got you placed in my bunk. You'll do well now, I hope.'

I replied that I already felt much better, thanks to his kind care, and asked his name.

'Ned Bath,' he answered. 'I've only done to you what I'd have expected another to do for me, so don't talk about it.'

He then inquired my name. I told him, giving him an outline of my history, how I had been carried off from my wife, and how cruelly I had been disappointed in my efforts to get back to her.

'You shan't be this time if I can help it, Will,' he said ; 'and as soon as we get into Plymouth, I'll help you to start off for Portsmouth. I've got some wages due, and you shall have what money you want, and pay me back when you can.'

I thanked him heartily, feeling sure that Uncle Kelson would at once send him the money, and accepted his generous offer. I could not help

hoping that we might meet with a foul wind and be compelled to put
into some nearer port; but the wind held fair, and we at length sighted
the Eddystone, when, however, it fell calm. Not far off lay a frigate
which had come out of the Sound. Several other vessels were also
becalmed near us. I was looking at the frigate, when a boat put off
from her and pulled towards one of the other vessels. She then steered
for another and another, remaining a short time only alongside each.

'She's after no good,' observed Ned; 'I shouldn't be surprised if she
was picking up hands. We've all protections aboard here. You'd better
stow yourself away, Will. Jump into my berth and pretend to be sick,
it's your only safe plan.'

This I did not like to do, and I guessed if Ned was right in his conjectures, that the officer who visited us would soon ascertain there was
one more hand on board than the brig's complement. Unhappily he was
right—the boat came alongside. It was the old story over again. Just
as I had expected to obtain my freedom, I was seized, having only time
to give Ned the address of my wife, to whom he promised to write, and
to wish him and my other shipmates good-bye, when I was ordered to
get into the boat waiting alongside. She, having picked up three or
four more men from the other vessels becalmed, returned to the frigate,
which was, I found, the *Cleopatra*, of thirty-two twelve-pounder guns,
commanded by Captain Sir Robert Laurie, Bart., and bound out to the
West Indies.

I very nearly gave way altogether. In vain, however, I pleaded to be
allowed to go on shore. I acknowledged that I belonged to the *Glatton*,
and promised faithfully to return to her as soon as I had visited my wife.
My petition was disregarded, my statement being probably not even
believed. A breeze springing up, all sail was made, and the *Cleopatra*
stood down Channel.   ⌟

I must pass over several weeks. They were the most miserable of my existence. Three times I had been pressed, when on the very point, as I supposed, of getting free. I began at last to fancy that I never should return on shore. Though my spirits were low, I retained my health, but I did my duty in a mechanical fashion. My shipmates declared that for months together they never saw me smile.

At length, after we had visited the West Indies, we were cruising in search of an enemy, when soon after daybreak we sighted a ship standing to the eastward, we having the wind about north-west. Instantly we made all sail in chase. Every one was sure that she was an enemy, and from her appearance we had no doubt that she was a big ship. She, observing that she was pursued, stood away from us before the wind. All day we continued the chase. Everything was done to increase our speed. We began to be afraid that the enemy would escape us. The sun went down, but there was a bright moon, and numbers of sharp eyes were constantly on the watch for her. We marked well the course she was steering. Anxiously the night passed away. When daylight returned, the watch on deck gave way to a shout of satisfaction, as in the cold grey light of dawn she was seen right ahead rising out of the leaden waters. One thing was clear, we were overhauling her surely, though slowly. We went to breakfast, the meal was quickly despatched, and we were all soon on deck again to look out for the stranger. In a short time there was no doubt about her character. The order was given to clear the ship for action. As I heard the words, I felt more cheerful than I had done since I came on board. Strange as it may seem, my spirits rose still higher when the stranger was made out to be a forty-gun frigate. By half-past eleven he shortened sail, and hauled his wind to allow us to come up with him, and hoisting his colours at the same time, we now knew him to be a Frenchman. Probably he had run away at first thinking that we were the biggest ship, whereas in reality, as we afterwards discovered, he was vastly our superior, not only in the number of his guns but in weight of metal, for they were eighteen-pounders, and while we had only 200 men fit to work our guns, he had 350. The *Cleopatra* measured only 690 tons, while the enemy's ship, which was the *Ville de Milan*, measured 1100, and carried forty-six guns. We also shortened sail ready for action, and directly afterwards began to fire our bow-chasers, which the enemy returned with his after-guns. Thus a running fight was carried on for some time, we in no way daunted by the vastly superior force with which we were engaged.

At about half-past two we were within a hundred yards of the *Ville de Milan*, when she luffed across our bows and poured in a crashing broadside, while we, passing under her stern, returned her fire with good interest. We now ranged up within musket-shot, on the starboard side of our big antagonist, and thus we kept running parallel to each other, sometimes on a wind and sometimes nearly before it—we trying to prevent her from luffing again across our bows or under our stern, and she not allowing us to perform the same manœuvre. Never in a single combat was there a fiercer fight. We worked our guns with desperate energy—not that we ever doubted that we should be the victors, but we knew that we must fight hard to win the victory.

For upwards of a couple of hours we had been hotly engaged, when a loud cheer broke from us. We had shot away the enemy's main-top sail-yard. We, however, had suffered greatly, not only in spars, but our running rigging had been literally cut to pieces. A number of our men, also, lay killed and wounded about our decks; and though the latter were carried below as fast as possible, their places were rapidly supplied by others doomed to suffer the same fate.

The loss of the enemy's main-top sail-yard caused us to forge ahead, but unhappily, from the condition of our running rigging, we could neither shorten sail nor back our main-top sail. Our captain therefore resolved to endeavour to cross the bows of the *Ville de Milan.*

The order was given to put the helm down. At that moment, a shot struck the wheel, knocking it to pieces and killing one of the men standing at it. There we lay, with the ship utterly unmanageable and at the mercy of our opponent. It was enough to make us weep with sorrow, but instead of that we set to work to try and get tackles on to the tiller to steer by.

'Look out, my lads! stand by to repel boarders!' sang out our captain.

At that moment the enemy bore up and ran us on board, her bowsprit and figure-head passing over our quarter-deck, abaft the main rigging. I was on the quarter-deck. As I saw the bows of our huge enemy grinding against our sides, our ship rolling terrifically, while the other was pitching right at us as it were, I felt that never were British courage and resolution more required than at that moment. It was put to the test.

'Repel boarders!' was the shout. On came the Frenchmen, streaming in crowds over their forecastle. We met them, cutlass and pistol in hand, and with loud shouts drove them back to their own ship. They must not have been sorry to get there, for every instant it appeared that our gallant frigate would go down under the repeated blows given us by our opponent. I do not believe, though, that such an idea occurred to many of us. We only thought of driving back the enemy, of striving to gain the victory. All this time our great guns were blazing away, and the marines were keeping up a hot fire of musketry, while the enemy were pounding us as sharply in return.

Not a minute of rest did they afford us. Led on by their officers, with shouts and shrieks they rushed over their bows and down by the bowsprit on to our deck. Every inch of plank was fiercely contested, and literally our scuppers ran streams of blood.

Try and picture for a moment the two ships rolling, tumbling, and grinding against each other, the wind whistling in our rigging (for it was blowing heavily), the severed ropes and canvas lashing about in

every direction; the smoke and flames from our guns, their muzzles
almost touching, the cries, and groans, and shouts; spars and blocks
tumbling from aloft; the decks slippery with gore; the roar of big guns,
the rattle of musketry, the flash of pistols, the clash of cutlasses as we
met together; and some faint idea may be formed of the encounter in
which we were engaged.

Once more the enemy were driven back, leaving many dead; but we
also suffered fearfully. Still we persevered. For an instant I had time
to look round. I saw the shattered condition of our ship, my brave
companions dropping rapidly around me, several of our lieutenants
severely wounded, and for the first time the dread came over me that we
must strike our flag or sink at our quarters, for I felt convinced that
the ship could not stand much longer the sort of treatment she had been
undergoing.

Again the shout was raised, 'Repel boarders!' 'Steady, my brave
lads, meet them!' cried our gallant captain. We saw the Frenchmen
hurrying along the waist, leaping up on the forecastle, and then in dense
masses they rushed down on our decks. We met them as bravely as
men can meet their foes, but already we had nearly sixty men (more
than a quarter of our crew) either killed or wounded, and, terribly over-
matched, we were borne back by mere force of numbers.

The way cleared, the Frenchmen continued pouring in on us till our
people were literally forced down the hatchways or against the opposite
bulwarks, while our cutlasses were knocked out of our hands, no longer
able to grasp them. The bravest on board must have felt there was no
help for it, and no one was braver than our captain. The British
colours were hauled down.

When I saw what had happened, I felt as if a shot had gone through
me—grief and shame made my heart sink within my bosom. The
Frenchmen cheered; we threw down our weapons, and went below. We

were called up, however, to assist in getting the ships free of each other. This was a work of no little difficulty. Some of our people were removed aboard the *Ville de Milan,* and she sent about forty men, including officers, to take possession of the *Cleopatra.*

Some of the Frenchmen told us that their captain had been killed by one of the last shots we fired. We had four lieutenants, the master, and the lieutenant of marines wounded, as well as the boatswain and a midshipman, though not an officer was killed. Of the seamen and marines, we had twenty-two killed and thirty wounded. Another proof that we did not give in while a chance of victory remained was, that scarcely were we free of the Frenchman than our main and fore masts went over our side, and very shortly afterwards the bowsprit followed, and our gallant frigate was left a miserable wreck on the waters.

The French lost a good many men, and their ship was so knocked about, that her main and mizzen masts both went over the side during the night, and when day broke, to all appearance she was not much better off than the *Cleopatra.*

We at once were summoned to assist the prize crew in getting up jury-masts, and the weather moderating, we were able to do this without difficulty. Both frigates then shaped a course for France. Even now I scarcely like to speak of what my feelings were when once more all my hopes were cruelly dashed to the ground, and I found myself carried away to become the inmate of a French prison.

I sat most of the day with my head bent down on my knees, brooding over my grief. I certainly felt ripe for any desperate adventure; but nothing else would, I think, have aroused me. The Frenchmen did not like our looks, I conclude, for they kept a strict watch over us lest we should attempt to play them a trick, and would only allow a few of us on deck at a time. This was very wise in them, for had they given us the chance, we should certainly not have let it slip.

CHAPTER XXVI.

A Friend in need—The Frenchmen catch a Tartar—The tables turned—Return to Old England—Off again to sea—England expects that every man will do his duty—Battle of Trafalgar—Wreck of our prize—My enemy found—Home—Conclusion.

I OUGHT to have said that the larger portion of the ship's company and all the officers had been removed at once on board the *Ville de Milan*. I, with about sixty or seventy others, remained on board the *Cleopatra*. I would rather have been out of the ship, I own. I could not bear to see her handled by the Frenchmen. Often and often I felt inclined to jump up and knock some of them down, just for the sake of giving vent to my feelings. Of course I did not do so, nor did I even intend to do so. It would have been utterly useless, and foolish in the extreme. I only describe my feelings, and I dare say they were shared by many of my shipmates.

Nearly a week thus passed, when one morning, as I was on deck, I saw a large ship standing towards us. What she was I could not at first say. The Frenchmen, at all events, did not like her looks, for I observed a great commotion among them. The two frigates had already as much sail set on their jury masts as it was in any way safe to carry, so nothing more could be done to effect their escape should it be necessary to run for it, by the sail in sight being, what I hoped she was, a British man-of-war.

How eagerly I watched to see what would be done! The French officers kept looking out with their glasses, and constantly going aloft

Soon the two frigates put up their helms and ran off before the wind, and almost at the same instant I had the satisfaction of seeing the stranger make all sail in chase.

One, at all events, was certain of being captured, for, knocked about as they had been, they made very little way. Anxiously I watched to ascertain to a certainty the character of the stranger. The Frenchmen, I doubted not, took her to be an English man-of-war, and I prayed that they might be right, but still I knew that their fears might cause them to be mistaken.

Most of the English prisoners were sent below, but I managed to stow myself away forward, and so was able to see what took place. On came the stranger. Gradually the foot of her top-sails, and then her courses rose out of the water, and when at length her hull appeared I made out that she was not less than a fifty-gun ship, and I had little doubt that she was English. The Frenchmen looked at her as if they would like to see her blow up, or go suddenly to the bottom. I watched her in the hope of soon seeing the glorious flag of Old England fly out at her peak. I was not long kept in doubt.

As soon as the ship got near enough to make out the French ensign flying on board the *Cleopatra* and *Ville de Milan*, up went the British ensign. Forgetting for the moment by whom I was surrounded, I could scarcely avoid cheering aloud as I watched it fluttering in the breeze. The Frenchmen, in their rage and disappointment, swore and stamped, and tore their hair, and committed all sorts of senseless extravagances, and I felt that it would be wise to keep out of their sight as much as possible, as some of them might, perchance, bestow on me a broken head, or worse, for my pains.

The two frigates closed for mutual support, but when I came to consider the condition they were in, I had little doubt that the English ship would be more than a match for them. The stranger had first been seen soon after daybreak. The people had now just had their break fasts. They were not long below, for all were anxious to watch the progress of their enemy. The weather had been all the morning very doubtful, and thick clouds were gathering in the sky. My earnest prayer was that it would continue moderate; I began, however, to fear that my hopes would be disappointed. The clouds grew thicker and seemed to descend lower and lower, while a mist arose which every instant grew denser.

At length, when I had for a short time turned my head away from our big pursuer, I again looked out. What was my horror and disappointment not to be able to see the English ship in any direction! I looked around and tried to pierce the thick mist which had come on, but in vain; and again my heart sank within me. The Frenchmen also searched for their enemy; but when they could not find her, they, on the contrary, began to sing and snap their fingers, and to exhibit every sign of satisfaction at the prospect of escaping her.

One or two of my shipmates had slipped up on deck, and they returned with the sad tidings below. After a little time I joined them. I found them all deep in a consultation together. It was proposed that we should rise upon the French prize crew, and, taking the frigate from them, go in search of the English ship. Some were for the plan, some were against it. It was argued that the *Ville de Milan* would, at every risk, attempt to stop us—that, short-handed as we were, we could not hope to hold out against her—that we might very probably miss the English ship, and then, if we fell in with another Frenchman, we should very likely be treated as pirates.

I rather agreed with these last-mentioned opinions; still, as I have said, I felt ready to undertake any enterprise, however desperate. Hour after hour passed away. The Frenchmen kept walking the deck and rubbing their hands, as the prospect of escape increased.

Sad only we heard them stop. I slipped up again on deck; a breeze had carried away the mist, and there, right away to windward, was the English ship, much nearer than when she had last been seen. I did cheer now, I could not help it. The Frenchmen were too much crest-fallen to resent by a blow what they must have looked upon as an insult, but an officer coming up, ordered me instantly to go below.

I was obliged to comply, though I longed to remain on deck to see what course events would take. The people below, as soon as they heard that a friend was in sight, cheered over and over again, utterly indifferent to what the Frenchmen might say or do. They did utter not a few *sacrés* and other strange oaths, but we did not care for them.

The two frigates were, as I said, at the time I went below, close together, with the French ensigns hoisted on the main-stays. The British ship was coming up hand over hand after them. We tried to make out what was going forward by the sounds we heard and the orders given. Our ship was before the wind. Presently a shot was fired to leeward from each frigate, and a lad who had crept up, and looked through one of the ports, reported that the *Ville de Milan* had hauled her wind on the larboard tack, and that we were still running before it. We all waited listening eagerly for some time, and at last a gun was fired, and a shot struck the side of our ship. Then we knew full well that our deliverance was not far off. The Frenchmen *sacré'd* and shouted at each other louder than ever. Our boatswain had been left on board with us. He was a daring, dashing fellow.

'Now, my lads, is the time to take the ship from the hands of the Frenchmen!' he exclaimed. 'If we delay, night is coming on, and the other frigate may get away. If we win back our own ship, it will allow our friend to go at once in chase of the enemy.'

The words were scarcely out of his mouth when we all, seizing hand-spikes and boat-stretchers, and indeed anything we could convert into weapons, knocked over the sentry at the main hatchway, and springing on deck, rushed fore and aft, and while the Frenchmen stood at their guns, looking through the ports at their enemy and our friend, we over-powered them. Scarcely one of them made any resistance. In an instant we were on the upper deck, where the officers, seeing that the game was up, cried out that they gave in, and hauled down the French flag.

On this, didn't we cheer lustily! The ship which had so opportunely come to our rescue was the fifty-gun ship *Leander*, the Honourable John Talbot. Her crew cheered as she came up to us, and her captain asked us if we could hold our own against the Frenchmen without assistance. We replied that we could, and against twice as many Frenchmen to boot. We thought then that we could do anything. He told us we were fine fellows, and ordering us to follow him, he hauled his wind in chase of the *Ville de Milan.*

We took care to disarm all the Frenchmen ; and, you may believe me, we kept a very sharp look-out on them, lest they should attempt to play us the same trick we had just played them.

The *Ville de Milan* had by this time got some miles away, but the *Leander* made all sail she could carry, and we had little doubt would soon come up with her. Still we could not help keeping one eye on the two ships, and the other on our prisoners. In little more than an hour after the French flag had been hauled down aboard the *Cleopatra*, as we hoped, never to fly there again, the *Leander*, with her guns ready to pour forth her broadside, ranged up alongside the *Ville de Milan.* The Frenchmen were no cowards, as we had found to be the case, but they naturally didn't like her looks; and not waiting for her to fire, wisely hauled down their colours. Then once more we cheered, and cheered again, till our voices were hoarse. People have only to consider what the anticipation of a prison must be to British sailors, to remember that we fancied that we had lost our gallant ship, and that we were smarting under a sense of defeat, to understand our joy at finding ourselves once more at liberty. I had a joy far greater than any one, or at least than any one not situated as I was (and perhaps there were some as anxious as I was to return home), of feeling that I had now a far greater chance than had before occurred of once more setting foot on the shores of Old England, and of returning to my beloved wife.

The three ships all hove to close together, while arrangements were made for our passage to England. The *Leander* put a prize crew on board the *Ville de Milan*, strengthened by some of our people, and our gallant captain, Sir Robert Laurie, and his officers once more took possession of their own ship. It was a happy meeting on board the *Cleopatra*, you may depend on that; and on the first Saturday afterwards, as may be supposed, there was not a mess in which 'Sweethearts and wives' was not drunk with right hearty goodwill. Some, and I trust that I was among them, felt that we owed our deliverance to a power greater than that of men, and thanked with grateful hearts Him who had in His mercy delivered us from the hand of our enemies. And oh! my fellow-countrymen, who read this brief account of my early days, I, now an old man, would urge you, when our beloved country is, as soon she may be, beset with foes, burning with hatred and longing for her destruction, that while you bestir yourselves like men and seize your arms for the desperate conflict, you ever turn to the God of battles, the God of your fathers, the God of Israel of old, and with contrite hearts for our many national sins, beseech Him to protect us from wrong, to protect our native land, our pure Protestant faith, our altars, our homes, the beloved ones dwelling there, from injury. Pray to Him—rely on Him—and then surely we need not fear what our enemies may seek to do to us.

Once more, then, we were on our way to England. I did believe that this time I should reach it. I could not fancy that another disappoint-

ment was in store for me. The weather, notwithstanding the stormy
time of the year, proved moderate, and we made good way on our homeward voyage. While the boats were going backwards and forwards between the ships, I had observed in one of them a man whose countenance
bore, I thought, a remarkable resemblance to that of Charles Iffley. Still
I could not fancy it was Iffley himself. I asked some of the *Leander's*
people whether they had a man of that name on board, but they said
that they certainly had not, and so I concluded that I must have been mistaken. The man saw me, but he made no sign of recognition, but neither,
I felt, would Iffley have done so had he been certain of my identity.
Still the countenance I had seen haunted me continually, and I could not
help fancying that he was still destined again to work me some evil.

'Land! land ahead!' was sung out one morning, just as breakfast
was over. The mess-tables were cleared in a moment, and every one not
on duty below was on deck in a moment looking out for the shores we all
so longed to see. It was the coast of Cornwall, not far from the Land's
End. Point after point was recognised and welcomed, as, with a fair
breeze, we ran up Channel. Then the Eddystone was made, and the
wind still favouring us, we at length dropped our anchor close together
in Plymouth Sound. I could scarcely believe my senses when I found
myself once more in British waters. Oh! how I longed to be able to go
on shore and to set off at once for Portsmouth; but, in spite of all my
entreaties, I could not obtain leave to go. The captain was very kind,
and so was the first lieutenant, but they were anxious to get the ship
refitted at once, to be able to get to sea to wipe out the discredit, as
they felt it, of having been captured even by so superior a force. All I
could do, therefore, was to sit down and write a letter to my wife to tell
her of my arrival, and to beg her to send me instantly word of her
welfare. I entreated her, on no consideration, to come to meet me; I did
not know what accident might occur to her if she attempted to come by

land or by sea. Travelling in those days was a very different matter to what it is at present. Even should no accident happen to her, I knew that before she could reach Plymouth I might be ordered off to sea. I felt bitterly that I was not my own master. I did not blame anybody. Who was there to blame? I could only find fault with the system, and complain that such a system was allowed to exist. Fortunate are those who live in happier days, when no man can be pressed against his will, or be compelled to serve for a longer time than he has engaged to do.

The three ships as we lay in the Sound were constantly visited by people from the shore, and the action between the *Cleopatra* and the *Ville de Milan* was considered a very gallant affair, and instead of getting blamed, the captain, officers, and crew were highly praised for their conduct. Our captain, Sir Robert Laurie, was presented with a sword of the value of a hundred guineas by the Patriotic Fund, as a compliment to his distinguished bravery, and the skill and perseverance which he exhibited in chasing and bringing the enemy to action. Indeed, we obtained more credit for our action, though we lost our ship, than frequently has been gained by those who have won a victory. The *Ville de Milan* was added to the British Navy under the name of the *Milan*, and classed as an eighteen-pounder thirty-eight-gun frigate, and Sir Robert Laurie was appointed to command her. Our first lieutenant, Mr. William Balfour, was also rewarded by being made a commander.

Day after day passed away, and I did not hear from my wife. Dreadful thoughts oppressed me. I began to fear that she was dead, or that, not hearing from me, or perhaps believing me lost, she had removed from Southsea. Indeed, I cannot describe all the sad thoughts which came into my head, and weighed down my heart. Then the tempter was always suggesting to me, ' Why not run and learn all about the matter? What harm is there in deserting? Many a man has done it before. Who will think the worse of you if you do?' But I resisted the temptation, powerful as it was. I had undertaken to serve my country, and to obey those placed in authority over me ; and I knew that their reasons were good for not allowing me to go on shore. Still I own it was very, very hard to bear. I had yet a sorer trial in store for me.

Things were done in those days which would not be thought of at the present time. Men were wanted to work the ships which were to fight England's battles, and men were to be got by every means, fair or foul. Often, indeed, very foul means were used. While we were expecting to be paid off, down came an order to draft us off into other ships. In spite of the bloody battles we had fought, in spite of all we had gone through, our prayers were not heard—we were not even allowed to go on shore ; and, without a moment's warning, I found myself on board the *Spartite*, 74, commanded by Sir Francis Laforey, and ordered off at once to sea. I had barely time to send a letter on shore to tell my wife what had occurred, and no time to receive one from her. Well, I did think that my heart would break this time ; but it did not. I was miserable beyond conception, but still I was buoyed up with the feeling that I had done my duty, and that my miseries, great as they were, would come some day to an end.

We formed one of a large squadron of men-of-war, under Lord Collingwood, engaged in looking out for the French and Spanish fleets. We continually kept the sea cruising off the coast of Spain and Portugal, and occasionally running out into the Atlantic, or sweeping round the Bay of Biscay. From August to September of this memorable year, 1805, we were stationed off Cadiz to watch the enemy's fleet which had taken shelter there, and in October we were joined by Lord Nelson in his favourite ship the *Victory*. We all knew pretty well that something would be done, but we little guessed how great was the work in which we were about to engage. The French and Spanish fleets were inside Cadiz harbour, and we wanted to get them out to fight them. This was a difficult matter, for they did not like our looks. That is not surprising, particularly when they knew who we had got to command us. Lord Nelson, however, was not to be defeated in his object. Placing a small squadron in shore, he stationed other ships at convenient distances for signalling, while the main body of the fleet withdrew to a distance of eighteen leagues or so from the land.

The enemy were deceived, and at length, on the 19th and 20th, their whole fleet had got out of the harbour. No sooner was Lord Nelson informed of this, than he stood in with his entire fleet towards them.

At daybreak on the memorable 21st October 1805, the combined French and Spanish fleets were in sight, about twelve miles off, the centre of the enemy's fleet bearing about east by south of ours. At 6 A.M. we could from the deck see the enemy's fleet, and, as I afterwards learned, the *Victory* was at that time about seven leagues distant from Cape Trafalgar. At about 10 A.M. the French Admiral Villeneuve had managed to form his fleet in close order of battle; but owing to the lightness of the wind, some of the ships were to windward and some to leeward of their proper stations—the whole being somewhat in the form of a crescent. We had at an early hour formed into two columns, and bore up towards the enemy. The *Victory* led the weather division, in which was our ship. We had studden sails alow and aloft; but the wind was so light that we went through the water scarcely more than two knots an hour. I am not about to give an account of the battle of Trafalgar, for that is the celebrated action we were then going to fight. It has been too often well described for me to have any excuse for making the attempt. Indeed, when once it began, even the officers knew very little about the matter, and the men engaged in working the guns knew nothing beyond what they and their actual opponents were about. All I know is, that Lord Nelson was afraid the enemy would try and get back into Cadiz, and in order to prevent him, he resolved to pass through the van of his line.

At 11.40 A.M. Lord Nelson ordered that ever-memorable signal to be made—' ENGLAND EXPECTS THAT EVERY MAN WILL DO HIS DUTY.' Nobly, I believe, one and all did their duty; and, oh! may Englishmen never forget that signal in whatever work they may be engaged. It was received with loud cheers throughout the fleet both by officers and men. The *Royal Sovereign*, Lord Collingwood's ship, led the lee division, and at ten minutes past noon commenced the action, by passing close under the stern of the *Santa Anna*, discharging her larboard broadside into her, and her starboard one at the same time into the *Fougueux*. These two ships fired at her in return, as did the *San Leandro* ahead, and the *San Justo* and *Indomitable*, until other ships came up and engaged them. The action was now general. All that could be seen were wreaths of smoke, masts and spars falling, shattered sails, shot whizzing by, flames bursting out with a tremendous roar of guns, and a constant rattle of musketry; ships closing and firing away at each other, till it appeared impossible that they could remain afloat.

In the afternoon I know that we and the *Minotaur* bore down on four heavy ships of the combined squadron, which we hotly engaged, and succeeded in cutting off the Spanish *Neptuno*. She was bravely defended; but in two hours we compelled her to strike her flag, with the loss of her mizzen mast and fore and main-top mast. No seamen could have fought more bravely than did the Spaniards on this occasion; but their bravery did not avail them. As the spars of the enemy's ship went tumbling down on deck, and his fire slackened, we one and all burst into loud cheers, which contributed not a little to damp his courage. I forgot my own individuality, my own sorrows and sufferings, in the joy of the crew at large. I felt that a great and glorious victory was almost won—the most important that English valour, with God's blessing, had ever achieved on the ocean. I felt certain that the victory would be gained by us. My spirits rose. I cheered and cheered away as loudly as the rest. Many of our people had been struck down and carried below, though comparatively few had been killed outright. I saw my messmates wounded; but it never for a moment occurred to me that I should be called on to share their fate. Suddenly, as I was hauling away at my gun, I felt a stunning terrific blow. I tottered and fell. I was in no great pain, only horribly sick. The blood left my checks. It seemed to be leaving me altogether. ' Carry him below,' I heard some one say. 'He's not dead, is he?' Then I knew that I was badly wounded; I did not know how badly. I was almost senseless as I was conveyed below, where I found myself with a number of my shipmates, who had lately been full of life and activity, strong, hearty men, now lying pale and maimed or writhing in agony. One of the surgeons soon came to me and gave me restoratives, and I then knew where I was, and that my left arm was shattered, and my side wounded. I thought at that time that I had suffered a very great misfortune; but I had reason afterwards to believe that I ought to have been thankful for what had occurred. I said that we were engaged with the Spanish ship the *Neptuno*. In spite of the hammering we gave her, her people continued to serve her guns with undaunted courage. At length, when we had knocked away her mizzen mast and main and fore-top masts, and killed and wounded a number of her people, and sent many a shot through her hull, her crew, seeing that numbers of the combined fleet had already succumbed to British valour, hauled down their colours. I heard the cheering shout given by my shipmates, and discovered the cessation of the firing from no longer experiencing the dreadful jar which the guns caused each time they were discharged. As soon as any of our boats could be got into a condition to lower, the prize was taken possession of. I found afterwards that my name was called over to form one of the prize crew; but when it was known that I was wounded, another hand was sent in my place. I had been selected by the first lieutenant, who looked on me as a steady man, and wished to recommend me for promotion. I give an account of what befell the prize as narrated to me by a shipmate.

'You know, Weatherhelm,' said he, when I met him some months afterwards, 'that I formed one of the prize crew sent to take possession of her. Before we got her sufficiently into order to be manageable, we fell on board the *Téméraire*, one of our own squadron. We little thought at that time that our beloved chief was lying in the cockpit of the *Victory* mortally wounded. He had been struck by the fatal bullet at 1.25, while walking his quarter-deck, and at 4.30 he expired without a groan. Lord Nelson had directed that the fleet with the prize should anchor as soon as the victory was complete; but Lord Collingwood, who now took the command, differed on the subject, and ordered the ships to keep under way, being of opinion that the less injured ships might the better help the crippled ones. Our ship was less injured than most; for we only had our main-top masts wounded. Our prize, however, was in a very crippled condition. She had lost her fore and mizzen masts by the board, and as it was late in the afternoon before we took possession of her, after which we had to secure the prisoners and send them on board our ship and the *Minotaur*, it was nearly night before we could begin putting the ship to rights. We had then in the dark to work away to set up a jury, fore, and mizzen mast. We laboured all night, and by the morning had them both standing. The morning after that never-to-be-forgotten battle broke dark and lowering, giving every indication of a gale. How little prepared to encounter it were the greater portion of the ships which had been engaged in the desperate struggle! Down came the gale upon us from the westward. Every instant it increased, and very soon our two jury masts were carried away, leaving us a helpless wreck on the raging waters. The Spanish coast was under our lee, and towards it we were rapidly driving.

'A lee-shore, on any occasion, is not a pleasant object of contemplation, but still worse was it for us when we remembered that it was inhabited by our enemies, whose ships we had just so soundly thrashed. We tried to range one of our cables to bring up, but it was useless to trust to it a moment, it had been so much injured by the shot. It soon became evident that if the gale continued, we should drive ashore or go down. Anxiously we looked out to windward, but in the prospect on that side there was very little to cheer us, and still less was there on the other side, where a few miles off only the sea broke on the rock-bound, inhospitable shore. Towards that shore we were rapidly driving. The gale came down on us stronger and stronger. "There's no help for it!" exclaimed our commanding officer with a deep sigh, for he felt, as we all did, that it was very hard to win a prize and to have helped to win a great victory, and then to lose our prize and perhaps our lives. "Up with the helm—keep her dead before the wind!" he added, going forward with his glass, as did the other officers, looking out for a spot free from rocks into which to run the ship. Evening was coming on, and he saw that it was better to go on shore in the day-time, when we might take advantage of any chance of saving ourselves, instead of at night, when our chance would be small indeed. Orders were given for every man to prepare as best he could to save himself. On we drove towards the shore. We had a large number of prisoners on board. As we approached the land they were all released, the danger pointed out to them, and they were told to try and save themselves, the officers promising that they would try and help them.

'There was little time for preparation. Every moment the gale was increasing. The roar of the surf on the shore was terrific, sadly warning us of the fate of the ship once cast within its power. Even the bravest

turned pale as they saw the danger. The Spaniards, bravely as they
had fought, tore their hair, shrieked, and called on their saints to help
them, but did little to make ready for the coming catastrophe.   We, with
our axes, tore up the decks, and each man provided himself with a spar
or bit of timber on which he might float when washed overboard, as we
expected soon to be.   Darkness overtook us sooner even than we had
calculated.   In thick gloom, with a driving rain and a howling wind, the
ship was hove in among the breakers.   She struck with terrific violence.
The sea broke furiously over us.   I know little more.   I received a blow
on my head, I suppose.   When I came to myself, I was lying on the
beach and unable to move.   Then I saw lights approaching, and I found
myself lifted up and carried to a cottage, where my head was bound up
and food was given me.   I found the next day that not ten of the prize
crew had escaped, but that of the Spaniards upwards of forty had been
washed safely on shore.   I was treated kindly, but afterwards carried off
to prison.   A Spanish prison is one of the last places in which a man
would like to take up his abode; and, my dear Weatherhelm, you may
believe me, I am right glad to find myself exchanged and once more
treading the shores of Old England.'   Such was the account my old shipmate gave me; and then I felt, as I have said, that I should be thankful
for what had happened to me.   To return to my own adventures.   Our
ship had a long passage home, for in her crippled condition we could
carry very little sail.   This gave me a longer time to recover before
landing.   From my abstemious habits, I did not suffer as much as many
of my companions in misfortune, several of whom died of their wounds
from inflammation setting in, caused by their previous intemperate mode
of life.

We at last reached Plymouth, and I was carried to the hospital.   I
longed to write to my wife, and yet my heart sank within me when I
thought that I should have to tell her what a maimed and altered being

I was. I fancied that she would not know me, and would look on me with horror. When the surgeon saw me, directly I was carried to the hospital, he bid me cheer up, and said that he thought I should soon be strong enough to move. Scarcely had he left me, when I heard a man groaning heavily in the bed next to mine. The groans ceased. I asked the sufferer what was the matter with him. I was startled when he answered in a voice which I knew at once, 'I am dying, and going I know not where, with a thousand sins on my head unrepented of and unforgiven.' It was Iffley who spoke. I was not certain whether he knew me. I answered, 'There is forgiveness for the greatest of sinners. Repent. Trust in Christ. His blood will wash away all your sins.' There was no reply for some time. I thought that he had ceased to breathe.

'Who are you who says that?' he exclaimed suddenly; 'you think that I do not know you. I knew you from the first, and I believe you know me. Can you forgive one who has injured you so severely—who would have injured you still more had he found the opportunity? Weatherhelm, I ask you, can you forgive me?'

I was silent for some minutes. There was a severe strife in my bosom. I prayed earnestly for God's Holy Spirit. I uttered the words, ' Forgive us our trespasses as we forgive them that trespass against us.' I felt that I could reply with sincerity, 'Iffley, I do forgive you—from my heart—truly and freely.'

'Then I can believe that God will forgive me,' he cried out with almost a shriek of joy. 'Yes, the chaplain here and others have talked to me about it. I could not believe them. I felt that I was far too guilty, and too wretched an outcast; but I am sure that what man can do, God will do. Yes, Weatherhelm, you have given a peace to my heart I never expected to dwell there. Go on, talk to me on that subject. Pray with me. I have no time to talk on any other subject, to tell you of my past

career. That matters not. My hours are numbered. Any moment I
feel may be my last on earth. Go on, go on.'

I did talk long and earnestly to him, and what I said seemed to increase his comfort. Our conversation was interrupted by a visitor who
came round and read and talked to the poor wounded occupants of the
wards. He came to my bed. I looked up in his face, and recognised in
him my old friend and commander, Captain Tooke. He had left the sea,
I found, and having a competence, thus employed himself in visiting
hospitals, especially those which contained seamen, and in other works of
a labouring Christian. I told him what had occurred between me and
Iffley. He sat by the bedside of my former shipmate, and talked, and
read to him, and prayed with him. His voice ceased. I saw him bending over Iffley. Slowly he turned round to me. 'He is gone,' he said
in a low voice. 'He placed his hope on One who is ready and able to
forgive, and I am sure that he is forgiven.' Captain Tooke promised
to write to my wife to break to her the news of my wound. I got
rapidly round,—indeed, the doctors said I might venture to move to my
home whenever I pleased. Just then business called Captain Tooke to
Portsmouth, and he invited me to accompany him. We found a vessel
on the point of sailing there. We had a quick and smooth run, and in
two days we were put on shore at the Point at the entrance of the
harbour. A hackney coach was sent for, and we drove to Southsea.
When I got near the house where I had left my uncle and aunt, and
where I hoped to find my beloved wife, I felt so faint that I begged to be
put down, thinking that the fresh air would revive me. Captain Tooke
thought the same, and so, getting out of the carriage, he told me to sit
down on a low wall near at hand, while he went on to announce my
coming. While there, a little rosy, fair-haired boy ran laughing by, as if
trying to escape from some one. I sprang forward, and putting out my
hand, he took it and looked up in my face. I cannot describe the

tumultuous feelings which came rushing into my bosom when I saw that child. 'Who are you, my little fellow? What's your name?' I asked, with a tremulous voice.

'Willand—Willand Wetherholm,' he answered plainly.

Yes, my feelings had not deceived me. I took him up, he nothing loth, though he looked inquiringly at my empty sleeve. 'And your mother, boy, where is she?' I asked, still more agitated.

'In there,' he answered, pointing to our old abode. 'She no guess I run away.'

I now went up to the house with the child hanging round my neck. I was blessed indeed. There was my own dear wife, still pale from her anxiety about me, weeping, but it was with joy at seeing me; and there were my kind uncle and dear Aunt Bretta, just as I had always known her.

My tale is ended. I never went to sea again, but in a short time obtained the same employment in which I was engaged when I was pressed. Never after that did I for a moment doubt God's good providence and loving-kindness to all those who put their trust in Him. He afflicts us for our good. He tries us because He loves us. Reader, whatever may occur, trust in God and in His Son, whose blood can alone wash away all your sins. Love Him, confide in Him, and let your great hope, your chief aim, be to dwell with Him for eternity.

THE END.

RICHARD CLAY & SONS, LIMITED,
BRUNSWICK STREET, STAMFORD STREET, S.E.,
AND BUNGAY, SUFFOLK.

BOOKS FOR BOYS

PUBLISHED BY

HENRY FROWDE and HODDER & STOUGHTON

THE HERBERT STRANG SERIES

Many of Mr. Herbert Strang's Books are issued in German, Danish, and Swedish

The Air Patrol : A Story of the North-West Frontier. Illustrated in Colour by CYRUS CUNEO. Demy 8vo, cloth, gilt top, 6/-.

In this book Mr. Strang looks ahead—and other books have already proved him a prophet of surprising skill—to a time when there is a great Mongolian Empire whose army sweeps down on to the North-West Frontier of India. His two heroes luckily have an aeroplane, and with the help of a few Pathan miners they hold a pass in the Hindu Kush against a swarm of Mongols, long enough to prevent the cutting of the communications of the Indian army operating in Afghanistan.

The Air-Scout : A Story of National Defence. Illustrated in Colour by W. R. S. STOTT. Demy 8vo, cloth, gilt top, 6/-. Picture boards, cloth back, 4/6.

The problems of National Defence are being discussed with more and more care and attention, not only in Great Britain, but also in all parts of the Empire. In this story Mr. Strang imagines a Chinese descent upon Australia, and carries his hero through a series of exciting adventures, in which the value of national spirit, organisation, and discipline is exemplified. The important part which the aeroplane will play in warfare is recognised, and the thousands of readers who have delighted in the author's previous stories of aviation will find this new book after their own heart.

> LORD ROBERTS writes :—" It is capital reading, and should interest more than boys. Your forecast is so good that I can only hope the future may not bring to Australia such a struggle as the one you so graphically describe."
>
> LORD CURZON writes :—" I have read with great pleasure your book, 'The Air-Scout.' It seems to me to be a capital story, full of life and movement : and further, it preaches the best of all secular gospels, patriotism and co-operation."
>
> " We congratulate Mr. Strang on this fine book—one of the best fighting stories we have read."—*Morning Post.*

THE HERBERT STRANG SERIES

Humphrey Bold : His Chances and Mischances by Land and Sea. Illustrated in Colour by W. H. MARGETSON. Crown 8vo, cloth elegant, olivine edges, 6/-. Special Presentation Edition, 7/6 net; also cloth, 3/6.

In this story are recounted the many adventures that befell Humphrey Bold of Shrewsbury, from the time when, a puny slip of a boy, he was befriended by Joe Punchard, the cooper's apprentice (who nearly shook the life out of his tormentor, Cyrus Vetch, by rolling him down the Wyle Cop in a barrel), to the day when, grown into a sturdy young giant, he sailed into Plymouth Sound as first lieutenant of the *Bristol* frigate. The intervening chapters teem with exciting incidents, telling of sea-fights with that redoubtable privateer Duguay Trouin; of Humphrey's escape from a French prison; of his voyage to the West Indies and all the perils he encountered there.

"Mr. Strang is undoubtedly the best writer of this class of story that we have to-day. He has never done anything better than 'Humphrey Bold.'"—*Newcastle Chronicle.*

"Undoubtedly one of the strongest historical stories we ever remember to have read."—*Schoolmaster.*

Palm Tree Island. Illustrated in Colour by ARCHIBALD WEBB. Crown 8vo, cloth elegant, olivine edges, 6/-; also cloth, 3/6.

In this story two boys are left on a volcanic island in the South Seas, destitute of everything but their clothes. The story relates how they provided themselves with food and shelter, with tools and weapons; how they fought with wild dogs and sea monsters; and how, when they have settled down to a comfortable life under the shadow of the volcano, their peace is disturbed by the advent of savages and a crew of mutinous Englishmen. The savages are driven away; the mutineers are subdued through the boys' ingenuity; and they ultimately sail away in a vessel of their own construction. In no other book has the author more admirably blended amusement with instruction.

"Written so well that there is not a dull page in the book."—*The World.*

THE HERBERT STRANG SERIES

Rob the Ranger : A Story of the Fight for Canada. With Illustrations in Colour and Maps. Crown 8vo, cloth elegant, olivine edges, 6/-. Presentation Edition, 7/6 net; cloth, 3/6.

Rob Somers, son of an English settler in New York State, sets out with Lone Pete, a trapper, in pursuit of an Indian raiding party which has destroyed his home and carried off his younger brother. He is captured and taken to Quebec, where he finds his brother in strange circumstances, and escapes with him in the dead of the winter, in company with a little band of stout-hearted New Englanders.

General Baden-Powell, in recommending books to the Boy Scouts, places "Rob the Ranger" first among the great scouting stories.

One of Clive's Heroes : A Story of the Fight for India. With Illustrations in Colour and Maps. Crown 8vo, cloth elegant, olivine edges, 6/- ; also cloth, 3/6.

Desmond Burke goes out to India to seek his fortune, and is sold by a false friend of his, one Marmaduke Diggle, to the famous Pirate of Gheria. But he escapes, runs away with one of the Pirate's own vessels, and meets Colonel Clive, whom he assists to capture the Pirate's stronghold. His subsequent adventures on the other side of India—how he saves a valuable cargo for his friend Mr. Merriman, and assists Clive in his fights against Sirajuddaula, are told with great spirit and humour.

"An absorbing story. . . . The narrative not only thrills, but also weaves skilfully out of fact and fiction a clear impression of our fierce struggle for India."—*Athenæum.*

Settlers and Scouts : A Story of the African Highlands. Illustrated in Colour. Crown 8vo, cloth, olivine edges, 5/- ; also cloth, 3/6.

An Englishman and his son emigrate to a remote part of British East Africa, where they settle down as farmers and stock-raisers. The story tells of their difficulties through the depredations of wild beasts, and the yet more formidable attacks of an Arab engaged in the ivory trade. The story is a worthy successor to "Tom Burnaby," also an African tale, by which Mr. Herbert Strang made his reputation as a writer for boys.

"Boys will love to read through these pages, and they will find in them much that is instructive and useful."—*Record.*

"The boy who begins to read it will certainly read it to a finish."—*Literary World.*

3

THE HERBERT STRANG SERIES

With Drake on the Spanish Main.

Illustrated in Colour by ARCHIBALD WEBB. With Maps. Crown 8vo, cloth elegant, olivine edges, 5/-.

A rousing story of adventure by sea and land. The hero, Dennis Hazelrig, is cast ashore on an island in the Spanish Main, the sole survivor of a band of adventurers from Plymouth. He lives for some time with no companion but a spider monkey, but by a series of remarkable incidents he gathers about him a numerous band of escaped slaves and prisoners, English, French and native ; captures a Spanish fort ; fights a Spanish galleon ; meets Francis Drake, and accompanies him in his famous adventures on the Isthmus of Panama ; and finally reaches England the possessor of much treasure.

"Mr. Herbert Strang bids fair to become to the present what the late G. A. Henty was to the past generation of young folk ; in fact, his stirring romances, though, like Henty's, worked up on a sound historical basis, are far better written."—*The Lady.*

"Another of Mr. Herbert Strang's masterful stories of adventure and romance."— *School Guardian.*

Barclay of the Guides :

A Story of the Indian Mutiny. Illustrated in Colour by H. W. KOEKKOEK. With Maps. Crown 8vo, cloth elegant, olivine edges, 5/-.

Of all our Native Indian regiments the Guides have probably the most glorious traditions. They were among the few who remained true to their salt during the trying days of the great Mutiny, vying in gallantry and devotion with our best British regiments. The story tells how James Barclay, after a strange career in Afghanistan, becomes associated with this famous regiment, and though young in years, bears a man's part in the great march to Delhi, the capture of the royal city, and the suppression of the Mutiny.

"Mr. Strang has been truly described as 'a born teacher of history,' and this Story of the Indian Mutiny is an additional proof of the truth of the observation."— *Schoolmistress.*

The Motor Scout :

A Story of Adventure in South America. Illustrated in Colour by CYRUS CUNEO. Large crown 8vo, cloth, olivine edges, 3/6 ; picture boards, 2/6.

In the interest aroused by the solution of the problem of flying, the motor bicycle has been entirely overlooked by story-writers. Happily Mr. Herbert Strang has now thought of making it the pivot of a story, and for the scene he has hit upon one of the Latin States of South America, which have been somewhat neglected as a background for romance. Mr. Strang tells the story of an Irish boy who is living in this State just at the time when one of the periodical revolutions breaks out. He is forced to take sides, and with the help of his motor-cycle is able to assist his friends, but not without running risks unknown to scouts provided with less novel means of traversing the country.

THE HERBERT STRANG SERIES

Round the World in Seven Days. Illustrated in Colour

by A. C. MICHAEL. With Map. Crown 8vo, cloth, olivine edges, **3/6**; picture boards, **2/6.**

The science of aviation is making such rapid progress that the subject of Mr. Herbert Strang's first 3*s.* 6*d.* book perhaps anticipates a very near future. A young naval officer, learning that some relatives of his are in desperate peril on an island in the Pacific, sets off from England at a few hours' notice to convey help to them by aeroplane. He is due back to his ship within seven days. How he flies " Round the World in Seven Days," what adventures he meets with, what checks he triumphs over—these are here recounted in the author's vivid and picturesque style.

Jack Hardy : or, A Hundred Years Ago. Illustrated in Colour. Crown 8vo, cloth extra, **2/6**; picture boards, **2/-.**

The old smuggling days ! What visions are called up by the name—of stratagems, and caves, and secret passages, and ding-dong fights between sturdy seamen and dashing King's officers ! It is in these brave days of old that Mr. Herbert Strang has laid the scenes of his story " Jack Hardy." Jack is a bold young middy who, in the course of his duty to the King, falls into all manner of difficulties and dangers : has unpleasant experiences in a French prison, escapes by sheer daring and ingenuity, and turns the tables on his captors in a way that will make every British boy's heart glow.

" Herbert Strang is second to none in graphic power and veracity. . . . Here is the best of characterization in bold outline."—*Athenæum.*

ROMANCES OF MODERN INVENTION

In this series Mr. Herbert Strang effectually demolishes the theory that the days of romance are restricted to the mediæval ages when knights in armour met each other in the lists, or delivered fair maidens who languished in turret chambers; and he proves that the modern world, in which the clash of arms is largely superseded by the whirr of machinery, is as full of wonder and romance as the ancient. Each of the following stories is concerned with some particular discovery of modern science, such as the aeroplane and the submarine, which is made use of in the working out of the plot ; and the heroes of these adventures, who face dangers that were unknown in olden times, cannot fail to make a strong appeal to boys of to-day.

THE HERBERT STRANG SERIES
ROMANCES OF MODERN INVENTION

The Flying Boat : A Story of Adventure and Misadventure. Illustrated in Colour by T. C. DUGDALE.
Crown 8vo, cloth, olivine edges, 3/6 ; picture boards, cloth back, 2/6.

The Cruise of the Gyro-Car. Illustrated in Colour by A. C. MICHAEL.
Cloth, 2/6 ; picture boards, 2/-.

(The Gyro-Car, which is a road vehicle or a boat at pleasure, is the logical outcome of the gyroscope applied to the bicycle.)

Swift and Sure : The Story of a Hydroplane. Illustrated in Colour by J. FINNEMORE. Cloth, 2/6 ; picture
boards, 2/-.

"It is one of the most exciting of this season's works for boys, every page containing a thrill, and no boy will leave it to a second sitting if he can help it."—*Teacher.*

King of the Air : or, To Morocco on an Aeroplane. Illustrated in Colour by W. E. WEBSTER. Cloth, 2/6 ;
picture boards, 2/-.

"One of the best boy's stories we have ever read."—*Morning Leader.*

Lord of the Seas : The Story of a Submarine. Illustrated in Colour by C. FLEMING WILLIAMS. Cloth, 2/6 ;
picture boards, 2/-.

"A good deal of fun pervades the story, while there are plenty of thrilling episodes and startling encounters."—*Teacher's Aid.*

THE UNIQUE EDITION

Robinson Crusoe. Illustrated with Twenty-four Plates in Colour, mounted, by NOEL POCOCK. Royal
8vo, cloth, 7/6 net.

No edition of "Robinson Crusoe" hitherto published has been illustrated on the lavish scale of the present one. Mr. Pocock is in thorough sympathy with his subject; his illustrations possess great originality of design and excellence of workmanship; and they bring home with peculiar force and pathos the circumstances of Crusoe's solitary life. Printed on good paper in a bold type, and strongly bound in cloth, this book is one to delight the heart of any boy.

6

THE ROMANCE OF THE WORLD SERIES
Edited by Herbert Strang

The Romance of Canada   The Romance of Australia
The Romance of India

640 pages.   Illustrated with 16 Plates in Colour and 4 Maps.   Demy 8vo, cloth, gilt top, 6/- each.

Each volume in the Romance of the World series contains a graphic account of the rise and progress of some one of the great countries forming part of the British Empire. The Editor has not attempted to compile an exhaustive history of these dominions: his aim has been to present, as in a series of pictures, a story that will interest boys and girls, and at the same time teach them something of the manner in which the foundations of our Colonial greatness were laid. The interest centres in the men of action and the outstanding events in which they played a leading part. The conquests of Clive in India, the taking of Canada by Wolfe, and the discovery of Australia by Captain Cook are given due prominence, side by side with the work of explorers and settlers and others who have helped to make history.

CLAUDE GRAHAME-WHITE AND HARRY HARPER

With the Airmen : Illustrated in Colour by Cyrus Cuneo, and with numerous black-and-white Illustrations and Diagrams.   Demy 8vo, cloth, gilt top, 6/- ; cloth, 3/6.

Mr. Grahame-White has not only repeatedly proved his skill and daring as a pilot, but the well-known type of biplane bearing his name shows that he is in the forefront of designers and constructors. With his practical and technical knowledge is combined the somewhat rare ability to impart his knowledge in a form acceptable to boys, as he has already shown in his "Heroes of the Air." This time he has written a *vade mecum* for the young aeroplanist, who is conducted to the aerodrome and initiated into all the mysteries of flying. The structure of the aeroplane, the uses of the different parts, the propulsive mechanism, the steering apparatus, the work at a flying school, the causes of accidents, and the future of the aeroplane are all dealt with.

CAPTAIN CHARLES GILSON

The Lost Empire : A Tale of many Lands. Illustrated in Colour by Cyrus Cuneo. With Map. Crown 8vo, cloth elegant, olivine edges, 6/-.

To found a great Empire in the East was one of the designs of Napoleon Bonaparte, and he might possibly have carried it out, had not certain events happened, which are related in this story. Amongst these were the Battle of the Nile, and the discovery of Napoleon's plans of campaign, in each of which incidents the hero, Mr. Thomas Nunn, Midshipman, was concerned.

"It is a magnificent story, with not an error of phrase or thought in it . . . is not only relatively good, but absolutely so."—*Daily News.*

7

CAPTAIN CHARLES GILSON

The Lost Column : A Story of the Boxer Rebellion. Illustrated in Colour by CYRUS CUNEO.
With Map. Crown 8vo, cloth elegant, olivine edges, 6/-.

At the outbreak of the great Boxer Rebellion in China, Gerald Wood, the hero of this story, was living with his mother and brother at Milton Towers, just outside Tientsin. When the storm broke and Tientsin was cut off from the rest of the world, the occupants of Milton Towers were compelled to retire into the town. Then Gerald determined to go in quest of the relief column under Admiral Seymour. He carried his life in his hands, and on more than one occasion came within an ace of losing it ; but he managed to reach his goal in safety, and was warmly commended by the Admiral on his achievement.

"An excellent piece of craftsmanship."—*Outlook.*
"All the sketches of Chinese character are excellent, and we read the book with delight from the first page to the last."—*Ladies' Field.*

The Pirate Aeroplane : Illustrated in Colour by C. CLARK, R.I. Crown 8vo, cloth, olivine
edges, 5/-.

The heroes of this story, during a tour in an entirely unknown region of Africa, light upon a race of people directly descended from the Ancient Egyptians. This race—the Asmalians—has lived isolated from other communities. The scientific importance of this discovery is apparent to the travellers, and they are enthusiastic to know more of these strange people ; but suddenly they find themselves in the midst of exciting adventures owing to the appearance of a pirate aeroplane—of a thoroughly up-to-date model— whose owner has learnt of a vast store of gold in the Asmalians' city. They throw in their lot with the people, and are able in the end to frustrate the plans of the freebooter.

The Lost Island. Illustrated in Colour by CYRUS CUNEO. Crown 8vo, cloth, olivine edges, 3/6 ; picture
boards, 2/6.

A rousing story of adventure in the little-explored regions of Central Asia and in the South Seas. The prologue describes how Thomas Gaythorne obtained access to a Lama monastery, where he rendered the monks such great service that they bestowed upon him a gem of priceless value known as Guatama's Eye. Soon after leaving the monastery he was attacked and robbed, and only narrowly escaped with his life. "The Lost Island" describes the attempt of one of Thomas Gaythorne's descendants to re-discover the missing gem ; and he passes through some remarkable adventures before he succeeds in this quest.

8

WILLIAM J. MARX

For the Admiral. Illustrated in Colour by ARCHIBALD WEBB. Crown 8vo, cloth elegant, 3/6; picture boards, cloth back, 2/6.

The brave Huguenot Admiral Coligny is one of the heroes of French history. Edmond Je Blanc, the son of a Huguenot gentleman, undertakes to convey a secret letter of warning to Coligny, and the adventures he meets with on the way lead to his accepting service in the Huguenot army. He shares in the hard fighting that took place in the neighbourhood of La Rochelle, does excellent work in scouting for the Admiral, and is everywhere that danger calls, along with his friend Roger Braund, a young Englishman who has come over to help the cause with a band of free-lances. This story won the £100 prize offered by the *Bookman* for the best story for boys.

"It is much the best book of its kind sent in for review this season, and stands head and shoulders above its rivals."—*Academy*.

DESMOND COKE

The Bending of a Twig. Illustrated in Colour by H. M. BROCK. Crown 8vo, cloth elegant, olivine edges, 5/-.

When "The Bending of a Twig" was first published it was hailed by competent critics as the finest school story that had appeared since "Tom Brown." It is a vivid picture of life in a modern public school. The hero, Lycidas Marsh, enters Shrewsbury without having previously been to a preparatory school, drawing his ideas of school life from his imagination and a number of school stories he has read. How Lycidas finds his true level in this new world and worthily maintains the Salopian tradition is the theme of this most entrancing book.

"A real, live school story that carries conviction in every line."—*Standard*.
"Mr. Desmond Coke has given us one of the best accounts of public school life that we possess. . . . Among books of its kind 'The Bending of a Twig' deserves to become a classic."—*Outlook*.

9

DESMOND COKE

The School Across the Road.
Illustrated in Colour by H. M. BROCK.

Crown 8vo, cloth 3/6.

The incidents of this story arise out of the uniting of two schools—"Warner's" and "Corunna"—under the name of "Winton," a name which the head master fondly hopes will become known far and wide as a great seat of learning. Unfortunately for the head master's ambition, however, the two sets of boys—hitherto rivals and enemies, now schoolfellows—do not take kindly to one another. Warner's men of might are discredited in the new school; Henderson, lately head boy, finds himself a mere nobody; while the inoffensive Dove is exalted and made prefect by reason of his attainments in class work. There is discord and insurrection and talk of expulsion, and the feud drags on until the rival factions have an opportunity of uniting against a common enemy. Then, in the enthusiasm aroused by the overthrow of a neighbouring agricultural college, the bitterness between them dies away, and the future of Winton is assured.

"This tale is told with a remarkable spirit, and all the boys are real, everyday characters, drawn without exaggeration."—*British Weekly*.

The Worst House at Sherborough.
Illustrated in Colour by H. M. BROCK. Crown 8vo, cloth elegant, 5/-.

Dick Hunter, the most popular boy in the School House at Sherborough, on the last day of one Easter term learns that his father, Colonel Hunter, has suddenly become too poor to send him back for the summer. The Head Master interviews the Colonel, tells him that one of the Houses—that known to the boys as "Weary Willie's"—is badly in need of a boy to lead it, and suggests that Dick, owing to the extreme difficulty and importance of the work, could in no way be considered a charity-boy if he lived there without any boarding fees being paid. The Colonel, believing that an ordeal of this kind would be of great benefit to Dick, reluctantly consents. In the summer term Dick sets to work to reform his new House, and the story tells of his struggles with its former leaders and of the misunderstandings, inevitable in the circumstances, with his old friends in the School House. He finds at the end of the term that his father has managed to get out of his money difficulties, and he is able to take his choice between staying to help "Weary Willie" and returning to the happy, tranquil life at the School House.

A. C. CURTIS

The Voyage of the " Sesame " : A Story of the Arctic. Illustrated

in Colour by W. HERBERT HOLLOWAY. Crown 8vo, cloth elegant, olivine edges, 5/-.

The three Trevelyan brothers receive from a dying sailor a rough chart indicating the whereabouts of a rich gold-bearing region in the Arctic. They forthwith build a craft, specially adapted to work in the Polar Seas, and set out in quest of the gold. They do not have things all their own way, however, for a rival party of treasure-seekers have got wind of the old sailor's El Dorado, and are also on the trail. In the race and fighting that ensue, the brothers come off victorious ; and after a voyage fraught with danger from ice, hunger, cold, and wild beasts, the *Sesame* returns home with the gold on board.

" The building of the stout ship *Sesame* at Dundee is one of the best things of the kind we have read for many a day."—*Educational News.*

" The Voyage of the *Sesame* is thrilling from cover to cover."—*The Standard.*

D. H. PARRY

Kit of the Carabineers : or, A Soldier of Marlborough's. Illustrated in Colour by ARCHIBALD

WEBB. Large crown 8vo, cloth, olivine edges, 5/-.

No period of English history was more productive of stirring deeds than the early years of the reign of Queen Anne, when the reputation of British arms reached its greatest height. This story tells how Kit Dawnay comes under the notice of the Duke of Marlborough while the latter is on a visit to Kit's uncle, Sir Jasper Dawnay, an irritable miserly old man, suspected, with good reason, of harbouring Jacobite plotters and of being favourable to the cause of the exiled Stuarts. Kit, instructed by the Duke, is able to frustrate a scheme for the assassination of King William as he rides to Hampton Court, and the King, in return for Kit's service, gives him a cornet's commission in the King's Carabineers. He goes with the army to Flanders, takes part in the siege of Liège ; accompanies Marlborough on those famous forced marches across Europe, whereby the great leader completely hoodwinked the enemy ; and is present at the battle of Blenheim, where he wins distinction.

11

GEORGE SURREY

Mid Clash of Swords : A Story of the Sack of Rome. Coloured Illustrations by T. C. DUGDALE. Crown 8vo, cloth elegant, olivine edges, 5/- ; cloth, 3/6.

Wilfrid Salkeld, a young Englishman, flees from Rome as a result of a quarrel with an Italian, and he travels hither and thither in the hope of finding some service to which he can devote himself. He has been trained to arms, and as a swordsman is second to none in Italy. He enters the employ of Giuliano de' Medici, the virtual ruler of Florence, whom he serves with a zeal that that faint-hearted man does not deserve ; he meets Giovanni the Invincible ; and makes friends with the great Benvenuto Cellini. He has many a fierce tussle with German mercenaries and Italian robbers, as well as with those whose jealousy he arouses by his superior skill in arms.

"Told as it is with unflagging spirit, the story is one to delight the heart of any normally constituted boy."—*Dundee Courier.*

" A tale of the most rousing description."—*Liverpool Courier.*

FRANK H. MASON

The Book of British Ships. Written and Illustrated by FRANK H. MASON, R.B.A. Crown 8vo, cloth, olivine edges, 5/-.

The aim of this book is to present, in a form that will readily appeal to boys, a comprehensive account of British shipping, both naval and mercantile, and to trace its development from the earliest times down to the Dreadnoughts and high-speed ocean liners of to-day. All kinds of British ships, from the battleship to the trawler, are dealt with, and the characteristic points of each type of vessel are explained.

"Mr. Mason lays down his facts so clearly and simply that the attention of the most harebrained of his young readers should be fixed and held."—*T. P.'s Weekly.*

Rev. J. R. HOWDEN

Locomotives of the World. Containing 16 Plates in Colour. 5/- net.

Many of the most up-to-date types of locomotives used on railways through-out the world are illustrated and described in this volume. The coloured plates have been made from actual photographs, and show the peculiar features of some truly remarkable engines. These peculiarities are fully explained in the text, written by the Rev. J. R. Howden, author of "The Boy's Book of Locomotives," etc.

"Illustrations simply splendid, and letterpress teems with interest."—*Irish Independent.*

JOSEPH BOWES

Comrades. Illustrated in Colour by CYRUS CUNEO. Large crown 8vo, cloth, olivine edges, 3/6; picture boards, cloth back, 2/6.

This book describes the adventures of three boys in the northern territory of Australia, whither they go with their uncle to gain health and acquire experience of farming and stock-raising. The life that awaits them is interesting and varied. They go on expeditions in search of natural history specimens, and assist in rounding-up cattle. Their great opportunity of adventure presents itself when a party of natives drive off a considerable number of cattle. The boys start in pursuit, and go through some dangerous scouting operations before they return successful.

THE ROMANCE SERIES

The Romance of the King's Navy. By EDWARD FRASER.

Illustrated in colour by N. SOTHEBY PITCHER. Crown 8vo, 3/6.

"The Romance of the King's Navy" is intended to give boys of to-day an idea of some of the notable events that have happened under the White Ensign within the past few years. There is no other book of the kind in existence. It begins with incidents afloat during the Crimean War, when their grandfathers were boys themselves, and brings the story down to a year or two ago, with the startling adventure at Spithead of Submarine B4. One chapter tells the exciting story of "How the Navy's V.C.'s have been won," the deeds of the various heroes being brought all together here in one connected narrative for the first time.

"Mr. Fraser knows his facts well, and has set them out in an extremely interesting and attractive way."—*Westminster Gazette.*

The Romance of Every Day. By LILIAN QUILLER-COUCH. Crown 8vo, Illustrated, 5/-; cloth, 3/6.

Here is a bookful of romance and heroism; true stories of men, women, and children in early centuries and modern times who took the opportunities which came into their everyday lives and found themselves heroes and heroines; civilians who, without beat of drum or smoke of battle, without special training or words of encouragement, performed deeds worthy to be written in letters of gold.

"These stories are bound to encourage and inspire young readers to perform heroic actions."—*Bristol Daily Mercury.*

The Romance of the Merchant Venturers.
By E. E. SPEIGHT and R. MORTON NANCE. 5/-.

Britain's Sea Story. By E. E. SPEIGHT and R. MORTON NANCE. New Edition, Illustrated in Colour by H. SANDHAM. 5/-; cloth, 3/6.

These two books are full of true tales as exciting as any to be found in the story books, and at every few pages there is a fine illustration, in colour or black-and-white, of one of the stirring incidents described in the text.

Edited by HERBERT STRANG

Early Days in Canada	Pioneers in Australia
Pioneers in Canada	Early Days in India
Early Days in Australia	Duty and Danger in India

Crown 8vo, cloth, olivine edges. Each book contains eight plates in colour. Price 3/6 each; picture boards, 2/6 each.

The story of the discovery, conquest, settlement, and peaceful development of the great countries which now form part of the British Empire, is full of interest and romance. In this series of books the story is told, in a number of extracts from the writings of historians, biographers, and travellers whose works are not easily accessible to the general reader. Each volume is complete in itself and gives a vivid picture of the progress of the particular country with which it deals.

MEREDITH FLETCHER

The Pretenders.
With Coloured Illustrations by HAROLD C. EARNSHAW. Crown 8vo, olivine edges, 3/6.

A tale of twin-brothers at Daneborough School. Tommy Durrant (the narrator) has been a boarder for about a year, when Peter arrives upon the scene as a day-boy. The latter's ill-health has prevented him joining the school before, and, being a harum-scarum youngster, his vagaries plunge Tommy into hot water straight away. The following week, unaware of all the mischief he has made, the newcomer, who lives with an aunt, urges his twin to change places one night for a spree. Tommy rashly consents, and his experiences while pretending to be Peter prove both unexpected and exciting.

"Mr. Meredith Fletcher is extremely happy in his delineation of school life."—*People's Journal.*

V. E. JOHNSON, M.A.

Playbooks of Science :
Chemistry and Chemical Magic
Mechanics and Some of its Mysteries
Flying and Some of its Mysteries
Electricity and Electrical Magic

Crown 8vo, cloth, 1/6 each.

These books are sure to prove fascinating to boys with a liking for Science. Mr. Johnson deals with the lighter side of the many subjects with which he is intimately acquainted, and shows how the knowledge acquired in school laboratory or workshop may become a source of infinite pleasure and entertainment. The first book contains over 150 chemical experiments, many of them of a quite simple character, with which the reader can hold an audience interested on winter evenings. The second deals with the laws of mechanics, illustrated by the action of such things as spinning tops, designographs, pendulums, gyroscopes, etc. The third explains some of the mysteries of flying, and balloons, kites, parachutes, and model aeroplanes are dealt with in turn. The fourth book, which has just been added, explains how the budding electrician may derive an infinite amount of recreation from his hobby ; the experiments cover a wide field and show what may be done in the way of entertainment with magnets, induction coils, Geissler tubes, and simple wireless apparatus. The text is illustrated with numerous figures.

Herbert Strang's Historical Series

This Series is quite unique. Its aim is to encourage a taste for history in boys and girls up to fourteen years of age by giving all the important events and movements of a reign or period intermingled with a rousing story of adventure. While the stories are worth reading for their own sakes, they are also worth reading—especially on the eve of an examination—by a boy or girl who in class or in school text-book has worked up the "dry history" of the period. Each volume contains, besides the story, a general summary, a chronological list of important events, and a map. Much care has been devoted to the "get-up" of these books. They contain about 160 pages each, with four beautiful illustrations in full colour, and are issued in two styles:—

> (*a*) In cloth, with coloured cover design, 1/6.
> (*b*) In picture-board bindings, with cloth backs, and gilt-foil lettering, 1/- net each.

In the New Forest: A Story of the Reign of William the Conqueror. By HERBERT STRANG and JOHN ASTON.

Lion Heart: A Story of the Reign of Richard I. By HERBERT STRANG and RICHARD STEAD.

With the Black Prince: A Story of the Reign of Edward III. By HERBERT STRANG and RICHARD STEAD.

Claud the Archer: A Story of the Reign of Henry V. By HERBERT STRANG and JOHN ASTON.

For the White Rose: A Story of the Reign of Edward IV. By HERBERT STRANG and GEORGE LAWRENCE.

A Mariner of England: A Story of the Reign of Queen Elizabeth. By HERBERT STRANG and RICHARD STEAD.

One of Rupert's Horse: A Story of the Reign of Charles I. By HERBERT STRANG and RICHARD STEAD.

With Marlborough to Malplaquet: A Story of the Reign of Queen Anne. By HERBERT STRANG and RICHARD STEAD.

Roger the Scout: A Story of the Reign of George II. By HERBERT STRANG and GEORGE LAWRENCE.

"These stories, which are bright and stirring, are sufficiently simple to be within the grasp of the children, the descriptions of life and manners are accurate, and the history of the period is interwoven in a skilful manner."—*Practical Teacher.*